THE OTHER SIDE OF TRUST

A NOVEL

BY

NEIL ROBINSON

Burning Chair Limited, Trading As Burning Chair Publishing
61 Bridge Street, Kington HR5 3DJ

www.burningchairpublishing.com

By Neil Robinson
Edited by Simon Finnie and Peter Oxley
Cover by Burning Chair Publishing

First published by Burning Chair Publishing, 2022

ISBN: 978-1-912946-24-2

For Elizabeth

ONE

The interview room might have been created for a cheap television drama: a single table and four chairs of tubular aluminium and chipped MDF, strip lights hanging from a 1960s foam-tiled ceiling. One side wall was mirrored down its whole length, the watchers on the other side needing no introduction. Only one of the chairs was occupied, and the man sitting in it looked tired and irritable. He was a youngish man of about thirty, of no more than average height, perhaps a little less in truth. His straw-blond hair and blue eyes gave him something of a Scandinavian appearance and his face—round, unlined and soft-featured—would surely have been quite pleasant to look at had he not appeared, at that precise moment, so terribly weary. His clothes hung off him as though he had shrunk since putting them on. Perhaps they weren't his own clothes at all. Sebastian Friend flexed his fingers and massaged his aching wrists. His hands were no longer manacled, but he didn't feel any less the prisoner.

Friend had thought it was the VIP treatment at first: the officer from Special Branch picking him up at Passport Control and ushering him wordlessly out through the back rooms of HM Customs to the unmarked police car outside. It had come as a relief to him after weeks on the run in enemy territory. No hero's welcome, but a serious and business-like transfer from his incoming flight at Heathrow to one of the SIS debriefing centres somewhere on the outskirts of London. There he would be stuck for a day or two while the details of the report he had sent in—from the office of the Service's representative in Oman—were dissected and confirmed. But no sooner had he settled himself on the back seat than he felt the handcuffs close over his left wrist and the man, who moments earlier had introduced himself as Inspector Hemming, told him that he was under arrest. For what? For murder. Of whom? Linus Martinson. Martinson! Friend had to choke back a laugh at the thought of it. Martinson! The whole thing was preposterous.

And then the police car—if that's what it was—had not driven him as he now expected to Polar Park police station on the northern perimeter of Heathrow, or even to the secure suites of Paddington Green in West London. Instead, it had cruised out onto the Cranbrook by-pass and from there to the M4, heading west, away from London, before turning off at Windsor and winding through the pretty Berkshire countryside to the south. As soon as they had passed through Windsor, Friend was certain of their destination.

Lambrook House, standing on its own in an unremarkable corner of Berkshire north of Bracknell, was a dingy late Victorian red-brick manor house built by a local industrialist for his retirement. As a home it had not long survived its first owner's demise in the early 1900s. Death duties, followed by the loss of both natural heirs in the First World War, led to the house and its grounds being sold off. For the next fifty years it served a variety of purposes: girls' school, officers' hospital and recuperation centre during the Second War, and latterly as a psychiatric hospital of the less enlightened kind, which had given the place the ugly atmosphere it retained to the present day. In the mid-1970s the house had been acquired by the government for the use of the Secret Intelligence Service. It was then, and remained now, a principal reception and training centre for operational recruits, those who were unlikely to be forging a career in the carpeted offices of Vauxhall Cross. In recent years no one had cared for the place particularly. Each year when budget submissions came around it was slated for disposal; each year, somehow, it remained on the books and rotted a little more.

Friend himself had spent six weeks there in the first year of his service. The secure, self-contained north wing of the house included a number of subterranean suites used for training in the arts of performing and resisting interrogation. It had also been used, at times, for genuine debriefings carried out with agents returning from operational duty, as well as defectors from foreign services. But in recent years its principal use had been for training, and it might have been in that very room, certainly in one very like it, where Friend had received his first, harsh, lessons in how to survive an interrogation.

He had been back at Lambrook for an hour, he thought, although this was pure guesswork since his watch was taken from him, along with his shoelaces, upon his arrival. They had looked for a belt too, and the sight of Friend's oversized trousers sliding down his skinny hips had caused the nearest thing to genuine mirth that could be achieved in that place. All that had taken a mere five minutes. The rest of the hour had been spent in the room, waiting.

He heard the door open behind him and two sets of footsteps approach. He did not bother to turn his head. A man and a woman sat down across the table from him; the woman pretty in a stern sort of way: pursed, disapproving lips, mid-brown hair bobbed around the chin, a dark tailored jacket pulled across an ivory silk crew neck. The man had the sort of scrubbed appearance and beaming bonhomie that suggested he had come directly from his weekly wet-shave and hair trim at Trumpers: ageless with babyish pink skin and curly blond hair. His suit was unseasonable dove grey flannel with a bold chalk stripe, drape cut for comfort. Both wore lanyards around their necks, the badges describing them as *'Visitor'*. Neither had brought with them any files or documents, nor even anything on which to make notes.

"So, Mr Friend," began the man. So it was to be real names then. Fine. "You had a pleasant journey, I trust? Shall we begin?"

Friend shrugged. "I have no other commitments today."

The comment brought a sour smile from the other man.

"I'm glad to hear it. Well, let's begin with the introductions. My name is Lascelles, and this is Ms Wilton, from our legal department."

"Are you from our legal department too?" asked Friend.

"Not exactly."

"Well, if I'm to be charged with murder shouldn't I have my own lawyer present?"

Lascelles seemed genuinely shocked at the suggestion.

"Charged with murder? What on earth gives you that idea?"

"Oh, the fact that Inspector Hemming mentioned a murder charge and read me my rights not more than two hours ago."

"Inspector Hemming? I'm not sure we know an Inspector Hemming, do we?"

He turned to Ms Wilton for confirmation and after a short delay, during which the woman from the legal department seemed oblivious to the question asked of her, she slowly turned to Lascelles and gave a brief shake of her head before returning her empty gaze to a point on the wall somewhere behind Friend.

"Hemming was the man who handcuffed me on the way here from the airport," explained Friend patiently, as if to a child.

"And where are those handcuffs now?" Lascelles paused for impact. "You are not being charged with anything at the moment, nor are you on trial here. Isn't that right, Ms Wilton?"

The nod came more immediately this time, and Wilton allowed her eyes to focus on Friend for an instant.

"There are, however, certain issues raised by your actions in Iran and not altogether clarified by the report you submitted…"

"Have you read the report?"

Lascelles chose his words carefully.

"We have been apprised of its contents, insofar as they are relevant to this enquiry. Or perhaps I should say to this debriefing. You will probably find it easier just to consider this process as a perfectly regular debriefing of the kind you might undergo after any assignment."

"I've had regular debriefings after all my assignments, but I'm fairly sure that we never needed the lawyers to be present."

"Ms Wilton is present only because your most recent assignment has led to some interest from external parties, intelligence agencies both friendly and not so friendly. There are, shall we say, political implications, should this interest reach governmental level."

Friend turned to Ms Wilton directly.

"So you are here to represent whom, exactly? The Minister? The Cabinet Office? Not me, I presume."

He might as well have spoken to the wall for all the reaction he got. Wilton showed not a flicker of concern on her face, nor any intention of responding. Lascelles continued instead.

"She is here to represent the interests of the Service, Mr Friend. As are we all. Our only purpose here is to establish the truth, so that those in a position to do so can make the appropriate decisions. I might add that, since Ms Wilton is representing the interests of the Service, she is also representing your own. It is in all our interests that you participate in this process as fully and openly as possible."

"You'll find the truth in my report," said Friend.

"Perhaps. But is that all of it? We are here to verify if possible, to clarify where necessary and to establish whether anything of import should be added."

Listening to Lascelles, Friend began to understand why he tended to leaf through civil service briefing documents so quickly. "I'd like to speak to the Director," he said.

"And why is that?" asked Lascelles patiently.

"It's a question of trust."

"Your report was eyes only to the Director and 'C', was it

not? You received your travel instructions in direct response to this and your presence here is the end point of those instructions. Surely that is enough to suggest to you that this process has been authorised both by the Director and at the very highest levels of the Service, is it not?"

Friend remained impassive.

"But if you insist, I am authorised to permit you to make one telephone call." He pulled a mobile from his jacket pocket and slid it across the table to Friend. Two minutes later, Friend returned it, as satisfied as he could be and not greatly reassured by what he had heard.

"Shall we proceed?" asked Lascelles, returning the phone to his pocket.

Friend nodded.

"Good. Then let's begin before you went to Iran. Let's begin with Cambridge."

TWO

The old man was very nearly dead when they found him, barely conscious and gasping for air on a park bench. But even if they had reached him earlier, fifteen or twenty minutes, say, it would have been a long shot to hope that the paramedics who reached him first or the doctors in the local hospital would have been able to make an accurate diagnosis in time to give the necessary treatment. It was perfectly understandable, on a warm early summer's day, that an elderly man strolling in Christ's Pieces might take a breather on a vacant bench and doze off in the sun. Nobody disturbed him. By the time they did, it was too late. Almost forty-eight hours then passed before the cause of death could be properly established, and by that time the park had already been sealed off and the old man's body, together with everyone who had come into contact with it, placed into strict quarantine.

But, for the first few of those forty-eight hours, there was nothing to suggest that anything other than natural causes was involved. The victim had succumbed to respiratory collapse, probably the result of an underlying heart or lung condition; the paramedics had given him oxygen and with heroic effort managed to keep his lungs going until he reached hospital. There he had lingered, in a deep coma, for a further six hours. Towards the end he had begun to suffer from convulsions, and it was only then that one of the duty physicians monitoring the case began to suspect the involvement of a nerve agent. The patient was stripped and scrubbed clean, his clothing and possessions placed in hazard bags. Diazepam was administered to counteract the convulsions, atropine to combat the as-yet-unidentified poison, arrangements for secure transportation to a specialist unit at Addenbrookes Hospital were put in place; it was to no avail. Death was recorded at 10:17pm on Thursday 4th June.

Twenty minutes earlier, the paramedics who treated him had returned to A&E complaining of breathing difficulties.

By nine the following morning, a total of seven members of medical staff at the hospital had been placed in isolation due to direct contact with the victim. Five were experiencing mild symptoms of respiratory difficulty and disorientation. What was now a murder investigation had been passed swiftly from Cambridgeshire Constabulary to the Metropolitan Police's Counter-Terrorism Command, otherwise known as SO15.

Initially at least, identifying the murderer was some way down the investigating team's list of priorities. When Detective Chief Inspector George Wetherby first addressed his team in an operations room hastily converted from an unfinished paediatric surgical unit on Friday afternoon, he began by highlighting what to him was the very heart of the case. "The first priority is identifying the poison used and how, when and where it was administered. The first part of that falls to the pathology team here. We have an expert in toxicology coming in from Porton Down to assist. But the second part is down to us. It won't be easy. Most weaponised nerve agents vary in the time they take to cause symptoms, depending on how they were administered and how much was used: a few seconds if vapour was inhaled; minutes or even hours in the case of a liquid that penetrates the skin. So we could be looking for something sudden that happened in the park, or something quite subtle that took place earlier in the day. My hunch is the latter. Using vapour involves too much risk to the perpetrator and anyone walking around a city park in full haz-chem gear and carrying a spray gun is liable to attract attention."

"What about that North Korean guy who got hit with VX in Malaysia?" piped up a keen-looking Detective Sergeant.

"Kim Jong-Nam. Good question." Wetherby perched himself on the edge of a table and began to explain. "That was one of the puzzling things about the case, but the most plausible theory about the method also explains why the Koreans used two young women to carry out the 'prank' hit rather than just one. If you remember, one of them placed a cloth over his face from behind while the other sprayed him with a vapour from in front. Neither suffered any serious ill effects, so it's likely that the cloth was treated with a liquid which together with the fluid in the spray bottle combined to form VX. In isolation neither substance was remotely harmful, but together they were deadly. I have to say I doubt whether that exact method was used in this case; Mr Kim knew what had happened immediately and sought medical attention, which failed to save his life.

"Our victim made no such attempt. Perhaps the attack was too sudden, but the only witness statement we have so far suggests that he was just walking in the park and sat down on the bench as anyone might do. So we need more witnesses, we need to know his exact movements over the course of that day, and especially who he was in contact with. These people need to be isolated and questioned. They might be suspects or just witnesses, but even more importantly they might have been contaminated themselves. That means eyes on every CCTV camera in the city centre, public and private, that means speaking to his neighbours, that means some of you lucky people will need to suit up and go through his home and office and identify any object that might have been introduced from outside in the last few days. Then we need to seal everything off for decontamination. The park has already been sealed off and we have the army coming in to help with the rest. Let's hope we don't have to decontaminate the whole city centre. And just in case the perpetrator was contaminated in the act, however slightly, we need every hospital in the country on the lookout for anyone displaying similar symptoms. Any questions?"

Wetherby was met with silence. The twenty men and women before him knew the procedure; a handful of them had been through it before and the rest had received the benefit of that experience in training.

"Right, item two on the agenda: our victim. He was Professor Mansour Sadaghiani, senior lecturer at Cambridge University's Department of Chemical Engineering and Biotechnology. Born in Iran 1958, applied for political asylum in the UK 1987. UK nationality granted 1997. Widower. Lived alone in a semi-detached house just off the Histon Road. The whole street is being evacuated as we speak. He had an office with the rest of his department at the West Cambridge site. Thank heavens it's a weekend and nearly the end of term; we'll probably have to seal that off for decontamination as well."

"So the working theory is an Iranian government hit, then?" came a voice from the back.

"Very likely. We don't have anything yet to suggest he was political, but I'm sure we'll turn something up. I'm no expert on how ugly university rivalries can get, but I'm pretty sure I never saw chemical weapons used on Inspector Morse." A ripple of subdued laughter passed across the room. "That being the case, we can probably expect the company of the funny boys and no doubt the OPCW will want to have their representatives on board too."

"Do we have any idea what killed him yet?"

"No. The manner of death suggests a nerve agent of some description, but so far we have no idea which one. Samples have been taken from the body and clothing; they're being analysed now. We should know more by this time tomorrow. Any more questions? Right then, DI Harrison will give you your individual assignments. We'll have a daily briefing in here at oh-eight-hundred hours. And now if you'll forgive me I have two minutes to get to a press conference with the Head of Counter-Terrorism and the Home Secretary."

Wetherby strode towards the door amid murmurs of amusement, but as he pushed through it and walked out into the empty corridor he felt the mobile phone in his pocket begin to buzz. Reading the message through twice, he felt the sweat begin to form on his brow.

"Oh, bloody hell," he said.

*

It did not take long to become obvious that the world's media would not be relying for their copy on the bland banalities produced by press conferences, and that their own investigations would be carried on in parallel with the official one. The press conference had produced the same direct questions for Wetherby that had come from his team: "Who was the victim?" "Was he political?" "Was this yet another government-sponsored assassination carried out on British soil?" And for the Home Secretary, the uncomfortable "How long would the British Government permit such atrocities to be carried out before serious action might be taken?" They all dead-batted as much as they could. Wetherby with an increasing feeling of foreboding, since he now knew just how political Professor Sadaghiani had been.

The weekend headlines were another clear demonstration that the media were not prepared to wait for the investigation to be concluded before they apportioned blame: *'Iran murders émigré Professor in Cambridge'*; *'Another state-sponsored chemical attack on British soil'*; *'PM under pressure to condemn Iran murder'*. But there was another shock to come. By Sunday evening details were emerging of the deaths of another two prominent Iranian émigrés: Dr Aziz Qarib had been killed by a hit-and-run driver near his home in upstate New York, Dr Javad Nassirian shot dead on a backstreet in Hamburg. In the latter, the helmeted assassin made his getaway on the back of a waiting motorcycle bearing falsified licence plates. The motorcycle was finally discovered two days later, parked discreetly near the railway station in Lübeck. Ballistics analysis of the two bullets found in Dr Nassirian's body suggested that the weapon used had been an obsolete automatic of Czech manufacture. There were no suspects.

There was, however, plenty of speculation about the reasons for this sudden spate of violent deaths affecting the more prominent members of the Persian diaspora, and into the connections between the three victims. An article by The Observer's longstanding commentator on intelligence matters, Tom Westerman, got closer to the heart of things than most.

Since the recent spate of deaths in Cambridge, New York and Hamburg, speculation has been rife into the connections between the three victims. It can now be revealed that such a connection did indeed exist, and it was such that linked their destinies from very early in their lives until the days of their deaths. According to sources in more than one major Western intelligence agency, Professor Sadaghiani, the Cambridge academic with links to Iran's nuclear programme, Dr Qarib, the leading cardiologist and Dr Nassirian, the successful academic publisher, were students together at Tehran University at the time of the Islamic Revolution. Initially supporters of the overthrow of the Shah's regime, which towards the end was the subject of widespread disgust among all levels of Iranian society for its corruption, brutality and extravagant mismanagement of the country's finances, the three young men soon grew disenchanted with the increasingly puritanical direction of the revolutionary regime, its focus on theological purity, disdain for modernity and overt hatred of the West.

Each of them left his native land in his late twenties or early thirties, but although their new lives in exile saw them settle in various parts of the globe, a common bond continued to hold them together. Indeed, it had been a bond forged before they left. As early as 1985, it is thought, they were at the heart of an influential group of young, dissident intellectuals, challenging government orthodoxy, promoting independent thought and circulating forbidden literature. Indeed, his role in distributing illegal works such as Salman Rushdie's 'The Satanic Verses' earned Dr Nassirian a spell in prison during which he was repeatedly tortured. When he claimed asylum in Germany two years after his release, the scars he bore on his back and the soles of his feet were a powerful testimony in support of his case.

Their dissident activity took on a new form in exile. They became the public face of opposition to Iran's authoritarian regime. The Tehran Committee, as it was now known, had been born in student resistance within Iran, but it found new expression in its leaders overseas. The Committee was a Troika. Nassirian may have been its most public face—a gifted speaker with a natural flair for public relations he was the obvious front man—but Sadaghiani and Qarib were no less important behind the scenes. In the corridors of power in Washington, Whitehall and Berlin, and in many other Western capitals, the Committee came to be seen as little less than a government in exile, the representation of the hidden democratic will of the Iranian people.

But it was much more than that. Over the years the Committee grew into a resistance movement within Iran, co-ordinating anti-government protests, circulating illegal newspapers and broadcasting illegal radio, doing its best to counteract the official government narrative through its own information channels. Was it propaganda? Of course. Was it pro-Western? Undoubtedly, for the most part. While the Committee gathered significant funds from sympathetic donors across the world, the bulk of its funding was provided by secret disbursements from western intelligence agencies. Since 1989 the CIA alone has funnelled more than one hundred and thirty-five million dollars into the Committee and its various offshoots, *in return for which the Committee used its connections inside Iran to assist with CIA and other agencies—including Britain's Secret Intelligence Service—intelligence demands. How deeply involved the Committee was in US and UK secret operations within Iran is not clear, but the fact of its involvement has been confirmed to me by several sources.*

This had long been the charge levelled at the Tehran Committee by the Iranian regime; invariably met, by the British government at least, with the traditional line that they do not comment on intelligence matters. The Committee's links with Western intelligence made it an obvious target for Iranian reprisals, and mean that the prospects for its remaining operatives within Iran must now be especially bleak. But why now, rather than at any other time in the last thirty years?

According to my information, the reason may be two-fold. Firstly, Iran's senior intelligence organisation, the Ministry of Intelligence, is currently smarting after the defection of an un-named senior officer to the CIA. Reprisals against Western intelligence would be a natural response to this development and in line with the Ministry's previous actions. Secondly, the forthcoming presidential election in Iran, now just four weeks away, has seen hard-line forces including the leadership of the Revolutionary Guard giving their official backing to one of the most hawkish figures to emerge in Tehran politics in many years. Were former Mayor of Tehran Ali Reza Mohajerani to become President of the country, it is widely considered that this would be a disaster for relations with the west and a potential security risk for the region. But his rabble-rousing style and anti-Western rhetoric has proved popular with the masses and put ever more pressure on the unstable, relatively liberal government of Hassan Abdollahi. The temptation for the Abdollahi government to demonstrate its ability to stand up to 'Western imperialist provocation', as these things are usually termed, must have been immensely strong in recent weeks. These operations against three of their most high-profile expatriate critics could well have been their response.

The downside of such action for Abdollahi is obvious. The damage to relations with Western governments will be significant and the risk of even harsher sanctions being introduced is higher than ever. This, rather than the likelihood of a few tit-for-tat diplomatic expulsions, is likely to be weighing on minds in Tehran this evening. Disappointing and tough though this would be for the Iranian people, especially after two years of general thaw between Iran and the west and the sense that a new deal on the country's nuclear programme might have been in the offing, it is unlikely to have discouraged the regime overly. Tehran remains on good terms with both the Kremlin and Beijing, neither of whom is likely to react to the events of recent days with more than a shrug, both of whom can supply Iran with much of the economic support it requires. Since it is impossible to conceive of any individual ever being prosecuted for the murders of Professor Sadaghiani, Dr Qarib and Dr Nassirian—the perpetrators are undoubtedly back in Tehran already—one must ask whether these atrocious acts of violence will ever be suitably punished.

All of which was read assiduously in the corridors of Vauxhall Cross and had its thousands of secretive employees gazing at each other over their coffee mugs and asking themselves "Who on earth is Westerman talking to?"

THREE

"By the time I got to Cambridge," said Sebastian Friend, "the investigation was already more than a week old. There was very little investigating for me to do. My job was to speak to the DCI leading the team and try to interpret the facts in the light of everything else that was going on."

"By everything else, you mean all our networks in Iran being blown sky high," suggested Lascelles.

"Our networks and Derrick Halsgrove. He was blown sky high too."

"Of course he was. Did you know him before? Or about the Iran networks?"

"I'd heard of Halsgrove of course. Who in the Service hadn't? But I'd never met him, and I knew nothing about the networks. Not until I was briefed."

"Is that usual?"

"For my department, yes. You don't send an operational agent into hostile territory with his head stuffed full of intelligence he doesn't need. I had no need to know about our Iranian networks until I went there, and then only because part of my job involved finding out what had happened to them."

"All right then, I suggest we continue with the same week. The Cambridge murder has just become headline news, and then the news comes through from Tehran. Shall we talk about that?"

FOUR

Even as he opened it, Henry Blake was aware of a suspicion at the back of his mind that the second bottle of champagne of the evening was likely to be a mistake. And not just because he had forgotten his wife's usual injunction to open anything fizzy over the kitchen sink; forgotten until the contents foamed out over the living room carpet and his neatly brushed suede shoes.

The first bottle had been an accompaniment to dinner at their favourite restaurant in Putney, a tradition on their wedding anniversary. And since Blake had booked leave for the following day, he had assumed he was on fairly safe ground for the next few hours. But Blake was Head of Middle East Desk at SIS's Vauxhall Cross headquarters and knew only too well that there was no such thing as a guaranteed day off, even when you have been marked down for 'emergency contact only' on all internal systems. Before turning the lights out, his finger had hovered over the mute button on his work mobile without ever quite pressing it. When, in the deepest hour of sleep somewhere around a quarter-to-four in the morning, it had begun blaring out its familiar tune, he had recognised the end of a romantic interlude in the sharp jab of his wife's elbow in the vicinity of his ribs. Then came the onset of a splitting headache, whose growth behind his eyes he could visualise like a time-lapse photo sequence of a nuclear fireball in the seconds after the line went dead and his mind began to process what he had just heard.

With a whisper of "Sorry, darling", he lifted his legs out of bed, felt blindly around the floor for his slippers, and padded softly out to the bathroom, tripping over his discarded trousers on the way. He stood under a tepid shower for five minutes, hoping the headache would pass, then managed to disturb his wife again as he hunted in the wardrobe for an uncreased set of clothes, earning a pillow flung at his retreating back in retribution. The Uber was waiting for him by the time he made it downstairs. He told the driver to drop him at the top of Glasshouse Walk, from where he could walk to Vauxhall Cross in five minutes, and then set about rousing the rest of his team from their slumbers. It was going to be a long day for all of them.

The Night Duty Officer, Mary Hopkin, was waiting for Blake inside the security gates and walked with him up to his office on the third floor.

"Sorry to have to call you in," she said as they trotted up the steps towards the lift. "I know you had today booked off."

"Well, better this morning than last night, anyway. I checked the IFP website on the way in but there was nothing much. What are the details so far?"

"Signals intercept from GCHQ about midnight our time. Six Revolutionary Guard units were being deployed to arrest what were termed 'anti-government elements'. Some sort of internal purge, they thought at first, so they kept it to themselves. But then two or three hours later they got wind of the story coming out through the Farsi language media. Online outlets mostly but it seems Kayhan is leading with the story in its early print edition."

Blake nodded. "Makes sense. Kayhan has pretty good links with the IRGC. More or less an official mouthpiece. Must have had a tip-off in advance to make their early edition though."

They stepped into the lift together and Blake stifled a yawn. He rubbed his temples with his fingertips and tried to make his eyes focus on the lift buttons.

"Struggling?" asked Hopkin.

"Yeah, just a bit. Listen, Mary, you don't happen to have an aspirin on you, do you? My head's giving me a bit of drum 'n' bass."

"I may have some paracetamol in my desk. I'll have a look for you."

"Thanks. What else is there?"

"According to GCHQ, Kayhan is running the line that more than fifty western spies, terrorists and provocateurs have been arrested as heroic IRGC forces break up a plot to disrupt or influence the presidential election."

"Any of our people involved?"

"We don't know yet. I think that's what you'll have to find out."

"Fine. Who else is in?"

"No one from your desk. I suppose they're on their way. And Burgsmuller's been trying to contact you. Wants you to give him a call back as soon as you can. He's in his office."

"Burgsmuller?" Blake looked at his watch. Ken Burgsmuller was his counterpart with CIA at Langley. "Christ. What time is it there? I can't think."

"They're five hours behind, so it's coming up to midnight. He said he'd wait."

"He'll have to."

The lift opened at the third floor, and they peeled off towards their respective sections. The door that led through to the suite of offices occupied by Middle East Desk was protected by dual security; Blake first keyed in a four-digit code, then held his security pass up to the reader and heard the click of the lock. At the end of the grey corridor, Blake's personal office also unlocked at the tap of his pass. He turned on the lights and walked behind his desk, switching on his PC as he sat down. Using an old metal key, he unlocked his bottom desk drawer and pulled out a small Nokia mobile. He hit the power switch and laid it on the desk before him, leaning back in his chair and closing his eyes. For a few seconds he dozed, until the ping of an incoming text message snapped him out of it. As he reached to pick the phone up there came another, and then another. He held the phone in front of his eyes and stared at it, aghast, as message after message flashed on the screen. At last the flood stopped. Nineteen in all; each of them arriving in the last three hours from an Iranian number. Slowly he began to scroll through them, nausea rising in his gullet as the truth became clear.

"Jesus," he said softly. "Oh, Jesus Christ!"

The little Nokia phone, a 'burner' containing a pre-paid SIM from a Lebanese network, was used for receiving final emergency signals from SIS's Middle Eastern assets. If an asset sent a single, individually assigned code word by text message to this phone, it meant he was blown and going dark, if he had time to do so. Blake was looking at nineteen of them. Nineteen individual code words received since GCHQ's intercept of Revolutionary Guard movements that night. Nineteen agents blown and probably arrested. If it were true, and it most certainly looked like it was, then most of the assets in SIS's various networks across Iran had been rolled up in a single night. Three decades of patient network building and intelligence work had gone up in smoke.

Blake was dumbstruck. A terrible sense of guilt swept over him. The mobile was kept as an emergency measure; it was supposed to be kept on his person, or a member of his team's, at all times. It was a rule he had always been strict about. He had imposed it himself. For several minutes he stared vacantly at the phone's screen, long after it had gone dim and the red flag from the last of his agents had faded to blackness. Then somehow he roused himself and painstakingly went through the log-on procedure for his PC. Slowly, he moved through the mental and physical gears that took him away from the state of total inertia that shock, interrupted sleep and a champagne hangover had left him in, and by the time the first of his team popped his head around his door he was back to something like normal.

Of course it was Nima. It had to be Nima, himself the son of Iranian refugees with grandparents still in Shiraz. The loss of the networks would be more personal to him than anyone else on the Desk.

"I'm in, boss," he said more cheerily than could be expected at this hour. "What's going on?"

"All our Iranian networks are being rolled up as we speak, that's what. Red flags have gone up from nineteen agents. I'm emailing you the list now. Emergency contact procedures for everyone. Focus on the ones we haven't heard from yet. Maybe we can warn them in time. Divide it up between the three of you. And get someone monitoring the news outlets in Tehran; we can't wait for GCHQ to drip-feed us the latest whenever they get round to it. You can brief the rest of the team when they come in, divide the jobs up between yourselves however you want. I'll be on the phone for the next hour or so I expect."

"Right boss." Nima showed no sign of shock or upset. Good lad, thought Blake. You could always rely on him to get on with the job.

No sooner had Nima disappeared than Mary Hopkin walked through the door carrying a packet of tablets and a glass of water.

"I only had ibuprofen; I hope that's okay."

"Fine, bless you." Blake took the tablets from her and immediately punched two out of their blister strip, swallowing them whole and washing them down with water. Mary Hopkin was still standing there. "Something else, Mary?"

"Yes. More trouble on your patch, I'm afraid. News coming in from Reuters. There's been a car bomb explosion in Baghdad, in the green zone."

In the green zone? Car bombs were ten a penny in Baghdad, but one in the green zone was more unusual.

"Any casualties?"

"Nothing on that yet."

"Well, it can wait then. Bigger things on our plate at the moment. Log it for now, and I'll pick it up later."

"Righto." Hopkin headed for the door but paused on the threshold and said, "Hope you feel better soon, Henry."

Blake acknowledged the comment with a nod of the head as he picked up his desk phone. "Some chance," he said to the closed door behind her.

Blake spent the next twenty minutes on the phone to the Head of Station at the Embassy in Tehran but learned nothing of value. They were relying on the same information sources to work out what was going on and using the same emergency contact procedures to establish whether any member of any of the networks was still at liberty. They had received no response. The Head of Station had tried to reach a journalist contact, not an asset as such but a man who could usually be relied upon to give an accurate steer about events, but this too had proved fruitless. The man's phone was dead. He would keep at it and let Blake know if he heard anything.

Blake then called Ken Bursgmuller in Langley. He got on well with Ken, although they had never met in person. He imagined him as a lean, Teutonic type who played tennis at the Philadelphia Club on weekends and kept his wife and three kids in respectable comfort on some gated estate. Perhaps it might have disappointed him to learn that Burgsmuller was in fact a portly African-American who shared his home with a male interior designer half his age and had a penchant for patterned silk waistcoats, or vests as he called them. Either way, the two were in regular communication with the approval of their superiors and shared a basic level of understanding of each other's operations. It was now past one in the morning on the eastern seaboard, but the CIA man picked up the call on the first ring.

"Sorry I couldn't call you back sooner, Ken," said Blake, "but it's been a hell of a night here and I'm still trying to get an idea of what's going on."

"You too then," replied Burgsmuller sadly. His voice sounded tired and dry, as if this call were just one more in a long line of despairing conversations that had brought him no relief. "Sorry to say it, Henry, but it seems like all our agents just got rolled up in the space of one night."

"No one got out?"

"Well, we don't know for sure, but given that we haven't heard so much as a squeak out of anyone it sure as hell looks like it."

"Dammit! Same at our end. We had red flags go up from nineteen agents across every network. No response since then from any of them."

"Well, not that I want to get all competitive about it, but it's more than sixty here, and no sign of it stopping yet. A dollar to a dime that by sun-up we don't have a man, woman or child in Iran who can tell us a damn thing."

"Hell, it's a mess. How can we go thirty years without losing an agent out there to suddenly losing everyone in a single night?"

"Beats me, I don't mind telling you."

"I... oh hang on just a second will you Ken?" He put his hand over the mouthpiece and looked up at Mary Hopkin who was standing quietly in the open doorway, a look of profound shock on her face. "What is it, Mary?"

"It's that car bomb in Baghdad..."

"What about it? I told you it could wait."

"Yes, but there's more come in from Reuters. They say only two casualties, but one of them's Derrick Halsgrove."

"Halsgrove?"

"Yes, Henry. Derrick's been killed."

FIVE

Even Reuters cannot be right all the time. Derrick Halsgrove had not been killed, and no one was more surprised by this fact than Halsgrove himself. In fact, at first he was not completely certain that he wasn't dead. At first, he was not aware of being able to see, hear, smell or feel anything at all; his entire identity and experience reduced to the simple awareness of self, and nothing more. Slowly, he became conscious of his own breath: slow, rhythmical, in and out. It was calming in a way. Then a kind of remote whistling noise in his left ear became apparent; soft and constant like an old steam kettle boiling away somewhere on the other side of the house. Not getting shriller or boiling dry and running out of steam, just *there*. That much was positive. Corpses neither breathed nor heard, he was fairly sure of that, but it concerned him that he could not feel anything. He had an idea that he was lying down, that his eyes were closed, or bandaged in some way. But he had none of that sense of pressure on his frame that comes from lying even on a soft mattress and he could feel no bandages around his face. He couldn't even feel his eyelids, come to that. He tried somehow to *will* his eyes open, but how can you open your eyes if you can't feel them? How can you move a muscle you are no longer certain you have?

Time passed, he sensed that at least. He drifted. He tried to remember: but what? The noise in his ear was stronger now, as if the kettle had been brought into the room or he had been wheeled somehow closer to it. If they moved him, would he even notice? Then more drifting, not sleep as such or even dozing but a sense of time elapsed without conscious thought. But now something was different: a dizziness, a disorientation. Pain. Pain searing up his left side from his knee right up to his face. A hot, burning, sticky pain that seemed to have coagulated around him. What had happened to him? His heart began to race. His eyes, he could feel his eyes now. Pain-free but heavy and stuck closed as if with glue or dried blood. He struggled with them and at last freed first the right lid and an instant later the left. He was met with a blinding whiteness which made him clamp both eyes shut again. His retinas seemed to be burning from it. He felt himself wrinkle his nose and utter a weak groan. And then from somewhere inside the whistling he heard another noise: a rapid beeping of machinery then a confused clatter of footsteps. Then silence.

When he next became aware of himself, Halsgrove noticed that the pain was gone, but his other sensations remained. Less acutely, but there all the same. He could feel the mattress underneath him and probed the rest of his body for other responses. He couldn't move. There didn't seem to be anything holding him down, but none of his limbs, none of his digits, would respond. He didn't seem to have any feeling at all below the shoulder, nor could he turn his head on the pillow. He was lying slightly more to his right side than otherwise; did that account for the pain he had felt on his left side earlier? All he could do was move his face, wrinkle his nose, his forehead, open his mouth just enough to lick his dry lips. Beyond that his jaw refused to co-operate. That he could open his eyes he already knew, but next time he would do it gradually. Then he heard the voice.

"Derrick?"

For some reason the sound of it terrified him. It was a gentle voice, filled with concern, and it spoke his name. But he wasn't ready for it. He didn't want it to be there. He wished it would go away.

"Derrick? Are you awake?"

It wasn't going away. He felt he ought to open his mouth and bark back "It's Mr Halsgrove to you!" at whoever it was, but he had neither the strength nor the will. He opened his lips a fraction and felt a stream of saliva drip down to the pillow. Dear God, was this him now?

"I think you can hear me Derrick. Don't try to move. You've been sedated. You're in hospital and you've been here two days. You were caught in an explosion and you had a rough coupla days, but you'll live. Hear me? You're gonna be okay."

Okay? He was going to be okay? When had okay ever been enough for Derrick Halsgrove? And where in God's name was he? Had they shipped him back to Britain? The voice was American, he thought, so he was probably still overseas. Where had he been? He tried to remember. It was vital to him to know. He tried to think rationally, to build up a picture of the situation he found himself in that was as factual as possible. What the doctor (if he was a doctor) had said was plausible. Certainly he had been in some sort of dreadful incident like an explosion; perhaps he was in hospital. The lack of feeling in most of his body surely spoke of injury and sedation; was the nausea from morphine? But he couldn't remember where he had been or what he was doing. The odds were heavy that he had been overseas on an operation when it had happened, whatever it was. And operations meant one thing: hostile territory. That meant it was more than likely that the hospital he was in was under opposition control. The fact that the doctor's voice sounded American meant nothing. People all over the world sounded American when they spoke English. He might be in Vladivostok or Shanghai for all he knew. The conclusion was inescapable. He must say nothing. He must listen and learn, but better that his memory should not return at all than that it should come back when he was under enemy control. If the memories started to come back to him he must bury them, and bury them deep.

After two days, Halsgrove found he was able to move his head around a little to get a sense of his surroundings, even to murmur a few words of thanks or acknowledgement to the medical staff. He had seen the cast on his arm, the tubes running into his side, the monitors flashing and beeping away. They told him he was in Number 25 Combat Support Hospital in Baghdad. He was on his own in a private ward and there were four of them taking care of him: the doctor who had spoken to him and three nurses. They all looked and sounded American enough and all wore combat uniform under their scrubs. One of the nurses, a jolly black woman who introduced herself as Aisha, said she came from Louisiana and sounded like it.

The Major didn't sound like that at all. He arrived on the third day wearing the uniform of the 1st Signal Regiment and spoke with that singular accent—halfway between Thames Estuary and a bad Eton drawl—which is unique to forces personnel who have spent half their lives stationed on bases around the world. He said his name was Protheroe, that he was attached to the Army Intelligence Corps and had authority from 'C' to conduct an initial debrief. He held a military ID close to Halsgrove's face just long enough for him to see it for what it was. Halsgrove was unimpressed. It was going to take more than a well-tailored uniform, an easily forged ID and a decent bit of voice coaching to get him to talk, even if there were anything he could tell them.

"Is there anything you can remember?" asked Major Protheroe. "Anything at all that might help?" Halsgrove shook his head. "You can't recall what you were doing in Baghdad?" Another shake. "Oh well," the Major seemed resigned. "At least there are one or two things I might be able to tell you. For one thing, it was a car bomb that got you."

Well, that makes sense, thought Halsgrove. *Baghdad and car bomb go together like, well, strawberries and cream.* The Major went on. "Only one other casualty besides yourself. An Iranian journalist: Reza Ghollamhossein. Does the name mean anything to you?"

Halsgrove's blank expression signified another "no".

"I see. Well, he was killed outright, I'm afraid. He was in the car and triggered the explosion when he started the engine. You were about five yards away on the pavement at the time. Whether your presence was a coincidence or not, I suppose we will never know. There was a lamppost between you and the car which gave you some sort of protection from the blast. I suppose it saved your life. You'll probably be here for a few weeks yet before you can be shipped home to begin rehabilitation. It's marvellous what they can do these days. I suppose that's one thing we can thank these God-awful wars for."

The Major paused when he saw Halsgrove was trying to speak. He edged his chair a little closer and bent his head towards Halsgrove's mouth. The words came out in a strangled whisper.

"What's wrong with me?"

The Major jumped back in his chair with a start.

"What, haven't they told you? Oh sod it, what have I done now? Well look, you'll have to get the details from the medical staff but basically the blast hit you from the left: arm, leg, left side of spine. That's why you're propped up a bit on your right side. I can't tell you how bad the damage is, but I know it's nothing terminal. You're not in any danger and you will get better."

The Major prattled on for another few minutes, before remarking that his visit was probably tiring Halsgrove out and bolting for the door. "Thank you and goodnight," mouthed Halsgrove to his immaculately jacketed back, "and do come again." He had been oddly comforted by the encounter. The Major was too much of a fool to be anything but English.

The next few days saw Halsgrove make good progress. He gained more movement in his upper body and was able to prop himself up on one elbow. He began to chat with the nurses and one of them came in to read Steinbeck to him for half an hour each day. He received messages from home wishing him a speedy recovery. All this cheered him. But his memory still had not returned. Those which seemed recent were a jumbled, inconsistent mess. He had a strong impression of a meeting with the Head of Station in Riyadh, but when it had taken place and what had been discussed there were a mystery to him. There was nothing incongruous about his going to Riyadh, or even being there in Baghdad (he had at last accepted that he was in Baghdad); the Middle East, North Africa, the major part of the Islamic world from Morocco to Kashmir was very much his operational territory, but it frustrated him not to be able to put a finger on why.

Dr Kriegler told him not to worry. The memory loss was a function of shock, and would almost certainly pass. The immediate circumstances of the explosion might never come back—which was surely no bad thing—but the rest of it would. There was no sign of any neurological damage, only the damage to the hearing in his left ear. He was less certain about whether that would return in time. The prognosis with his other physical injuries was still unclear. His left arm had been shattered by the blast, but they had operated as soon as his condition stabilised and Kriegler was confident he would regain something like full use. The shrapnel damage to his legs and back was nasty but superficial. Of more concern was the nerve damage to his spine. In most cases of this kind, the damage was temporary but not in all. The improvement in Halsgrove's upper body was encouraging. It would just be a case, he said, of wait and see.

But the doctor hadn't even finished speaking before Halsgrove had reminded himself that wait-and-see had never been his policy. With him it had always been decide-and-do. Halsgrove would never be satisfied with spending the rest of his life in a wheelchair, or in bed. And so he set about curing himself, slowly starting to exercise the muscles and limbs he could feel and using his imagination with those he could not. He imagined sinking his toes into warm sand or cool water, the sensations of touch and movement, heat and cold; he brought back the vividness of exercise, of sprinting on the track, skipping, kickboxing, bare feet pounding the punch bag until reddened and sore. He recalled blisters and calluses, toenails torn by poorly fitted boots until the remembrance of pain was as dear to him as pleasure or joy. And when, two weeks later, he felt first a tingle, then a minute spasm of contraction in a single toe, it was something like the greatest triumph of his life. The next morning they told him of the arrangements for sending him home.

*

The news of Derrick Halsgrove's death had spread through Vauxhall Cross like a shockwave. He had been one of those legendary field-agents whose exploits, never officially discussed, were known about and exaggerated around every water-cooler in the building. He was the sort of hero that the general public imagined defending their lives and their country and who inspired the keen young field agents who were starting out in their careers. News of the car bomb and its victim cast a pall over the building that might have been smoke from the explosion itself. When this initial report proved to be false, so significant was the news that 'C' himself saw fit to announce the good tidings in an email to the entire service. Amid the resulting jubilation, it was easy to understand why the details of the bomb's one true fatality were largely overlooked. And it was there that Henry Blake redeemed himself for his night of champagne domesticity and for what he felt to be his culpability for the loss of the Iranian networks. It came to him in a sudden flash of intuition during another call with the Head of Station in Tehran and it was rather like, he later recalled, understanding that two and two actually make three hundred and seventeen instead of four.

"That friendly journalist you were trying to contact the other night," he said. "His name wasn't by any chance Reza Ghollamhossein, was it?"

SIX

"How many agents were lost in the end?" asked Lascelles. "Twenty-four," replied Friend. "Nineteen had time to send up their red flag but the other five did not. It made no difference. All our networks lost every single member. Overnight we went from significant penetration of Iranian military, scientific and political establishments to not having a single agent left at large in the country. Overnight. It was unprecedented. When I spoke to Henry Blake, he told me he didn't think he would ever get over it. It was like being in charge of the British Army on the first day of the Somme. The biggest single operational disaster in the Service's history."

"It was that damaging, you think?"

"It's not simply a question of damage," Friend explained. "Philby, Burgess and Maclean caused greater damage over a longer period. But think of it as a shock to the system, a single, brutal hit to our self-belief. I couldn't help thinking at the time that the Iranians had done it this way for exactly that reason. They might have been in a position to break any one of the networks earlier, perhaps years earlier, but waited until they had them all for the sheer shock and embarrassment it would cause."

"An interesting theory but I'm not sure it fits too well with your official report. Did you have anything to back it up?"

"Not a thing. And you're right, it doesn't fit well. Not least because it relies on the assumption that the Iranians knew these networks were all we had. But it's what I felt at the time and what Henry Blake felt too. He took it very personally."

"I see. So this is the point where you began, where your department was called in?"

Friend nodded.

"We have a chain of events: the murder of Professor Sadaghiani in Cambridge, the rolling up of our networks in Tehran, and the blowing up of Derrick Halsgrove and an Iranian journalist in Baghdad, all in the space of less than a week. When exactly were you given your brief?"

"Two days after the news broke about the networks."

"You were briefed by the Director?"

"No. The Director was present, but the initial briefing came personally from 'C'. Over lunch at the Travellers Club. The Director filled in the details later, over still water in his office." He laughed at the memory.

"You find something amusing, Mr Friend?"

"Just the contrast between brief and debrief. More striking than usual. If you'll forgive the observation."

Lascelles ignored the quip. "Is that usual? A personal briefing from 'C', I mean."

"No. I'd never met him before."

"So how do you account for it?"

Friend shrugged. "Difficult to say. I suppose he wanted to stress the importance and sensitivity of the job. It's not normal for me to be sent on an assignment that's front-page news."

"I see. Were you told why you were given the assignment?"

"If you're asking why me personally, then no, you'd have to ask the Director. As for why it was my department, I think we were the obvious choice. We're trained in operations and investigations, we operate overseas and at home, we don't carry any superfluous intelligence about in our heads, as I've already explained, so we can be sent into hostile territory with less risk to the Service." He paused and smiled at Lascelles for the first time. "Sometimes it also helps that we're off the official books and not based at Vauxhall Cross. Makes us more deniable. But of course you know all that already."

Lascelles smiled back at Friend, leaving him uncertain how much the other man really did know about his curious branch of Britain's intelligence services.

.

SEVEN

The existence and nature of Friend's department was not widely known even among the denizens of Vauxhall Cross and Thames House, although it did business with both of those more publicly visible bodies. Born amid the frenzied preparations for war of the late 1930s, it had been absorbed during the subsequent conflict into the Special Operations Executive and had participated in Churchill's plan to "set Europe ablaze" with enthusiasm and success. The end of the war had seen it, along with the rest of SOE, become part of a larger SIS, but it had nevertheless retained its structural and operational independence, thanks perhaps to its deliberately limited size and the solidity of its cover. Its employees, few in number, were recruited exclusively through SIS, where HR records listed them as having transferred out of the Service. The destination of these transfers, as with every other reference to the Department in SIS records or communications, was both vague and coded. The code had changed over time and had included such designations as simply *The Department, Box 1200, The Bureau* and most recently *The Audit Department*.

Based away from Vauxhall Cross for security reasons, it boasted its own offices on a quiet street in Mayfair, under the guise of a genuine and historic private bank. The Head of Department was always known simply as the Director. The present incumbent was the sixth in line and had been in post for more than a decade. He had been an obvious choice; a distinguished RAF career having been followed by a number of senior posts in the City. Friend was one of five operational members of the department who reported to him and were generally briefed by him on the details of every assignment they were offered. The number never rose above five, and if one of the number resigned, transferred out or was incapacitated or killed it might stay below it for some time. Suitable recruits for the department were few in number; suitable missions rarely were. More often than not the Director was obliged to select a particular operative for an assignment simply because he or she was the only one available.

So it was that Sebastian Friend got the Tehran job. Friend had been something of a lost soul when he joined the Service, still failing to cope with the demons left by a military career which had ended in tragedy. He had so many of the qualities that the Director habitually looked for: bravery, intelligence, resourcefulness, a natural flair for languages. But there was an impatience and a restlessness too; Friend was temperamentally unsuited to the painstaking, long-term work of a standard field agent or handler. Put him behind a desk and he would implode. Drop him into a hostile situation with limited briefing or back-up, however, and he would thrive in a way that few others could. He wasn't the sort of investigator who could master a thousand tiny details of evidence and keep them at his fingertips, but in a funny way his instincts often seemed to lead him to the heart of the matter. That, in the Director's experience, was the rarest and most valuable of gifts.

"Will he take orders?" 'C' had asked.

"I don't want him to take orders!" the Director had responded, rather too forcefully for 'C's taste. "I want him to keep his wits about him and think on his feet. His orders end when we put him on the ground. The rest is up to him. If that means he goes off script, so be it. He's in a better place to judge whether the script was accurate than we are, stuck behind our desks a thousand miles from the action. That's true for all my people."

The fact that it was truer of Friend than most, that Friend had a habit of trusting his instincts and following them even to the extent of contravening his instructions, the Director kept to himself. 'C' was unlikely to agree that this very independence of thought was Friend's greatest asset.

'C', as he so often did, sensed the Director's implied rebuke. He was one of nature's office dwellers. So there was more than a touch of irony about the fact that, having spent almost his entire Service career around Vauxhall Cross and Whitehall and having no major overseas posting on his record, he frequented the Travellers on Pall Mall. Since his appointment as Head of the Secret Intelligence Service, Sir Richard Graves had eschewed the more public profile of his immediate predecessors and reintroduced the Service's original focus on security and discretion. When meeting colleagues based elsewhere he would never invite them to his offices at Vauxhall Cross, but arrange a discreet rendezvous on neutral territory. This had in practice meant alfresco discussions in London parks, however inclement the weather, until a recent chance encounter with a Press Association photographer in the rose garden at Regents Park had led to a change of tack.

The change in Sir Richard's attitude to indoor meetings may also have been influenced by his acquisition of a new gadget. The Service's technical section had lately developed an app which, when activated on a Service mobile, turned it into a short-range jamming device against electronic signals, effectively obstructing any attempts at eavesdropping and ensuring that conversations remained private. A side effect was that it also blocked any mobile phone and Wi-Fi signals within the same fifty-foot range. This could be inconvenient at times, but it gave Sir Richard no end of private amusement when dining with his children.

"Shall we go dark, gentlemen?" was 'C's announcement that the jamming app was now active as he welcomed them to a corner table in the Travellers' plush first floor 'Coffee Room' with its line of grand sash windows overlooking Pall Mall. In this case the choice between security and connectivity was an easy one: a club rule strictly forbade the use of mobile phones within the building.

There were no introductory pleasantries and no attention was paid to the menu. Without consulting his guests, 'C' ordered a bottle of house claret and cold roast beef with new potatoes. He proceeded to quiz Friend on his progress in the Service: his background, family, education, early career. Friend answered each question as simply as he could, without elaboration. He knew they were of no particular significance to the prospect before him, apart from allowing 'C' to appraise him as an individual before briefing him for the task. The Director sat and listened quietly and approvingly while sipping at a glass of claret. It pleased him that Friend was concise and professional in his answers. He only raised a discreet eyebrow once, when he heard Friend describe his old company comrades from Third Battalion, The Rifles as being "scattered to the four winds". Aside from Friend's taste for overly poetic description, it seemed to him a rather cold-blooded way of recalling how five men from his unit had been blown to pieces by an improvised explosive device before his very eyes.

"I'm glad we've had this chance to chat," said 'C' after the waitress brought their food and refilled the glasses. "I know it's not the usual form for you to get a briefing from the Head of the Service, and after today you will report to the Director in the normal way. He will fill you in on any additional details and keep you up to speed with new developments as you progress. I really wanted to see you in person to get the measure of you, so to speak, because of the particular difficulties of this assignment. Both for the Service and for you. The Cambridge murder has been splashed all over the front pages, including Professor Sadaghiani's association with the Tehran Committee and, through that, with the Service. That puts us in the news again, which is exactly what I've been trying to avoid since I've been in this position. But it also means that the media will be on the lookout for any sign of incompetence on our part, and no doubt the inquisitive little buggers will also be expecting someone like yourself to turn up in Cambridge during the investigation. So you'll need to try and blend in the with police team while you're there. I'm told the officer in charge is a good man, is that right, Director?"

"Yes. Wetherby," said the Director. "He did eight years in Special Branch and our paths have crossed more than once. Like most of them, he views our kind as a nuisance. But he's discreet and more helpful than most."

"Fine. You'll liaise directly with this Wetherby, then. Get him to take you through the evidence. Make your own judgement if you can, but don't share it with him. What we need to know is whether this really was another political assassination by a foreign government on British soil."

"Is there any real doubt about that, sir?"

"Not as far as the media is concerned. But unlike the media, and certain politicians I could mention, I prefer to assess all the evidence before I make a judgement. And certainly, before I suggest any response to the Minister, even if he has already made his mind up. It will be your job to check whether there are any other lines of enquiry the police ought to consider, any evidence which doesn't fit the preferred narrative. If there is, report it to the Director."

"I understand, sir."

"Good. Then we have the other side of the business. Twenty-four agents, the guts of our networks in Iran, rolled up in one night. Similar stories coming out from the Americans, French and Germans. The Tehran Committee looks like it's finished, and those lovely Revolutionary Guard people are gearing up for the biggest set of show trials since Stalin's purges. Then one of our own men, Derrick Halsgrove, gets himself badly injured by a car bomb which killed an Iranian journalist. Hardly a coincidence,

I'm sure you agree. I don't think I can possibly exaggerate how much damage we have suffered in the last few days, both to our operations and to our reputation." 'C' leaned forward, his fingers gripping the edge of the table. "Just about every intelligence agency in the West will be conducting its own inquiry. There's probably nothing we can do now to save our agents, but I want to know who is responsible. Somebody somewhere has been talking out of turn. Whoever they are, they have handed over the whole Tehran Committee and every western intelligence agent in Iran over to the Revolutionary Guards on a plate. I very much want to find out that it wasn't one of our people. But if it was, he'll have so much blood on his hands that a little of his own won't matter."

'C' sat back in his chair, his fury spent. He took a sip of wine and dabbed at the corner of his mouth with a napkin. The Director watched him impassively.

"I think I understand, sir," said Friend. "But there'll have to be a lot of digging around before we get to what happens next. And for what it's worth I think it's unlikely the leak would have come from one of our people."

'C' cast a doubtful look at him. "Really? Why do you say that?"

"Well, if I understand the facts correctly, the Americans seem to have fared even worse than we have." He paused, waiting for the other men to make the connection.

"True. Go on."

"And my guess would be that our information sharing with the CIA is not completely even-handed. I mean to say that they know more about our operations than we do about theirs."

'C' said nothing. The lack of balance in the transatlantic intelligence trade was something of a running sore for him. But it was not an issue he felt like being drawn into discussing with operational agents, even if it did have a bearing on the case. Which he doubted.

"Although it doesn't necessarily follow," Friend continued,

THE OTHER SIDE OF TRUST

"that because it couldn't be one of ours it must have been one of theirs. It might just as well have been someone from within the Committee itself. An Iranian government mole, for example. And of course I can't be absolutely certain that it wasn't one of our people. Not yet, at least."

'C' sat quietly for a moment. There was something oddly compelling and persuasive about this young Mr Friend. He didn't look like a man of action, but his record spoke for itself. He looked too pleasant to have real gravitas, but he clearly thought logically and expressed himself well. If he had the knack of getting the truth out of people without giving too much of his own agenda away, then he should do a good job. The Director had been right.

"So," he said at last, "your first priority is to establish whether anyone from our side could have had detailed enough knowledge of American networks to blow them as well as our own. The rest will follow from there."

"I'll need your authority to interview the relevant people," said Friend.

"You'll have it. You'll have whatever you need. Speak to anyone you want. Just do it away from Vauxhall Cross if you can."

"I may need to consult Records as well."

"I'll have you cleared for access to any files on the Committee or Iranian ops, of course."

"I may need the paper archive at Vauxhall Cross too, sir. I don't know how far back I'll have to go and some of the older files may never have been digitised."

"Oh very well. If you need to come in, then I suppose you'll have to. I'll grant authority. But you know the protocols for externals, I presume." Friend nodded. "It's just possible you may need to go out to Iran as well," 'C' added. "But I'll leave that to the two of you to work out."

"Just one more thing, sir," Friend sensed that 'C' was about to declare the subject closed. "Do you happen to know how many Iranians we still have in the country with links to the Committee?"

"I'd have to look it up, but I believe it's somewhere between two hundred and two hundred and fifty."

"Well, we'll need to sweat them, sir. At least as many of them has had access to the right information. It's just possible a leak might have come from one of them. I'll need some help though; two hundred and fifty is a bit much for one man."

"Don't you worry. That's what we have the Security Service for. I'll get them on to it."

And that was it. They pushed the food around their plates for another few minutes before declining coffee and trooping sombrely back down the stairs. Friend cast a quick glance at the sketchy portrait of Patrick Leigh Fermor which hung at the bottom of the staircase. Perhaps if he kidnapped an Iranian general in Tehran and smuggled him back to London, they might hang his own portrait up there too. Posthumously.

EIGHT

It was with little enthusiasm that Sebastian Friend travelled by train up to Cambridge. He felt that the Sadaghiani murder was a sideshow to the main event, that his real work would be the patient research into who had access to or knowledge of Iranian operations. It would be a case of poring over paperwork and meticulous questioning, not tiptoeing around the edges of a very public murder investigation. The Cambridge angle was likely to lead in only one direction: back to Iran. An Iranian assassin would have done the job. It would have been a quick in-and-out by a suitably obscure route. All of that seemed certain. The odds were long on the killer ever being identified, but if he were it would be by solid police work rather than his own efforts. After that, it would be up to the politicians to decide how to respond. None of that would get him an inch closer to knowing who was really responsible. But the Director had insisted he cover all angles, and so he was there to make himself known to the senior investigating officer, and to find out what he could.

It was also the fact that he simply wasn't in the mood to be diplomatic. His briefings by 'C' and the Director had been followed by a long-planned but disappointing visit to Sadler's Wells. He had gone at the behest of the friend who accompanied him, to see a visiting Russian dancer she had long admired but never before had a chance to see. Friend had been persuaded at the time, but sitting through the performance had been an experience first baffling, then at last deeply irritating. It had been one of those modern, minimalist pieces with a score played on solo piano by a composer who desired his audience to absorb the full import of each note before he proceeded to the next, and choreography which involved a pair of dancers writhing and crawling over and around each other's bodies with excruciating slowness. It was supposed, the publicity had claimed, to make the audience question their assumptions about the nature of art and dance. It left Friend questioning whether he hadn't seen and heard it all too many times before. Then when his friend had gushed her approval over a drink at the end of the performance, he had almost quarrelled with her.

He wanted nothing more than to get home and relax with a whisky in silence, but even in this he was foiled. The flat he called home was a spacious three-bedroomed affair in Belsize Park. He had spent the early part of his childhood there, before a change of ownership on the left-wing newspaper his father edited had coincided with the death of his grandfather and the family's relocation to a sprawling and draughty farmhouse on the edge of the Cheviot Hills, from where Friend senior continued his career remotely as a respected progressive columnist and opinion former. The London flat, for some years rented out, was now shared between Friend and his elder sister Isobel, a doctor whose frequent absences for her work with *Medecins sans Frontiers* were as much of a relief to Friend as his own overseas trips were to her. But Isobel had been back in London for some weeks, and when he arrived home from the ballet it was straight into the middle of a dinner party still in full swing.

Isobel invited him to join them as gracefully as she could, and in the same spirit he accepted. He pulled his mother's old piano stool up to the table and accepted a glass of pinot noir poured by his neighbour, a journalist of some kind from a new media outlet whom he vaguely recalled meeting, and taking an instant dislike to, once before. The rest of the party were strangers to him, but he quickly realised they were cut from identical cloth. There were eight of them in total; a typical gathering of the modern young intelligentsia of London, well-dressed, well-mannered and terribly well-meaning. Friend supposed it was a scene the flat's spacious living / dining room had seen many times in their father's day. He still recalled tiptoeing out of his bedroom and listening through a crack in the door to conversations he never understood with people he never recognised. There had been opposition politicians and Cabinet ministers, trade unionists, prominent journalists and broadcasters, even churchmen. Once, his father claimed, a young Tony Blair had been among the guests. Friend did not remember, but he did wonder whether the atmosphere then had been quite so uniformly earnest as it seemed to him now.

Friend's own politics were not the old Labour shibboleths of his father's day, but a mixture of both left and right-wing attitudes. Those few people he shared them with condemned his position as confused; he countered that it wasn't a position at all and that anyway he preferred to think of it as 'nuanced'. He did not feel like sharing his views tonight. Instead, he sipped at his wine and listened as the issues of the day were discussed and dismissed, each point reinforcing the last and never a contrary view expressed. The more he listened, the more he found it all profoundly disconcerting and he wondered from where the attitude had arisen that those in opposition to their views were not just misguided but basely motivated and immoral. He felt that, if he had spoken his mind, it would have been greeted like an outbreak of blasphemy at a bible meeting.

"You were very quiet tonight," said Isobel after it was over.

"Your friends seemed to have all the answers," he replied. "There didn't seem much I could add."

Isobel gave him a look. "You needn't be so hard on them," she said. "They have strong convictions, just like me. That's why I like them."

45

"Strong convictions? Careful sis, you'll start to sound like Uncle Johan."

Friend was referring to their mother's older brother, a Lutheran pastor of greater than usual moral rigour.

"What the hell does Uncle Johan have to do with anything? Jesus, it's so infuriating trying to talk to you sometimes. Everything's just a joke to you, isn't it?"

"What makes you think I was joking? What I listened to tonight reminded me of all the worst aspects of religious faith. Everyone seemed to have the same unquestioning belief in their own righteousness that Uncle Johan does. It didn't sit well with me, that's all."

"Unquestioning? Who on earth are you to call them unquestioning? At least they believe in something, in the improvement of society, of humanity. What do you believe in, Sebastian?"

Friend felt the rise of an old, familiar tension; his own and his sister's emotions gaining dominance over their reason, the presence of an almost uncontrollable temptation to wound. He forced the feeling back down and smiled in what he hoped was a conciliatory and affectionate way.

"I'm sorry. I don't mean to be hard on your friends. I don't disagree with them about everything, or with you. Perhaps I just envy you all your certainties."

"Certainties?" Isobel laughed, and Friend wished that just occasionally he might hear her laugh out of joy rather than scorn. "You're a fine one to talk about certainties, swanning around the world all the time dispensing violence by government order!"

Friend rarely gave way to anger, but this was too much. "What are you talking about? I'm not a bloody assassin! What do you think I do?"

There was a pause, until Isobel said, coldly and firmly, "I know what you do."

But did she? Friend wondered. Of course she knew the broad outline, that her brother's job was secret, that it involved overseas travel for extended periods; travel from which he sometimes returned bearing wounds that her doctor's eye could not fail to identify. But what did she know of the autonomy he enjoyed in thought and action? Of how his actions in the field were the result of his own deductions and judgement? Did she really think of him as some kind of human drone, little more than a killing machine to be directed against any target his masters thought fit?

A long silence settled upon them, each dreading the next word spoken, a word which might lead to an outburst of the kind that had peppered their relationship with anguish and regret.

"You know what your trouble is?" said Isobel at last. "You've got a brain but you're too lazy to use it. You always reach your opinions through gut instinct instead of subjecting them to rational analysis. That's why you've got such a confused mess of attitudes in your head. If you took the trouble to think about things properly you might have some sort of coherent philosophy, instead of random opinions that don't get you anywhere."

"Perhaps you're right; perhaps it is a bit of a mess in here." Friend tapped his temple for emphasis. "But at least it's my mess. I've reached each of my opinions through my own personal judgement instead of filtering them through some preconceived notion of righteousness. I don't rely on anyone else's judgement to reach my own. I'm immune to groupthink. That might seem like intellectual confusion to you, but to me it feels like having a personality."

Which, Friend realised as he saw the flame begin to burn behind his sister's eyes, was exactly the wrong thing to say. Why, he wondered, could they not be like some of the couples he knew who seemed to have a gift for knowing what to say and do for each other at moments of stress? How could they build such trust and understanding in just a few years together, when he and his sister had spent a lifetime on a knife-edge of emotion? Perhaps it was the result of the natural caution both parties would feel at the beginning of a romance, the knowledge that one word out of place might shatter the growing feeling of compatibility. He and

Isobel, united by blood and shared experience, had only learned the need for reticence amid the debris of a hundred stalemated battles.

The problem didn't stem from lack of love; whenever one of them returned from overseas their joy at the reunion was perfectly genuine. It was, in part, an expression of relief since each knew that the other's work carried with it more than a measure of risk. But there was also comfort in the renewal of the lifelong bond they shared between them. Yet there was relief too in the departures, in the temporary end to the squabbles, the painful words said and the even more painful ones held back but nonetheless understood.

As he stared at his sister, Friend rehearsed in his mind all the possible paths this evening's argument might take and each one seemed to him like a minefield stretching far into the distance. Whichever path he took, the explosion was surely inevitable. And, even if he were to turn around and walk away, they would both know why, and what damage he wished to avoid. There had been a time when he would have pushed on regardless of what lay ahead, determined not to submit, too proud to allow himself to appear the weaker character. But now he wanted it to stop. There were more important things in life than being right, and if there was one thing in life more exhausting than arguing with someone you had no hope of convincing, it was arguing with the people you love. He apologised, held up his hands in surrender and went off to load the dishwasher while Isobel glowered into her final glass of wine.

The next morning he was dressed and almost out of the door before he saw her, bleary-eyed and still in pyjamas and a loosely tied dressing gown. She came straight up to him in the hallway, threw her arms around his neck and planted the softest of kisses on his cheek. Then she disappeared into the bathroom without saying a word. It only added to Friend's feeling that the greatest puzzle of all was his own family.

*

Detective Chief Inspector George Wetherby was in no mood to be diplomatic either. The previous evening he had argued with his wife over a trivial domestic matter affecting their home in Brentford, and had slept badly as a result. The sage old advice that you should never go to bed on an argument was difficult to heed when you spent so many nights separated by distance and incompatible working hours. Now he was uncomfortably aware of being the image of the stereotypical detective: bedraggled hair, stubbled chin, clothes that looked as though he had slept in them because he *had* slept in them. The taste of last night's whisky stubbornly unremoved from his palate by the morning's coffee; the vague, semi-permanent feeling that something was not right with his health.

So when, in the unfinished hospital wing his SO15 team had taken over as their operations centre, the receptionist announced that a Mr Simon Collins of the Foreign Office was here to see him, he had risen from his desk with reluctance and trudged his way down the corridor weighed down by a sense of futility and wasted time. His mood was not improved when the so-called Mr Collins of the so-called Foreign Office rose from his cheap plastic bucket chair and held out a hand in greeting. He wasn't what Wetherby had been expecting at all. He knew from long experience that someone from the 'funny boys' would be dropping in on him before long, but he had anticipated someone considerably older and more lived-in. One of those drab little men in ill-fitting overcoats who look like they are carrying half the secrets of the world in their pockets. This Mr Collins looked too young, too slim, too presentable. Spies were not supposed to wear nicely pressed suits or have carefree smiles that showed their dentistry from twenty feet away.

A more lived-in type of visitor would also have better suited his mood. Wetherby was feeling a little lived-in himself. Instead he found himself faced with this one-man advert for Colgate and clothes brushes; this grinning fair-haired youth who must have risen at four in the morning to have shaved and dressed so carefully and made it here from whatever part of London he lived in by nine-thirty. Professional considerations aside, George Wetherby was perfectly disposed at that moment to hate Mr Collins of the Foreign Office and to demonstrate this strength of feeling by spitting on his highly polished shoes.

"Your name Collins?" he grunted.

"That's right." The smile was followed by an extended hand which Wetherby gave a perfunctory shake before finding himself possessed of an urge to try and straighten his tie. His hand tugged at it uselessly before he remembered that his collar button was undone and gave it up.

"You'd better come with me, then," he said, turning and leading the way down the corridor.

Friend walked calmly in Wetherby's wake, alert to the curious eyes which followed him down the corridor as Wetherby's team of investigators bustled to and fro. It was clear that the impending arrival of Mr Collins of the Foreign Office had been announced and that everybody knew he wasn't really from the Foreign Office and his name wasn't really Collins. The futility of pretence in certain moments of his job was so absurd that at times you could only treat it with amusement. He felt a subversive urge to raise an ironical eyebrow in response to the stares he attracted.

The investigating team from SO15 had set themselves up in a half-built new wing on the hospital's eastern fringe. Intended to provide specialist paediatric care, it was a single-storey extension connected to the main hospital building by a single corridor, shielded from the road by mature trees and a well-tended garden. The structure had been weatherproofed and already benefitted from electricity, water and several telephone lines. But the walls were unpainted, there was no heating and Wi-Fi coverage was patchy at best, which had already caused frustration to Wetherby's team.

Wetherby led him halfway down the corridor until he reached

the small room which served as his private office. Like everywhere else in the new extension, the walls were of bare plaster that still bore the blush of recent work and left a cloying humidity in the air. There was a desk with a computer and a telephone, and a single plastic chair of the kind Friend had sat on in reception, which had creaked alarmingly even under his modest frame. More chairs were stacked in a corner in case Wetherby might need to entertain. A kettle and some plastic beakers sat on a small table by the window to serve the same need. A large map of Cambridge was pinned to the wall and the window was shaded from the outside world by a cheap, white venetian blind. That was it. It was a depressing little room; however little time Wetherby might spend there.

Without waiting to be asked, Friend took a spare chair from the top of the stack and carried it over to the desk.

"Before we get started," said Wetherby as he sat down behind his desk, "let me make myself clear. This is my investigation. Mine and my team's. I won't have any of you funny types coming in here interfering and wasting resources. If you can help, help. If you need to know something, ask and I'll tell you what I can, but…"

Friend held up two hands in supplication. Somehow Wetherby's prickliness had defused his own frustration and now he just wanted to get the job done.

"Please, Detective Chief Inspector. The last thing I want to do is get in your way. I'm not here to run a parallel investigation of my own. I'm here to find out what the facts are, as far as you've been able to establish them, and to hear your interpretation of those facts. Then I'll take the information back to my department and give you my details so you can let me know how things progress. That's all. I don't intend to be here any longer than it takes to do that, so you needn't worry about having me in your pocket for the next fortnight."

Wetherby was embarrassed. He had got off on the wrong foot and it was entirely his own fault. Collins was being perfectly pleasant and reasonable. It was time to unbend a little.

"Well, that's fine then. I'm glad to hear it. And I'm sorry if I came across…"

"No need for apologies at all. And while we're sitting here," Friend nodded in the direction of the kettle, "how about some coffee?"

Wetherby dug into a desk drawer and pulled out a small package.

"How about green tea? We've only got instant coffee here and it's pretty rancid. Anyway, I had enough coffee at breakfast. My wife always sends me away with a packet of green tea. I think she hopes it'll keep me healthy."

Green tea would be fine, said Friend. He watched curiously as Wetherby pulled out a small glass teapot and two small mugs from another drawer. He carefully heaped a single teaspoon of loose tea into the pot's filter compartment and took everything over to the kettle. He waited until the kettle began to rattle and steam before pouring hot water into the pot.

"My wife tells me that green tea should never be brewed at a temperature of above seventy-five degrees. It's not easy to judge exactly with this thing, but I do my best. She also says you shouldn't brew it for more than a minute, or it stews" he said, pouring the liquid into the mugs a moment or two later. "Are you married, Mr Collins?"

"No."

"I'm sorry, I shouldn't pry. Asking questions is an occupational hazard."

"Just as trying not to answer them is for me. Don't worry about it. I can't tell you much about myself, except that I don't really work for the Foreign Office and I've only been Mr Simon Collins since I left London this morning. But of course you knew that already." He paused to take a sip of tea. "And your wife was right, by the way."

"Of course," shrugged Wetherby. "She usually is." He walked over to the map and gestured for Friend to join him. "There isn't much I can tell you at the moment. A week may be a long time in politics but it's the blink of an eye in a murder investigation. The first days are all about collecting evidence. Actually sifting through it all and beginning to understand it takes much longer, even with a team the size I have. But we do have a good idea of Sadaghiani's movements on the day he died now." He pointed to an area of the map, north of the city centre. "He lived here: Avery Close, just off the Histon Road. Decent sized property, modern three-bed semi which he shared with his wife until she died two years ago. Cancer. Since then he's lived alone. He had no other family, not in this country anyway. Occasional visitors, but no one regular. Didn't really mix much with his neighbours, but then that's hardly unusual these days. He gave tutorials to students in his office at the university, never at his home. It's a quiet street, a cul-de-sac, so anyone going in there is going in for a purpose. I only wish I could say it was full of those retired busybodies who spend their days peeking out through net curtains, but it isn't. It's mostly professional people. They noticed him leaving for work around eight-thirty because enough of them were leaving home at the same time. Everybody seems to have been operating on their usual routine. He got into his car, alone, and we have CCTV footage picking him up on Histon Road a few minutes later heading towards the city centre. From there we can follow him pretty much all the way to his office. He didn't stop anywhere.

"He arrived at his office at eight fifty-four. Said hello to the department secretary on the way in, a couple of the other academics saw him arrive. Went straight to his office and, judging from his computer records, spent the morning looking through research papers and reading emails. Everything that morning seems to have been connected to his university work. It looks like he kept his political interests totally separate from that. Just after ten he came out of the office to make himself a cup of coffee. One of his colleagues bumped into him in the kitchen and they exchanged a few words about a student with mental health issues. Then Sadaghiani went back to his office with his cup of coffee and a biscuit. Apparently he was a chocolate hobnob man—make of that what you will. Back in his office he carried on working as before, until about noon. No appointments, no visitors, no one else saw him until he left about noon. He said goodbye to the secretary and mentioned he would be back between three and four." Wetherby paused and turned to Friend. "Now here's a curious thing. For some reason, instead of going straight to where he has lunch, he drives home. We can follow him on camera again, at least we can follow him up the Histon Road so it's a fair assumption he was going home."

Friend interrupted. "Do you know whether he had any phone calls or mail delivered that morning?"

"Yes, there were two incoming calls, both from students. He called one of them back not long before he left. He didn't make any other calls. I don't think there's anything there. Mail is more interesting. Regular post arrived at around eleven but there was nothing for him except a notification of an expenses claim for a trip to Nottingham that had paid out. Then at eleven thirty-five we have a recorded delivery parcel arrive for him. The secretary signed for it and took it to his office. She remembers it was an A5 size padded envelope with some kind of box or cylinder inside. We found the envelope in his waste bin but not the contents. It was posted the previous morning in a village just outside Ely with guaranteed delivery before 1pm the following day. The post office staff there don't remember anything about who posted it. It was pension day and there was a long queue of locals waiting to pick up their money."

"I see. Thank you."

"So the professor is on his way home for some unknown reason. He can't have been at his house more than thirty minutes, because by 1pm we see him on his way back into the city centre. He drives straight to the Grafton West car park, finds a place on level two and prepays £3.80 which gets him two hours' parking at off-peak rates. Long enough for him to enjoy his lunch at a

Turkish restaurant on King Street, which is here.' He pointed to it on the map. 'Now we get to curious fact number two. To get from the car park to the restaurant the obvious route is to come out on Fair Street and then turn down Willow Walk, skirting along the north side of Christ's Pieces. But he doesn't do this. Instead, we have a camera picking him up walking south on the east side of New Square. Completely the wrong direction. Ten minutes later he's going north on Emmanuel Road before turning left onto Willow Walk and completing the expected route to the restaurant. Where he went, and what he did there, we just don't know yet."

Wetherby left the thought hanging and Friend pondered it for a moment, sure he was being tested.

"You say you never found the contents of that envelope he received?"

"That's right. He didn't leave it in his office and we didn't find it in his home or his car, or at least nothing that matches the description of the small box or cylinder the secretary described. Whatever was inside it might be hiding in plain sight and the container could just have been thrown away."

"Or he could have gone out of his way to pass the container and whatever was in it on to someone else."

"Right! My thoughts exactly. But I'm damned if I know where yet. There's no one who lives or works in those streets who has any obvious connection with the professor and the cameras don't give us any more clues. But maybe something will turn up. My team are drawing up detailed profiles of every individual and business based round here, checking every possible social, financial or business connection. If any one of them so much as shared a bus ride with Sadaghiani in the last six months we'll know about it, given time."

"Well, let's leave that for now. What about the restaurant?"

"He arrives at about one forty-five and leaves just before three. Eats an Imam Bayildi and a chicken kebab and drinks a beer. Follows up with Turkish coffee, pays his bill by debit card and leaves. The staff say he was alone and sat quietly reading the latest issue of New Scientist. He seemed perfectly normal. He was something of a regular there; came in a couple of times a month, mostly alone but sometimes with one other person. Not anyone in particular though. This time he was alone. No sign of any illness or distress. When he leaves, he turns down Milton's Walk into Christ's Pieces, strolls past the playground, finds a bench overlooking the bowling green and sits down. One witness thinks she remembers him looking a bit tired and not too steady on his feet when he went up to the bench, but it didn't look like anything serious to her. But that's where he sat down and that's where they found him, almost dead, over an hour later."

"Did anyone speak to him while he was on the bench?"

"No one has said so."

"So who called it in?"

"An elderly woman passing by didn't like the way he was sitting, sort of slumped to one side. When she went to take a closer look, she didn't like the way he was breathing so she called an ambulance. Lucky she didn't try to touch him."

"Well, that's that then. One very dead professor in a park, but at least you know most of what he did that day. What else is there?"

"I suppose we come on to what killed him. According to the Porton Down people it's not an exact match for anything they have samples of so they're running more tests to see if it's closely related to anything they've seen before or if it's something completely new. That might give us an idea of where it came from, but it will probably take weeks." He paused, a show of caution and reluctance when it came to asking a question of his visitor. "I would assume that even if it was the Iranians who did this, they're as likely to have got the stuff from China or Russia as to have made it themselves."

Friend tried to be encouraging but non-committal. "Yes, very likely," he said. "Or from half a dozen other places."

"So that might not get us very far at all, and there's no point holding up the investigation while we wait for it. The other question is delivery. How did they get it into him? The post-mortem found traces on his hands and around his mouth and nose, as if he'd rubbed his face shortly after getting his hands exposed to it. So there was penetration through the skin of his hands and face but also some traces inside his mouth, eyelids, nose and airways…"

"I'm sorry," Friend put in. "Does that mean it was administered as an aerosol, sprayed at him for example, and he got some on his hands when defending himself? Or did he touch a contaminated object and just breathe in what he got on his hands?"

Wetherby shrugged. "Inconclusive is the word I was given. So far as the tests go, it could mean either. But if you ask me the spray theory is pretty unlikely. Call it plod's instinct if you like, but it seems to me that if he had something sprayed at him he would have done something about it. Gone to hospital. Called the police. He wouldn't just have sat there and let himself die. He would have had time. These aren't quick weapons; even a high dose given as a spray would take several minutes to have any effect. To my mind he had no idea what was happening until it was too late. That means the poison got into him between one and two hours before he collapsed. My bet is it happened at home. We found traces on the handle of his front door and in various spots inside: hallway, study, downstairs WC. Nothing in his office though, nor in his car either."

"Really? My money was on the cylinder he received in the post, but if there were no traces in his office then…"

"Perhaps. But maybe he doesn't open it until he gets home. Then his patience runs out and he opens it before he's got through his front door, smearing the stuff on the handle. Either that or he contaminates the handle on the way out."

"Did he normally use the handle on the way out?"

"Good question. I don't suppose any of the neighbours will have noticed, but perhaps the manufacturers might have an idea how people use their doors. I'll get someone to check it."

"What about the restaurant?"

"No traces on the table he used, and the kitchens and the staff were clean. No one else used the table that lunchtime and it doesn't seem that he used the toilet."

Friend was puzzled. "So he's got nerve agent all over his hands, he drinks a beer and has a meal in a restaurant but neither the glass nor the cutlery is contaminated and whoever cleared them from his table is clean too?"

Wetherby shrugged. "Beats me," he said. "For now, anyway. We'll get to the bottom of it eventually."

"Fair enough. Anything else? Any suspects?"

"Not yet. We've got CCTV coverage over half the city and we can track the professor on foot and in his car for much of the day, but we've seen nothing you could call a suspicious interaction. Border Force and Special Branch are sifting through the details of every Iranian who entered the country through an airport in the week leading up to the day. But then we have to try and match a passport or visa photo with thousands of blurred faces on CCTV images from the areas of the city where the professor was on the day he died. We've got the latest facial recognition software of course, but it will still take days, maybe weeks."

"And maybe our killer was in the country longer than a week planning this. Maybe he was living here already like the professor himself. Or maybe he wasn't Iranian at all but a proxy from Syria or Lebanon." Friend stopped abruptly. Such reflections were valid, but not especially helpful.

"I know, I know." Wetherby ran a hand through his greasy, unwashed hair. He seemed to have aged ten years in the space of a few minutes' conversation. "It's the scale of the thing. An investigation like this, I mean. You can't let it get to you. You can't let yourself confront it all at once. It's like running blind into a desert without a map. You've got to just plug away, step by step, fact by fact, day by day until you get to the end of it. Hopefully then it makes sense. Not always. If you have any suggestions I'm all ears."

"Well, there is one thing that occurs to me."

"Yes? What is it?"

"If you're checking on Iranians coming in to the country, you might want to check on those leaving it after the event. Your perpetrator may well have wanted to get out of the country as quickly as possible after the job was done. The next bit might be a long shot, but perhaps concentrate on flights to northern or western Germany although probably not Hamburg itself."

"You mean the same person might have killed the professor and Dr Nassirian?"

"Could be. There's no way all three killings could be the work of one man—the timings for New York won't fit—but Hamburg just might."

"And if your theory is correct, you don't think our man would have taken the most direct route?"

"Mr Wetherby, I think you've dealt with enough people from my line of trade to know that we never do anything by the most direct route."

Wetherby allowed himself a laugh. In years of working with the 'funny boys' he had rarely come across one who was capable of being funny.

"No," Friend continued. "If I were planning a double hit like this, I would be sure to use a less obvious route both times. I wouldn't come straight into London from Tehran, for example. I might hop over to Qatar and fly from there, or better still fly somewhere in Europe with a good-sized Iranian population. Somewhere I might be expected to have family to visit: Stockholm, Paris, Berlin, say, then come on to London from there. Perhaps even to a provincial airport rather than Heathrow. Then after I'd done the job here, I'd go on to Hamburg via Bremen or Lübeck, maybe Hanover. You could try Holland and Denmark too, either would be close enough. Anywhere but Hamburg itself. Any Iranian flying direct from London to Hamburg between the two killings would be too obvious for the police to miss."

"More work, then," said Wetherby.

"More work. I'm afraid so."

"All right, let's look at this from a practical point of view. We can't be certain when the professor was poisoned but if he picked up the stuff from his front door handle then we have to assume it was smeared there between him leaving home at eight-thirty and arriving back at twelve-thirty. So if twelve-thirty is the latest our man could have done the deed, does that give him time to get to Hamburg and be in position to commit his second murder of the day by eight-twenty the same evening? And that's local time of course."

"I think it does. Just. But it will narrow the range of airports down."

"If he wanted to get out in a hurry then Luton or Stansted would be quickest."

"Probably. But it may depend on flight times."

"And we don't even know whether it was the same man who committed both murders anyway."

"No. I'm sorry if I'm making things more complicated. But if you do find someone who fits that travel profile then it might speed things up for you. It would certainly be a lot quicker than sifting through the details of every Iranian to enter the country in the space of a week."

Wetherby nodded. "You're right enough there. All right, I'll put one of the team on it. Anything else I can help you with this morning?"

"Well, that diversion the professor took on the way to the restaurant troubles me. Can I have a look around the area?"

"I don't see why not. It's still cordoned off, but the decontamination crews haven't found much to worry about there. I can run you down myself. It'll do me good to get away from this dreary place for a while."

*

They drove into the city centre in Wetherby's unmarked Peugeot. The cordoned off area around Christ's Pieces and King Street was relatively small and much of the city seemed to be going about its normal business in the sunshine; students and shoppers mingled on the pavements, traffic hummed up and down the streets. Professor Sadaghiani might never have existed. Then they came to the barricade and everything stopped. A uniformed constable pulled the barrier back for them and Wetherby drove through and parked at the top of Fair Street by the entrance to Salmon Lane.

"That's where he ought to have gone," said Wetherby, pointing across the street to the narrow terrace of Willow Walk and the northeast corner of Christ's Pieces beyond.

"Where did the camera pick him up?"

"Just up ahead there on the east side of New Square, then a few minutes later coming back up Emmanuel Road towards the west side of the square, about where Elm Street ends."

"Any other cameras on Emmanuel Road?"

"At the bottom end where it meets Parker Street. And no, it didn't pick him up."

"Could he just have turned along Elm Street, or the next one after that, whatever it is?"

"Why would he do that? He wasn't meeting anyone and didn't have a reservation at the restaurant, so he didn't need to kill time. He must have walked down there with a purpose."

"Yes, no doubt you're right. So let's do the same."

Together, they walked slowly down the middle of the empty street. Friend felt Wetherby's eyes on him. He knew the policeman had probably taken this very walk himself already, marking every house, shop, tree or bench that might have had significance for the professor, trying to put himself in the same mental space as the dead Iranian. Was Wetherby hoping that Friend would spot something he himself had missed, or praying that he wouldn't? Perhaps he was just curious about how his mind worked.

The camera was on the left, pointing towards them as they walked down New Square. Perfect for seeing where the professor had come from, but no use for where he was going. *Now we're in uncharted territory,* thought Friend. The utter quiet, the absence of any sign of life brought to mind the still tangible horrors of Afghanistan; patrolling through empty villages where Taliban activity had been reported, the streets just as eerie and deserted, the few inhabitants who hadn't fled cowering indoors. Friend shook his head to rid it of the image. No snipers taking aim from the windows here, no landmines hidden in the sand, no booby-traps on the doors. This is England; no danger here. Unless your name is Professor Mansour Sadaghiani, and your door really is booby-trapped.

From New Square they walked down Jesus Terrace and on to Clarendon Street.

"This is Elm Street on either side of us now," said Wetherby. "Down there to the right is where the next camera picked him up heading towards the restaurant again."

"So we're entering the key area now. Suppose he had walked straight from here down Elm Street to where the camera spotted him, without stopping or making any diversion, how much earlier would he have got there?"

Wetherby sucked some air in through his teeth as he thought about it. "I'm guessing, but probably no more than four minutes."

"So we must be close then. Whatever he did, it didn't take him long."

It didn't take them long to find it. Even before they came to the next junction, they saw the narrow alley leading between high walls that separated the back yards of the buildings on Elm Street from the precincts of a local church.

"That goes all the way down to Eden Street," said Wetherby. "There's a pub down the other end, the Elm Tree, rather a good watering hole as it happens, but nothing before that. We had swabs taken all the way down, but there was no sign of any contamination."

"Well, he didn't leave much in the restaurant either. Come on," Friend grinned at Wetherby. "When in doubt, head to the pub."

Friend led the way down the alley. He went slowly; he seemed to want to examine every bit of brickwork, move every bin or wooden pallet, he poked, prodded and scraped, seemingly careless of the effect on the threads of his suit or the implications of the lingering smell of stale urine. They were only a third of the way along when after pulling another wheelie bin away from the wall he crouched down to below knee level and deep in the shadow of the wall began pulling away at something with his fingers.

"I don't suppose you've got a pair of gloves and an evidence bag on you?" he said, looking up at Wetherby.

"Hold on." Wetherby dug into an inside pocket of his jacket. Pulling out a pair of thin, blue surgical gloves he passed them over to Friend who slipped them on and turned back to the wall. Wetherby bent down after a moment and saw Friend holding a complete red brick.

"Good grief!" he exclaimed. "You people don't still mess around with dead letter drops, do you?"

"Of course. Much more secure than electronic communications in this day and age. Anyway, look at this."

The gap left by the brick was no more than eight inches above ground level. His eyes struggling with the poor light, Wetherby could just make out the thin scratches on the edges of neighbouring bricks than Friend was pointing to with his finger.

"There's no mortar left. Probably it was loose and crumbling already and that's why they chose it, but they've scraped the rest away with a metal tool of some kind, leaving a loose brick, low down in the wall of a quiet alley, hidden behind a wheelie bin. It's perfect, as long as you're not being followed." His hand disappeared into the hole. "And plenty of room to hide a cylinder, or whatever else was in that package he received. How about that evidence bag?"

Wetherby pulled a clear plastic bag out of his jacket and held it open. Friend carefully placed the brick into it before dropping the surgical gloves in on top.

"Nothing in it I'm afraid, but better get the brick tested for his fingerprints, and any traces of the nerve agent."

"And you'd better get your hands washed, too. I know it's been a week, but you can't be too careful."

"Good point," agreed Friend. "I don't suppose that pub is open?"

Wetherby nodded. It was proving to be a much more interesting day than he had expected.

NINE

"And what did they find?" Lascelles asked Friend. "The professor's smudged fingerprints all over the brick. And the minutest traces of the same nerve agent that killed him. Barely enough to register."

"Smudged? Why smudged?"

"The thinking was that whoever cleared the drop probably wore gloves."

"Might the professor have been clearing the drop himself? Are you certain he was leaving something rather than picking it up?"

"It couldn't be ruled out. Not absolutely. The smudging was certainly caused by someone else moving the brick after the professor left his prints on it, but that could have been me. They didn't find anything particular on his body, but perhaps he passed something on to someone in the restaurant without anyone else noticing."

"I suppose it would be naïve of me to ask what an Iranian dissident was doing with a dead letter drop in what he ought to have considered perfectly friendly territory," said Lascelles.

"Not necessarily. He wasn't on our payroll, not directly. The Committee received funds and assistance from our government, but it wasn't in any way under our orders. They co-operated with us, and we did with them, but they were partners rather than subordinates."

"Which means?"

"Which means they had their own way of doing things. And someone like the professor must have expected that the Iranians would be watching him, even here in Cambridge. That was how I rationalised it."

"So not a particularly suspicious circumstance, in your opinion."

"Oh, I wanted to know the reason for it, all right. But I wouldn't put it any stronger than that."

For a moment Lascelles looked as though he were considering pressing that point further, but then he decided to move on.

"All right. What about the traces of nerve agent found in the dead letter drop? Were they consistent with what was found on the professor and at his home?"

Friend paused before answering and Lascelles wondered whether the question had even occurred to him before.

"That was something that puzzled Wetherby. Not so much the traces left in the alley but there was something funny about the traces at his home, and on his body. How can I put this? The strongest concentration that was found was on the door handle of his home. The lab said that the sample taken from there was 'of high purity, persistent and resistant to weather conditions,' or words to that effect. The samples were taken the afternoon after the Professor died, and there had been heavy rain overnight, so let's just say there was a lot of the stuff. There were two theories as to how it got there. The first was what Wetherby suggested to me: that the contents of the package the professor received at the office had been contaminated and that he left the traces on the door handle himself after opening the package outside his house. But the pattern of the traces didn't match that. They were wider than the professor's hand. He would have had to rub his hand all over the handle to get the stuff distributed the way it was and there's no earthly reason why he should have done that. So that left us with the theory that the package had nothing to do with it, that the killer had smeared the nerve agent directly on to the door handle sometime that morning while the professor was in his office."

"Would that not be extremely dangerous for the killer?"

"Potentially, yes. The pattern of the traces suggested smearing with an impregnated cloth, rather than being sprayed from an atomiser, which is a slightly safer process, but he would still have needed special gloves and containers and some method of removing the gloves without contaminating himself. Whoever he was, he would have needed a lot of training in how to apply the stuff safely. Either that or he'd be dead himself soon afterwards. Anyway, we have a high concentration of nerve agent on the door handle, but the traces inside the house weren't nearly as pure and strong, even though there had been rain overnight which you would think would have diluted the samples on the outside of the door. The lab also thought that the high concentration on the door handle should have killed him rather sooner than it did."

"And what was the explanation?"

"Wetherby thought the professor must have washed his hands in the downstairs WC as soon as he came in, and that all the traces left inside were degraded because of that."

"And what did you think?"

"It seemed reasonable."

"At the time?"

"At the time."

"But now?"

"You've read my report."

Lascelles just smiled. "As I said earlier, I have been apprised of its contents. Well, never mind, let's move on to our killer now. Did your theory about flights to Hamburg bear any fruit?"

"No."

"A pity. It was a nice theory."

"It didn't matter in the end. They found their suspect."

TEN

"I don't think I'll ever get over it," said Henry Blake abstractedly. The Head of SIS's Middle East Desk was sitting with Sebastian Friend on the tiled patio area which looked out over the small, private garden of his split-level Putney maisonette, the pair of them perched uncomfortably on wrought-iron chairs with a French press full of coffee and two plain china mugs on the matching round table between them. He looked as though he hadn't shaved in at least three days and probably hadn't slept for even longer. He wore a dirty grey sweatshirt and jogging pants that gaped open at the knee. He smelled horrible. He seemed to be living on strong coffee and roll-up cigarettes. At times, he would stub one out no more than half-smoked and immediately begin the process of assembling another, as if this minor act of creation helped take his mind from the destruction going on inside his head. He must have been about the same age as Friend, but to Friend's eye he looked a good fifteen years older.

"You must tell me all about it," said Friend as sympathetically as he could. "Better to let it all come out."

Blake continued as if Friend were not even there: "It will be the same as it was with Cochrane. Pushed out, just pushed out, poor sod."

"Cochrane?"

Blake looked up and seemed to register Friend's presence for the first time in several minutes.

"Of course, you wouldn't know him. It was years ago. I'd only been in the Service eighteen months myself. The fresh-faced new boy on Middle East Desk. Brian Cochrane was our top man then. Highflier, would probably have been on course for 'C's office if it hadn't been for the almighty cock-up that got him his marching orders."

"What happened?"

Blake looked Friend in the eye for the first time. "I'm not sure I should tell you," he said.

"I have full authority from 'C'," said Friend, pleasantly. "He wants me to go back as far as I think necessary, asking anything that occurs to me. He knows I'm here now and he's in his office available for calls if you have any doubts."

Blake coughed out a mixture of smoke and derisive laughter. He stubbed out another cigarette. "Call 'C'? I've never called him directly in my life! Even speaking to his PA gives me the shivers." He paused, collecting his thoughts as the memories washed over him. "It must be a dozen years ago now. They called it the Cochrane Affair, one of the most legendary catastrophes in the long and proud history of our Service. Questions in the House, diplomatic protests from the Iranians, quite a storm in the press. I'm surprised you missed it."

Friend said nothing. A dozen years ago he had been a young lieutenant in the Rifles, cut off from all the world save for the monastic brotherhood that had been his unit.

"God help us if we ever have another Cochrane Affair, they used to say," Blake went on. "And now we've had one. A Blake Affair, worse luck. Oh well. I can't remember the details very well; there will have been an operational codename, but I can't tell you what it was. That's can't, not won't. Cochrane had some hot tip about a new source in the Ministry of Intelligence. A sample of the promised material was provided, and it was good enough for Cochrane to jump at it. The source wanted a personal meeting with his handler, so that they could establish trust before working together. A rendezvous was arranged, but when the handler turned up he found the source dead: shot, if I remember correctly. Then there are sirens everywhere and he realises he has been caught in a trap. *'British agent murders Iranian army officer for secrets'* was the line in the papers. Hell of a stink worldwide. Very embarrassing for the Service and the government too. No bloody wonder they found some heads to roll. They always do. And now that I'm on 'gardening leave', pending the results of this enquiry, I expect mine is next on the block."

Friend ignored the comment. He needed to keep Blake talking about the past, not worrying about the future. "Who was the handler? Not Cochrane himself?" he asked.

"God no! It was Halsgrove, Derrick Halsgrove."

"Halsgrove? But how come it didn't finish his career as well as Cochrane's?"

"Because he came back from the dead. The Iranians didn't get him. God knows how, but he slipped through the net. All they had was his work name and a passport photo that looked more or less like my uncle Tony. They put this huge manhunt together, but they never found him. As for us, we'd given him up for dead, but then a month later he turned up in Basra, at the army base. Two stone lighter than when he'd last been seen and dressed in rags. He'd only bloody well walked across the Iran-Iraq border! All the way from Isfahan, so they said."

"So that was Halsgrove's long walk to freedom?"

"Yes, exactly. The origin myth of the Halsgrove legend."

Friend watched in silence as Blake poured himself some coffee and rolled another cigarette. With part of his mind, he reflected that he would need to fumigate his clothes, and his lungs, when he got home; with another he pondered the coincidence of Derrick Halsgrove having been involved in the two major catastrophes to have affected SIS's Middle Eastern operations.

'So who was this dead prospective source, exactly?' Friend asked at last.

"Sorry, I can't remember. It'll be in the file."

"But Halsgrove didn't kill him; you're sure of that."

"Sure? Sure as I can be based on the guy's reputation. I don't know anything more about it than that. I mean, they sweated him for an age when he got back. An agent goes missing in hostile territory for weeks, you've got to be careful, right? He might have been turned, or tortured and spilled the beans. Anything could have happened to him over there."

"What beans did he have to spill?"

"Everything! Between him and Cochrane there was hardly an asset in Iran at the time who wasn't recruited by them. Them and the Committee, of course."

"How were the Committee involved?"

"The first contact to a new network usually came from them. They'd give us a lead to a potential new source, Cochrane and Halsgrove would follow it up. If the source worked out, sometimes they'd be able to build a network around them, other times they stayed solo."

"I understand."

"Right. And the point is, Halsgrove knew what Cochrane knew. He was his number two and they worked together for years. If Halsgrove had been turned, or if they had beaten the information out of him, then the networks would have been finished from that point on. But they weren't finished. They all kept going for years afterwards. Until quite recently in fact. Ergo, Halsgrove didn't blow them, willingly or unwillingly, ergo the story he told about his long walk to freedom was true."

"I take your point. But what if the Iranians did get the information they wanted out of Halsgrove, then they turned all our agents and let Halsgrove go to maintain the deception?"

"Now you're being ridiculous! Do you think they could keep that up for more than a decade? Two dozen agents going double on us, and we don't have a sniff of suspicion for that length of time?' Blake dismissed the idea with a shrug. 'Anyway, how could they be sure Halsgrove wouldn't simply tell us what happened when he got home? No one would have blamed him for cracking. We could even have turned it to our advantage. Even if we knew that what our networks were feeding us was rubbish, at least we would know what Tehran wanted us to know.'

Blake paused and Friend waited while he took a gulp of coffee and followed it with a long drag at his cigarette, his eyes glazing over as the smoke drifted in the air.

"The point is," he said at last, "that Halsgrove didn't blow the networks. Someone else did that, not more than a few weeks ago."

"Do you have any idea who?"

"Not a clue, pal. If I did, I wouldn't be sitting here smoking myself to death, I'd be off somewhere with my fingers tightening around the bastard's throat."

"You take it very personally."

"Of course I bloody well do! They were my people. Cochrane and Halsgrove may have done the initial recruitment, but I handled them for years: arranged for pick-ups, made sure they were paid what we owed them, listened to their gripes and worries and tried to reassure them that they were doing valuable work for us, and in the longer term for their own country. Most of them were patriots, really, working for a democratic, liberal Iran sometime in the future. So yes, I cared about them and I do take it personally."

Because they were his people, thought Friend, *and also,* perhaps uncharitably, *because they were his career.* Blake spat out the tattered remnants of a cigarette and rinsed out his mouth with coffee.

"So tell me about them,' said Friend. 'Who were they? What were they providing?"

"You want every agent in detail or just the outline?"

"The outline will do."

"Well, if you need more you can always come back. Or check

the files. I'll start with the areas they covered: military, scientific, political, security. Usually we tried to have more than one group of sources in any given sector, so they could corroborate each other's information. Sometimes there was a little crossover between sectors. We had two networks in the military: codenamed Persepolis and Rahir. Persepolis consisted of five sources, Rahir had only three. There used to be a fourth, but he died about two years ago. Heart attack. Persepolis was good for High Command strategy, internal politics, expenditure, that sort of thing. Rahir was good on weapons research. Their big coup was a series of reports on the chemical weapons programme in the early 2000s. A while ago now but we still got some good material from them from time to time.

"The scientific network was codenamed Asfarani, after a medieval Persian physician. It was the largest we had in the country: ten individual sources all feeding material through a single conduit, going right to the heart of the nuclear programme. Huge results from them over a long period. That was Professor Sadaghiani's area, of course. He was instrumental in setting it up. We didn't have a political network as such but two individual sources, one a journalist and one an official in the energy ministry. Together they gave us everything from political gossip to oil output forecasts and advance warning of Iran's position leading into OPEC meetings. Really useful stuff.

"Lastly, on security we had sources in both the Revolutionary Guards Intelligence Service and the Ministry of Intelligence, the first an individual source code-named Timur, the second a network of three sources codenamed Pahlavi. They were all pretty low level, I'm afraid, so the grade of intelligence we got from them didn't match the other sources. But all the same that's twenty-four sources spread across four different areas of intelligence gathering. All now gone. Poof!" He made a gesture to indicate their having disappeared in a cloud of smoke.

Friend ignored the theatrics. "Sounds pretty comprehensive," he said.

"It was. Not much in numbers but in the variety of intelligence we got from them, I'd say that pound for pound they were the most productive the Service had anywhere in the world."

"And you hadn't lost a single one of them in all that time? No one got careless, no one lost their nerve, no one got too greedy and was cut loose? That's remarkable."

"Oh there were a few who had an attack of the jitters from time to time, and once or twice we had to play hardball over the budget. But we nursed the nervous ones through and stuck to our guns with the greedy ones. Eventually they all came round. That's the trick in this business: knowing when to be the nursemaid and when to be the boss, when to back off and when to insist. And no one got caught. Not one. Of course there were a few changes in personnel over the years: old sources dropped out and new ones came in. We had a couple who died—natural causes, mind—and a few who retired. We had one officer in Persepolis who was with us twenty-five years. Cochrane recruited him as a young lieutenant and he retired as a full colonel about four years ago. But that hardly counts as losing an agent; he was never caught."

"And how was the Tehran Committee involved?"

"Just as I told you. They provided the introductions and we built each network from there. Most of the sources were Committee affiliates anyway. And on a day-to-day basis they often helped us out with transport: getting material out and payments in. I'm not saying it would have been impossible without them, but working with them made things a hell of a lot easier."

"And they did the same thing for the Americans?"

"Yes. I don't know the ins and outs of that relationship, but I think it was much the same as ours. Bigger scale of course. They helped out the French and Germans too, probably others."

"So what made them offer certain sources to us and others to the CIA?"

Blake gave a shrug. "Who knows? Maybe they gave the

greedier ones to the Yanks. They always were better payers than us. Probably it was personal preference as well. If you think you may have to get out of Iran in the end and you'd rather settle down in Colorado than, say, Kent, better spy for the CIA instead of us."

"I see. So what about the quid pro quo with the Committee?"

"The what?"

"What did they get from us?"

Blake barked out the kind of hollow laugh that made it clear he saw no humour in the matter. "Money!" he said. "Money for agents, for introductions, for information received, for assistance with operations. Stipends for their officials in the UK. Training too: how to avoid electronic surveillance, that sort of thing. We even gave the professor a laptop and mobile phone so he could keep his academic work separate from what he did for the Committee."

"A Service laptop?"

"No, just an ordinary business grade HP and a Samsung mobile. Nothing fancy. No Service apps, no access to our systems in case they fell into the wrong hands. We just paid the bills. We even cleaned up the hard drives for him free of charge every couple of years when he traded them in for new ones."

Friend made a mental note to ask Wetherby if his team had found the devices in the professor's home. "So what about the opposition in Tehran? What are they like?"

"Well that's a surprising thing," began Blake. "There are two major agencies in Iranian intelligence, as well as various small departments of military intelligence, domestic security and the like. But the main ones are the Ministry of Intelligence, which used to be Intelligence and Security, and the Revolutionary Guards Intelligence Organisation. When I started as a junior on Middle East Desk, we always thought the Ministry was the better opponent. They grew out of SAVAK, the old intelligence service of the Shah. Khomeini had ninety percent of SAVAK killed when he came to power, but they kept the other ten percent on for their particular expertise. First it was called SAVAMA then VEVAK, now it's VAJA, but it's all the same thing and they're a huge organisation of real pros. It's one of the biggest government ministries in Iran and probably as close to the old cold war KGB as anything in the modern world. Extensive networks of foreign-based agents, whole departments working on disinformation campaigns, terrorism, assassinations. Prison facilities not unlike the dear old Lubyanka. Their charter specifically tasks them with monitoring dissidents: political, religious, social, even ethnic.

"But it wasn't them who rolled up our networks and destroyed the Tehran Committee. No, that was the Intelligence Organisation of the Islamic Revolution Guards Corps. They've really grown in the past decade or so. They were the prime beneficiaries when Ayatollah Khamenei reorganised domestic security back in 2009. They managed to absorb some of VAJA's functions and even managed to get some of their officials removed from office. So of course the IRGC and VAJA hate each other. I mean *really* can't stand each other. There's no clear dividing line in their areas of responsibility and they just don't like working together at all. More often they work against each other. Although weirdly VAJA does sometimes work with one branch of the IRGC, Quds Force, in overseas operations." He paused and took another mouthful of coffee. "Ever heard of Abd al-Rasoul Dorri Esfahani?"

Friend shook his head.

"Ah, well that's an instructive little tale." Blake drew deeply on his cigarette and let the smoke seep gently back out of his nose. "Esfahani was—is—an Iranian-Canadian who worked at the Central Bank in Tehran and was part of the team representing Iran in the nuclear negotiations back in... 2016 I think it was. He got caught up in one of the IRGC's periodic witch-hunts for foreign spies, was publicly accused in various IRGC-sponsored media outlets and eventually put on trial. The Minister of Intelligence, the man who runs VAJA no less, made a public statement that Esfahani was innocent and doing good work in the negotiations. But it made no difference. Esfahani was part of a delegation flying to Ankara. He was arrested on the plane and flown straight back to Tehran. The trial was a sham. He got five years. I don't know whether he was spying for the Canadians or not, he was just unlucky to get caught up in the crossfire between two intelligence services who seem to think their common enemy is each other."

"Interesting."

"Isn't it. Actually you can forget the Soviet analogy I just drew, it's really more like Nazi Germany in a way. The IRGC are like the SS, the personal security force of the Supreme Leader and reporting directly to him. No other arm of government has any real influence over them. VAJA are part of the main government bureaucracy, responsible to the President. So the direct competition between the two agencies mirrors the divide in power at the very top. I could try and explain the dynamics involved, but by the time I'd finished the election would probably be over."

"So what do you deduce from the fact that it was the IRGC rather than VAJA who arrested our people?"

"What do I deduce? You don't have to be Sherlock Holmes to work out it's bad news. Just look at the timing. A few weeks before a presidential election. The whole thing is perfect for making the Ministry and the current government look incompetent. A whole nest of western spies nestling in the heart of the establishment. You can bet your life the trials will be set up to emphasise the point. The IRGC have their own preferred candidate, and this'll do no end of good for his chances. And that means a new hard-line regime in Tehran, back to the dark days of Ahmedinejad, and worse relations with the west. Full speed ahead on their nuclear weapons programme and no way of monitoring their progress. Yep, that's bad news in my book."

"All right. Last question, for now. What about liaison with friendly agencies? Who are the other players in Iran and how much business do we do with them?"

"Ah, well now, as you might expect the two major players are the CIA and Mossad. A few others are active there: the Canadians, Swedes, Germans and French but on a very small scale. Then of course there are the not-so-friendlies, the Russians and Chinese. They're more or less co-operating with the locals, but still spy on them. As for the business we do, in terms of raw intelligence most of what we receive is freely traded with our Five Eyes partners and we don't get much in return from anyone except the Americans. I suppose the others repay us in other areas, but my desk doesn't see much benefit from it. And of course I can't guarantee that the CIA gives us everything they get. Rather less than most of it, I suspect. I get on all right with Ken Burgsmuller, my oppo in Langley, and we have a regular catch-up every three months but given the size of the operation they have... or rather had out there... there's no way we're getting everything.

"As for the Israelis, we have very little to do with them. I don't think they've trusted us since Suez. The only time I can recall us getting any sort of information direct from them was years ago, to do with some Israeli-American flying into Heathrow who was wanted on kiddy-fiddling charges in Florida. We got Special Branch to pass it on to Border Force; he was picked up at Immigration and extradited. A nice little result, but hardly the day job. The only Mossad-generated material that I ever see is what gets passed on to us by the Americans. They've always worked closely together out there. In fact it was the two of them working together who helped the Shah set up SAVAK. So you might say we're living with the consequences of their co-operation to this day."

Blake blew out a lungful of smoke and smiled at Friend through the cloud. Friend coughed up half a lung, then finished his coffee.

*

Friend couldn't help being amused by the coincidence when he got the call from the Director on the train back into Vauxhall. The CIA were claiming to have come into possession of information which might shed light on the murder of Professor Sadaghiani. A rendezvous had been arranged.

The American was waiting for him, hunched impatiently on a bench in a dreary stretch of pseudo parkland a short walk along the Thames bank from the moated glass excrescence that was his country's new Embassy in London. He was blond and Ivy League, a sitting advert for American polish and presentation, from his Brooks Brothers blazer and slacks to his chestnut Alden brogues. He was looking out across the grey river and drumming his fingers on a folded copy of the *Evening Standard* that lay next to him on the bench. Friend strolled casually up to him.

"Excuse me, would that be today's Standard you've got there?" he asked.

The American looked up at him and seemed to run an appraising eye up and down Friend's frame. His tone of voice suggested that he didn't like what he saw.

"No. It's tomorrow's. The weather report was better." He picked up the paper to make space on the bench for Friend. "Spare me the clichés and take a seat. You're Friend, I suppose."

Friend nodded and sat down, now rather dreading this routine encounter. Why did some Americans have to force their sense of superiority on you all the time?

"Well, my name's Bradley. How come I don't know you?"

"Probably because we've never met before. That's usually how it works."

"Oh really? Well I was kind of expecting a familiar face from liaison to come down from your big ugly building to our big ugly building. It threw me out a tad to hear I was meeting someone new."

"I'm sorry to hear that. But I'm glad there's something we can both agree on."

"And what's that?"

"That your new Embassy is as much a blight on this city's skyline as our headquarters."

Bradley unbent a little and allowed a crooked smile to break across his face. "I guess that's right. You know, when I was stationed in Paris I used to love spending time by the river. All those historic buildings; such a sense of history, such beauty. Here it's getting to be just line after line of glass towers. All those so-called luxury apartments for people who want a riverside view and all they get is a view of the apartments of other people who wanted a riverside view."

"If there's anybody living in them at all," said Friend. "Half of them seem to be empty investments."

"Is that so? Well, God bless capitalism." Bradley laid down the paper on the bench between them. "It's all in here."

"All what, if you don't mind me asking?"

"Details of an Iranian agent who arrived in England two days before the Cambridge murder and left the evening after it. Travelling on a genuine Iranian passport but probably under an assumed name. Our information is that he's Ministry of Intelligence, or VAJA as they call it, so he could be your man."

Friend took the paper and slipped it inside his jacket.

"Thanks. Where does this come from?"

"Our friends in Tel Aviv." Bradley spoke with his face to the river, as if by not looking at Friend he could disguise the fact that they were talking together. "There's not much detail to it, so don't ask me why the Israelis think it's significant. The name and date of birth don't mean anything to us and there's no photo yet. But he would have needed a visa to come here so there'll be a photo with his application for sure. If you pass it back to me when you have it, we'll see if we can find a match."

"That would be appreciated, thank you."

"You're welcome. How's the investigation going?"

"It's early days yet. We can't even be certain how the professor was poisoned."

"You'll get there. If there's one thing you Brits do well it's a good detective story. I love all that Agatha Christie stuff. Not that there's much of a whodunit about this case though. It's got Tehran's fingerprints all over it and all you need is the fingers they belong to. My guess is you'll find them in there."

"Maybe we will. But how are things progressing at your end? The hit-and-run driver who killed Dr Qarib in New York?"

Bradley sighed. "Hardly anything to go on. No witnesses, no cameras. It happened in the dead of night, and we haven't even been able to trace the car. You'd expect them to use a stolen vehicle and then ditch it somewhere afterwards, maybe torch it to get rid of any forensic evidence. But we've got zip. Without the car we've got no chance of getting the driver. Unless we get a lucky break from Mossad or somewhere else, we'll just be shining a spotlight on every Iranian on the eastern seaboard until our friends in the Commissioner's Office decide it's no longer worth the effort. And I don't suppose that'll take long."

"You have my sympathy."

"Well, it's not my problem anyway. But thanks. And let me know if you have something more useful than sympathy."

"I will. How's Ken Burgsmuller taking it? I expect he lost pretty much all of his sources just like we did."

Bradley paused and glanced sideways at Friend. Then he seemed to overcome his caution.

"I guess it's no secret. We lost ninety percent over there in one night. Quite a shitshow. As to how Burgsmuller's taking it, I can't say. Don't know the guy personally. But how would you feel? Same as anyone, I guess. Your whole life's work goes up in smoke overnight. Not a nice thing to happen. The likes of you and me should be glad we don't have any skin in that game. Liaison work in friendly territory is so much easier on the soul." He got to his feet, fastening his blazer buttons against the stiff riverside breeze that tugged at his thinning blond hair. "Even in your wonderful climate," he concluded. "What is it you Brits say? Brisk? Be seeing you, Friend. Saunders in liaison will tell you how to reach me."

Friend counted down three minutes on his watch before he followed Bradley back along the path, feeling the paper folded tight against his chest and wondering what it contained.

ELEVEN

"It was just a single sheet of paper," said Friend. "Folded up inside a copy of the *Evening Standard*. Printed on it were a name, passport number, and flight details, both inbound and outbound. The only other thing on it was a single line of commentary."

"I would have thought something like a USB drive would have been considerably more practical," observed Lascelles.

"It surprised me too at first, but then my job doesn't often involve receiving product from allied intelligence agencies. Blake told me later that it was quite common for CIA to pass on material in this way. Electronic data is more easily traceable, and it's difficult to be certain that the drive you're passing it over with is entirely clean. There's very little you can read into a piece of ordinary printer paper."

"I see." Lascelles consulted his notes for a few moments. Ms Wilton meanwhile was leaning back in her chair, hands folded across her abdomen and staring at the ceiling. She might have been asleep.

"So you had a name, flight details and a passport number. Was that enough to go on?"

"Yes. All Iranian nationals entering or transiting through the UK require a visa, with the exception of diplomats, merchant seamen and flight crew. All we had to do was supply the name and passport number to the visa section of the Embassy in Tehran and within forty-eight hours we had a copy of the Visa Application Form. That gave us a photo. And with a photo, Wetherby and his team could use CCTV and facial recognition software to try and trace the suspect's movements after his arrival."

"Which they managed successfully?"

"For the most part, yes. There were black spots, but it gave them enough to reconstruct most of his movements while he was here."

"And what else did the application form give us?"

"That our suspect was a well-travelled thirty-six-year-old businessman working for one of the leading spice exporters in Iran. The visa was a five-year multiple entry issued eighteen months earlier. He had a well-established travel history going back more than eight years, repeat visits to many western European countries, Canada, the USA, even Russia. He had visited the UK for meetings with their main import partner twice previously. They remembered him well, but they hadn't been expecting him this time. And they're based in Southall, West London. There was no reason for him to be in Cambridge."

"But would Border Force not have questioned him about the purpose of his visit when he arrived?"

"Naturally. But with a wealthy, well-travelled man like him the questions were likely to be perfunctory. It would have been different if the information from Mossad had come through before his arrival, of course."

"And so perhaps we should turn to the final piece of information that Mossad gave us, the single line of commentary you mentioned."

"All it said was that the subject's travel history was thought to be a cover for his work with Department 15 of Iran's Ministry of Intelligence."

"Department 15? Did Blake mention that organisation when you interviewed him?"

"No, he didn't. But he did co-author the Service briefing paper on them."

TWELVE

**EXTRACT FROM *SIS BRIEFING PAPER 2004.171*
(*OVERVIEW OF INTELLIGENCE SERVICES OF THE
ISLAMIC REPUBLIC OF IRAN*)
*DEPARTMENT 15: A DIVISION OF THE MINISTRY OF
INTELLIGENCE OF THE ISLAMIC REPUBLIC OF IRAN***

'Department 15' was founded by Iran's newly installed Islamic regime as a modern equivalent to the eleventh century Ismaili Shiite sect of northern Persia, known as the Nizari. The Nizari, under their leader Hasan Sabah, fought back against the oppression of the Sunni Seljuk regime which dominated Persia, becoming the most feared and ruthless killers of their time. Skilled at infiltration and terrorism, they became the first recorded sleeper agents in history. Most such sleepers were installed to observe enemy strength and positions, but a few were infiltrated into the very highest echelons of Seljuk society from where they could report back on strategic thinking and future threats. In many cases, the purpose of a sleeper was to lie low for years, before emerging to strike a fatal blow against an individual enemy.

Their weapon of choice was the dagger. In this way they made the act of murder as silent as the years-long approach to it. To the Seljuks, and the other enemies they encountered in their two hundred years of terror before they were overrun by the Mongols of Genghis Khan, they were like a terrifying phantom, appearing out of nowhere and disappearing just as quickly after they struck. In many cases they forewarned their victim of his fate; a dagger might appear under his pillow with no one able to account for how it got there. Rarely did such a warning help the victim avoid death, and the knowledge of its approach, together with the Nizari reputation for brutality in dispatch, only added to the terror for the appointed target and for anyone else who feared they might be next.

Such is the modus operandi of Department 15 today. And the enemies of Iran's Islamic leaders both at home and abroad live in constant fear of its vengeance. It wasted no time in establishing its reputation. The first dramatic murder attributed to its functionaries took place in December 1979, just months after the revolution which toppled the last Shah. Its victim was Prince Shahriah Shafiq, nephew to the Shah, who had at first attempted to resist the revolution from inside Iran but later affected a dramatic escape from the country, piloting his own hovercraft through a fierce naval barrage to the safety of Kuwait. Continuing his counter-revolutionary activities in the west, Prince Shahriah was sentenced to death in absentia by an Islamic court and gunned down outside his mother's Paris home by a masked assassin.

As well as political assassinations, Department 15 is tasked with 'exporting revolution', to which end it maintains relations with various Islamic terror groups worldwide, as well as other terrorist groups whose aims match the Iranian regime's of destabilising the west. Its technical and weapons support for the IRA is just one example of this. To these ends, operatives of Department 15 have been infiltrated into many Western countries under the guise of students, journalists, refugees and even construction workers, but its domestically-based operatives also travel abroad with great frequency under a variety of covers.

Department 15 has been linked with a number of successful and unsuccessful assassinations overseas, from the shooting of dissident Ali Akbar Tabatabaei in Bethesda, Maryland in 1980 to a foiled plot to blow up the Saudi Ambassador to the USA in a popular Washington restaurant in 2011. This latter plot was proven to be a collaborative effort between Department 15 and the Quds Force of the Islamic Revolution Guards Corps. By far the most notorious series of murders carried out by Department 15 was the so-called 'chain murders', which took place inside Iran between 1988 and 1998 and led to the deaths of more than eighty dissidents, writers and intellectuals. An exemplar of the style of killing employed by Department 15 was the double murder of human rights activist Dariush Forouhar and his wife Parveneh in November 1998, one of the last in this brutal sequence of political assassinations. The couple were found dead in their Tehran flat: Forouhar at his desk with eleven stab wounds to the chest. His wife lay on the floor nearby, in her case there were no fewer than twenty-four stab wounds to her chest. The absence of any defensive wounds on either victim, together with a toxicology report suggesting that both had been sprayed in the face with an unknown substance, indicated that the couple were either unconscious or immobilised when the fatal wounds were inflicted. The calculated brutality of this attack could only have been intended as a warning to other enemies of the state, as if they needed any further reminder of what the regime was capable of after the decade of killings that preceded it.

Nizari-style stabbings were not the only methods employed during the chain murders. Others included strangling by garrotte, faked car crashes and heart-attacks simulated by the injection of potassium. One attempt which failed, ignominiously and even comically, was a plot to dispose of twenty-one members of the Iranian Writers' Association en-route to a literary conference in Armenia by driving their bus off a cliff above a one-thousand-foot-deep ravine. After the first attempt, which was foiled by a well-placed boulder by the side of the road, the driver apologised for falling asleep at the wheel and the passengers agreed to resume their journey. But a few minutes later they found the bus again accelerating towards the cliff edge, and were only saved by an alert passenger grabbing the handbrake. In the confusion the driver somehow managed to disappear without trace. Security forces then appeared on the scene and forced the passengers to sign a document obliging them never to disclose what had happened. Only after the Forouhar killings exposed the chain murders two years later did the events of that strange journey come to light.

The chain murders became a very public scandal, leading to the trial of alleged 'rogue elements' in the Ministry of Intelligence and the resignation of the Minister, proving that even such a dictatorial state as Iran cannot be entirely dismissive of public opinion. The supposed mastermind of the rogue elements, Deputy Intelligence Minister Saeed Emami, conveniently died in custody before he could be brought to trial. Emami was said to have committed suicide by drinking a bottle of hair remover. Eighteen suspects were tried (including Khosro Barati, the driver of the writers' bus), several of them implicating the Minister directly in their confessions. It is no coincidence that the public trial and the resignation of a hard-line Minister came just a year into the presidential term of the reformist Mohammad Khatami.

In the two decades since the chain murders, Department 15 has rarely been in the public eye, but it is known to have remained extremely active. It continues to advise, assist and supply major terrorist or 'liberation' networks worldwide, notably Hezbollah. In the last five years at least three European-based Iranian dissidents have been murdered by their agents: in December 2015 Mohammad-Reza Kolahi was murdered in the Netherlands where he had been living as a refugee under the assumed identity of Ali Motamed; in April 2017 Saeed Karimian, a TV executive and dual British national, was shot dead in Istanbul along with his Kuwaiti business partner—a killing which may have been carried out with the assistance of the IRGC Quds Force; then in November 2017 Ahmed Mola Nissi (an Arab-separatist campaigner from Iran's south western

Khuzestan province) was gunned down outside his home in The Hague. Department 15 agents are also thought to have been responsible for the ambush of Service operative Derrick Halsgrove near Hesa air base outside Isfahan in 2006 and the killing of agent Mansour Khan at Peshawar in 2013.

While Department 15 may have gone about its business more discreetly since the beginning of the century, it remains a significant element within the Ministry of Intelligence and a powerful and feared organ of Iranian state power. No information is available on its leaders or membership, but it seems clear that in terms of numerical strength and budget it survived largely unaffected the re-organisation of Iranian intelligence post-2009, while in global reach, method and efficiency it continues to perform a role most readily compared to that of SMERSH in the Stalin-era NKVD.

Brian Cochrane, Middle East Desk, 2004.
Revised and updated by Henry Blake, 2018.

THIRTEEN

LAMBROOK HOUSE
TUESDAY 21 JULY, 1422 HOURS

"So Blake didn't mention Department 15 to you, but he had personally updated the briefing paper on them quite recently?" asked Lascelles.

"Correct," replied Friend. "But his contribution was fairly minor stuff. Just a few details relating to the Department's numerical strength and confirmation of their involvement in the more recent assassinations. It was information received from CIA, who said they had received it during debriefing sessions with a recent defector from the Ministry of Intelligence, Dr Kamal Sirjani."

"Did Blake say anything else about the Sirjani debrief?"

"He seemed surprised that it had produced so little, or perhaps I should say that we had got so little from it ourselves. It was only three updates in something like eight months and didn't really go beyond internal politics and personalities, relations with other government ministries, financial planning and disbursements among the ministry's various departments. A few snippets about collaboration with Russia and China. Blake had been hoping for some detail of VAJA operations against the UK and other Western allies, but there was nothing. And when he asked for more, CIA—to be precise my old friend Damon Bradley—pretty much shrugged off his request. Gave him the usual guff: debriefing a defector is a long and frustrating process, more like a negotiation than an interrogation. There would probably be more to come eventually, but for now they had given him everything they were authorised to give. Blake thought they gave themselves away with the last point; he guessed that they were keeping back much more than they were giving us."

"And there was nothing at all about Department 15?"

"Not a thing. Nor anything much to add to our knowledge of VAJA in a wider sense. What we know about the Ministry and its various directorates that isn't in the public domain you could write on the back of a postage stamp. We've got a supposedly accurate list of all the Directorates culled from a paper in the Library of Congress in Washington, but we don't know which Directorate Department 15 sits under, or if it sits under any of them at all. There's a Department of Disinformation which is supposed to be the largest in the entire Ministry, but we don't know where that slots into the hierarchy either."

"You make it sound as though the loss of our agents inside Iran's security establishment was not much of a loss at all."

"Do I? Well, that's what Blake said about it. We hadn't penetrated very deeply into VAJA despite almost forty years of trying. It was the one area of our Iranian operations that were considered disappointing."

"And it wasn't much better with IRGC?"

"Worse, if anything."

"You see, I hope I'm not being obtuse Mr Friend, but I'm struggling to grasp the relationship between VAJA and IRGC and how it affected your thinking on the case. I mean, let me ask you this: if Tom Westerman was right about the destruction of the Tehran Committee and the breaking-up of western intelligence networks being a direct response to the defection of Dr Sirjani, then why, when Dr Sirjani was a VAJA official, was this response the work of IRGC? And if IRGC mopped up the networks, why was the simultaneous execution of Dr Sadaghiani carried out by an officer of VAJA's Department 15? If I have this right, VAJA is shorthand for the Ministry of Intelligence while IRGC—the Islamic Revolutionary Guards Corps to give them their full title—are the personal security force of the Supreme Leader. So they are completely separate organisations and not just that but, according to what Blake told you, bitter rivals."

Friend said nothing at first, so Lascelles pressed him further.

"What I mean is, everything Blake told you, everything in those briefing papers you studied, speaks to a historical rivalry between these two organs of state. And yet the chain of events we are dealing with here seems to suggest them working in concert with each other; co-ordinated to the highest degree."

"True, but of course they have worked together sometimes. Quds Force is part of IRGC, and they are specifically tasked to co-ordinate with VAJA in overseas operations."

"But the IRGC part of this operation was not overseas, was it? It was purely domestic. Surely that didn't make sense to you?"

"No, it did not."

"So why mention it?"

"It was part of my thinking at the time."

"And what about Blake's point that the IRGC rolled up the networks just before the election to make VAJA look incompetent?"

"Blake had a theory that IRGC were trying to take over as the primary intelligence service from VAJA. They blamed VAJA for not clamping down on the public protests after the 2009 elections and all the instability that followed. There was a review after that which gave IRGC a certain amount of control over VAJA's internal security processes. They had a chance to influence recruitment, promotion, structural relationships within their rival. From there I suppose it might have been a short step to influencing operations."

"Well there you are then!" Lascelles beamed in satisfaction. "The whole thing was an IRGC plot to humiliate VAJA and take over its functions. A classic power grab."

Friend shook his head. "So why is the Sirjani defection not

headline news in Tehran? It's never been publicly admitted, but what could be better calculated to show VAJA as a nest of traitors and incompetents? If IRGC came up with this whole plan themselves, surely that would have been the first thing they would do."

This time Lascelles shook his head. "You're over-reaching, Mr Friend. Projecting your own theories onto events and ignoring the facts that don't back you up. But the weight of evidence is against you."

"The evidence didn't make sense unless you made a whole lot of lucky guesses about what might be going on in Tehran," countered Friend angrily. Then, more softly, he added "Besides that, my instincts told me something about it wasn't right."

"In fact, you had a hunch, Mr Friend. Isn't that the truth of it? You let your instincts get in the way of proper judgement. And what did it matter? It was an IRGC job or a VAJA job—either way it was the Iranians at work. There was no suggestion of anything else in play."

There was a lengthy silence, which Ms Wilton filled by stifling a theatrical yawn.

"Listen," said Friend at last, "I think we're getting a little ahead of ourselves. All I felt at this stage was that something didn't add up. I couldn't put my finger on what it was."

Lascelles gave a tired shrug. "All right, we'll move on. Whoever was the driving force behind the arrests and the killings, someone betrayed our agents in Iran. What were your thoughts about that? Did you suspect a traitor in the Service, or a mole in the Committee?"

"A mole in the Committee made more sense to me. The Committee was the common factor between ourselves and the CIA. We both used them as an intermediary, so someone inside the Committee would be better placed to betray both sets of networks. When Brian Cochrane was Head of Middle East Desk, he suspected a mole as well. Had done for years."

"It was Cochrane who brought the Committee to us in the

first place. What made him think it had gone bad?"

"Years of working with them. But I suppose it started with Vienna."

FOURTEEN

Brian Cochrane perched himself awkwardly on the stile and laced up his boots. It didn't matter how tough your feet were, how many miles you had put them through in the past, breaking in a new pair of boots was always a bugger. The Compeed plaster would take care of the one on his right heel, but the one just behind the toe where his instep had rubbed against the vamp of the boot was going to be hell until he got home. If he could prevent it bursting before then, he knew a trick that would cure the skin and leave it toughened and ready again by the next morning. But that would mean suffering agony for the remainder of the walk. The alternative was to slash through it with his pocketknife now and drain all the liquid away. Pop a plaster over the top and he could walk the last half mile or so in comfort, but then the skin would be ruined for days afterwards and there would be nothing he could do. Choices, choices. He was close enough to home to choose the first option without too much hesitation, but still. These new boots were practically indistinguishable from the old pair he had just consigned to gardening duty after more than twenty years' hard service and two full resoles. But they were still awkward interlopers rather than familiar friends.

He shrugged the small rucksack off his shoulders and pulled

his water bottle out of a side pocket. Taking a long pull at the liquid, he rinsed it around his mouth before swallowing. Then, slowly and with due consideration, he took a small leather hipflask from the cargo pocket in his trousers and washed the water down with a chaser of neat brandy, mouthing an habitual silent apology to Leila as he did so. It was all right, he insisted, it was only a couple of tots on a good long walk and the occasional longer drink in the evening. These days it was rare for him to finish a bottle in under a fortnight. Not everyone got out so easily, he reminded her, and himself. He felt his cheeks redden at the tired justifications. Leila had never ceased to make him feel that somehow he had fallen short of her standard; even death hadn't stopped her.

Ahead of him, the dark, angular roof of Christmas Place, the former home of playwright John Osborne, peeped out above the high wall that enclosed it. He remembered reading somewhere that Osborne had ended up drinking something like a bottle of brandy a day during his disastrous fourth marriage. So he raised the hipflask once more, with a toast of "Cheers, you old sot!" before stowing it back in his pocket and slipping backwards over the stile with a practised ease unbecoming in such a large figure.

Cochrane zigzagged through the fields of ripe young peas and corn, past the handsome facade of Shernden Manor and out along a narrow furrow between the pods down towards the village of Marsh Green, where he made his home. He turned along the road towards the church, exchanging nods with old Dorothy as she sat in her window seat, as was their habit, noting the cars parked along the lane. Dorothy's battered old Nissan was the first in line, caked in rust and sagging on its ancient axles. It must have been two years at least since she had driven, but still the car sat there outside her home like an abandoned dog waiting for its master to return. Nobody at this end of the village drove a smart car. The narrow, semi-detached cottages leading up to the church were not occupied by those kinds of people. Mr Verity's scrupulously cleaned Peugeot and Cochrane's own silver

Saab, one of the last to have rolled off that particular production line, were about as good as it got. The weekend always brought visitors of course, many of them attracted by the kind of walk Cochrane himself always enjoyed, but it was rare in midweek for an unfamiliar vehicle to be parked on the narrow lane that separated the church from the village green.

So the dark grey Jaguar XE parked just a few feet along from Cochrane's garden gate set off a familiar alarm in his head. It was facing towards him, so whoever had driven it had entered the lane from the far end where the green stretched beyond the limits of the village. The lane had always been too narrow for turning; in one way and out the other was how it was done. So, it was a strange car on a weekday, that was the first thing; it was parked as closely as possible to Cochrane's house (his own Saab was parked directly outside), that was the second. And the third clinched it. Wedged under one of the windscreen wipers was a small triangular piece of pale blue card. So whoever it was had also done their homework. The card had been the idea of source Qasim, an army officer whom he had run for a while in Tehran, back in the day. Leila had been to university with him, before the revolution, and had vouched for him. "He's a good man, Brian," she had assured him. "A patriot. Our kind. He won't give you anything that weakens Iran as a country, only what weakens the regime. He wants a strong, independent Iran that can stand up for the interests of the whole region, not just itself. Don't let him think you want to turn us into a vassal state of American imperialism, or he won't work with you. That's why he chose us, not the Americans."

And where is the dividing line? he had wondered. The line which marks how far you can go when you only want to betray a little bit. One false step and you were too far across it to ever go back. But Qasim to his credit had never made that step. His material was entirely political, strategic, revealing Tehran's thoughts and likely areas of aggressive action. There was never anything on military strength or sites of installations, anything which could have been used by Britain or its allies to aid a military strike against his country. Perhaps, if it had ever come to that… Cochrane abandoned the thought. It never had come to that.

The blue triangle had been his signal. Sometimes it was a folded over leaflet tucked under a windscreen wiper, sometimes a sticker affixed to a window or a chalk mark on a wall or any one of a dozen other things that gave the all-clear. It meant the meeting was safe, he hadn't been followed; the dead letter drop had been made, so proceed to pick-up. How old would Qasim be now? The same as Leila, he supposed, sixty-two or so. Surely no longer on active service. Hadi—that had been his real name. Lieutenant Hadi.

Cochrane needed a moment to think. He ducked through the low wooden gate into the deserted churchyard and stooped down behind a gravestone unlacing and adjusting his boots, his eyes scanning the lane and the village green beyond. He never expected the pleasant English voice that came from behind him.

"Those boots look new. Still breaking them in?"

Cochrane's head whipped round, but at first he could see no one. But then his eye caught a flicker of movement from the entrance to the church and he watched as a slender pair of chino-clad legs uncrossed themselves and a slim, fair-haired man in a green linen jacket emerged from the gloom of the porch, smiling as he walked towards him.

"Who are you?" Cochrane asked uselessly as he straightened himself.

"Sebastian Friend. Are they Scarpas? Good boots. I had a pair myself a few years ago, but they were a little tight across the vamp. I wear Zamberlans myself these days."

"Really? When you're not driving a Jaguar, I suppose. Is the one over there yours?" The Mancunian accent was still distinct, Friend noted, even though it must have been forty years since Cochrane last lived there.

"Yes. Or to be strictly accurate, no. I don't own it, but I did drive it here."

"And parked it outside my house."

"Yes. Oh, I do hope I didn't block anyone's access."

The young idiot seemed to find the situation amusing. Cochrane did not.

"What do you want?"

"I have a letter for you, Mr Cochrane."

"Oh yes? Who from?"

"'C'," said Friend.

"Well, give it here then." Cochrane held out his hand.

"I put it through your door when I got here. I'll wait here while you go and read it and take whatever precautions you feel necessary. Then I'll be along in ten minutes or so."

"How do I know I can trust you?"

"The letter will explain everything." Friend paused, but seeing that the statement did not seem to be enough for Cochrane he added, "Do you think we'd be standing here talking if I'd been sent to kill you?"

Cochrane shook his head. "Being killed isn't what worries me," he said.

All the same he probed the edges of his front door carefully before he entered. As he turned the key he dropped to his knees and pushed through on his haunches. The empty, dark hallway stared back at him mockingly. He had already trodden on the envelope. It was plain white, rectangular with his name handwritten on the front in familiar green ink. The single sheet of paper inside carried a signature in the same colour. The letter itself introduced Mr Friend of something called the Audit Department and absolved Cochrane of any responsibility in relation to the Official Secrets Act when talking to him. This was an official enquiry and Cochrane was to co-operate with it as fully as he could. But neither this nor the green ink absolved the letter writer from a potential charge of what modern terminology might describe as 'phishing'. The only thing that did that was the telephone number printed at the bottom of the sheet of paper, which Cochrane was to ring for confirmation. It was a number he already knew. He had carried it in his head for almost fifteen years.

Closing the door behind him, Cochrane moved through to the small living room and punched in the numbers on his mobile phone. The number had been given to him as an emergency contact when he left the Service. He had always assumed that using it would be a laborious process of codenames and double-checks, identifying him to some low-grade newcomer who had never heard of Brian Cochrane, who for twenty years had been the Service's number one man on Middle East affairs. Only now his call was expected. Moments later he was speaking to 'C's personal assistant, who put him straight through to Sir Richard himself. Cochrane was impressed. There was no way for 'C' to have known exactly when the call would come, and in all his years in the Service Cochrane had never known an attempt to contact the Chief without an appointment take less than half an hour. Young Mr Friend clearly had some pull at headquarters.

The conversation could hardly have been briefer. Cochrane was to understand his obligations as specified in the letter. The matter was of vital national importance. That was all; no "Hope you're doing well", no "Dreadfully sorry to hear about your wife". The line went dead. Brian Cochrane unlaced his boots and walked over to the small sideboard where he emptied the contents of his hipflask into a square cut glass tumbler. Then he sat down to wait for the soft tap on the door that announced Friend's arrival.

There was no doubt in Friend's mind that this was the house of a single man. The furnishings were too basic and did nothing to lift the cottage out of the gloom that its narrow situation and small windows granted it. There were no pictures on the walls. It lacked a woman's touch, and surely no woman would have chosen the place to start with. Cochrane looked nothing like the high-flier from HQ that Blake had painted him as. He was burly and bearded, more than six feet of muscle and aggression clad in a loose-fitting khaki t-shirt and matching cargo trousers. The beard was full but neatly trimmed and only just beginning to show flecks of grey. And yet he must have been over sixty. Friend wondered why the man was keeping himself so fit. Was it purely for his self-esteem or in preparation for something?

He turned down Cochrane's offer of a brandy and followed him through to the kitchen while he made coffee instead. A photograph of a younger, clean-shaven Cochrane with a dark-skinned woman was fixed to the door of the fridge with a plain magnet. It was a holiday snap, taken somewhere in the Middle East judging by the minarets visible in the background. They looked happy together.

"Where's this? Istanbul?" he asked.

"Amman," said Cochrane curtly.

"And that must be Leila with you."

"And what do you know about Leila?'

"Not much. Only that she was your wife. And she died."

"Tact not your strong point, is it? Yes, she died. Six years ago. But you didn't come here to talk about my private life, I hope." Cochrane poured hot water into the cafetiere and gave it a stir.

"No, but it helps to make a little conversation to get things moving. Did you live here with her?"

"If you must know I moved here after she died. We had a place just up the road in Edenbridge, ran a little bookshop there together."

"And after she died you felt you had to get away, I suppose. It was a car accident, wasn't it?"

"Yes, if you must know."

"I suppose it was really an accident?"

Cochrane placed the two mugs he was holding down on the worktop with a crash.

"Of course it was a flaming accident! Why the hell wouldn't it be? She was knocked down by a car and killed. End of story. I've had just about enough of young idiots like you trying to stir up trouble." And then the flame seemed to die out as quickly as it had sprung to life. Perhaps he was over-reacting. "Look," he said, more calmly now, "I'll talk to you to help your bloody enquiry because I've been asked to. But don't push your luck. I have my limits and my personal life is beyond them."

Friend shrugged. "All right, I'm sorry. Forget I mentioned it." But inwardly he smiled. No one's personal life was going to be off-limits in this business. Brian Cochrane's least of all, especially when he seemed so touchy on the subject.

"What do you want to know?" asked Cochrane as they sat facing each other in the living room's two armchairs.

"Let's begin at the end," said Friend. "Tell me about Isfahan, about Operation Trust. The operation that cost you your career, and nearly cost Derrick Halsgrove his freedom."

"What do you mean it 'cost me my career'?"

"That you got the blame at the enquiry and they forced you out as a result. That's what Henry Blake said at least."

"Blake said that? Idiot! He doesn't know what he's talking about. Yes, it's true there was an enquiry, but I didn't stick around for the end of it. I resigned as soon as it became clear to me that they weren't prepared to listen."

"What weren't they prepared to listen to?"

"To my explanation of what I believed had gone wrong, had been going wrong for years."

"I was under the impression that our operations in Iran had gone more smoothly than most, ever since the 1980s."

"Oh yes, they were smooth all right. Too bloody smooth."

"What do you mean by that?"

Cochrane looked as though he were about to launch into a lengthy tirade, but he paused and collected himself, sipping at his coffee before placing the mug down carefully on a side table and fixing his eyes on Friend.

"It's a long story, and maybe an incoherent one. Time was I could have marshalled my facts just like that," he snapped his fingers together so sharply Friend almost jumped, "but I've been out of the game for fifteen years and my memory isn't quite so sharp on the details." He paused again, trying to find the right point of entry to begin his tale. "Look, I can't really tell you about the end unless I tell you about the beginning. It's the only way it makes sense. So I won't start with Isfahan, I'll start with Tehran. Tehran was my first overseas posting. It made my reputation. I'd travelled there in my student years, not long before the Shah was overthrown. I was fluent in Farsi and almost as good in Arabic, so it was a natural fit for me. It was 1981, not long after the revolution and the place was in chaos. It's easy to forget now but it wasn't just the Ayatollah and his religious hotheads behind it. There was a whole load of different factions as well. You had these weird coalitions like the National Front, which was a mixture of right-wingers, clerics and socialists. You had anti-Soviet socialist groups like the Mujahedin-e-Kalq who were part of it, then there was the pro-Soviet Tudeh party. Somehow all these different groups ended up campaigning together to get rid of the Shah. Tehran in 1979 was like Petrograd in 1917, and just as the Russians had Lenin lurking overseas, the Iranians had Khomeini. And just as there was an interim between the Tsar and Lenin, so there was between the Shah and Khomeini. The Shah appointed one of the National Front leaders as his new Prime Minister, Shahpur Bakhtiar, and then fled into exile a few days later. But once Khomeini returned, Bakhtiar didn't last long."

"So Bakhtiar plays the Kerensky role in this analogy."

"Exactly. Only he was even less successful. He couldn't even get the rest of the National Front coalition in line behind him, and the army refused to support him. The strikes and demonstrations continued, and when Khomeini returned from France, he simply ignored Bakhtiar and appointed his own prime minister. Just like Lenin, he was going to make sure that his own faction came out on top to the exclusion of all the others. Within weeks Iran had become an Islamic republic; Bakhtiar had to flee, and so did most of the other secular opposition leaders. Bands of religious zealots called

Komitehs started patrolling the streets handing out summary justice for non-Islamic dress or behaviour—so it's ironic really that we ended up with our own Komiteh in the form of the Tehran Committee."

"And where did the Tehran Committee come in to it?"

"At the beginning, nowhere. They grew out of the aftermath of the revolution; they simply didn't exist before it. The only opposition group to actually survive the revolution in any significant form was the Mujahedin-e-Kalq, or MEK, a bunch of left-wingers who had been in opposition to the Shah since the 1960s. They're still going, as it happens, if you can call a camp in Albania filled with ageing paramilitaries and their disappointed wives still going. They'd all but cleared out of Iran itself when I arrived in eighty-one and no one had heard of the Tehran Committee yet. It was a hell of a situation for a young agent to arrive in."

"So what did you do?"

"I lived my cover. I mean bloody well lived it. We'd broken off diplomatic relations, so I had commercial cover. Like all revolutionary regimes, the Iranians were desperate for hard currency and foreign trade, and that meant selling oil to the west. So I became an oil man. For a couple of years I was an oil man first and a spy second, if at all. I had no real choice, given how the local hoods were all over me from day one, as they were with just about every Westerner left in the country at that time. There weren't many of us. It must have been about the end of 1983 I think when I felt the pressure start to ease off. I wasn't being followed as routinely, post and telephone intercepts didn't seem as regular. They must have figured out that I was exactly what I said I was. And I was. For that whole period my intelligence value was precisely nil, and the Service didn't get anything from me that it couldn't have got from the Reuters correspondent I used to drink mint tea with in the Gol Rezaieh café."

Cochrane paused and took another sip of coffee, a couple

of fugitive droplets settling on the bristles of his beard. "But it was top-class training for me; learning how to flush out the watchers without letting them know I'd done it. If I'd just once shown an ounce of tradecraft to them, they'd have known at once I was a fake and I'd have been finished. All it takes over there is a single accusation of spying, they don't even have to prove anything. So I learned to be subtle, and I never stopped being subtle even when they weren't paying me the same attention as before. And not long after that, I made my first real breakthrough: Leila."

"Leila? Your wife?"

"Yes. She'd been on the streets with the rest of the student radicals in '78 and '79. She was part of the MEK at the time but hadn't fled the country with the rest of them, partly because she was too junior to have come to anyone's notice but also because she felt someone had to stay behind and carry on the fight. Then there were her parents of course. She didn't want to leave them."

"So how did she contact you? It can't have been easy for a woman in that atmosphere."

"It wasn't. But she was clever. She was tall and slim, so she cut her hair short and when she wanted to go out incognito she dressed as a young male student. Pretty convincingly too, and she had one of those voices that was just about deep enough to pass for male as long as she spoke in an even tone and didn't get too excited. She got herself some good counterfeit papers; there was already a healthy trade in them for women who wanted to get around without the Komitehs beating them up for it. So there I am, riding the bus into town one morning and she sits next to me and says quite openly, in English, that she represents an opposition group in Iran who are looking to get in touch with Western intelligence. It wasn't till our second meeting I worked out she wasn't a feller."

"Did you consider she might have been an agent provocateur?"

"That's exactly what I thought. I'd had a couple of approaches like that in my first few months in Tehran, but they were painfully obvious. There'd been nothing like that for over a year, but I still played a dead bat. She went on to say that I was one of a handful of Westerners they had been observing for several months before making an approach. They were satisfied that the local hoods had lost interest in me and come to the conclusion that I was the likeliest man on their list."

"So did you buy it?"

"Not at first. I said I had nothing to do with Western intelligence and no idea how to get in touch with anyone who did. But when she came back a week later, again just brazenly coming up to me in a city park, then I bit."

"What was the bait? An introduction to MEK?"

"No, she'd broken with them a few months earlier when the MEK leader Masud Rajavi offered support to Saddam Hussein during the Iran-Iraq war. Every Iranian I've ever met has been a patriot at heart and that was too much for them. It disgusted them. From that point on, MEK's support within Iran just haemorrhaged. It's never recovered. No, what she offered was something entirely new. A group of liberal, Western-sympathetic intellectuals who wished to undermine and, in the longer term, overthrow the new Islamic regime and build a modern Iran on the lines of Atatürk's Turkey."

"The Tehran Committee."

"The Tehran Committee. I got to meet all three of the main characters: Sadaghiani, Qarib and Nassirian, over the next few weeks and it's from those meetings that our networks in Iran began to grow. From the end of '83 until I was recalled to London in '89 to take over the Middle East Desk, more or less the whole structure of our intelligence operation in Iran was put together by Leila and me. Of course new agents came into the mix both in my time and later, and some retired or lost access to whatever it was they were giving us, but if what I've been reading in the papers over the last couple of weeks is correct then the basic structure we put together lasted more than thirty years."

"It sounds like something you should be proud of, rather than talking about something having gone wrong."

"Well... I suppose I am proud of it, but there was still something wrong by the end."

"By Isfahan?"

"Isfahan was just the final straw. There were plenty of other signs."

"Signs of what?"

"That the whole beautiful structure that Leila and I had put together had been penetrated by Iranian intelligence."

"Penetrated? Do you mean deeply?"

"I mean someone right at the heart of it had turned double. Could even have been double right from the beginning. That's what I thought."

"Do you have any idea who?"

"No. I never had any doubts about any one individual. Everyone seemed absolutely genuine in their desire to work against the regime. Some were nicer people than others, I couldn't stand Sadaghiani on a personal level, but I couldn't say any more than that. Any one of them might have had a relative, or a lover, who was being held by the authorities to force them into co-operation. But I could never find out anything to support the theory."

"So what made you suspicious?"

"The first thing was the quality of the material coming through. For the first four or five years it was excellent, really hot stuff. But then it began to tail off. Hardly so as you'd notice, but the real good stuff became less and less frequent until by about '91 or '92 we were pretty much left with the filler. It was still useful, but not really attention grabbing, much less tradable. We'd still get the odd really good snippet, but towards the end I got the feeling we were being thrown a bone to keep us happy whenever that happened."

"Did you take your concerns upstairs?"

"Of course. Quite a few times. It never did any good. Once or twice I got the blame for not pushing my agents to produce better material, other times they pointed to the last good report we had and said how vital it had been. I got the feeling that the Committee had a really good fix in with Whitehall, and there was nothing we in the Service could do to dissuade them of their value."

"I see. Was there anything else that made you suspicious?"

"Yes. For a start the fact that everything seemed to run like clockwork. For years. Our agents all seemed to follow career paths that were totally predictable. If one of them went for a promotion he always seemed to get it. We didn't always get the higher grade of intelligence we were hoping for as a result but still, in years of managing the networks you would have to expect at least one of them to be frustrated by a lack of progress. But no, it never happened. And then there was Vienna."

"Vienna?"

"Oh, you don't know about that? I assumed young Blake would have told you, but then I suppose it wasn't long after he started on Middle East Desk, and he wasn't directly involved."

"So what happened?"

"A bomb, that's what. Bloody nearly killed me."

Cochrane was silent for a while, staring into space as he communed with his memory. Friend found himself listening to the twittering of birds in the garden outside and the soft ticking of the grandfather clock in the hallway behind him. He felt like a bored child sitting in the living room of an elderly and unloved uncle, waiting for the compensation of buttered crumpets and fizzy pop. Cochrane, too, seemed lost in a distant world locked somewhere inside his memory.

"It was in the restaurant of the Sinzendorf Hotel," he continued. "Near the main railway station. 1994. Just after Dr Nassirian was granted refugee status in Germany. The Committee held its first, and as far as I know only, international conference.

All completely secret, of course. Access was restricted to the top level of the Committee, that is the big three and about a dozen others, plus a handful of invited guests and observers from CIA, the Austrian and German intelligence services and ourselves. I was the representative from the Service."

"What about Mossad?"

"No official representation, but if I remember correctly the CIA man might have held a listening brief on their behalf. Anyway, it was just a one-day affair: a meeting with presentations in a small conference room, sandwich lunch, some break-out sessions for private meetings in the afternoon and a dinner in the restaurant in the evening. Most of it was pretty dull, my paper included. I think the only useful thing I got out of it was a chance to sit down with the German guy and talk about general headquarters stuff. We were both going through a pretty heavy series of cuts at the time. Anyway, the Austrians had laid on some decent but low-key security and everything seemed to be fine until the dinner in the evening. The whole restaurant was booked out by our party, we were all sat along one long table and I think they'd just cleared away the starters when this young lad came charging through the kitchen doors screaming blue murder. Everyone stopped eating and turned to look at him. He was dressed like kitchen staff so at first we all thought it was just some sort of problem among the staff. There was this moment when everyone just froze, wondering what to do next, including the bomber. He was looking at us, we were looking at him. Then off he goes with his 'Allah-u-Akbar!' and starts charging towards one end of the table. The German and Austrian guys were already on their feet and they managed to take him down, but they didn't stop him from pulling the cord on the suicide vest he was wearing under his chef's smock. Five killed in total: the bomber himself, the two guys who took him down, one of the second rank Committee men and the guest representative from MEK. As luck would have it, the big three had left the room for a conference call with someone, I forget who, that was scheduled between courses."

"Who was the bomber?"

"Some young Lebanese hothead. He'd been granted refugee status in Austria three years before and was working as a pot washer in the Sinzendorf kitchens. The Austrians ran a full background check on him, of course, but they found nothing to link him to any particular group or any indication of where he might have got his hands on a suicide vest. I got the impression they didn't even know much about who he'd been in Lebanon, which rather makes you wonder why they gave him refugee status."

"Probably nothing else they could do with him," said Friend. "How long had he been working there?"

"That's the thing. The hotel had only taken him on a few weeks before, something like seven or eight, I can't remember exactly. But the point is that it was before the date and location were confirmed to us or the CIA or any of the other delegates, but after the Committee had arranged everything with the Austrians. That means if there was a leak, and I have no doubt of that whatsoever, it could only have come from the Austrians or the Committee itself. I don't think it was the Austrians."

"Was there an official verdict?"

"The official enquiry left the matter open. Even the Committee couldn't decide who was responsible. Sadaghiani insisted it was an MEK plot to regain their role as the main opposition group. The other two blamed Iranian intelligence but couldn't agree on which department. MEK said it was the Committee itself who had set it all up, citing the death of their representative and the convenient absence of the big three from the room when the bomb went off. Nobody took them seriously."

"Did you?"

"Not when I thought about it. I know it was almost thirty years ago, but that scene is as clear to me now as it was then. I was sitting facing the kitchen doors, so I must have been one of the first to see the bomber come through. The big three were at my end of the table, or rather their empty chairs were. I think that's why he stopped when he came through the door. He looked in our direction, I'm quite certain of that, and when he saw that his main targets were absent, he headed for the other end of the table to take out the second string leadership and the MEK."

"Why didn't he just go back into the kitchen and try his luck again later?"

"No, that wouldn't work with the psychology of the suicide bomber. You've got to psych yourself up for the big moment, and there are no second chances. Then there's the fact that pot washers aren't supposed to show their faces in the restaurant. He'd breached his own protocols in coming through those doors and he would have had too many awkward questions to face if he'd gone back through them again. No, from his point of view it was the right decision to reassess his target and go ahead anyway. But coming back to who was responsible, our man in Beirut did hear from a local source a year or two later that the bomber had actually been Hezbollah, acting on instructions from our old friends in Department 15. You're familiar with them, I presume."

"Yes, I am. So your case is that a traitor within the Committee tipped off Department 15 about the conference and they took the opportunity to try and eliminate several senior opposition figures in one fell swoop."

"Exactly. And it very nearly worked. They never had another chance. Ever since then the Committee acted like the Royal Family, never too many of them in any one place. I don't think any of the big three ever met each other again after Vienna. So you can understand why I was convinced it was the work of a traitor. And that same traitor probably over a period of years blew most, perhaps even all of our networks in Iran so that all we were getting is what Tehran wanted us to have."

"That's quite a statement. Did you tell your superiors?"

"I told 'C' herself, as she was then. She didn't buy it. To be fair to her, we didn't have the information from Beirut at that stage and by the time we did there was a new broom in charge and it was old news. She told me it was far more likely to be an opportunist attack; the Committee must have scouted the hotel in advance and could have been spotted by VAJA agents, perhaps our pot washer had even heard about it after he came to work at the hotel and had time after that to acquire the necessary material to carry out the attack. Any European city the size of Vienna has a resident community of Islamist fanatics. That's what she said anyway."

"She may have had a point."

"She may, if this were an isolated incident. But it wasn't."

"So you've said. Did you share your suspicions with anyone else?"

"One or two of the staff on my desk. And Dr Nassirian."

"Nassirian? But why not Sadaghiani? He was your local man. Nassirian was based in Germany."

"I told you, I didn't like Sadaghiani. He was a snob. Came from the old aristocracy and behaved like everyone else should still defer to him. I'm just a simple grammar school lad from Cheadle Hulme, hardly up to scratch for the likes of him. Qarib wasn't so bad, a bit of a bore, but decent enough. I actually liked Nassirian. He was good company; interested in literature, music, art. He'd been planning to stay on in Vienna for a couple of days after the conference to see the museums and visit the opera house, but of course after the bomb he had to pack that idea in and get back to Hamburg as quick as he could."

"He was back in Hamburg when you spoke to him about it?"

"Yes. It was just over a month later. I flew over to see him."

"And what did he say?"

"Not much. He'd had no suspicions himself and wanted to know if I suspected anyone, which of course I didn't. He said he would have a think about it and try to put together a list of every member of the Committee who had known the date and location of the conference. But I never heard any more about it from him."

"Did you give any thought to whether Nassirian himself might have been the traitor?"

"Hardly. If he had been I can quite imagine that he would have made sure he was out of the room when the bomb went off, but I don't see why he would have arranged to take the other two with him. They would have been the main targets for sure. By the same token I think we can absolve Sadaghiani and Qarib from suspicion."

"Unless all three of them were traitors," said Friend.

"Please tell me that's not a serious suggestion," said Cochrane.

"All right. So who else within the Service knew about the conference?"

"Quite a few people. Just about everyone on Middle East Desk, everyone upwards from me to 'C', transport section, finance who gave me an imprest for travel and subsistence."

"Was Derrick Halsgrove among their number?"

'Derrick? No, he didn't join the Service until two or three years later.'

"And what about Leila?"

"Leila? What do you mean?"

"You say your wife was involved with the Committee, so I'm sorry I have to ask but was she there or did she know about it in advance?"

Cochrane was silent again for a few moments, but he showed no sign of the anger Friend had expected in response to his question. Instead, he sipped at his coffee and stared into space, as if the subject were not personal at all and could be answered just as dispassionately as any other.

"It's all right," he said at last. "I can understand why you asked. And no, she wasn't in Vienna. We didn't get her out of Iran until 1996 and then we didn't get married until two years after that. Her vetting took quite some time. But she was still involved with the Committee then and, as for how much she knew about the conference, I simply don't know. I expect she must have known something but as for the full details, who can say? The whole thing was organised from outside Iran so there was no real need for those on the inside to know the details. They weren't sending any delegates. And I'm afraid I never asked how much she knew. By the time we got her out it didn't seem important anymore."

"Did she carry on with her work with the Committee after leaving Iran?"

"Officially no. I had to declare our relationship, of course, and that was one of the conditions placed on us by the Service. But Leila was an expat in a big city, and you couldn't keep someone like that isolated from others in the same position. She got a job with a charity, helping newly arrived asylum seekers with accommodation, legal help, and so on. Took a particular interest in the Iranians of course, and after a while she started hosting social events for them: cosy chats in coffee houses, that sort of thing. Very little of it had any bearing on intelligence work, but there were one or two occasions when she let me know that she thought someone new wasn't quite what they claimed to be."

"And what happened then?"

"We put the security boys on to them. In most cases I think their asylum claims were rejected, but whether that meant they got kicked out, I couldn't say."

"So she had no contact with her old friends in the Committee?"

"No, I wouldn't say that exactly. She'd known many of them for years. She didn't entirely keep them at arm's length."

Friend waited, hoping that Cochrane would elaborate. And when he didn't, he asked, "So, was it a social or a professional relationship?"

"Oh social, I should say. Definitely social."

"And did it continue after you left the Service and moved to Edenbridge?"

"We were already living in Edenbridge before I left. But to answer your question, no. I got the impression it petered out gradually after we started getting busy with the shop."

Friend was not so sure. For the first time during their

conversation, he had the distinct impression that he was being lied to. Nothing Cochrane had said earlier had struck him in quite the same way, except that there was an occasional impression of forced ease, of the old spy wanting to give the appearance of being more relaxed and open than he really was. Something was being held back. Friend could only guess what it might be.

"Let's move on,' he said, after waiting for more detail that never came. Cochrane did his best not to look relieved. "What can you tell me about Isfahan?"

"It's an historic city in central Iran." Friend did not smile. "Sorry, that was flippant," Cochrane went on. "What do you want to know?"

"The purpose and genesis of Operation Trust. And why you think it went wrong."

"It went wrong because it was a bloody trap from the start. And I fell right into it!"

"Why would the Iranians set a trap for you?"

"My guess would be that they wanted to get rid of me, and probably Derrick too. He was my field man, doing jobs for me all across the Middle East, maintaining the old networks and building new ones, running ops. Good man, Derrick. He was just as sure as I was that there was a traitor somewhere in the Committee."

"So what happened?"

"I received a tip-off, direct from Mossad."

"Mossad?"

"Yes, a rare event in those days."

"And what did it say, this tip-off?"

"That a source in the Ministry of Intelligence was prepared to make a one-time sale of information to the Service. The information related to the Tehran Committee and was available for a price of fifty-thousand US dollars. Well, I thought, what else could that mean but the identity of the traitor in the Committee? I had twelve hours to signal my acceptance of the price and a further forty-eight to make the specified rendezvous. That gave me a headache because to get approval for the operation and a budget would have taken at least five days. Luckily I had some funds set aside for agent pay-offs elsewhere so I was able to reallocate some of those without troubling the finance department. I hoped I'd be able to make good the loss if the operation was successful."

"But you must have suspected it might not be."

"Of course, but the fact it came through Mossad made me feel more bullish about it, and to be frank by that stage I was gunning for the traitor. It had been eating away at me for years. I just had to take the chance."

"So why was the source using Mossad as a go-between?"

"My understanding was they were offered the deal first but weren't interested. They never had any time for the Committee or any of these émigré groups. It just wasn't their scene. So they hawked it on to us in the hope the source might go back to them again later when he had other material to sell."

"But why us rather than the CIA? They're usually freer with their money than we are."

"True, but the honest answer is they were more likely to get a bite from me. It was their liaison man, Gaby Cohen, who brought it to me. I'd known him for years and he knew pretty well about my suspicions where the Committee was concerned. The CIA were probably less likely to pay good money for a story they didn't want to believe."

"I see. All right, so you took the bait. How did you make the arrangements?"

"It took me six hours to sort the money out. After that I called Gaby and signalled my agreement. He gave me the details of the rendezvous, which was at a farmhouse a mile or two away from one of the airbases on the outskirts of the city. I suppose there was some sort of safety and recognition protocol, but I can't remember. You'll find it in the file. The only man I could realistically send out at such short notice was Derrick. He knew the territory; he'd been in and out of Iran on journalistic cover for the past two or three years. Luckily he was available. Of course, I didn't have time to get the usual clearances, which is what got me into trouble in the end."

"Couldn't you have got verbal authority at least? From 'C' or someone else at the top table?"

Cochrane seemed to swallow his next words before they came out of his mouth. He took a moment to compose himself before continuing.

"I suppose so. The truth is I didn't want to risk it. They might have said no."

"So you were prepared to risk your career on such a long shot as this?"

"Yes!" Cochrane was emphatic. "Don't you see, it was probably the only chance I was ever going to get to find out who the traitor was? If it worked, I would have been vindicated, if it didn't I knew I could never stay on anyway. It would have felt like working for the other side. That's why the enquiry didn't matter to me. Once it went belly-up, I was always going to hand in my cards. How is Derrick by the way?"

"Not too bad, I understand, considering."

"What do you mean, 'considering'?"

Of course, thought Friend, the Baghdad bombing had been kept out of the papers.

"I'm sorry, I assumed you knew, but of course you don't. He was injured in a car bomb attack in Iraq just a few hours before the IRGC started rounding up our agents."

"Bloody hell! I don't suppose that was a coincidence."

"Probably not, but how it might be linked I couldn't say."

"Will he be all right?"

"I think so. His life isn't in danger, that much I do know."

"Glad to hear it. He was a good lad, young Derrick."

"Did you keep in touch?"

Cochrane laughed. "No, that wasn't his style. I was long gone by the time he got back. He sent me a postcard from London to let me know he'd made it. I've still got it somewhere, I think. But that was the last I heard from him."

"So tell me about the rendezvous."

"There isn't much to tell from my angle. Derrick flew off to Tehran the day after I'd made arrangements with Gaby. The cash went off on the same plane by diplomatic courier and Derrick picked it up from the Embassy the same evening. He spent a peaceful night in a decent hotel, then took a train to Isfahan the next morning. The rendezvous was fixed for 10pm that night, which is six-thirty our time. I was at my desk, following the GPS signal from his phone. No one else had an idea that anything was going on. I checked on him from time to time during the day; most of the time he was bumming around central Isfahan, probably seeing the sights, but about three hours before the rendezvous he headed north. I could see him scouting around the area for a while, then with just over an hour to go he sits tight. Probably some place with a good view of the rendezvous. Bang on time, he starts to move, makes it to the rendezvous, then he's motionless for a couple of minutes, then nothing. No signal, blank screen, everything just dead, including Derrick for all I know. I tried calling, but the phone was dead, and that was it. I stayed in the office, tearing my hair out, until gone midnight. That was when Iranian state TV started howling about Western imperialist criminal provocation and the Head of Communications called me in for a friendly chat. Exit Brian Cochrane. For the rest of it, you'll have to ask Derrick, if he's up to it."

Friend had finished his coffee and was rising to leave when he noticed the photograph. It was tucked away on a bookshelf, propping up a row of novels: a simply framed black-and-white print of four happy young people posing informally outdoors. A young woman in a headscarf and a long shirtdress, together with three young men: all dark, one rather portly and already balding, a pair of wire-rimmed spectacles perched halfway down his nose, his shirt open-necked, exposing a tuft of chest hair; the second rather cool and aloof, his expression unreadable behind the darkest of dark glasses, a pencil-thin moustache immaculate above his upper lip; the third, pictured in the centre next to the girl, in a light tailored jacket was the only one smiling, not caring about the heavy lock of dark hair that had been caught by a stray breeze and sent flying backwards from his forehead, an honest, open face captured in a carefree moment. Even in this still image his natural charisma was apparent. It was Dr Nassirian, although perhaps not a doctor yet, and beside him the portly figure was the medical man Qarib. Sadaghiani was obviously the aloof man in the dark glasses. The woman, of course, was Leila; a Leila of twenty or so, happy and still unaware of the drama of her life to come.

"Yes, that's her," said Cochrane, anticipating the question. "With the three she introduced me to. They were all students together at the time of the revolution. She didn't bring much with her when we got her out, but that photograph was very dear to her."

"What was her subject?"

"Mathematics. Afterwards she taught. Even under Khomeini they still believed in education for girls; they didn't start clamping down on that until Ahmadinejad's time."

Friend nodded and Cochrane thought his ordeal was over as his guest made his way down the hall towards the front door. But, as if struck by a parting thought, Friend stopped and turned towards him, a curious gleam in his eye.

"Before I go, there is one more thing I should ask you. I almost forgot. Has anything changed for you?"

"Changed for me? What do you mean by that?"

"Since the killings and arrests, I mean. The wholesale destruction of the Tehran Committee."

"Sorry, I still don't follow."

"I mean that your assumption of a traitor in the midst of the Committee must have been tested by what just happened. If the Committee and our networks had been so badly compromised by some deep penetration agent that they were actually doing more good than harm to the Iranians, why have they just put our agents on trial for espionage and murdered all the Committee's senior people?"

Cochrane looked back in silence. There was no answer he could give. He stood in the doorway and watched Friend drive off, but his thoughts were far from the smart young Englishman in his executive car. They were back in Tehran with his early years in the Service; back with Leila and her friends, watching them as they posed for the photograph. Why did he choose to keep this one among all the pictures he had of her on display? There were dozens of others that better captured her looks and her spirit, or brought back memories of their life together. But they had never come out of the box he had carried down from Edenbridge, the box which remained untouched in the loft. Of all of them, he had chosen this one, taken before he even knew her, standing with the men who had shaped her future life and his own. Perhaps it was his own way of punishing himself for his sins.

Secrets: that was what had brought them all together. And it was too many secrets that had killed them. All of them, except one.

FIFTEEN

Friend was more than halfway back to central London when he took the call from Wetherby. He dropped the car off at the Service pool in Croydon and rattled back into London Bridge on a train that smelled like it hadn't been cleaned since Harold Wilson was prime minister. Leaving the station, it was a ten-minute walk to the Royal Oak where he found Wetherby sitting alone at a wooden table nursing a pint of Harvey's Mild and looking as though the white heat of technology had entirely passed him by. At least until he got his laptop out and opened it on the table between them.

"We've made some progress since you came to Cambridge," he said, once Friend had settled down with a pint of his own. It was just after four and the bar was nearly empty; the barman lounging idly on a stool and working his way through a newspaper crossword. Like the train carriage Friend had travelled up from Croydon in, the Royal Oak had a distinct vintage feel to it. But whereas the train had carried with it a heavy sense of neglect and overuse, the Royal Oak was immaculately maintained; a living relic of the kind of spartan, socially-levelling public house that used to proliferate in the towns and cities of Britain. Welcoming, homely places unsullied by televisions or sound systems, where the only noise was a buzz of conversation and the occasional thud from the dartboard. *My kind of place*, thought Friend.

"Here he is," said Wetherby, as the grainy image of a dark-haired young man appeared on the screen. It was a video clip lasting less than two seconds, just long enough to give Friend an impression of a smartly dressed Middle Eastern man in his late thirties, wheeling a small, carry-on suitcase through a set of electronic gates in some airport terminal, and looking helpfully up at the camera as he did so.

"Omid Sourian, that was the name we were given. Age thirty-six, resident Tehran, occupation businessman. This is him arriving at Heathrow Terminal Three direct from Tehran on Iran Air flight 711 at fifteen hundred hours on Tuesday 2 June, that's forty-eight hours prior to the murder of Professor Sadaghiani. The immigration officer didn't remember him particularly, it was a very short interview, but luckily she made a note that he was staying two days on business. And of course we already know that his usual business connections weren't expecting a visit from him at all."

The screen moved forward to another short clip showing the same man walking through the arrivals hall towards the exit for the Heathrow Express. Friend remained silent as he watched further clips of the man buying a ticket, waiting on the platform at Heathrow and then walking down the platform at Paddington Station. In each clip he seemed relaxed and unhurried; he was making no attempt to disguise his appearance or avoid the camera. If it had been Friend he would have ducked in behind some other passengers at Paddington and walked as close on their tail as he could, hoping to go unnoticed as part of a larger group. But this man strolled on his own at an even pace, straight down the middle of the platform, giving the other arriving passengers as wide a berth as possible. Friend simply couldn't understand his behaviour.

"The cameras follow him through the station to the taxi rank outside," Wetherby continued. "He takes a taxi to the Belton House Hotel near Kings Cross where he is booked in for the specified two nights. It's on a little back street, so not much camera coverage there but I guess he's tired after his journey because there's no sign of him for a couple of hours until we pick him up again on Pentonville Road just after nineteen hundred. He goes into an Indian restaurant and eats Chicken Dhansak washed down with a whole bottle of cheap Bulgarian cabernet. No wonder the waiter remembered him. Leaves the restaurant just before nine, walks a little unsteadily back to his hotel and that's the last we see of him for the day."

The next image was a still, taken inside a railway station ticket office; the same young man queueing with other commuters, then another taken from behind the ticket office counter showing him face on, smiling at the ticket clerk, credit card in hand poised for payment.

"This is all I'll show you from Wednesday. He clearly believes in planning ahead, our Mr Sourian. He's booking an advance return ticket to Cambridge for Thursday. Outward journey at oh-eight forty-two, return at twelve forty-four, giving him a total of three-and-a-quarter hours in the city. Pays using a Visa card registered in his own name, same as he used at the restaurant the night before. The rest of the day is not important. Tourist stuff. A trip to the British Museum, a walk in Regents Park, later he strolls down Bond Street and browses watches in the Breitling boutique but doesn't buy anything. Fish and chip supper in a pub near his hotel." Wetherby looked up with a smile. "Funny how many foreigners go for that sort of thing," he said.

"So then we come to Thursday." Wetherby led Friend through another series of still and moving images of the same man, Sourian, arriving in Cambridge and travelling through the city, first on foot, then by bus. "From the station he starts off walking the natural route into town: straight up Station Road then right onto Hills Road, but then he does something interesting. Instead of carrying straight on, he cuts across Parker's Piece and here we see him just beyond there, at the junction with Clarendon Street. We can't be sure, but it looks like he might be about to take a right turn along Clarendon Street," he minimised the window and brought up on screen a detailed street map, "which is here."

"But that's where…"

"Exactly."

Friend stared at the image as Wetherby brought it on screen again. Omid Sourian, wearing a short summer raincoat and carrying a compact rucksack over one shoulder, was staring to his right, towards the entrance to Clarendon Street. If he had taken that turning, it would have led him up towards Jesus Terrace and straight past the entrance to the alleyway where the two men had found the dead letter drop used by Professor Sadaghiani a few days before. The time stamp on the screen read 09:57, twenty-three minutes after Sourian had left the station.

"So could it be that Sourian was making a drop-off and the professor came along to make the pick-up later?"

Wetherby shrugged. "If that were the case, then what happened to whatever it was that he picked up? There was no sign of a handover in the restaurant or in the park afterwards. And what happened to the cylinder he received in the post that morning? Besides which it doesn't explain what he did next."

Wetherby brought another video clip up on screen: Sourian seen walking up to a bus shelter, consulting the timetable, checking his watch, sitting down on the plastic bench to wait.

"This is Emmanuel Street, east side of Christ's Pieces. 10:14am. He waits seven minutes then boards a number eight bus which takes him north. He doesn't get off anywhere in the city centre, but carries on until we get here."

Friend watched as another clip showed a figure that might have been Sourian getting off the bus, the camera being too distant to give a clear picture. Then luckily the figure turned and walked closer, running a hand through his hair as he approached and finally glancing up at the camera just before he passed. It was Omid Sourian, without a shadow of a doubt. The time stamp read 10:52.

"This footage comes from the camera of a petrol station

forecourt on Histon Road, about two hundred yards short of the turning to Professor Sadaghiani's home. The direction he was walking in would have taken him to that turning. We don't have anything closer. And that's the last we see of him for over an hour. We next pick him up on Bridge Street, by the Round Church at twelve oh-four. Forty minutes left before his train back to London. He's probably done what he came to Cambridge to do so he's doing a little sightseeing on his way. Maybe he realises he'll never get another chance. So he carries on south, more or less direct, getting to the station with just over ten minutes to spare. I won't bore you with the rest. He gets back to Kings Cross, collects his luggage from the hotel, taxi to Paddington, Heathrow Express back to Terminal Three and checks in for his return flight to Tehran.

"Any thoughts? We'll be going public with all this tomorrow, together with an appeal for witnesses. We may be able to fill in some of that missing hour with any luck. Either way, the file is going up to CPS in the morning and I've every expectation that a murder charge will be formally made within forty-eight hours. Not that it will help much; I don't see the Iranians sending him back to us any time soon."

Friend sat back in his chair. The case was about as open and shut as it could have been. He felt almost disappointed by how easy it was.

"I don't suppose there's any way they could have met, is there? Sourian and the professor, I mean," he asked.

"Pretty much impossible, time-wise. Sourian can't have got to the professor's house before eleven, and by twelve oh-four we have him back in the city centre. The professor didn't leave his office until about the time we find Sourian back on Bridge Street, and the timing of his car journey home doesn't leave enough for him to have detoured into the city to meet there. Chances are we would have picked it up on camera anyway if he had. No, I don't think that works. But what does work is the idea that Sourian was keeping a container of nerve agent in his backpack and smeared it on the professor's front door handle just an hour before the professor got back from the office."

"He wasn't wearing any protective equipment."

"And he'd have looked bloody silly on the bus if he had been! No, he probably had that in his backpack too."

"And put it on in front of the professor's house?"

"It's possible. He'd be partly shielded by the porch and, as I said before, it's a cul-de-sac with mostly professional residents. Most of the neighbours were out at work. Nobody saw him there, wearing protective equipment or not. Or he might have changed into it on the inside."

"Inside?"

"That laptop and mobile phone you asked me to check on—there was no sign of either of them inside the professor's home or anywhere else. If he did keep them at home, someone must have turned the place over in a very professional way. Our people could find no evidence of forced entry and there was nothing inside the property that couldn't be linked directly to the professor or one of his known visitors. Fingerprints, clothing fibres, hairs, you name it. But all the same there wasn't a damn thing inside the house that connected the professor with the Tehran Committee. It's like he had nothing to do with them at all. So, let's suppose it's Omid Sourian who does the professional clear-out of the professor's house, then before he leaves he suits up and smears his nerve agent on the door, doing it from inside, well out of sight of the neighbours."

"Could be," admitted Friend, more reluctantly than otherwise. "What about his backpack—could he have fitted the laptop inside?"

"The images we have from CCTV don't really tell us anything about whether his backpack was fuller on the way back from the house, but we do have footage of him going through security at the airport. It shows him clearly placing a laptop and two mobile phones in the tray. Now of course there's nothing to say that he hadn't brought all of that kit with him from Tehran."

"And lots of people carry two mobiles. One for work, one for personal use."

"Of course they do. But still the footage is consistent with the theory of how Sourian probably did it."

Friend's pursed lips and troubled expression showed clearly enough that he did not agree. "You know what isn't consistent?" he said. "The idea that Omid Sourian could enter and strip the professor's home so professionally and yet leave such an amateurish trail for us to follow."

"I know what you're thinking," said Wetherby after an age of silence. "It's too damn easy."

"You feel the same way?"

"On the whole, no. I'll admit the thought crossed my mind, largely because it's contrary to what you said about the likely movements of a professional killer. But I'm an experienced enough copper to know that it's usually a mistake to over-think these things. If something seems straightforward that's usually because it is."

"Perhaps that's all it is," said Friend, reflectively. "The idea that our killer could have behaved with such... such criminal incompetence, that's the only way I can describe it, offends my professional sensibilities."

Wetherby gave a soft laugh.

"No, I'm serious," Friend went on. "I mean he's supposed to have come here to commit a dreadful crime, carrying a deadly poison in his backpack, knowing that the killing will be headline news all over the world and yet he takes the most direct and easily traceable route imaginable and parades in front of every CCTV camera he can find like he's actually auditioning for the role of prime suspect. It's inexplicable. Whoever taught him his tradecraft deserves to be shot."

"Well," said Wetherby, "no doubt you know more about these things than I do, but tell me this: are the Iranians really so professional that they've never made a mistake? Have they never had a job go so badly wrong that it made them look like fools?"

Friend was about to respond with a charge sheet of the crimes attributed to Department 15, but then an image came to mind of a coach full of journalists perched on the edge of a precipice and of an apologetic driver who claimed to have fallen asleep at the wheel. There, at least, the fabled organ of Iranian terror had shown itself capable of almost comical incompetence.

"Perhaps you're right," he conceded. "After all, nobody's perfect."

SIXTEEN

LAMBROOK HOUSE
TUESDAY 21 JULY, 1613 HOURS

"But what you failed to take into account," said Lascelles, "is that Omid Sourian was no ordinary murderer. He was a professional, state-sponsored assassin and it was not necessarily in his interest to evade detection."

"You mean that by killing Professor Sadaghiani, the Iranian government was sending a message that it could do whatever it liked on British soil and there was nothing we could do to prevent it, or respond to it. They were thumbing their noses at us and at the same time sending a warning to all dissidents at home and abroad: nowhere is safe." Friend shrugged. "It's a theory I suppose."

"A theory consistent with what we've seen from the Russians, among others, in recent years. And a theory which you don't seem to be prepared to argue against. Or am I wrong?"

"I wouldn't presume to argue against such masterful logic," said Friend, his smile treacle-thick with insincerity. "But it's still just a theory. Supposition, based on your reading of the evidence from a particular point of view."

Lascelles threw up his hands in despair. Friend thought he detected a smirk from Ms Wilton.

"All right, Mr Friend. We will pass over that for now. There is another important factor we have yet to really touch on: the fate of those middle and lower ranking members of the Tehran Committee domiciled in this country. I believe there were more than two hundred of them?"

"Two hundred and thirty-seven."

"The most senior of whom was Ali Rezaei, the Deputy Treasurer?"

"Correct. The Committee's senior Treasurer was Dr Qarib, in New York. Rezaei was his deputy and handled income and distribution of funds for western Europe. It was small beer compared to the amount of money Qarib was handling—the Americans were showering the Committee with cash—but he was still handling millions of euros every year."

"And he, like the rest of them, was supposed to be interviewed by the Security Service in the aftermath of the killings here, in Germany and the United States."

"That's right."

"And when did you get the first indication that something was not quite right with Mr Rezaei?"

"A couple of hours after I met with Wetherby in the Royal Oak. I got a call from our liaison man at Thames House: Jadon Rivers."

"And what did Mr Rivers say?"

"That Ali Rezaei had disappeared and it looked like he had emptied the Committee's bank accounts in London before he went on the run."

"Can you put a little flesh on those bones, please? What can you tell us about the chain of events?"

"Rivers told me that his office had made initial contact with Rezaei four days after Professor Sadaghiani's death. By contact I mean something like a routine health-check over the telephone; making sure he was all right, asking if he'd noticed anything unusual recently, urging him to take extra security precautions. They fixed a follow-up appointment a week later at a police station in the City, for a proper debrief. But he didn't show. When they ran their usual checks, they found his phone was dead and he hadn't turned up for work since the day they first contacted him."

"His work was…?"

"He lectured at the LSE. Worst of all, when they checked with the Committee's bankers in the City, they found that all three accounts had been virtually emptied the day after they spoke to him. More than eight hundred thousand pounds had been transferred out on the same day, five days after Professor Sadaghiani's murder. It was the same across Europe. Accounts in Frankfurt, Stockholm and Madrid all cleared on the same day. Just under two million euros in total."

"And the money went where? Tehran?"

"No. Iran's under sanctions so no European bank can send money there directly. But it was the next best thing. Every transfer was made to an account at Blom Bank in Beirut where it was drawn out in cash the following day."

"By whom?"

"A local businessman, believed by our station chief to be a paymaster for Hezbollah."

"So, if I understand this correctly, the Tehran Committee's treasurer in Europe transferred all of the Committee's funds in Europe to a known Iranian front in Lebanon."

"I'd say you understand it perfectly."

"Don't tell me you had your doubts about this as well?"

Friend gave no answer. Instead, he folded his arms across his chest, looked up at the ceiling and let out a long, expressive sigh.

"Oh good grief!" Lascelles sank back in his chair, aghast. "What do you want? A signed confession from the Ayatollah?"

"If you must know, I thought the timing was reactive rather than otherwise."

"Meaning what?"

"Meaning if Rezaei had been in on the plot to close the Committee down, both the money and he would have disappeared within twenty-four hours of the professor's death. The fact that neither of those things happened until almost a week later, and he still took a call from Rivers' team in the interim, suggested to me that he hadn't made any such arrangements before the murder. Which meant he hadn't been aware of it in advance."

"All right. So what did you do?"

"I asked Rivers whether they'd had a look through Rezaei's apartment yet. They hadn't, so I arranged to meet him there. My hope was that if he left in a hurry, he might have left something behind. The sort of clue we might have found if Professor Sadaghiani's house hadn't been turned over after he was poisoned."

SEVENTEEN

LONDON
TUESDAY 16 JUNE

"I've always hated this area," said Sebastian Friend, peering out from under the rim of his umbrella at the rain-soaked concrete walkways and towers of the Barbican. "If you ask me, we'd have been better off settling for how the Luftwaffe left it rather than building all this."

"Pretty it ain't," agreed Jadon Rivers, turning up the collar of his overcoat as the rain blew sideways across the concrete walkway that carried them over the road from the Tube station. "I've got a bit of a soft spot for it myself, though. You know I lived here for a while when I was a kid?"

"No, really?"

Rivers nodded. "Seddon House, one of the terrace blocks. I don't really remember it. I was only three when we moved out. When my dad came over from Dominica he got his first job as a porter at St. Barts, just up the road. My mum was a nurse there. That's how they met."

"Did they like it here?"

"Yeah, I think they did. But my old man missed the sea, so we moved down to Southampton. Nice place to grow up. But I still come down here sometimes and wonder what it would have been like. The gardens are nice on a summer's day; you get a much better impression of the place than when it's pissing down of an evening like this. You know, we've actually got a little outstation around here somewhere."

"Really? Doing what?"

"Search me," said Rivers, then adding, after an enigmatic pause, "It's not supposed to be one of the most sought-after postings in the Service."

"Which one of these oversized tombstones does our friend Rezaei inhabit?" asked Friend, thinking it was time to bring the conversation back to the matter at hand.

"Lauderdale Tower. Straight ahead of us. Eighteenth floor. Crazy place for a hood to live, if you ask me. Difficult to get out of if you're cornered and anyone with half-decent tradecraft would know it. There are three flats to each floor, each making up one side of the triangle. Access via a shared central lobby with three lifts and three emergency stairwells, which you can also get to via the balconies. No faster way of making an exit unless you're an expert with a low-level parachute. On the other hand, it is very private."

"How long has he lived here?"

"Eight years. God knows how much he pays in rent. But if we're right about him, I suppose he claims it back from his paymasters in Tehran."

They rode up to the eighteenth floor in silence, then Friend kept watch in the triangular lobby while Rivers fiddled with the lock on the flat's front door. It was only a few moments before he heard the click of the lock springing open.

"All clear," said Rivers.

Friend followed him into the central hallway and Rivers took him through the layout: kitchen, living room and dining room to the right, main bedroom and two bathrooms to the left. The three spare bedrooms lined the corridor ahead of them. Friend chose left, and entered Ali Rezaei's bedroom, in search of any personal items he might have left behind him.

Rezaei had left in a hurry, but he had been thorough. The bedroom was stripped clean of anything movable or personal.

Not a scrap of clothing remained, but none of the furniture—Rezaei's own—had gone and even the bedding lay as Rezaei had left it, crumpled and thrown to one side as if a troubled night's sleep had given way to a hurried morning departure. But the room yielded no further clues about the man who had slept there for eight years. Friend stepped out through the sliding windows onto the balcony that ran the full length of the apartment. He leaned on the rail and stared down eighteen floors of concrete through the encroaching darkness to the concrete below. The wind whipped at his face and spat rain in his eyes. Rezaei must have had a good head for heights, as well as finance, to have lived in this lonely tower.

Friend walked along the balcony, staring in turn at each of the spare bedrooms. It was a big flat for a single man and Friend wondered why he had needed the extra space. The first two rooms looked empty, but the third was set up as some kind of storeroom. He stepped back inside and found himself looking at a large, metal bookcase. A number of books and bound magazines in a variety of languages were grouped on its shelves, all of them devoted to Iran and the wider region. In among them were a number of clamshell storage boxes, but Friend found them all empty, the only clue to their former contents a scribbled code on its front. Opposite the bookcase stood a bare wooden desk and matching chair, while an old-fashioned grey, metal filing cabinet occupied a place in the corner. The cabinet was locked and when Friend tried to rock it back to open it from underneath, he found it screwed to the floor by two metal brackets. Surely it was unlikely that Rezaei would bother to lock a filing cabinet that contained nothing important. Perhaps Rivers' little bunch of skeleton keys might include something that could help them open it.

He found Rivers in the dining room, crouched behind the back of a desk which must have been Rezaei's main workspace. Whatever else he had managed to grab before leaving, he had left his desktop computer behind.

"Any luck?" Friend asked from the doorway.

"Looks like the hard-drive's gone," said Rivers. "There's something odd about this wiring though. Not sure what to make of it…"

The frame of the doorway was the only thing that saved Friend. One moment he was watching Rivers work at something at the back of the PC with a small pocketknife, the next he was lying amid the ruins of a glass coffee table in the middle of the living room. For a moment he couldn't work out what he was doing there, but then he heard the fire alarm ringing in his ears and felt the rain blowing in from the shattered windows. He struggled to his feet and brushed the broken glass from his clothes. There was a gaping hole in the partition wall that separated the living and dining areas; a black fog of smoke still hung in the air, an awful smell of roasted flesh. Feeling the bile begin to sting at the back of his throat he compelled his legs to move towards the gap in the wall, forced himself to look through it and see the broad, black slash across scorched wall and ceiling, the twisted, mutated mass of furniture and man where moments before Jadon Rivers had been at work. This is England. No danger here.

Then something inside him seemed to break and he turned and fled through the shattered windows to the balcony, steadying his shaking hands on the cold metal rail and gulping down lungfuls of air as the rain spattered his face, until at last he leaned forward and vomited all of it—blood, smoke and horror—eighteen storeys down to the earth below.

EIGHTEEN

VAUXHALL CROSS
THURSDAY 18 JUNE

Day after day through any English summer, crowds of cricket fans can be seen pouring out of Vauxhall Station in the shadow of SIS headquarters, streaming across the busy road junction and making their way down Harleyford Road towards the Oval. As a boy, Sebastian Friend had often been among them and he, like most of his fellow travellers, had never offered more than a passing glance at the short and rather shabby parade of shops on the corner approaching Harleyford Road. The five shops were, unsurprisingly, all leased from a single landlord; recorded at the Land Registry as Vauxhall Properties (1996) Ltd. Anyone who wished to find out more about this firm could view their list of Principal Officers quite openly on the Companies House website, but nobody ever had taken that trouble. The parade of shops at Vauxhall was the firm's only commercial holding, and a singularly unimpressive one it was too.

The sandwich bar and the newsagent did a reasonable trade, especially on cricket days. The dry cleaners looked dirty and neglected, although it did enjoy the custom of some SIS employees whose expectations rose no higher than the removal of soup stains from their one and only tie. The camera shop was very quiet, and the last on the row, Amos Sporting Trophies Ltd, was hardly ever open; a hand-scrawled *'Back in 30 minutes'* seemingly as permanent a fixture on the locked front door as the tarnished pewter and plastic trophies were in a window display unchanged in twenty years.

The busy road junction adjoining Vauxhall Station is not a place where anyone is inclined to linger and observe, but if someone had been doing just that at nine-thirty in the morning, thirty-six hours after Sebastian Friend had staggered out of Lauderdale Tower and lost himself in the chaos of a fire evacuation, he might have seen a slim, blond haired young man wearing a fawn coloured suit and pale blue shirt coming out of the newsagent with a copy of that morning's Daily Telegraph. The guilt of Omid Sourian was declared in bold print across the paper's front page. Tucking it under his arm, the young man strolled along the parade until he came to the trophy shop at the end, where he pulled a key out from his trouser pocket and unlocked the door. Even the most jaded observer would have been surprised to see this; the young man did not look anything like the sort of person who would be expected to work in a shop of that kind.

Sebastian Friend locked the door behind him and made sure the blind was firmly pulled down. Then he walked through to the back of the shop and into an office behind. Switching on the light, for the office had no windows, he walked over to a battered wooden desk which was bare save for a single telephone. He lifted the receiver, ignoring the absence of any dial tone, and entered an eight-digit code; when he heard a click from the right hand wall he replaced the receiver and walked over to the wall. In the middle of the wall stood a door, which remained locked at all times until the correct code—changed routinely each month—was entered on the office telephone. Friend went through the door and stepped carefully down a spiral stairway, lights coming on in stages as he made his descent.

At the bottom of the stairs, Friend found himself at the end of a long, straight passageway no more than seven feet high and barely wide enough for two people to walk side by side. The walls were barrel-shaped, as if made for a London Underground train, and finished in bare concrete. The floor, too, was bare concrete, and sang in hollow fashion under Friend's leather soles. The only other feature was the lighting above; a single naked bulb every thirty feet connected by black cables running the length of the tunnel. The tunnel was too long for the far end to be visible, but Friend knew where it led. Very rarely did he need to use this route to enter the Vauxhall Cross headquarters of the Service, known as the 'tradesman's entrance' since it was reserved for those who worked at outlying stations or whose cover would be compromised by accessing the building in full public view. Friend was covered by either stipulation.

Every time he made this lonely walk, he imagined to himself the traffic overhead, the pedestrians crossing the junction, the trains passing over the viaduct in and out of Vauxhall Station. Sometimes he would feel a distant reverberation and remember that the tunnels of the Victoria Line were only a few hundred feet away. Mostly he heard his footsteps ringing on the concrete and wondered whether they could hear him coming in Vauxhall Cross. It seemed to him loud enough to be heard on the fourth floor.

His pass card gave him entry through a sliding steel door at the other end of the tunnel. This brought him into a dimly lit vestibule where a sleepy security guard roused himself and asked for Friend's identification, before telling him to place his watch and keys in a tray before they passed through the security scanner. Friend himself then passed through a body scan. The guard issued him with a dark green lanyard attached to which was a simple yellow card. It said *'Visitor'.*

There was nothing ahead of Friend but a wall with a single lift. Friend wondered what the guard would do if the lift were out of order, and what lay behind the wall. He was on level B2. He got into the lift, held his pass card to the reader, and pressed the button for the fourth floor.

'C' greeted him with unprecedented warmth.

"Ah Sebastian, thank you for coming in. Glad to see you looking so fit. Come and have a seat. Terrible business about poor Rivers."

"Yes. He was a good man." Friend strode across the thickly carpeted floor to where Sir Richard was seated at his desk and sat down opposite him. It was the first time he had ever been inside 'C's office and he allowed his eyes to wander over to the full-length window with its view across the Thames. The layout of the office had been carefully planned: 'C's desk occupied the side wall, offering a clear view of the door to the left and the window, to the right. A small leather sofa and two armchairs were placed around a glass coffee table by the window for more informal meetings. On the opposite wall stood a wooden sideboard bearing pots of fresh tea and coffee, bottled water and a selection of china cups, saucers and glasses. The closed part of the sideboard underneath, Friend suspected, probably concealed the booze. Not having expected any, Friend was not disappointed when Sir Richard failed to offer him a drink.

"How did you survive the blast?"

Friend shrugged. "The Director says it's a knack I have."

"Well, that's very useful in our line of business. Listen, Sebastian, I'm not sure how much may have filtered through to you while you were in hospital, so I'd better update you on everything that has happened since your visit to the Barbican."

"I thought the Director would be briefing me, sir."

"Yes, that would be the normal procedure. But given the seriousness of the situation we are in and the nature of the course of action I am going to propose, I thought it better to brief you myself, in person. Sometimes it's better to know that your instructions are coming straight from the top."

Now, what the hell does that mean? thought Friend.

"First of all I should tell you that the computer was not the only thing in Rezaei's flat that was booby-trapped. Several of the kitchen drawers and the living room light switch were also wired-up and there was a filing cabinet that contained enough Semtex to take out the entire floor. So you were doubly lucky." 'C' paused as if waiting for some reaction from Friend, but none came and so he continued. "I'm not sure I really understand why he did it, what he and his masters hoped to gain. Perhaps just trying to cause maximum damage to us before he left. Notwithstanding all that, I'm afraid we're no nearer knowing where Rezaei has gone. It's a safe bet he's no longer in the country, but how and when he left, where he went to and what documents he used, we simply don't know. Yet. We've got Border Force going through passenger records and Special Branch sifting through the CCTV footage at ports, but that could take days, weeks even. However, I think it's fair to assume that he was a VAJA mole and that he is even now on his way home to Tehran via some complicated safe route they worked out for him."

Friend nodded his agreement.

"Whether he had anything directly to do with the Sadaghiani murder is difficult to say. We have nothing linking him to Sourian."

"I don't think he knew anything about it, sir. Not in advance, anyway."

"Why do you say that?"

"He left in a hurry, sir. All right, he had time to leave some nasty surprises behind but there was no evidence that he made any preparations to leave before Sadaghiani was killed. The exfiltration was likely a longstanding emergency plan."

"Well, I dare say VAJA wanted to limit knowledge of the assassinations. That's only to be expected."

"Of course, sir."

"I should also mention that Rezaei was not the only one. Of those two hundred or so Committee affiliates Rivers and his team were chasing up, fifteen remain unaccounted for. One or two may simply be away for quite innocent reasons, but we have to face the probability that a fair number of them were doubles just as Rezaei was."

"So it looks like Brian Cochrane was right, sir."

"About there being a traitor in the Tehran Committee? Yes, I'm afraid it does. Only instead of it being one bad apple it seems there was a whole barrowful. And then there is the matter of Professor Sadaghiani's missing laptop and mobile phone. If we assume that Omid Sourian delivered those back to Department 15 in Tehran then, together with what Rezaei and his comrades had been feeding them for years it doesn't take a genius to work out how the Iranians managed to round up all our agents just a few days later."

"The timing would suggest so," said Friend thoughtfully. "So I suppose that's that, then, sir. You won't need me to go to Iran after all."

"Don't be so hasty. I know it looks like game, set and match to Tehran, but we're not done yet. For a start we need to see if there is anything we can do to get our people back; some of them if not all. Some of the missing Committee people left families behind; we may be able to use them as leverage."

"I would have thought that was a job for Tehran Station, sir. Or the Embassy."

"Oh, don't be concerned, that isn't what I have in mind for you. I'm just giving you the bigger picture; we can open negotiations through regular channels. Although having said that, Tehran Station needs to keep its head down for the time being. It's a fair assumption they've been blown too. As for the Embassy, the Foreign Office is planning to expel a number of Iranian diplomats in retaliation for Cambridge. I've seen the list, and while many of them are known to have intelligence connections, not all of them do. We have to expect a certain amount of tit-for-tat, possibly even the severing of diplomatic relations. It's happened before. So I may need someone on the ground who can assess the situation for me, who isn't known to the Iranians and isn't connected with Tehran Station. There may be something you could do on that side of things."

"Sir, I still think…"

"Hold on, I'm not quite finished," said 'C', raising his hand

143

for emphasis. "There's also the question of our response."

"Response?"

"The Director of Public Prosecutions will be issuing a warrant for the arrest of Omid Sourian this evening, charging him with the Cambridge murder. But that's just a matter of form. Sourian is back in Iran with the rest of them and there is no way on earth that he will ever be handed over to us. Not even the PM has that amount of leverage over Tehran. I attended a COBRA meeting this morning and the decision has the full backing of the prime minister: we have to send a message that this sort of thing will no longer go unpunished. He's had enough of us being seen as a pushover by the rest of the world, and I'm bound to say I agree with him."

"What exactly are you suggesting, sir?"

"Don't be stupid, Sebastian. I'll admit this sort of thing is not usually in our line, in fact I've never asked anyone to do this before, but the PM has made it clear that we need to dispense justice to the killer of Professor Sadaghiani and punish Tehran for their criminal use of a deadly nerve agent on the streets of Britain. They might have killed hundreds. I'm asking you to find and kill Omid Sourian."

Friend swallowed hard and tried to keep his shocked reaction in check. He found he was gripping the arm of his chair tightly and had to consciously instruct his fingers to loosen their grip.

"With respect, sir, I've never killed anyone in cold blood before."

"I know. That's why I'm asking you, not ordering you. This is not a lawful act I am proposing. But if it is to be done it does need to be done by someone from your department. It's unlikely the Iranians will have a file on you, which makes it less risky for you, and if you're caught they're less likely to connect you with the Service, which makes it less risky for us. And you have killed before, in the course of duty."

Yes, thought Friend, *I have killed before, when there was no other way out, or to save an innocent life.* He recalled at once how Isobel had taunted him for swanning around the world dispensing violence by order and how her simplistic notion of his work revolted him. Could he ever again look her in the face after this? But then he thought about Jadon Rivers and his reminiscences of childhood; he thought about Ali Rezaei and Omid Sourian and his anger rose. Perhaps it hadn't been incompetence that Friend had spotted in the assassin's behaviour, perhaps it had been a simple disdain for consequences. Had he too been sending a message? That he and the rest of Department 15 could swan around Europe and do what they liked? Kill whoever they wanted? And that they knew that SIS and the rest could do nothing to stop them?

"What about Ali Rezaei, sir? He's responsible for a colleague's death."

"Once we know where he is we can make arrangements to deal with him as well. But for now we need to focus on Sourian."

"All right sir, I'll do it." The words seemed to have come out of Friend's mouth automatically, without any effort of will. It was too late to take them back.

Sir Richard looked visibly relieved. "Thank you, Sebastian. I hope I never have to ask this of you again. I think it best if we get you moving as soon as possible, so I've got you booked on an RAF transport for Baghdad out of Northolt tomorrow morning. That way you can have a word with Derrick Halsgrove on the way, if you still think it would be useful."

"Yes, sir. He knows the territory so I would like to talk with him."

"Good. Then you said Swedish cover, I think. We can get you on a Red Cross flight to Stockholm and then fly you in to Tehran from there. Your papers will be those of a journalist. That should account for your interest in Baghdad, and then in Iran you can always be there to cover the espionage trials, or the presidential election. Is your Swedish up to native standard?"

"Yes, sir. My mother is Swedish and I spent half my summer holidays as a child on my grandparents' farm in Värmland."

"Good. I'll get the Director to arrange the documents for you and have them couriered to Northolt in time for your flight."

"What about weaponry, sir?"

"Best if you go in clean, I think. Otherwise we risk you being blown before you even leave the airport. Besides which, you probably won't know the best way to kill the man until you've taken a look at him and got to understand his movements. Not much point sending you out there with a handgun if what you need is a sniper's rifle. No, you'll just have to use your initiative out there."

Friend nodded. "Will I be on my own, or do I have any local contacts in case of emergency?"

"I think it best if we avoid Tehran Station. We can't be certain they're not blown. But there is someone else who may be able to help you. Not an agent of course, more a semi-conscious asset. He was part of the Nassirian set at university but opted for a quieter life rather than properly joining the Committee. We've used him for the occasional information drop or safe house duty. Runs a bookshop in Tehran. Name of Reza Farahani."

"I've come across the name, Sir. I think he was spoken to when Leila Cochrane was being vetted."

"That sounds about right. I'll give you his details and the current recognition code we use with him. He's pretty well connected, I understand, and he may offer the best way of getting information back to us."

"Thank you, sir. By the way, on the subject of Leila Cochrane, was there ever any suspicion of foul play in her death?"

"Leila? Hmmm. They never found the car, did they? I don't recall any particular suspicion, but I suppose it couldn't be ruled out entirely. Of course it would have been an odd time for the Iranians to take their revenge on her. What was it, a decade or more after she came over to us? Long after she ceased to be of any intelligence value."

"Yes, that's rather what I thought, sir." Friend's mind returned to his interview with Cochrane, and the sudden flare of temper that had come at the merest suggestion that his wife's death might not have been an accident; temper that suggested Cochrane had been harassed by suggestions of foul play. But if the Service wasn't harassing him, then who was?

"Was there anything else, sir?'

"Yes, there was one other thing. I gather CIA already have someone out in Iran on much the same sort of mission. I don't know whether they have a prime suspect in the murder of Dr Qarib yet, they're playing their cards pretty close to their chest on that one, but since they've let us know they've got someone on the ground it could be useful for the two of you to compare notes."

"All right, sir. Is it anyone we know?"

"Just let me see, I've got the name here somewhere…" Friend waited while 'C' rifled through the small leather notebook he kept by his telephone. "Ah yes, here it is. No one we've worked with before in any serious way. His name's Linus Martinson."

NINETEEN

BRITAIN TO EXPEL IRANIAN DIPLOMATS IN RESPONSE
TO CAMBRIDGE NERVE AGENT MURDER
Tom Westerman

Revelations published on the investigative Bellingcat website this morning add to the already significant pressure mounting in Whitehall for a strong government response to Iran's use of a deadly nerve agent to murder one of its own citizens in Cambridge. Bellingcat journalists, hacking into the Farsi-language website of the Revolutionary Guards' Youth Organisation, found clear evidence that Omid Sourian, the Iranian 'businessman' charged yesterday with the Cambridge murder, is in fact the assumed identity of Jamshud Pirouzfar, a member of the Revolutionary Guards fanatical youth wing during his student years and more recently a senior member of what is known as Department 15 of Iran's Ministry of Intelligence, whose charter extends to revenge against counter-revolutionary elements and worldwide acts of terror in support of Iran's Islamist regime.

The Bellingcat exposé has of course produced furious denials out of Tehran. An official statement from the Ministry of Intelligence derided the report as 'an act of blatant and outrageous forgery' and 'fantastical in the extreme.' Tehran continues to deny any involvement in the murders of Tehran Committee leaders in Britain, Germany and the United States, and claims the accusations against them are aimed at 'diverting attention away from the widespread criminal espionage perpetrated by western imperialists within the Islamic Republic', by which it means of course the forthcoming trials of Western agents due to take place in Tehran in the next few weeks. Iran's vehement denials notwithstanding, the Bellingcat reports do tally with the conclusions reached by intelligence officials in both Washington and London.

It is understood that following a further COBRA meeting this morning, the Cabinet will approve a proposal by the Foreign Secretary to expel in excess of a dozen Iranian officials currently stationed at their Embassy in London. Tehran will no doubt look to respond in kind as relations between Iran and the west plumb depths not seen since the hostage crises of 1980…

*

"Where you from? America?"

It wasn't so much the questions that irritated Friend as the taxi driver's habit of turning his head to face his passenger while asking them, often in the middle of switching lanes on the busy Persian Gulf Freeway that led into the south of Tehran from Imam Khomeini Airport.

"No. Sweden," Friend replied, as calmly as he could.

"Sweden! No kidding. I have a cousin there. Works in a bakery in Örebro, do you know it?"

"Sure, it's a nice town."

"That's what he said. Peaceful. No crime, except sometimes the Kurds are fighting with the Iraqis. Not like here. Here it's crazy. Everyone is crazy."

Crazy like your driving, thought Friend, as the taxi veered across two lanes into a tiny gap between a BMW and a delivery van amid a howl of horns. He closed his eyes and tried to block

149

out the roar of the traffic and the driver's amiable chatter. All he wanted to do was get to his hotel and sleep. For forty-eight hours he had felt himself bouncing like a ping-pong ball between airport departure lounges, customs halls, hotels and taxi cabs; from London to Baghdad to Stockholm to Tehran until the whole journey became a dizzying, sweaty blur.

He had been less than six hours in Baghdad, two of which he had spent chatting with Derrick Halsgrove in the gardens of the British Embassy. Halsgrove had been a pitiful shadow of the man whose dark, brooding profile had prowled the corridors of Vauxhall Cross for years. The Halsgrove of legend had been a man of volcanic energy and determination: a pep talk from him could instil a monk with a thirst for battle; to find yourself on the receiving end of his displeasure could send you diving for the nearest trench. But the Derrick Halsgrove Friend had found waiting patiently for him in his wheelchair in the shade of a fig tree was a very different creature: a smaller-than-life character, quietly content within the limits of his new world, utterly docile in the acceptance of his fate. Had it not been for the puckered, reddened scar tissue running down the left side of his face, the dressings still covering his ear, the way one hand sat limply, uselessly in his lap, it would have been impossible for Friend to connect the passive invalid before him with the legend that was Derrick Halsgrove.

Halsgrove had tried his best to be helpful, been apologetic that he couldn't be more so. His memory had mostly returned but those parts of it that might have been useful remained a blank and his mind had a tendency to wander. His voice would trail off in mid-sentence and his expression lapse into vacancy. Invariably he would snap out of it after just a few seconds, but returning alertness brought with it no resumption of his train of thought. He remembered having come to Baghdad to meet Reza Ghollamhossein, and that the journalist had promised him vital information, but what that information was, or whether he had even received it before the bomb blast, he was unable to recall.

The old Halsgrove was gone, and the new one had only come to life when recollecting passages of time from years ago, like the details of his escape from Isfahan or his memories of Brian and Leila Cochrane. But even these were like the remembrances of an elderly don looking back wonderingly at his own undergraduate indiscretions, as if they were the product of a different time, a different personality. Friend had learned nothing of material value from Halsgrove, except for the implied warning of the fate that might await him, too, one day.

"Maybe I should go and live in Sweden too," the driver continued. "Drive a taxi or work in a bakery. Maybe my cousin could help me with a visa."

"You might find the winters a little cold."

"Cold? You kidding? You see those mountains up there?" His arm shot out of the open window and gestured north. "It gets pretty damn cold here too. Down to freezing sometimes. We get snow, too."

"Maybe, but in Örebro it usually gets down to minus ten or fifteen in winter. Further north it's much colder."

"Minus fifteen?" He cried out something in Farsi. "I hope my cousin got a good coat."

"We have a saying at home: there's no such thing as bad weather, only bad clothing."

That got a laugh, abruptly interrupted by a shout of anger and a pummelling of the horn as a battered Toyota ahead to the right got a little too close.

"So what you doing in Iran, anyway?"

"I'm a journalist, here to cover the elections."

"Ha! Why bother? It's all fixed."

"So who do you think will win?"

"Whoever Khamenei wants to win. My brother-in-law worked at a polling station the last time. They spent a whole week training them how to count the votes and how many each candidate would get. So what? Why worry? It's not interesting. I live my life. Okay?"

"Fair enough. What about all those spies they arrested. Is that interesting?"

"Who can say? They try them all in secret. Nobody knows where. Nobody will ever hear from them again."

*

Reza Farahani's bookshop stood on a pleasant, narrow alley that snaked its way up a hillside in the northern suburb of Niavaran. Friend made one slow pass with no alarms before ambling away along a roughly circular route through the busy, tumbling streets. He had checked in to his hotel in District Six just south of Salmas Square as dusk rapidly turned to nightfall and the dark mystery of an unknown and unfriendly city descended all around. But when he emerged the next morning it was into crisp, mountain air and an astonishing clarity of light. He wandered the streets breathing in their vitality and warmth, his ears clutching at the fugitive sound of an unfamiliar language, its tone tantalisingly familiar from the Pashtu he had picked up in Afghanistan, its words beyond his understanding.

At its upper end the alley curved away across the flank of the hill and then ran downwards again. Friend found a quiet café near the top and ordered a small cup of tea, using the Pashtu *coochny* for small and learning the Farsi *kučik* from a pleased proprietor in return. After ten minutes he left and began his slow walk down the hill, casting his eyes across the roofscape, dotted with trees, back towards the heart of the city.

There was no one outside the bookshop; none of the motionless watchers that Halsgrove had described to him, and Friend felt nothing of that distinctive tingle between the shoulder blades that always seemed to let him know when he was under observation. There was no one inside the bookshop either. Or so it seemed when he went in and found the cramped interior almost entirely taken up by bookshelves and hardly a space on any of them. But there was a mirror set high up in the corner of the wall and in its reflection Friend saw a grey-haired man watching him from the back of the shop.

"Can I help you with something?" Friend's blond hair made it pointless to ask the question in Farsi. Farahani's voice was soft and sibilant; words flowed from his mouth in a silken stream. The grey hair was no more than a horseshoe around a glistening bald crown; the skin around his eyes was creased with thin laughter lines. A pair of gold-rimmed reading glasses hung from a chain around his neck. It was a welcoming face.

"Just browsing, thanks."

"Browsing? Not American, then. British?"

Friend shook his head. "Swedish."

"Swedish? I don't have anything in Swedish."

"No matter. Quiet morning?"

Farahani shrugged. "I've been open two hours. You're my first customer. Since they opened that big new branch of Book City down the hill there hardly anyone comes up to me anymore. So I diversified, cut out the new books completely. Now I focus on second hand, antiquarian. Farsi, Turkish, Urdu, Hebrew, English, French, Russian. No Swedish though. It helped a little but, not so much." Another shrug and with it a weary smile. "I've been here thirty-six years. Soon I will retire."

Friend breathed in the heady combination of leather bindings and book dust, looked around at the shelves laden with unknown stories and listened to the silence broken only by the ticking of an unseen clock. He understood why Farahani had spent his life in this place.

"Well, I think it's a lovely place and I'd be sorry to think of it not being here after you retire."

"You are very kind, sir. Are you sure there is nothing I can help you to find?"

"Well, if you do stock antiquarian books from Europe then there is one thing I have always been on the look-out for."

"Yes?"

"A copy of the Caxton folio of the Four Sons of Aymon, printed in 1489."

Friend saw Farahani's eyes flicker for just a moment, but the recovery was almost instantaneous.

"I think you will be lucky to find one, my friend. As far as I know there is only one copy in existence."

"Yes, in the Spencer collection. But I believe one other copy has been referenced in literature."

Farahani gave a satisfied snort. "Then I may be able to help you. But first I think you had better attend to the front door and then join me in the back."

There was still nothing unusual to be seen on the street as Friend pulled down the blind and turned the key. He followed Farahani through into the back office where two comfortable armchairs sat either side of a battered old television.

"I know it's early," said Farahani as he pulled a bottle and two glasses from a cupboard behind the television set, "but after the shock you just gave me I could do with a drink. Will you join me?"

The second glass was already being poured before Friend had a chance to accept.

"It's good brandy. Armenian," said Farahani.

"Ararat?"

"Yes, you know it?"

"I've had it before, and I like it." He rolled the first mouthful around his tongue and swallowed. "As you say, it's early but welcome. How do you get hold of it?"

"A regular costumer brings me a bottle from time to time. He tells me a friend of his smuggles it over the border."

"Sounds like a useful man to know."

Farahani laughed. "You know I think that book must have been asked after more in this shop than anywhere else in the world. But it's been a long time since I last heard it mentioned. I thought all of this was over for me." A grave look came across his face. "Perhaps I'd prefer it if it was."

"I'm sorry to have to drag you back into it."

"So, who are you? What are you? Swedish or British?"

"Both. My name's Erik Lindgren."

"A Swede working for the British..."

"Half Swede, half British."

"And what do you want from me?"

"Firstly, to make contact. I may need help getting out of the country later. If I do, I won't want to waste time with introductions. Can you help me with that?"

"Possibly."

"There's a package I'd like you to hold for me if you would." Friend lifted the small canvas holdall he had brought with him and passed it over. Farahani took it but looked at it with suspicion.

"What's inside?"

"A change of clothes, a passport and some money. In case I need to get out of the country quickly." Friend had hidden his other escape passport neatly behind the wall-bracket of the television in his hotel room.

"This is a big risk you are asking me to take for you, Mr Lindgren. Tell me why I should take such a risk for you."

"You've taken similar risks for us in the past."

"Ah. I suppose I can take that two ways. One: why change my habit now? Two: if I refuse you can tell VAJA what I did for you in the past."

"I'm not here to make threats, Mr Farahani. I just want to know if you can help me."

Farahani said nothing for a moment. He looked down at the holdall and then up at Friend. At last, he got up from his chair and walked over to the cupboard, where he stowed Friend's holdall alongside the brandy.

"Thank you."

"Anything else?"

"I'd like to talk to you a bit about the recent troubles: the arrest of all our agents, the killings of the Tehran Committee."

"I don't know anything about that, apart from what I read in the papers."

"I just meant that in London we only get to hear what the official media say and think. Perhaps you could tell me what ordinary Iranians think, what you think about it all."

"Why should it matter what I think, what anyone else in this country thinks? We don't speak much about these matters with each other, except at the kitchen table."

"All right, so what is being said at the kitchen table about the Committee?"

"About the Committee? I think most people didn't know much about them until recently. A bunch of intellectuals living in the West. It wasn't relevant. Now they hear the Committee was helping Western spies steal secrets in Iran. I would say most people think they got what they deserved."

"Is that what you think?"

"Some of them were my friends. I knew them for a long time."

"But you weren't involved with them directly?"

"No. There was a difference between us, between me and them. In character I mean, not politics. They were ambitious: look at what they did, what they achieved. They were high achievers from the beginning. I wasn't like that. I was an average student and I just wanted an average, quiet life. That's why I came here. First it belonged to my uncle, now it belongs to me."

"So why didn't you break with them completely?"

"Because they were still my friends. So I did an occasional favour, like I'm doing for you now, and once you start doing favours like that it becomes difficult to stop."

"But if they were your friends surely they would have

respected your choice if you told them you wanted to stop?"

Farahani said nothing to this. He drained his glass and put it down steadily on the side table, his eyes never leaving Friend's for an instant.

"Someone threatened you?" Friend probed. Still there was no response. "Who was it?"

"What does it matter? They're dead now, aren't they? Javad, Leila, all of them."

Friend decided to change tack. He could have tried pushing a little harder on this point, but he felt the bookseller's willingness to co-operate waning.

"All right. Perhaps you can tell me about Leila."

"Leila?"

"She was part of your group at university, wasn't she? Was she a high achiever like the others?"

"Leila, Leila…" Farahani seemed about to lose himself in memories. "You know she helped me in here for a while, after I took over from my uncle. I liked Leila. She was different. Different from the others, different from me. Sadaghiani, Qarib, Nassirian, they knew what they wanted from the first day they arrived on campus. Never deviated. Leila never had that certainty, not at first anyway. I knew the others first, before her. We used to be part of a poetry society; we met every Tuesday evening at one of the cafés on campus. I wrote a bit myself and so did Nassirian. Neither of us was any good but he was a more confident speaker than me. I can still remember him reciting Omid's Winter to us one night. He had a way of holding an audience rapt, it was… it was almost magical, if you understand me. I don't know how long Leila had been coming before we noticed her. She used to sit on her own at the back and just listen. A tall, slim, silent girl in a simple headscarf. Neat, never a speck of dirt on her clothes. The four of us used to go for coffee together afterwards and one night Nassirian just went over and asked her to join us. He didn't tell us he was going to do it; I think he was intrigued by her silence, her lack of engagement. She just smiled, shook her head

157

and walked away. Not a word. But the next week she was back. The headscarf was gone and when Nassirian asked again she did join us for coffee.

"She was quite timid then. I don't think she quite knew who she was yet and didn't want to commit herself. She had come from the south, from quite a strict family and it was her first time away from their influence. She studied mathematics and loved poetry, running and netball. I watched her play netball once that first term and it was the first time I had seen her really come to life, forget herself. There was a joy and a vigour I had never seen in her before."

Farahani broke off and got up to pour another glass of brandy for each of them.

"She was closer to Nassirian than the rest of us. He had a kind of charm few people have. It was irresistible. There were lots of girls who wanted to get to know him. Some of them were probably jealous of Leila; she was no great beauty but she had something about her, like Nassirian did. Maybe that's why she stopped the netball. She started to drink a little, smoke, we all did. Then in her second year came the reaction, maybe some more of her parents' influence. The headscarf went back on, and she started attending religious group meetings. But it didn't last long. Sadaghiani and Nassirian decided to become socialist revolutionaries; I went along with them because they were my friends. I can't claim to have been a true believer. We took to the streets and Leila came with us. After the revolution was taken over by the religious fanatics, they formed the Committee together. That's it. I don't know what else I can tell you about her."

"Why do you think she stayed in Iran after the others left?"

"She wasn't in danger. She hadn't been a public figure like the others. She did her work quietly and she knew how to survive, how to protect herself."

"How did she know these things? They're not usual."

"Just part of her character, I think. She was always a cautious person."

"But she took a risk approaching Brian Cochrane openly."

"You think it's a risk? They were watching Cochrane for months first."

"When were you last in touch with her?"

"She came to see me about two weeks before she went to England. Sat in the same chair you're sitting in now. Told me about the conference she was attending, in Jordan, I think it was. Her voice was saying one thing, but her eyes were saying another. I didn't ask any questions, but I knew it was goodbye. I never heard from her again."

"So why did she leave then?"

"I don't know. She didn't say. Her parents were dead by then. Maybe she wanted to be with Cochrane. Your guess is as good as mine."

Friend took a moment and sipped at his brandy. He hadn't planned to ask about Leila, but even so the questions had come out, somehow they always did. What was it about her story that intrigued him? It was nothing more than a feeling, but it was a feeling that wouldn't let him rest. Leila Cochrane, Omid Sourian; the truth about these two was the heart of it all.

"I suppose it is," he conceded at last. "Perhaps there's something you can tell me about one other person."

"Oh yes? Who?"

"Omid Sourian."

Farahani placed his glass down carefully and turned a hard stare upon Friend.

"So that's why you're here. You're going to kill him."

"I'm not here to kill Sourian. Just to find out more about him."

And, just as he said it, Friend realised that it was the truth. That he could not simply obey the order he had been given without first satisfying himself of the man's guilt. And then? Was it any better to be an executioner than a disinterested assassin? Each was as cold-blooded as the other.

159

"I don't believe you," said Farahani, angrily. "They wouldn't send you all this way just to ask questions. If you're here to kill an innocent Iranian, then you can take your bag and go."

"What makes you say he's innocent?"

Farahani laughed scornfully. "You think a VAJA or Quds Force assassin would let himself be identified as easily as that? And that website those Western journalists are supposed to have found his real name on, nobody in Iran has ever heard of it. Someone has been playing your people for fools, Mr Lindgren."

"And who do you think that is?"

"No idea. It's your problem, not mine."

"Yes, it is. But if I can clear his name then I can make sure London starts looking for the people who are really responsible. Will you help me do that?"

"How can I help you? I know nothing."

"There's something else about Sourian you're not telling me, isn't there? You're so certain about his innocence. Do you know him?"

Farahani was silent for a long time. Finally, he gave a nod.

"He came into the shop a year or two ago, to collect something for a friend. We got talking, he was a nice guy; he liked the place. He's been back a couple of times since and bought books from me. He likes English detective stories and children's books. Omid Sourian is just who he says he is, a spice merchant from Tehran with a wife and eight-year-old daughter."

"This friend he was collecting for, who was he?"

"A contact from the Tehran Committee."

Friend leaned forward in his chair. "Are you telling me that Omid Sourian is part of the Tehran Committee?"

"Yes, he is."

"Then presumably you can tell me how to contact him."

"I can... I could. For someone who just wants to talk to him, to help him, I could. But for someone who wants to kill him, no." Farahani straightened his back and looked Friend in the eye. "You say you did not come here to kill him. How do I know

I can trust you?"

"You don't," said Friend. "That's what trust is."

TWENTY

Trust, that was what it came down to in the end. All the evidence, when he took the trouble to focus his intelligence and think about it, was damaging enough. It told him that Ali Rezaei had been the most senior of a whole nest of moles inside the Tehran Committee and that he, together with Omid Sourian and a host of other Department 15 operatives, had taken down the Committee worldwide before their colleagues in IRGC mopped up every Western network in Iran. But he didn't trust it. He couldn't form a convincing argument as to why, but he didn't trust it. There were answers to each of his most pressing questions, but he didn't trust them either. Why had Omid Sourian shown himself so brazenly to every surveillance camera he passed? What purpose had it served for Ali Rezaei to booby-trap his apartment? Why had Leila Cochrane died so suddenly (and suspiciously) years after her husband left the Service?

Friend had given his word to Reza Farahani; he had given his word to 'C'. Why did the one seem to count for so much more than the other? Because he had known in his heart when he accepted the job of killing Omid Sourian that he would make up his own mind whether to go through with it once he was in play. Because the alternative would have meant that someone else, perhaps a friend, might get the job of executing an innocent man. *Not executing: murdering*, he thought. *This thing should be called by its proper name.*

It came down to trust. Trust in the evidence and in the judgement of the people around him. But there was another side to trust: the trust he had in himself. The faith he had in his own instincts, his judgement of people and their motives. It was what made him good at his job. It was what kept him alive.

The questions lingered at the back of his mind all day. He kept them there. After leaving Farahani's bookshop he visited the Foreign Ministry building just north of City Park to formalise his press accreditation. He stretched his legs after a three hour wait with a stroll down the tree-lined Valiasr Street before turning off towards Razi Square where, in a cramped and dingy car hire office, he rented a noisy and battered little Vespa for a week. It didn't take him long to find out why motorbike and scooter hire was hard to come by in Tehran, and why the Vespa had so many dents to its bodywork. The chaotic and unpredictable traffic made biking a constant battle of nerves and he frequently found himself shunted over to the pavement as a car ahead switched lanes without warning.

He made his way east, towards the vast city bazaar where, in an anonymous, grey building just beyond the perimeter, Omid Sourian's supposed employers had their base. *Persia Spice* was one of those large, state-backed combines that had driven so much trade away from the bazaar since the revolution. It was not the sort of place where the passer-by could pop in unannounced to examine the wares, but the kind of large, secure warehouse with office space en-suite that catered solely to the wholesale trade. In front of the building and its single door showing the way to reception, there were parking spaces for a dozen cars, eight of them filled with a variety of business saloons and small, city-friendly hatchbacks. Friend might conceivably have walked straight in to reception and brandished his brand-new press card, asking for an interview with Sourian, but on the whole he thought it better to corner his quarry in private, when he would have less chance of hiding behind a corporate refusal. So he found a spot on the street with a good view of the front of the building, wedged the Vespa sideways between two parked cars and sat on the pillion to wait.

It was only four-thirty when Sourian emerged through the reception door; a thin, worried-looking man who scurried down the three steps and across the car park towards a dark blue Toyota parked nearest the exit. He seemed to have shrunk in comparison with the relaxed thirty-something seen on the CCTV footage from London and Cambridge. This was a middle-aged man, stooped and crumpled by the cares of life. Friend saw him crouch down as he got to the car, as if checking underneath for any sign of sabotage, or explosives, then he glanced around anxiously again as he pulled open the door. He did not spot Friend lurking in the shadow of a cypress tree.

Sourian didn't spot the Vespa either as it tracked him north through the crowded city streets, though its engine buzzed and spluttered enough to wake the dead and the traffic crawled so slowly that he might safely have spent more time looking back through his mirrors than forward through the windscreen. Once north of the centre, they turned onto an expressway and the going was easier. Friend was able to hang back, two or three cars behind Sourian; close enough to see his quarry without showing himself too obviously. He had already convinced himself that this was no professional he was tracking.

There were no diversions. Sourian drove directly to the north-eastern suburb of Narmak and pulled up outside his home. Friend coasted to a halt some fifty metres behind him. Sourian didn't get out of the car. Instead, after a minute or so, Friend watched as a tall woman in black jeans and a colourful headscarf emerged from the house, accompanied by a bare-headed young girl in a pretty yellow dress and white cardigan. Omid Sourian's wife and daughter got into his car and the family drove off together.

The procession continued further north, into Omid Town,

until the car finally parked at the Tehran Birds Garden. Friend pulled into the car park and stilled the Vespa's engine, watching as the family boarded the shuttle bus to the park entrance. He waited and took the next bus, sure of catching up with the family somewhere in the park but unwilling to give Sourian a close sight of him yet. He found them in a kind of wooden gazebo built on a stone jetty, looking out over a small lake crowded with flamingos. The girl was leaning over the railing, enraptured, while her father held her ice cream and waited. Friend tracked them around the park for almost an hour, until they decided it was time for dinner and headed back towards the entrance. This time Friend got ahead of them and was already seated in the shuttle bus when they got on board. He thought for a moment that Sourian caught his eye, a single, blond European man conspicuous among Persian families, but he ignored it and let them be. He had no wish to spoil their evening.

Friend didn't bother to follow the Sourians back to their home. Instead he headed back into town and parked the Vespa down a side street adjacent to his hotel. He found a small restaurant nearby and there sat and pondered on the fate of Omid Sourian over grilled chicken and saffron rice washed down with sparkling water. Sipping unenthusiastically at his water he recalled the flavour of Reza Farahani's Armenian brandy and wished with all his heart for a beer. Instead he got the American.

"Your name Lindgren?"

He was good. He had got this close to Friend's table without Friend seeing or hearing a thing until he saw fit to announce himself. He was really good. Or Friend was tired and sloppy. He looked up into a long, thin face beneath a greying salt-and-pepper fringe that must once have been jet black. The eyes were dark pools and the olive-skinned chin was covered in a week-long growth of stubble. Friend put him down as about fifty.

"That's me," he said, warily.

"I've got a message from your Uncle Charlie."

"Oh yes? And how is the old bastard these days?"

165

"He sends his greetings from Cove Bay."

Friend acknowledged the exchange of passwords with a nod and gestured for the American to sit down.

"Thanks, I won't eat though. I had something earlier."

"You must be Martinson."

"That's me, your cousin from across the pond. Here to help, if I can, within reason."

Martinson's appearance was dark and southern, but his voice had that sing-song quality that comes from the Canadian border states of the mid-west: Wisconsin or Minnesota.

"How did you track me down?" Friend asked him.

"Liaison gave me the name of your hotel. After that it wasn't difficult."

"You seem to know your business."

"And the territory. I've been working this parish for more than twenty years."

"Don't you think you might be at risk then, with all that's happened to our networks here?"

Martinson smiled. "I doubt it. All our people had were cover names. This one knew me as Harry, that one as Irfan; different appearances, different accents, if they can tie all that together into one Linus Martinson then they've earned their corn. But I don't think they will."

"Were you here when it happened?"

"Nope. I was back in Langley at the time. Don't ask me if that was a good thing or a bad thing. It's just the way it happened. How are you getting on here?"

"It's early days yet. I've only been here twenty-four hours. You've been here a long time. Linus Martinson's a funny sort of work-name for someone in this territory."

Martinson twisted his mouth into a knowing smile.

"From which I guess you've already worked out it's my real name. Nice work, Lindgren. On my father's side there were four generations of Minnesota Scandinavian until my grandpa married a Greek. Mom was straight up Persian. That's how you get me, Linus Martinson, the half-blood spy. What about you?"

"I'm part Scandinavian, just like you."

"Well isn't that nice," said Martinson cheerily. "Mongrels of the world unite! You made contact yet?"

"Contact?"

"With your man, Omid Sourian or whatever his real name is."

"No, not yet."

Martinson picked up on the caginess in Friend's voice. "Well, that is what you're here for isn't it? To serve justice on that sonofabitch?"

Friend shrugged. "Are you on the same mission? Justice for Dr Qarib?"

"Well since we're being so open with each other... Maybe I can help you." Martinson reached into one of the pockets of his worn old bush jacket and slid a slip of paper across the table. "Sourian's home address, courtesy of Uncle Sam."

Friend picked up the paper and looked at it. The address was the same one Farahani had given him that morning, the same he had trailed Sourian to just a couple of hours before. "Thanks," he said, pocketing it.

"You're welcome. Anyone else you're looking for while you're out here? Maybe I can help. I've built up lots of contacts here over the years."

Friend decided to take a chance. "Do you know a man called Ali Rezaei?"

"Rezaei?" Martinson pondered for a moment, then shook his head. "Nope. Don't know the name. Who is he?"

"He was the Committee's money man in Europe. Seems to have gone on the run, taking most of the cash with him."

"Has he now? Okay, I'll ask around." Martinson's smile was friendly, conspiratorial.

"Thanks. So has the investigation in New York made some progress then? When I spoke with your man in London he didn't seem to think there was much hope of identifying the killer."

"Let's just say that we know who is responsible and we're in the process of sending a strong message to our friends here in Tehran. If you ask me, it was a crazy move by your people naming Sourian and pressing formal charges. There's no way the Iranians will ever give him up and it just guarantees it'll make the headlines when you whack him."

"I see your point," said Friend, toying with a forkful of rice.

"But that's none of our business, right? We're just the foot soldiers. Do our jobs as quietly as we can and get home. Leave the thinking to those who are paid for it."

"Right."

"So, how you gonna do him?"

"I haven't decided yet."

"Got a gun?"

Friend shook his head, wondering what had happened to the concept of professional discretion.

"Bare hands merchant, eh? I respect that. Listen," he slapped one hand gently on the table as if in conclusion, "if you need any help, or you're in trouble, just give me a ring. My number's on the text message you just received."

Friend felt his phone buzz softly in his pocket and succumbed to a momentary sense of awe. Martinson's hands had been on the table the whole time.

TWENTY-ONE

"You didn't like Martinson from the beginning, did you?" said Lascelles.

"No."

"Why not?"

"He was all show. That business with the text message impressed me at the time. But when I thought about it, I realised he must have had a colleague sitting nearby in the restaurant. The text message was prepped and ready; him slapping the table like that was the signal to send it. It was nothing more than cheap theatrics."

"Nevertheless, he was the representative of an ally. He knew the job you had been sent there to do and freely gave you information that would help you get it done. It wasn't his fault that you had already acquired the information elsewhere."

"I felt he was pushing me into the job. Trying to influence my judgement."

"A job you had already agreed to do. Farahani told you that Omid Sourian was just an ordinary spice merchant with a family, and you believed him."

Lascelles was right. Friend had believed him. More to the point he had seen the man's family: the wife with the taste in colourful headscarves and the little daughter who loved watching birds. The idea of killing a man in cold blood had been distasteful enough on its own; now that he had seen the man's family he could begin to imagine the effect his actions would have on them. Friend had been far from certain he could live with that.

"And that," continued Lascelles, "is why you chose at this point to disobey your orders."

"It wasn't an order," said Friend. "It was a request. 'C' was quite clear about that."

"Don't split hairs." Lascelles sounded impatient. "It was a request you agreed to. You were sent out to Iran on the basis of your agreement to that request. At the taxpayer's expense, I might add."

"That explains the standard of my hotel," commented Friend sourly. The joke made no impression on Lascelles, but he thought he detected a flicker of amusement around Ms Wilton's upturned mouth.

"We are not here to discuss the standard of your accommodation."

"That's a pity. There are one or two things I have to say to the manager of this place."

"Mr Friend, if you are not happy here, I suggest you set aside your tendency to asinine quips and stick to the matter at hand. The sooner we can conclude this interview, the sooner we can all get out of here. Are we in agreement?"

Friend just smiled. This interview, as Lascelles put it, was already in its tenth hour and Friend was by no means certain that its conclusion would be followed by his own release from Lambrook House.

"All right then," Lascelles resumed. "Let's speak plainly. You were supposed to kill Omid Sourian, not interview him. So kindly explain why, having agreed to serve justice on him and having been transported out to Iran on the basis of that agreement, you decided on your own initiative not to do so."

Friend's manner changed abruptly. The flippancy was

dropped and he became serious. Forceful.

"One: because I wasn't certain that it would be justice I was serving on him. Two: because it's the nature of my job to use my initiative. That's what I'm trained for. When the Director sends me out into the field, he doesn't tell me to go to this place and carry out that action in precise detail. He tells me to go out there, gather information and then decide on the appropriate action. Isn't that right?" This last remark he made with his head turned towards the mirror on the long wall to his left, as if addressing it to the Director himself seated in the hidden room beyond. "And three: because it was not an order."

"It doesn't matter whether it was an order or a request."

For a moment both Friend and Lascelles were silenced, unable to believe that Ms Wilton had spoken, after nine hours without a word.

"It doesn't matter," she continued, "because the legal position is the same either way. If it was an order, it was an illegal one and you were not obliged to carry it out. Quite the reverse. And if it was a request the legal position is unchanged. There is no basis in English law for acts of assassination on foreign soil in peacetime. Whether ordered or requested, it's still conspiracy to commit murder."

Her point made, Ms Wilton folded her arms across her midriff and resumed her contemplation of the ceiling.

"You heard the lady," said Friend. "Whatever I agreed at Vauxhall Cross I didn't have to do it, if in my own judgement it was the wrong course of action."

"So when you made your first contact with Sourian you were in the 'gathering information' phase of your mission?"

"Exactly."

"And so, naturally, you had yet to decide whether ultimately it would be necessary to kill Omid Sourian or not."

Friend was momentarily flummoxed by this point. If the truth were to be told, he had already satisfied himself that Omid Sourian was not a government assassin and neither was Sebastian

Friend. But he had skirted around this revelation in his written report and, in the light of what happened later, he thought it best to remain silent.

"So can you please explain," Lascelles continued in the sweetest of tones, "exactly how this decision was supposed to be made easier by buying him lunch?"

TWENTY-TWO

TEHRAN
TUESDAY 23 JUNE

Getting Omid Sourian to trust him was never going to be an easy matter. He had seen the man's nervousness when he emerged from his workplace the day before. He was looking out for bombs under his car, watchers on the street; there was no sign of protection from the Iranian government and, if he really was a member of the Tehran Committee, no protection could be expected. Added to that, he had already seen Friend once, and a second sighting so soon after the first would be sure to spook him. He would probably put two and two together and make for the nearest exit as fast as he could. The only way to get his attention, Friend concluded, would be to pretend to be the very thing he feared and make him think that his only hope would be to talk his way out of it. At least that way they would be talking.

Friend had no idea whether Sourian was in the habit of lunching in his office or in a nearby restaurant. Just before midday he parked the Vespa close to where he had been the previous day and sat down to wait. If Sourian hadn't emerged by one-thirty he would give it up and come back at four. Just before twelve-thirty he saw him, as hurried and twitchy as the day before. Sourian came out of the car park gates and walked towards a pedestrian crossing some fifty metres up the road. Friend, his tell-tale hair covered by a neat white helmet, placed his hand on the loose chrome handlebar covering that vibrated so annoyingly on the road and began to unscrew it.

Sourian walked straight past Friend without any sign of recognition. Friend gave him ten metres then removed his helmet, leaving it dangling on a handlebar, and slowly walked after him, the five-inch chrome cylinder tucked discreetly in his pocket. Sourian led him towards the Grand Bazaar; he walked hurriedly, his shoulders hunched, everything about his body language speaking of anxiety and fear. But he never once looked behind him. Had he done so, he would surely have spotted the blond European he had seen at the Bird Garden the previous evening. He must, Friend thought, have reached that phase of terror where the fear of seeing his nemesis approaching was greater than his need to see who might be behind him. He was like a swimmer in tropical waters who scanned the ocean for shark fins before taking the plunge, then swam as fast as he could with his eyes clamped shut.

They entered the Grand Bazaar by the main southern archway, and even among its teeming crowds Friend had no difficulty tailing his mark. He had time to admire the vaulted ceiling and the brightly coloured glass windows set high up in the wall, and to breathe in the exotic air of spices and perfumes. Sourian walked along the same broad alley for a few minutes before he turned off to the right down a narrower corridor where the crowds were so thick that Friend had to force his way through the press of bodies to keep him in sight. At last they emerged into the open air and Friend found himself in a courtyard lined with trees and filled with people milling around drinking coffee and chatting.

Sourian made his way across the courtyard to a restaurant on the opposite side. The exterior looked dingy and unloved, but the queue of people at the door suggested that what met the eye outside was less important than what the taste buds would encounter inside. Sourian, striding more confidently now, ignored the queue completely and walked straight through the door. In the shadows Friend could just see the warm greeting he received from a member of staff. A regular, then, with privileged access. Friend gave it two minutes, then marched across the courtyard and, ignoring the muttered outrage of the queue, straight into the restaurant.

A man who might have been the head waiter was in front of him at once, a stern expression on his face and ready with a strong reproof for Friend's butting in ahead of the queue. Friend met him with a smile.

"Hello, I'm a guest of Mr Sourian. He'll be expecting me."

At once the atmosphere changed. "Of course, sir. A guest of Mr Sourian is always welcome. You will find him at his usual table." An expansive gesture with the arm showed Friend across to the far side of the busy room.

If Omid Sourian had been a trained hood, he could not have chosen a more likely table: tucked into a corner, his back to two walls, a short stride from the kitchen door with clear lines of vision to the entrance and the large window onto the courtyard. But his eyes were busy with his phone and he had not seen Sebastian Friend striding across the courtyard and talking his way past the head waiter. The first he knew of his presence was when he felt the hand clasp his shoulder and the barrel of a gun pushed into his back.

"No sudden moves please, Mr Sourian." The voice was soft and spoke perfect English. "Just stay calm and remain still. I'm going to sit down opposite you like we're business colleagues having lunch together. Then we'll have a little talk. But remember the gun will still be in my pocket. If you try to get away, I will shoot you. Do you understand?"

Omid Sourian found that every pore of his skin was exuding a freezing sweat. He felt himself shiver. He opened his mouth; he only wanted to say "Yes", to indicate that he understood, that he would do whatever this man wanted, but from his swollen and desiccated tongue not even that single word would come. All he could do was to jerk his head downwards once, more like a submission to the executioner's axe than a nod, but then the hand was gone and so was the metal cylinder below his shoulder blade, and when he raised his eyes again the Englishman was already settling himself in the seat opposite his own. He was young, blond and blue-eyed. It was a perfectly normal, even a nice face; not a trace of cruelty in it, which somehow made the situation all the more terrible. The gun was gone, but he could still feel the imprint of the metal in his back. He doubted the feeling would ever go away.

"You've been expecting someone like me, haven't you," said Friend.

"Y-yes." Uncertainly, but the word came this time. He began to feel that his muscles were relaxing a touch, that if he was to be killed it would not be quite yet and until then he might be able to move a little, to think, to speak. Emboldened, he spoke again. "You were there last night, weren't you? At the bird garden." Friend nodded. "You wouldn't shoot me here. Not with all these people around."

"Perhaps not. But how far do you think you'd get if you ran?"

That was true enough. Once they found you, there was no getting away. Unless somehow he could talk this man around.

"So, what happens now?" he asked.

"Now we have lunch," said Friend. "What's good here?"

They sat in silence until the head waiter appeared. He didn't bother to ask what Sourian was having; he was a known quantity, a regular customer at his regular table eating his regular lunch. Friend ordered whatever Sourian was having. As the waiter retreated, Sourian thought he could brave another question.

"So what do you want to talk about?"

"Two things: what you were doing in Cambridge and how you are involved with the Tehran Committee."

"What do you mean? I've never been to Cambridge; if I go to England my business is in London. And what is the Tehran Committee, please? I have never heard of it." Sourian threw the denials out there not thinking that they were likely to be believed, but as a first, desperate long-range effort before combat moved to closer and less comfortable quarters.

"Oh really?" Friend smiled indulgently. "And when were you last in London?"

"Well, let me see. I think it would be about nine months ago. September or October last year. My office will have the records. They could check for you."

"No, that won't be necessary." Friend gazed for a moment into the other man's terrified face. When he spoke again, there was genuine sympathy in his voice. "You're not very good at this, are you."

"I'm sorry? What do you mean?"

"You arrived in London on June second this year. You came on Iran Air flight 711 from Tehran and booked into the Belton House Hotel. Two days later you took an early morning train to Cambridge, and while there you took a bus up the Histon Road to where Professor Sadghiani lived. That's the Professor Sadghiani who was found poisoned in a park the same afternoon while you were on your way back to Heathrow. We have your passport details, flight records, credit card records and images of you from about two hundred CCTV cameras. We know exactly what you did every hour of your visit. There's no point denying you were there."

Sourian spread his arms wide as if making a last desperate appeal to a judge. "It wasn't me!" he said. "Someone faked my passport, stole my identity. Maybe the guy looked a bit like me as well. How should I know? What can you tell from CCTV?"

"It's no use."

"But you must believe me!"

A waiter arrived and placed a plate of minced kebabs and rice in front of each of them, along with two glasses of some steaming, fragrant infusion. Sourian looked down at the plate but made no movement to pick up his fork or his glass.

"Well it smells very nice," commented Friend. "Aren't you going to eat?"

"I don't feel so hungry."

"Then pardon me for starting without you." Friend sliced off a hunk of kebab with his fork and began to chew. As soon as he had swallowed his first mouthful he spoke again. "Seriously, this is really good. I can see why you come here regularly. Much better than that Indian place on Pentonville Road you visited. Go on, eat something."

Listlessly, Omid Sourian picked up his fork and began to eat. Friend ate a couple more mouthfuls, washing the spicy mixture down with some hot tea, then laid down his fork and leaned towards the Iranian.

"Mr Sourian, I have to decide whether you are a professional government assassin, or just an innocent citizen who got caught up in something he doesn't understand. I have to decide that here, today. And if I'm going to decide you're an innocent citizen then I really need to feel that you're being honest with me. Completely honest. Denying you were ever in Cambridge when the whole world knows you were, really isn't helping your case. Do you understand me?"

Sourian swallowed, too quickly, and began coughing. He picked up a napkin and spluttered into it. "Drink a little tea," suggested Friend, "and take your time."

Sourian sipped at his tea then dabbed at his mouth with the napkin, then folded it over and wiped the sweat from his face. How could this man be so calm, so relaxed? What sort of man were you if you were in a business like this and yet looked so untroubled by it all? His voice when it came at last was strained and hoarse.

"I'm an innocent citizen. I swear it."

"All right, so why did you go to Cambridge?"

"I was sent by the Committee."

"The Tehran Committee ordered you to go there?"

"No, the Committee never orders me. They ask me. If I say no, they get somebody else. But this time I said yes." He looked up at Friend with a nervous smile. "You see, I like England. I try to go whenever I can. If it's just a few days my wife doesn't mind. She has Miriam for company. My daughter."

Friend nodded. "So what did they ask you to do there?"

"It was a waste of my time. They use me as a courier. I collect and deliver packages: documents, money, photographs. That sort of thing. They said I was to collect a package in Cambridge and bring it back to Tehran."

"What sort of package?"

"They said it would be a metal cylinder, sealed inside a padded envelope. They didn't say what was inside, but they said it was perfectly safe for me to handle as long as I didn't try to open it. I asked what if the customs officers want to open it at the airport, but they said I was not to worry. They had it fixed so that I wouldn't be searched."

"You trusted them?"

"Of course. They never let me down before."

"Who was going to give you the package?"

"No one. At least, probably no one. I was supposed to collect it from a hiding place down an alley near the railway station. They made me memorise the location. I found it all right, but it was empty."

"So what did you do?"

"They said if the first pick-up went wrong there was a fall-back arrangement. A café on Histon Road. I was to be there at a certain time and a man would meet me and give me the package."

"What man?"

"I don't know. They didn't say. They just said he would know me and that's all. Listen, I didn't know that was where Professor Sadghiani lived. I didn't even know he lived in Cambridge. I never met him."

"All right, so there was nothing in the hiding place, so you got the bus to the café. Then what?"

"Then nothing. Nobody came. I sat there for forty minutes. Had some lunch. Then I took the bus back into town, looked around a bit and walked to the station."

"Were you annoyed? That they sent you all that way for nothing?"

"Sure, I got annoyed in the café. It wasn't such a nice place. But then I got to the city centre and walked through Cambridge. It was a nice day, sunny, and I got to thinking this is a beautiful little city and I'm glad I got to see it. I didn't pick up any package but at least I got a nice two-day holiday at the Committee's expense and I didn't have to worry about bringing anything back through customs."

"What were you supposed to do with the package when you got it back to Tehran?"

"Deliver it to the usual place. A bookshop in Niavaran."

Friend smiled to himself, so Reza Farahani had not been entirely honest with him about the degree of his involvement with the Committee or about how well he knew Omid Sourian.

"And was it Reza Farahani who asked you to make the trip to Cambridge?"

"Farahani? No. He is just, what do you call it? A post box. I collect from him, I deliver to him. But I get my instructions from Ali."

"Ali who?"

"I don't know. Ali is a voice on the telephone, a face in the crowd. Sometimes he calls me, but it's always a private number, so I can never call back."

"What if you need to get hold of him: in an emergency, say?"

"There's an email address. Not just for emergencies. If I have to go abroad for work, I always let them know by email. Then if they want me to do anything for them, I get a call from Ali."

Friend produced a notebook and pen from his pocket and asked Sourian to write the address down for him. He watched Sourian's hand shake as he did so.

"So was it unusual for Ali to contact you for a job without you having let him know you were going before?"

"It only happened once before."

"And you've never met Ali?"

"Oh I have. Twice in the five years I've been with the Committee. Once when I was introduced to him, by the old university friend who recruited me, and the last time when he gave me my instructions for Cambridge."

"Why did he want to meet this time?"

"He didn't give a reason, just asked me to meet him to discuss an assignment. I said okay and then he told me to be by the lake at Park-e-Mellat at 1pm the next day."

"When was this?"

"About three weeks before I went to Cambridge. I remember thinking it was all pretty hurried because I had to book holiday from my work and that takes two weeks at least."

"You were normally given more notice about an assignment?"

"At least a month. Work usually gives me a month or six weeks' notice if I have to travel anywhere."

"All right. Can you describe this 'Ali'?"

"Tall, thin, long nose, sunglasses. Expensive clothes, but always black or very dark grey."

"Hair colour?"

"Not sure. He wore a cloth cap. A black one. Kangol."

"Was he Iranian?"

"Oh sure! Tehran accent. Soft spoken guy."

"Anything else about him you can tell me? Anything unusual?"

Sourian shrugged. "Sorry, mister. I met him twice in five years and they were short meetings."

"Did you ever meet anyone else connected with the Committee?"

"No. Just him and Farahani. That's how my friend said it would be. Better for security that way."

"So how did you get involved with them?"

"My friend contacted me. Not long after I started work for *Persia Spice*. We spoke politics a lot when we were students. We were both anti-government. What they said in the papers about me being a student member of the Revolutionary Guards,"

Sourian's voice dropped to a whisper for the last two words, "it's all lies. I was never one of them. I never heard of Jamshud Pirouzfar. Anyway, my friend took me to a café and asked me if my opinions had changed. I said they hadn't. So he asked if I wanted to do something useful, something that could help build a better, freer Iran in future. I said sure, okay, what can I do? He asked if my new job would involve travel overseas. I said yes. Then he said that's what I could do, travel overseas and carry things for the Committee."

"Did he tell you it would be dangerous?"

"Yes, he told me if the government found out I could be arrested, but the chances were small. I never expected anything like this, to be prime suspect in a murder."

No, thought Friend. *You wouldn't have.*

"So who was this friend of yours?"

"Is it important?"

"I don't know. It could be."

"Okay then. He's a journalist. Reza Ghollamhossein."

"Thank you." Friend took a mouthful of kebab and tried to contain his excitement. It had been Ghollamhossein who had been killed in the car bomb attack that had crippled Derrick Halsgrove, and now it seemed that he too had been involved with the Committee. Did Sourian even know he was dead?

"When did you last see your friend?"

"Oh, two years ago. Maybe more. He said it was safer for both of us if we didn't meet often. Maybe twice since he introduced me to Ali."

The two men sat in silence for a few minutes and Friend chewed thoughtfully on his lunch. Sourian just sat quietly looking straight ahead, waiting for the verdict.

"You're not going to eat any more?" asked Friend.

Sourian shook his head. "I lost my appetite." He glanced at his watch.

"You need to be back at your office?"

"Yes. I'm late already."

"Don't go back to your office." Friend had made up his mind.

"What should I do? Are you going to kill me mister?"

"You're in no danger from me. I believe you. But someone wants the world to think that you killed Professor Sadaghiani and that someone probably wants you dead as well now. Is there somewhere outside Tehran you could go? You and your family?"

"My wife's family have a place in the mountains."

"Go there today. Call your office and tell them you're sick. Then go home, pick up your daughter from school and go to the mountains."

"How long for?"

"A week. Better make it two."

"I have to go back to the office to collect my car."

"Better to take a taxi."

"But mister, without my car how do I get to the mountains?" Friend cursed under his breath.

"All right then. Go get your car, but be careful. Go now. Don't worry about this," Friend gestured at their meal. "I'll take care of everything."

Sourian got up to leave, then paused.

"Wait," he said. "There's one thing I remember."

"Yes?"

"About Ali. He had a scar, a long thin scar just here," a hand waved airily upwards. "Behind his right ear."

Omid Sourian scurried away, ignoring the farewells from the restaurant staff. Friend felt sorry for him. He was just an ordinary man, dragged into a world he had no comprehension of. He hoped for his family's sake that he would get out of it safely. He reached over for Sourian's plate and spooned some of the Iranian's uneaten lunch onto his own. Then, as he continued eating, he laid his phone on the table and opened up the secure email server he used to keep in contact with SIS. He addressed his email to the Director and in the body of the message he typed the email address Sourian had given him with the comment *Request check*.

Satisfied, he returned the phone to his pocket and called for the bill. Omid Sourian was innocent. He was quite sure of that now. But if Sourian hadn't killed the Professor then who had? Who stood to gain from making it look like Sourian was a Department 15 assassin? Why had someone from inside the Tehran Committee wanted him to be a patsy for the killing of one of their own leaders? Now his mission in Tehran had an entirely new focus. He had to find 'Ali'.

TWENTY-THREE

Friend had almost forgotten the Presidential election, due in just ten days' time, but he was reminded of it when he spotted the marchers heading west down Mowlavi Street towards Meydan-e-Mohammadiyeh. He struggled to count them as they chanted and cheered their way down the centre of the road, banners waving in the air. Some of them bore the image of a studious-looking man in dark glasses. Friend had no idea whether this was the reformist candidate or the conservative, favoured and promoted by the political wing of IRGC; whoever he was, his supporters gave passionate voice to his campaign. The procession blocked Friend's view of the *Persia Spice* compound, but he hoped Omid Sourian's blue Toyota was no longer parked there and was instead on its way to pick up his wife and daughter just as he had said.

There was no use trying to steer the Vespa through such a crowd, so Friend sat himself down on the scooter and watched the marchers pass by. He had observed similar political rallies in the past, in Russia, Britain and America; some had been peaceful (mostly the Russian ones), but with others there had been a palpable sense of intent to provoke, to elicit a violent response from authorities and spark a wider confrontation. In the past he had found it easy to predict the intentions of a march from the demeanour of its participants, but this one was more difficult to read. There was an aggressive energy to much of the chanting, but at the same time he could see among many of the marchers a sense of simple comradeship and good humour. Small groups chatted among themselves, sharing jokes and gossip, and there was no sign of that wary observation of the police, the preparedness for things to turn ugly so that a quick escape might be made. What police presence there was seemed light; a few dozen uniformed officers patrolling the perimeter of the crowd, taking care that the marchers stuck to the prescribed route and avoided threats to surrounding people and property.

But then it seemed that Friend might have misjudged the mood. Of a sudden there came a distant crack and the sound of wailing up ahead on the Meydan. The crowd slowed its stride, then halted. Some turned around in confusion, others peered ahead. The police at the side of them melted away into the shadows. Then the shrieks grew nearer and panic broke out. The marchers began to turn and run, stumbling over each other in their hurry to escape. A flood of people came rushing back down the street, some jogging, some sprinting; taking to the pavements and leaping over cars to find a clearer path away from the crowds. Ordinary passers-by too began to run.

A moment later Friend saw what they were running from. A jagged line of helmeted men in dark green fatigues and heavy black body armour came down the street forcing the crowd back before them. They pushed with their shields and struck out with their batons, and when some unfortunate protester stumbled to the ground a group of four or five would surround him and begin to beat him heavily about the body and legs. Behind this infantry came an artillery of unmarked, dark green wagons into which the stragglers and the wounded were thrown.

It took barely a couple of minutes for the mêlée to reach Friend, still perched peacefully on the seat of his scooter and, like the good journalist he was supposed to be, filming the scene on his phone. Dozens of young men, scared or exhilarated, now darted past him. It was like standing in the middle of a stampeding herd of animals and Friend knew that if it weren't for the protection of the cars parked next to his Vespa and the trees by the side of the road he would have been knocked to the ground and crushed. Some of the older and slower marchers tried to make their way into the side alleys leading to the bazaar; a few made it, others Friend saw dragged back by the riot police. One young protester dodged nimbly between the cars parked at the roadside and made a dash for it along the pavement close to Friend. A single riot policeman came after him but, weighed down by his heavy equipment, he was never going to gain on the unencumbered escapee. Realising this, he turned his attention to Friend and darted towards him with his baton raised high.

"Press!" shouted Friend, thrusting his accreditation towards the policeman's face. The policeman stopped abruptly and thrust his baton back into his belt. He studied Friend's press card for a moment, then gave it back with a grunt.

"Your phone," he said, pointing at the device Friend was still holding in his left hand. Friend passed it over and watched as the policeman scrolled through the contents. Beneath his helmet the policeman had the wild eyes of a man in the fever of combat, on the edge of uncontrollable violence. His breath came in short, steamy gasps like a bull about to charge.

"You film this?" he asked.

"It's my job."

"And this is my job." He gave Friend a look of disgust then threw the phone to the ground and crushed its shattered body with the heel of his boot before running off to re-join his comrades.

The phone was dead, that much was clear to Friend even before he bent down to pick it up as the crowd still swelled around him. Nevertheless, he prized open what was left of the case and extracted the SIM card, which was undamaged as far as appearances could be trusted. If he could find a blank smartphone to put it in, then he could still retain a direct line of communication with London. If not, he would have to rely on Reza Farahani, or the Americans.

It took another fifteen minutes and two more confrontations with riot policemen wired up on adrenaline—or amphetamines—before he felt safe to wheel the Vespa up the street. He winced as he looked at some of the beatings meted out on unarmed marchers. The road towards the Meydan was still blocked by police vans and one more was parked outside the gates of *Persia Spice*, blocking any hope of his checking one last time for the blue Toyota. He shrugged and turned the Vespa down a nearby alleyway, slowly zigzagging round to Khayyam Street, north of the Meydan, where at last he started up the engine and rode the noisy little machine back towards his hotel. He would rest for a while, then, with the worst of the afternoon heat having passed, he would go out and try to find himself a new phone. Later he would head up to Niavaran to try and find out something more about Ali from Reza Farahani. Farahani was clearly more deeply involved with the Committee than he was admitting. If he knew anything about Ali, Friend would just have to get it out of him.

He was relaxed; he was in control. He had made his decision about Omid Sourian and he was comfortable with it. The damage to his phone was no more than a minor nuisance. It could either be replaced or Farahani and the American would relay anything he wanted back to London. Or maybe he wouldn't need them to. Friend was perfectly happy working a case on his own, without backup. He trusted his instincts to keep him out of trouble. He trusted those same instincts to lead him where he needed to go. Everything was going to be fine.

The hotel lobby was cool after the blistering summer heat of the Tehran streets. He walked up to the reception desk and smiled as he asked for his key. The young man behind the desk looked at him nervously, then nodded to someone over Friend's shoulder. Friend turned and saw two of the faces he had been expecting to see since his arrival in Iran: hard, unforgiving masks with eyes concealed behind dark glasses, thin, cruel lips, well-trimmed moustaches and dark, anonymous clothing. He remembered how Halsgrove had described them to him: "Cheap suits, shifty eyes that slide around the room even when their heads don't move. And an air of arrogance, superiority, like they think they're surrounded by dirt." As if operated by a single power switch, the two men got up in unison and walked towards Friend.

"Mr Erik Lindgren?" asked one of them. The pronunciation was as poor as might be expected.

"Yes."

"Please to come with us. You are under arrest."

*

Friend had been waiting in his cell for three hours when they came for him. Three hours he spent alternately cursing his luck and wondering how the hell they had got on to him. Was Reza Farahani under surveillance? In which case why hadn't they picked him up last night? Or the American, Martinson? But the same question would apply, and why hadn't they picked Martinson up before if they knew he was working for the CIA? Or could it have been Omid Sourian? Was he working for the Iranians after all? Had he run straight back to VAJA after Friend had bought him lunch? But then how had they found out his hotel so quickly? Somehow none of the options would fit. Not that it mattered. Knowing the answers wouldn't get him out of there any faster. Derrick Halsgrove had evaded VAJA for weeks, but they had managed to pick up Sebastian Friend in little more than forty-eight hours. As he sat staring at the bare cement walls of his cell, a shame grew inside him that was greater than fear.

Wordlessly, they had shoved him into the back of an unmarked car and driven him to a large police station in a part of the city he didn't recognise. The station was also being used as a processing centre for those picked up during the march, and after the presumed VAJA men dumped him at the front desk with barely a word to the harassed station officers he somehow got mixed up with a group of protesters and almost managed to talk his way out of trouble with the aid of his press card. He took advantage of the confusion to slide the notebook containing Ali's email address into the pocket of a fellow detainee. But then a new group of uniforms came along and shoved Friend, along with fifteen other prisoners, into a small cell designed for no more than four, where they were obliged to kneel on the hard concrete floor with their hands behind their heads for almost an hour before Friend was extracted, searched thoroughly, and taken to a cell of his own. The other fourteen men, he presumed, were still in the same uncomfortable position. He wondered whether their ultimate fate would be any worse than his.

The light was fading from the single barred window above his head when they came for him. Two bulky men marched into the cell and lifted him off the floor by his elbows. He did not resist. They dragged him down a dark corridor where no sound seemed to reach him from any other part of the building. Back in his own cell he had heard the persistent dull thud of truncheons striking human flesh and bone, the muffled cries of pain and despair, the calls for help that would not come, but here it was as if all sound had been sucked out of the world, all sound save for the crunch of police boots on solid concrete and the beating of his heart.

They reached the end of the corridor and Friend was dragged roughly up a flight of concrete steps before they entered a large, well-furnished room where a tall, fattish, grey-haired man stood looking out of the window onto the empty courtyard beyond. Friend recognised the epaulettes of a colonel's rank on the green army tunic, but the man did not turn round or show his face as they entered. The guards planted Friend in a chair before a large wooden desk and left the room without a word, but their footsteps could not be heard retreating down the corridor. Friend sat silently, composing himself, controlling his breath and recalling his training. It was two whole minutes before the colonel moved, but even then the man did not look at Friend. He turned away from the window and walked up to the desk. Picking up a battered leather briefcase he pulled out a notebook and pen and placed them on the desk. Then he placed the briefcase back on the floor and sat down. Only then did he look Friend directly in the eye. His face, puffy and sagging with middle age, showed no emotion; the voice when it came was soft and controlled.

"Good evening, Mr Lindgren. Allow me to introduce myself. I am Colonel Hadi of the Ministry of Intelligence. You won't have heard my name before, but I can tell you that I have had a long and productive career with the Ministry, culminating in my current position as head of what is known as Department 15."

Friend remained silent, his mind racing.

"I thought perhaps you might have heard of us," Colonel Hadi continued. "We have, regrettably, been mentioned in the Western media in recent weeks, in connection with certain killings in England, Germany and America. Of course we had nothing to do with any of them."

"Should I quote you on that? Is this an interview you're granting me?"

"No, no, no, Mr Lindgren," Colonel Hadi smiled with amusement. "This is not an interview; it is more of a conversation. A private talk between you and me. And I think I will be asking most of the questions."

"So what am I doing here? Why have I been arrested?"

Colonel Hadi ignored the outburst. Instead he continued calmly. "As I said, I will be asking most of the questions. For example, *hur är din svenska*?"

"*Ännu bättre än din*," Friend snapped back quickly. Colonel Hadi's English was flawless, but his Swedish was heavily accented. The Colonel seemed delighted by his prisoner's spirit.

"Even better than mine! Very good Mr Lindgren, you have sharp wits. Well, at least we have established that you speak Swedish, which not many English people do. At the same time, however, not many Swedish people speak English completely like a native as you do. For example, even such a simple word as 'is' would often be pronounced by a Swede more like 'iss'. You needn't be surprised. I spent some years in Sweden; a youthful exile during the reign of the late Shah, so I know what I am talking about. I wonder whether you might perhaps be of mixed blood."

Friend again held his tongue. Colonel Hadi was clearly a man capable of picking up on any small detail.

"Well, perhaps we might come back to that later. But you were wondering why you are here. I think I can satisfy your curiosity. Two very unusual things have happened this afternoon, Mr Lindgren. The first was that I received a telephone call, just as I was sitting down to lunch, informing me that a British agent masquerading as a Swedish journalist was in Tehran with the object of killing Omid Sourian, the unfortunate young man whom your government has most unjustly accused of responsibility for the recent murder in Cambridge. The astonishing thing about this is that the call did not come through to my office or to one of my subordinates, but to my personal telephone. Very few people are given access to that number, Mr Lindgren. Even the president has to contact me via the minister. My anonymous caller, who spoke in Farsi with a Tehran accent, withheld his name and number—not that this matters, my people will find him—but was kind enough to give me your name and the name of your hotel. And so I am wondering why this person would betray you in this manner. Can you enlighten me?"

"What was the second curious thing?" asked Friend, ignoring the question.

"The second thing was that just over an hour later, shortly after 3pm, Omid Sourian was shot dead in the car park outside his office. One of his colleagues heard two gunshots and saw Sourian's body lying on the ground through his office window, but saw no sign of the killer. There was a political march taking place on the street at the time and it seems that around this time two more shots were fired at riot police in the Meydan-e-Mohammadiyeh. Steps were immediately taken to disperse the crowd, of course. The killer may have used the chaos that followed to cover his escape. Normally this would be a simple police matter, but in the circumstances you will understand why I decided to take an interest myself. Which just leaves me thinking what I should do with you, Mr Lindgren."

"I didn't kill Omid Sourian."

"You amaze me. Can you give me any reason to believe you?"

"If I came here to kill him, I would hardly have bought him lunch today."

"You had lunch with him? Where was this?"

"In a restaurant just outside the bazaar. I think the name was Azadegan, or something like it, but it was Sourian's regular place. The staff knew him well."

"All right, Mr Lindgren. Perhaps that's a point in your favour, or perhaps it isn't. You just admitted to me that your presence here is connected with Omid Sourian."

"Not directly. I came here to cover the elections for my paper. But Sourian has been in the news in Europe recently and I thought I would try to get an interview with him as a side line. It would be quite a scoop."

"I see, so you weren't just having lunch with Sourian you were interviewing him."

"Yes and no, this was more an initial chat rather than a full interview. We agreed a later date for that."

"But surely if this were the case you would have been better prepared, Mr Lindgren. Sourian might well have said that you could have an interview with him now but later would not do. Any professional journalist in such circumstances would have had a recording device with him, or a notebook. Nothing of the kind was found among your possessions when you were brought in."

"I had my phone with me. I used that."

"No mobile phone was found on you either."

"No, I…" Friend stopped as he realised the implications of his phone having been destroyed by a policeman just across the road from where Omid Sourian had been shot. "I dropped it."

"That was careless of you. And it broke completely, I suppose? How unfortunate. But at least you managed to salvage the SIM card which was found among the possessions that were taken from you at the front desk. My people are looking at it now. It appears to be undamaged but encrypted. A perfectly natural precaution I am sure, but in the circumstances it would be helpful if you could let me know the password so that we can access the material it contains and corroborate your story."

"You can corroborate it with the staff at the restaurant."

"In part I expect we can. But the SIM card would tell us so much more. Where you were before, where you went after, perhaps even who you really are and what you are doing in Iran. So, please be so kind as to let me know the password."

"I want to speak to a lawyer."

"A lawyer? Oh, there are no lawyers for people like you, I'm afraid. We might let your embassy know, in time. Your people may want to exchange you. Although it's equally possible that they may prefer to pretend you never existed."

"I have nothing more to say."

"Then I won't prolong this conversation unnecessarily. My people will crack the SIM card eventually, with or without your help, but it would have made things easier for you if you co-operated. Your visa application may also tell us more when it arrives from Stockholm. I'm also having certain enquiries made there. Such things take time, but we have plenty of that. Omid Sourian is dead, and you are not going anywhere for a while. I suggest you think about that. My colleagues will show you back to your cell."

With that, Colonel Hadi got up and returned to the window. After a moment Friend too got up and walked to the door.

*

When Friend was thrown back into his cell, the brightness of the lights after the dark corridor initially blinded him. He groped his way to the wooden bench that served for a bed through clenched eyelids. He climbed on to the bench and lay down to think. His situation was not a happy one. Colonel Hadi had tied him in knots. It wouldn't be long until he was identified by the riot policeman who had broken his phone and then he would be right in the frame for Sourian's murder. The SIM card would not tell them much without the keys to the additional layers of encryption which he kept in his head, but there would be enough to suggest that he was no simple journalist. Enquiries in Stockholm might take a day or two, but before long it would be obvious that Erik Lindgren was a phantom rather than a journalist. And once his cover was gone...

The pain in his eyes was easing, so he gently opened them a fraction. His small, bare, concrete cell was lit by no fewer than six strip lights recessed into the ceiling, each emitting a powerful white light. Even after two or three minutes his eyes struggled to cope with the brightness or focus on anything. Just as he had processed this fact, the lights went out and the cell was plunged into complete darkness. Even from the single barred window not a sliver of moonlight could be seen, a heavy shutter on the outside wall had been drawn across it. So that was it for today; they had brought him neither food nor water, not even a bucket for toilet needs. Nothing to do now but turn over and sleep.

Friend rolled over onto his side and tried to clear his mind. He tried to forget about Omid Sourian and his wife and daughter strolling around the bird garden in the evening sun, he tried to forget about the fear on Sourian's face when he had sat down opposite him in the restaurant, or the hope he had seen in it an hour later when he got up to walk towards his death. He tried to forget about his sister and his parents and the Cheviot Hills and the taste of the Harvey's Mild he had drunk with George Wetherby in the Royal Oak. He tried to forget about all the things he loved and hoped to see again.

He found his thoughts turning to Derrick Halsgrove and the fantastical story he had told of his escape from Isfahan; his two-month long odyssey across the countryside to the Iraqi border. How he had escaped an ambush by shooting out the searchlights he was pinned down in, before losing himself among a grove of almond trees and fleeing across the runway of the adjacent airbase to the mountains beyond. How the next morning he had dared to walk back into the city, amply disguised in the full-length burka he had brought with him as an escape outfit, his pale eyes hidden behind dark glasses, bright red nail varnish concealing the masculinity of his hands. Friend had read Halsgrove's official account in the file on Operation Trust and had even listened patiently to his stuttering recollections as they sat together in the Embassy garden in Baghdad. There had been no operational necessity for this; he had done it purely for the entertainment value. Now, as Friend cowered in his cell, the forethought of Halsgrove's planning, the audacity of its execution struck him afresh. This was a true professional. And Friend? He had simply been picked up as he walked into the lobby of his hotel. It was a meek, tame ending to his mission. He felt his face redden with shame.

Shame gave way to hollowness and hollowness to exhaustion. Friend hovered on the boundaries of sleep. And then the music began. Loud, wailing Iranian folk music, coming from somewhere high up, but inside, certainly inside the cell. He stood up on the bench and tried to feel around the wall for the speaker, surely inset in the wall just as the lights were in the ceiling. The lights came on again and in the flash of blinding whiteness he stumbled backwards off the bench onto the hard concrete floor. Cursing, he got to his feet and looked up again, forcing his eyes open. High up around the walls there were half a dozen metal grilles that might have been for ventilation or might have concealed speakers. But they were too high to reach and even if he could have blocked them with something—his clothing?—he would perhaps only be blocking out his air supply as well as the music.

Friend returned to the bench and sat down. As he did so the lights went out once more and the music stopped, but instead of silence a new noise afflicted him. It was like a series of rapid, small explosions, the two-stroke engine of his Vespa spluttering into life, now quiet, now deafening. This was the game, then, he realised: disorientation, sleep deprivation, weakening body and spirit, slowly eroding resistance. It took him a while to work out that the pattern was entirely random. The lights might be on or off for a few seconds, a minute or five minutes at a time and endless variations between extremes. The same applied to the music and the six or seven varieties of ear-splitting noise they had prepared for him. It was impossible to predict the sequence and impossible to ignore. He endured four hours of it before they came for him. For all he knew it might have been four days.

The guards wore balaclavas, so it was impossible to tell whether it was the same pair who had come for him before. They dragged him down the corridor again, then carried him by the shoulders down a set of steps. Before they took him into the room, they tied a blindfold across his face. He never saw the room they led him into, nor did he hear a single voice. No questions were asked.

The persuasion was simple at first: beatings about the body and face. Friend tried to tell himself that they were causing pain but no damage. He wasn't sure he believed it. After the first couple of sessions when he showed no sign of begging them to stop or of shouting out the information Colonel Hadi had asked for, the methods became somewhat more refined. Friend was tied to a wooden stake and his body rotated over a heated metal element until he felt his flesh begin to roast. That was not so bad. Worse was when they bound his feet together and beat the soles with rubber truncheons. The pain was unlike anything he had ever experienced and after a while even the gentlest of touches on the bottom of his feet was enough to send him writhing into agony.

Still he did not talk. To his captors he seemed to have accepted his situation with a passivity that bordered on resignation. Once a day they brought him a small flatbread, some broth and some rice, together with a litre of water. It was the only way he had of marking the time. He began to wonder whether these deliveries too might be as random as the lights and noises; only the growth of his beard could reassure him that his mealtimes at least were regular. In between them he had no sense of the passing of time, of how long it might be until his next meal or his next appointment with the torturers. He consoled himself in the knowledge that his body would adjust and his hunger would tell him what stage of the day it was. Perhaps then his meals would become irregular.

Only one consideration was granted to him. Each time they took him downstairs they allowed him to visit the toilet and waited outside to give him privacy while he did so. But perhaps that was only to make sure he did not soil himself in their presence. Here at least he could get an occasional glimpse, through frosted glass, of daylight outside. It was not much help or comfort. He thought about breaking the glass, but what floor of the building was he on? Did he even have the strength to do it?

Colonel Hadi came just once, but it was not to ask any questions. He informed Friend that his mobile phone had been found and that a riot policeman had testified to an encounter with Erik Lindgren on the street outside *Persia Spice* shortly after the murder had taken place. Papers were being prepared for his prosecution. If he had anything else to say in mitigation he should do so now. Friend rolled over and turned his face to the wall.

By the fifth day he was almost broken; weakened by hunger and lack of sleep. His only rest came in the form of micro-naps; short periods when the programme controlling light and sound at random gave him a few minutes of stability, of unchanging environment which his brain could accustom itself to. They were rare, but blissful. This, and one other thing kept him going: the sense that his ordeal could not last forever, might already be drawing to its close. What was the point of torturing a man in perpetuity? In the end you just kill him and have done with it. And he had felt a slackening off in the severity of the beatings. It was two days since they had so much as touched his feet. The soles were still purple with bruises, but another day or so and he might even be able to walk on them. As it was, he could just about stand on tiptoe.

It was something like an hour after they had delivered his food that they came for him again. He gave himself up to the experience wearily, even holding his arms out for the guards to grasp as they dragged him off his bench and into the corridor. One guard propped him up as the other unlocked the toilet door. Friend shuffled painfully on tiptoe towards the urinals and heard the door click closed behind him. It was night, the moonlight streamed through the window and Friend could even see the countless stars shining down from the cloudless sky. He could see the stars. It took him a moment to process the fact and a moment longer to accept that he was not looking through frosted glass. The window was open. He moved closer to it and peered nervously out.

The toilet was at lower ground floor level, the window situated halfway down a series of steps towards an unlit basement door. There was no time to think. He levered himself onto the ledge and manoeuvred his way on to the steps, crawling up six or seven until he was almost at the top. He lifted his head cautiously above the parapet and looked around. He saw a courtyard, dark and empty, barely even a light from any of the windows, and on one side an archway leading out, maybe onto the street. There was no sign of movement, no gate blocking the archway. He scrambled up the final steps, turned towards the archway and, ignoring the agony screaming from his feet, sprinted out of sight.

TWENTY-FOUR

It took Friend three hours to reach Niavaran, and by then dawn was already lightening the sky. There were cars on the roads and people queuing at bus stops as the earliest commuters made their way to work. Friend stuck to the back streets and to what few shadows remained, knowing what an impression his appearance would make: barefoot with unshaven cheeks and unwashed hair, his face still livid with bruises and nothing but his prison clothes upon his frame. He wore only the thin grey cotton shirt and trousers he had been given when they took away his own clothes after his first night in the cell. They were cheaply made and flimsy, offering little insulation against the chill concrete and unheated air of the prison. The cold which had him shivering through most of the hours he spent in his cell was still with him in the mountain air of Tehran, which makes the early morning hours almost temperate even at the height of summer.

For the first thirty minutes after he escaped from the courtyard, Friend had wandered around blindly, disorientated by freedom and not knowing where the prison was in relation to where he wanted to get to. Then at last he had stumbled into one of the main north-south boulevards and the map of the city flickered to life in his brain. After that he had known where he was going, but the going was painful all the same. He could run on his toes, but he didn't have the strength to run any great distance. Slower going on the soles of his feet was agony. He tried to close his mind to the pain, but every few minutes such a spasm shot upwards through his body that it left him no choice but to crawl into the nearest doorway until it subsided.

It was only as he entered the familiar streets near Reza Farahani's bookshop that his brain began to work properly. Of course Colonel Hadi's men had let him go. Just as easily as if they had opened the front door and waved him goodbye. They had given him just enough time to digest his daily meal before they came, trying to make sure he was rested and fed before his escape. Obviously they meant to track him somehow, but he had seen no sign of pursuit. Perhaps they had planted something on him; it might be anywhere from the buttons of his shirt to the lint in the pockets of his trousers. He couldn't very well go naked through the city streets. He couldn't go back to his hotel. He had no means of contacting the American. He needed to change his clothes and smarten himself up somehow, quickly, and that left him with only one place to go.

The sun was over the horizon now, but the bookshop was still in darkness. There was no reply when Friend banged his fist on the door. He didn't know whether Farahani lived on site or came along to open up each morning; either way he couldn't afford to stand waiting on the street. There was a narrow alley to the side of the building and Friend crept along it until he found a single, ground-level window. It was locked, but it looked to be single glazed. He took off his shirt and wrapped it around his right fist and forearm and prayed that the glass wasn't toughened. He drew his fist back to the shoulder and took a deep inward breath, trying to remember the karate blows he had learned in training. At the top of the outward breath, he lunged. The corkscrew punch went through the window and Friend barely felt the contact; he knocked out the rest of the glass ignoring the noise he made and looked through into a small downstairs privy. Out through one toilet window and in through another, he thought to himself as he levered his body through the window frame and carefully placed his bruised feet between the jagged shards of glass that littered the floor.

No sound came from inside and at first Friend thought the building must be empty. But then he found Reza Farahani in the office. He lay in the middle of the floor, directly between the two chairs where he and Friend had sat drinking brandy together a few days before. One arm was splayed out to the side and the other lay across his chest, as if pointing with his fingers to the two neat bullet holes above his heart. To judge from the temperature of the body he had been dead at least twenty-four hours.

The pain in his feet forgotten, Friend quickly moved around the building, checking the other doors and windows. Everything was locked. There was no sign of a disturbance other than the disturbing sight of the bookseller's body on the floor. Farahani must have known whoever killed him, must have let him in willingly. The killer had considerately locked the door behind himself on the way out.

There was no time to lose. If they were tracking him, they would be waiting while he moved; once he was static they would move in. Then there might be two murders they could pin on him; he didn't place much hope in a defence based on time of death. He hardly dared think what he might do if the escape holdall he had left with Farahani were not still in its hiding place; he almost cried with relief when he found it right where he had seen Farahani put it, in the little cupboard behind the television beneath the office bookshelves. He stripped off his prison clothes and quickly put on the plain black t-shirt, jeans and trainers, stuffing the passport and money into the pockets of his jeans. The soft-soled trainers were heaven after the pain of walking barefoot on his bruised soles. The prison clothes he placed inside the holdall and zipped it back up. Maybe he could leave a false trail with it, but he would have to be quick.

He would have paid good money for food and a shower, but at least there was Farahani's Armenian brandy to hand. He grabbed the bottle and took a deep gulp, smarting as the liquor bit at his insides. It was then that he spotted the photograph. It was one among a dozen or so that dotted the shelves between books and ornaments, memories of friends and family and a life well-lived, and it would not have stood out from any of the others were it not for the fact that Friend had seen it before in the house of another Tehran veteran in a small village in northwest Kent.

But there was a difference. The print he had seen in Brian Cochrane's house had been unbalanced, empty space on the right by Professor Sadaghiani's left shoulder, cut off tightly at the left and missing part of Dr Qarib's right arm. Now he saw the reason why. Standing next to Qarib on the extreme left of the image was another man, a man a head taller than any of them. Perhaps Reza Farahani had been behind the camera, for it was not him on the edge of this group of friends, it was a man strong and athletic in build, his round face firm and gleaming with youth, his eyes burning with intelligence and purpose. The weight and care of middle age had done much to both face and frame, but there was no mistaking the presence of Colonel Hadi.

Friend pulled the photo from its frame, folded it once and slid it carefully between the pages of his passport. How long would it be before Hadi's men came for him? Perhaps they were outside already. He picked up the holdall and then reached for the brandy one last time. Even as the bottle was at his lips, he heard the crunch of broken glass under heavy boots.

For the next few seconds there was silence. Friend began to wonder if he had imagined the noise. He gently lowered the holdall to the floor and moved softly towards the door. He pressed himself against the wall and waited.

Now he heard footsteps, in the hallway getting closer. Whoever it was they were stepping softly, trying not to be heard. Was it only one of them? He could not be sure. The footsteps reached the door, then stopped. In a moment, he knew a hand was upon the doorknob; slowly, the door began to open. Friend heard the soft rustle of a foot stepping on carpet and raised his hand in preparation. A dark profile showed itself around the front edge of the door. Lower down Friend saw the dark shape of a gun.

Without thinking Friend brought the brandy bottle down on the man's gun hand then whipped its shattered neck up towards his face. He felt it make contact with something, but an instant later something was making contact with him: door, shoulder, mountain, whatever it was bounced him off the wall and landed him on his back. The two bodies grappled in a chaos of limbs, Friend underneath. Losing. Whatever was left of the bottle was no longer in his hands, but at least the other man had lost his gun. Friend knew he had little time because he had little strength; the days of torture by Hadi's men had taken it from him. All his assailant needed to do was get up from the floor, go and pick up his gun and Friend would be powerless to stop him. For now, he offered the pretence of resistance: used his arms to defend against the blows from the other man's fists, rocked his hips and shoulders to try and change the balance. He managed to bring up his knee up into the other man's groin and for a moment he found himself on top. But he was too weak to press home the advantage and the next thing he knew he was flat on his back again, his arms pinned to the ground, glass from the broken bottle cutting into his left hand. He felt the weight lift from his left arm as the man's right hand shifted to grip Friend's throat; a knee moved up towards his shoulder. With a last burst of energy Friend heaved upwards with the right side of his body and felt the man unbalance, toppling over to his right. Friend's hand closed around the broken glass and flashed upwards.

It was over in a matter of seconds. Friend watched as the man's fingers scrabbled at the piece of glass sticking out of his neck, urgently, then more weakly until he seemed to give up— the hand fell limply at his side and a moment later the breath left his lungs with a final, rasping wheeze. A tide of blood crept slowly across the tiled floor to where Friend lay, propped up on one elbow. The man's eyes stared back at him, but there was no light behind them.

For a moment Friend stayed still, regaining his composure and looking into the face of the man he had killed. The eyes and hair were dark enough to pass for Persian, but there was something about the shape of the face that didn't fit. Behind the gaping lips Friend saw a line of immaculate white teeth. It was not a face he had seen before. One of Hadi's men? But why would he come alone?

Friend got to his feet and walked through to the bathroom where he spent several minutes scrubbing the man's blood from his arm and hands. As far as he could tell he hadn't got any of it on his clothes, but it was difficult to be certain since everything was black. He couldn't stop his eyes from sliding away towards the window he had broken through just a few minutes before. The other man must have come in the same way too. Perhaps his friends were still waiting out there.

At last he finished and dried off his arms on a towel. There were still traces of blood in the sink, but it would be useless wasting time to wash them away. What did evidence matter now? Then he remembered the gun. He threw the towel down on the floor and went back through to Reza Farahani's office. The gun lay on the floor between the two bodies, as though they had died fighting over it. Should he pick it up? He took a step towards it, then hesitated. What would be the point? He could hardly shoot his way out of the country. Better to be stealthy, and smart. That was the way. It had been Derrick Halsgrove's way. And besides, there was a good chance that it was the same gun that had killed Farahani, that the man lying dead on the floor had been his killer. It would be a nice little puzzle for Colonel Hadi to solve. Friend left the gun on the floor and walked back through to the front of the shop. He wanted to have a look at the street before he plunged back into the world. He parted the venetian blinds with his fingers and peered out.

Life had returned to Niavaran while death had been visiting the bookshop. The morning commute was in full swing, and the pavements were alive with the bustle. But there was one man on this busy street who didn't seem to be in any hurry. He was standing right outside the bookshop, facing the road, the smoke from a cigarette drifting from his lips. Friend couldn't see his face, just a dark grey suit jacket over indigo jeans, a dark cap planted squarely on top of his head. He was close enough for Friend to touch him; he might have heard him breathing but for the glass between them. The man took a last drag at his cigarette then dropped it to the ground, crushing the stub with his shoe, and as he moved his head to look down Friend caught side of a long, thin scar behind his right ear. A scar behind the ear, a cloth cap on his head; he remembered Sourian's description. This must be Ali. The man who had been Sourian's contact in the Committee, the man who had sent him on his fatal mission to Cambridge, the man who had chosen him to be the fall guy for the murder of Professor Sadaghiani.

Before Friend could even complete his train of thought the man turned to look past the door of the shop to the end of the alleyway, and Friend saw his face in clear profile. Immediately he let go of the blind and took a step back, his heart racing, his brain fighting to keep up with it. The man with the long, thin scar behind his ear had a long, thin face in front of it. It was Ali waiting outside for the assassin to complete his work, and Ali was Linus Martinson.

What did it mean? Friend struggled to comprehend. His mind was racing too fast, trying to process too many facts on too little energy. Colonel Hadi with the men from the Committee, Martinson as Ali; none of it made any sense. When Friend dared to lift the blind again, he saw Martinson with an unlit cigarette in his mouth, looking down at his watch. He looked agitated. He took another look towards the end of the alleyway then turned and swept his eyes across the front of the bookshop.

Friend held his breath and hoped his fingers weren't shaking as he held the blind in place; even a hint of movement now might be fatal. He saw Martinson reach into his pocket for a lighter and hold the flame up to his mouth before he seemed to change his mind. The American strode towards the alley entrance. In less than a minute he would be coming through the window into the bathroom. There was no time to go back for the holdall. Friend gave him ten seconds to get around the corner, then he walked to the front door, gently drew back the bolt and stepped out into the bright morning sunlight.

*

Little more than fifteen minutes after Sebastian Friend left Reza Farahani's bookshop, the well-polished army boots of Colonel Hadi were crushing the shattered shards of window glass on the floor of the bathroom at the back. Glancing down, he noticed the little white button that had been ripped from Friend's prison shirt and, sliding a fingernail along the rim, he prized it apart, giving a resigned sigh as it revealed the tiny electronic wire inside. Still holding the broken button in his fist, he walked through to the office at the back, where three of his staff were patiently examining the scene. A young captain came towards him and gave a smart salute.

"It can't have been Lindgren who killed Farahani, colonel. The body's stone cold."

"I see. How long has he been dead?"

"I couldn't say, sir. A day, perhaps. No doubt the doctor will be able to give a more precise opinion. Shall I call him in?"

"No, not yet. What about the other man?"

"Less than an hour, I should say. The blood hasn't dried yet."

"Any identification?"

"No, sir."

Colonel Hadi smiled. "So we have two murders, in the same room, committed hours apart it would seem and probably by different people. Well, captain, if you ever wanted to be Tehran's answer to Sherlock Holmes this may be your chance. What about the gun?"

"A Glock-19, sir. Could be the same gun that killed Omid Sourian."

"Well, well. Did any of the neighbours see anything?"

"We've only spoken with two so far and neither saw or heard a thing."

"Take them in to custody anyway. They must have seen comings and goings in recent days. I'm sure they will remember something with a little encouragement."

"Yes, sir."

"Then put out an alert for Lindgren. Wanted in connection with the murder of Reza Farahani."

The captain saluted again and strode off to execute his orders. Colonel Hadi looked down at the body of the man he had known for so many years. He gave himself a moment to remember, then stepped across the body towards the bookshelf. The holdall was there, on the floor in front of the cupboard, but when he unzipped it there was nothing inside but a set of prison clothes. No matter, Farahani had told him all about the contents. Lindgren wouldn't get far.

Then he noticed the empty frame lying on the floor and bent down to pick it up. He had been in that room often enough to remember what had been in it. He turned again to look at his friend's body.

"Reza, you sentimental old fool!" he said. And forgetting, in his anger, his customary calm, he threw the broken button in the dead man's face.

*

By the time Colonel Hadi had recovered his composure, Sebastian Friend was beginning to have serious doubts about his judgement. He had picked up a taxi at the bottom of the hill and at first told the driver to take him back into the city. Then he changed his mind and told him to head west, towards the suburb of Zafaraniyeh. It was poor tradecraft; the driver would have no difficulty remembering a blond foreigner with his face covered in bruises, but Friend could hardly walk another step. The Metro would have been no better choice given the likely CCTV coverage.

What troubled him more was the thought that he might have misjudged the American. Could he be certain that Martinson was anything to do with the man who had tried to kill him? He might have guessed that Friend would try to reach the bookshop and turned up to wait for him there—or for Farahani to arrive so they could meet him together. He might have arrived after the assassin and had no idea what was going on inside. Perhaps the assassin had been one of Hadi's men after all. But no, why would Hadi have let him go just to have him killed elsewhere? And how did any of that tie in with Martinson being Ali; with him having put Sourian in the frame for the Cambridge poisoning?

No, this was no good. He gave his head a sudden, violent shake to try and clear his mind. The driver's eyes in the rear-view mirror widened with alarm. Friend had to get to somewhere quiet and safe; somewhere he could be undisturbed and think things out.

He had fresh clothes, a clean passport and plenty of money in his pocket. Everything that tied him to Erik Lindgren was either in the hands of Department 15 or zipped up in the holdall next to Reza Farahani's body. Everything, that is, apart from his very obvious appearance.

"Almost at Zafaraniyeh," said the driver. "Where you want me to drop you?"

"Palladium Mall."

TWENTY-FIVE

TEHRAN
MONDAY 29 JULY

Palladium Mall is one of the largest shopping centres in Iran: a one hundred thousand square metre temple of consumerism on the north-western fringes of the Islamic Republic's capital city. Friend might have chosen somewhere a little less glitzy—not to mention cheaper—but Palladium was the only mall whose name he could recall, and he had no wish to draw attention to himself by asking for somewhere more discreet.

At least, he thought as he paid off the taxi and walked into the mall's massive glass atrium, it was a busy enough place to get lost in. He had no illusions about being able to avoid the inevitable CCTV cameras, but he was rather more sanguine at the thought of how long it would take Colonel Hadi's men to trace him among the hundreds of hours of footage they collectively recorded each day, even assuming they would track him there in the first place. Friend had no intention of staying here more than an hour.

It took him the first twenty minutes weaving among the busy corridors to find a men's clothing store that more-or-less fitted his bill: cheap, basic and free of Western designer labels. He moved quickly, selecting two lightweight cotton blazers of roughly his size that varied only in colour: one in black, the other in stone, along with a cheap pair of wayfarer-style sunglasses and a wide-brimmed fedora hat. He paid in cash and asked the check-out assistant to remove the tags from everything. The stone-coloured jacket went into a large paper bag bearing the store's logo; he walked out of the store already wearing the rest. And if anyone thought he was trying to look like Van Morrison, that at least was better than trying not to look like Erik Lindgren.

He made one more detour to buy a disposable razor before he settled himself in a chair at one of the quieter burger joints and spent the rest of his hour gorging himself with carbohydrates, sugar and salt. It was a much-refreshed Sebastian Friend who exited the mall and hailed another taxi on the road outside; refreshed in body at least, but far from certain that the fair-haired foreigner had gone unnoticed and unremarked by the hundreds of ordinary shoppers and mall-dwellers he had mingled with for the past hour.

Friend's mood of cautious optimism lasted no longer than the time it took the taxi to cruise slowly down Ferdowsi Avenue, past the compound of the British Embassy. Traffic there was heavy, and the taxi slowed nearly to a halt. Friend peered cautiously out through the window, as sure as he could be that the hat and glasses would obscure his appearance. A typically bustling Tehran street scene met his eyes, but dotted around this busy tableau were several islands of stillness. There were five of them, at least. He spotted them easily enough: single men of about his own age with dark, watchful eyes. They were arrayed at various points around the scene, evenly spaced as if by design: one waiting at a bus stop for a bus that never came, others lounging in shop doorways, all with near perfect sightlines. Two of them stood smoking about thirty metres apart from each other on the same side of the street, either side of the tall red-brick pillars topped with bronze horses that bracketed the iron gates of the British Embassy. The taxi could drop him straight outside and he would still never make it through the gates before they got to him.

"Take the next right turn," he told the driver when they had gone a decent distance beyond the gates. He let the man drive another two hundred metres from the turn before he asked him to pull over.

Friend stepped out of the taxi into another bustling city boulevard. Scores of ordinary people hurried by, people with places to go, someone to see, someone to talk to. None of them on the run, in hiding, alone and scared. Friend put on a smile and told himself to be calm, be confident. Don't let anyone see how you feel. Along the parade of shops there was a stall selling cheap mobile phones. He walked over to it. The man at the stall spoke no English, no French, but a little Russian and Friend managed to make him understand what he wanted. Two minutes later he had paid three times the usual price for a decade-old Sony smartphone equipped with a pay-as-you-go SIM. A little further up the street he found a bench in the shade of a young fig tree and sat waiting while the phone powered up and connected with the network. He crossed his legs and turned his shaded face to the sun, just another citizen enjoying a few minutes' peace in a busy day. Now and again he sensed the eyes of a passer-by settle upon him, the foreigner, the stranger in their midst. Each time he felt a little flutter of panic behind his ribcage. He tried not to mind it.

He called the number he knew by heart. It had been expressly against 'C's instructions. Tehran Station was probably blown, he had said. Or if they're not blown, but you need them, then you're blown yourself. Either way, you're on your own. Friend would have accepted the situation had the Director himself not intervened. He was damned if he was sending a man into hostile territory without some kind of back-up. Of course he knew how that felt from his own experience. Iraq, it had been, 1991, a Tornado downed in the middle of the desert. That was the rumour anyway.

"Hello?" There was no other greeting. But the answering voice was English. That was something.

"Mr Baxter? This is the laundry. We have your shirts ready for collection."

"Oh yes? I'll be along shortly. Thank you."

The line went dead. Friend sat still and tried to picture the scene. Baxter putting the phone down and leaving his office, walking down the corridor or across the compound to wherever the station's secure communications suite might be, trying to keep his sense of urgency from communicating itself to the Embassy staff. Then, in a few minutes' time, he would call back, from a little lead-lined room in the basement or somewhere else that boasted the most sophisticated anti-electronic surveillance technology the Service could provide. That was one side of things; Friend's easily traceable mobile was the other.

It was six minutes before the return call came through. The voice was stern, still cautious.

"What name?"

"Friend, travelling as Lindgren." He heard the breath released at the other end of the line.

"Christ man, but you're hot. I'm surprised you haven't melted through the pavement. Your picture's been on every TV set in the country in the last hour."

"Anything you can do for me?"

"If we can get you inside."

"No good. They've got the street sealed up tight. I saw at least five of them when I passed by. Bound to be more. I'd never get through."

"All right, then maybe I can get out to you."

"Fine. Have you had anyone on your tail recently?"

"Yes, of course. But I'll send one of the boys out on an errand a few minutes before I go. That ought to draw one or two of them off. Then they'll have to leave some on station outside. Maybe I can lose the rest. Now, what do you need? Money? Do you still have your escape passport?"

"I'm okay for money, but I don't trust the passport."

"Why the hell not?"

"Because I don't trust the man who was holding it for me."

"All right," Baxter seemed to accept this view only grudgingly.

"I suppose I can cook something up for you from stock. We've got photos on file. But it'll take time."

"How much time?"

"Two hours at least. Do you know Barbod Alley?"

"I can find it."

"Good. There's a little café about halfway down. I'll be there at three."

"All right. What's the fallback?"

"No fallback, old boy. If I don't make it, it's because I couldn't shake the company. Then you're on your own."

There was nothing more to be said. It was almost eleven-thirty, more than three hours to kill before the rendezvous. Friend got up from the bench and looked around. The street seemed exactly as it had been a few minutes before. The foreigner in the black hat and sunglasses still aroused no curiosity in the busy streets of Tehran.

There was a flower shop about four doors down from where he stood. The shop assistant was busy with two chattering women, their pretty faces immaculately made-up, hair pulled back under colourful headscarves. She gave Friend a curious look as he stepped over the threshold, as if this wasn't a place accustomed to male visitors. He offered a weak smile and settled himself into the role of idle browser, sauntering around the little room with both hands clasped behind his back. He began to study a selection of lilies in a large metal bucket filled with water. After a moment, the assistant turned her attention back to her other customers, whose rapid chatter had continued without pause. Friend gave her a few seconds to reabsorb herself then, after a quick glance over his shoulder to check, he dropped his phone into the bucket and walked out of the door.

He had gone no more than twenty metres before he realised that without the phone he had no way of telling the time. He hadn't even bothered to ask Baxter if it had been set correctly.

*

215

Barbod Alley was about a quarter of a mile south of the Embassy, running directly between Ferdowsi Avenue and the next boulevard to the east. It looked like the best place in town to come if you wanted to get your TV repaired or pick up a refurbished 1970s HiFi. Friend had walked past four or five electronics stores before he found the café, carved discreetly out of the foyer of a long-abandoned cinema. He hadn't spotted any of the opposition on the way, but all the same he walked a loop far to the south of the alley before heading back towards it. He had run all the usual checks: ducking in and out of shops, doubling back on himself without warning, running to catch a bus and riding one stop back in the opposite direction.

The worst moments had been the fifteen minutes he spent in the toilet of a small shopping centre, painfully shaving off the stubble that had colonised his face while he was imprisoned. Luckily, no one disturbed him. He stopped a couple of times to check the reflection in a shop window. Choosing a jeweller's shop as he did had the added benefit of allowing him to check the time in the displayed watches. He saw no one and nothing to make him think he had been identified; even the militiamen on foot patrol seemed oblivious to his presence. It was just the feeling of being pressed in by the crowd, of being separate from all this teeming humanity. There was not a man, woman or child among them he could call a friend, or rely upon for the ordinary courtesies of human interaction, even as a stranger. It was a sense of isolation that operatives like Friend were trained to recognise and understand. Some could even learn to thrive in it, as Friend often did. Until they began to run out of options. That was when a sense of panic could take over, and then… Friend cast the thought away with as much disgust as he could summon. He hadn't reached that point yet.

It was ten minutes to three when he entered the café, a fact he could be sure of thanks to the wall clock above the cash till. Friend could see why Baxter had chosen it: the alley was quieter than the surrounding streets and the café had an old-world feel: widely spaced tables, many of them separated by large potted plants. For discreet, diplomatic conversations it was perfect. Friend chose a table on the side wall, towards the back. Foliage from one of the plants partially shielded him from the street and the door, but he would still see anyone who came in. He was no more than half a dozen steps from the staff door through to the back and he had a clear view of the clock. He took the risk of removing his dark glasses but kept his hat on to hide the blond hair, too thick and too long to shave away like the stubble on his chin.

He had made up his mind that he would give Baxter until half-past and then give up on him. And after that? The airport would be no good. He could take a train as far north as he could and try to slip across the border to Turkey or Armenia. Maybe south to Bandar Abbas and hop on a freighter to somewhere on the Arabian peninsula. Anywhere would do. The passport in his pocket might be no good for getting across a border, but he could always sell it if his cash ran out. There were always options. If Baxter came through he would have another passport. That wouldn't justify him risking the airport, but perhaps he could find a cheap hotel to lie low in for a day or two while the heat died down and his strength recovered.

A waiter approached and Friend managed to order coffee and a pomegranate salad with his few fragments of Farsi. He turned the printed menu over and saw that the reverse was blank. Even if Baxter couldn't guarantee him safe passage, at least he might get a message back to London. Friend signalled to the waiter and asked him to bring a pen along with his coffee.

All day Friend's conscious mind had been focused on instinct and training, keeping him alert to what he needed to do to stay ahead of his pursuers, to stay alive. Deeper down in his subconscious, Friend hoped, the evidence he had assembled had been forming itself into some kind of coherent picture. Now was the time to draw that picture out. He had a pen and a single sheet of A5 paper. Whatever he could write on it and give to Baxter might be the only thing that ever got back to London. He had to get it right.

So what was the evidence? Omid Sourian's innocence— established only by Friend's personal judgement; Sourian's testimony about being sent to Cambridge by Ali; Friend's identification of Ali as Linus Martinson; Martinson's apparent collusion with the killer in Farahani's bookshop; the photograph on Farahani's bookshelf. If there was a coherent picture you could make of all that, a coherent story, then every story has to have a beginning. Friend began it with the earliest piece of the jigsaw.

The photograph must have been taken around the time of the revolution. Perhaps Reza Farahani had taken it himself. All his closest friends were there: Dr Nassirian, Dr Qarib, Professor Sadaghiani, Leila Cochrane and Colonel Hadi. All of them dead now, all except Hadi, the man who ran Department 15. Had Hadi been the mole, undermining the Tehran Committee from the very beginning? It seemed likely enough, but then why would Department 15 blow a hole in the most successful operation it had ever run by killing its most important, unwitting, sources? It made no sense.

The next piece was Omid Sourian himself. Friend was certain the only reason he had been sent to Cambridge was so that he could be put in the frame for Professor Sadaghiani's murder. It was Martinson who sent him, so what did Martinson have to gain? Was he a traitor working with Colonel Hadi? But that made no sense either. If Martinson was a Department 15 mole inside the CIA then there was no more logic in him busting up the Committee than in Hadi doing it. That whole chain of logic could only hold together if the Committee had never been penetrated in the first place. And everything said that it *had* been: the photograph showing Hadi with all the others, the bomb that nearly killed Brian Cochrane in Vienna, the ambush of Derrick Halsgrove outside Isfahan. But if Linus Martinson wasn't a traitor then…

And then it struck him. Somewhere between his third sip of coffee and the arrival of his salad as his pen hovered uncertainly above the still blank piece of paper, the whole beautiful, insane scheme became clear to him for a second as if illuminated by a flash of lightning.

Martinson was no traitor. Who had sent Sourian to Cambridge? Not the Committee, but the CIA. Where had the details about Sourian and his travel history come from? Damon Bradley and the CIA. Of course they claimed they were just Mossad's middlemen, but how was SIS to know where the information really came from? Mossad had no involvement with the Committee, but the CIA were all over them, had bankrolled them for years. What could have changed? The evidence of a VAJA defector in Langley, telling them that the Committee was not what they thought it was. It never had been.

Colonel Hadi was no mole; he was a puppet-master. He hadn't infiltrated the Tehran Committee; it had been a Department 15 operation from the very beginning. There had been something similar, Friend recalled, in the early years of Soviet Russia. It was just after Bolsheviks had won the civil war and they still felt they were fighting on a dozen fronts to safeguard their revolution. They saw enemies everywhere, inside and outside Russia. The operation was the brainchild of Felix Dzerzhinsky, head of Lenin's Cheka. He set up his own opposition group and drew all the Bolsheviks' most dangerous enemies into the middle of it. Thousands of counter-revolutionaries, thinking they were part of a secure conspiracy to overthrow Leninism, little realising that they were being directed by the very people they sought to oppose. It worked so well that Western governments just threw money at it and the Bolsheviks' whole security operation was self-financing for a few years.

And now Department 15 had pulled off the same trick. Only they had kept it going much longer. Dzerzhinsky's operation had been closed down by Stalin soon after his rise to power. The

Committee had operated in harness with Western intelligence for more than thirty years. Friend had to stifle a laugh when he imagined the reaction in Langley when they found out: disbelief, denial, outrage, exquisite embarrassment. Hundreds of millions of dollars funnelled into an organisation that was working directly for Iran's theocratic regime. Decades of intelligence revealed to be worthless; hundreds of operations directed at phantom targets. It couldn't have been long before someone correctly estimated the reaction in Washington if they ever found out: heads rolling merrily down Pentagon corridors, funding slashed to the bone, investigations into misconduct, perhaps even treason.

If they ever found out... That was how it must have started: the mother of all arse-covering exercises. In its own way it was quite brilliant. Rather than reveal publicly that the Tehran Committee had been a sham, they took it down in such a way that it looked like the Iranians had done it. The more international outrage that could be generated the better—hence the use of a nerve agent—to pay Iran back for its deception. They had blown their own agents inside Iran—all worthless anyway—and in doing so no doubt found some amusement in watching IRGC mopping up one end of a VAJA operation. And then they had got SIS to tidy away the most inconvenient evidence: Sourian himself. Only Friend had refused to do it. And now Friend was that piece of evidence himself, and so Friend would have to die.

He didn't have all of the answers, but it was enough to make him a threat. Had Martinson been involved in any of the killings? His friend in the bookshop with the perfect, American dentistry behind his dark, semitic face? Probably; an operation like this was best restricted to as few people as possible. Had all three of the Committee's leaders been working for Department 15 from the beginning? And Leila too? What about Cochrane himself? Had he never once guessed? The answers to those questions would only be found in London. Somehow, he had to get back there.

He glanced up at the clock. Three-fifteen. No sign of Baxter.

As neatly as his shaking hands would let him, he began to summarise his thoughts on paper.

It was three twenty-four by the time he had finished. He lay the paper menu side up on the table and looked toward the door. No Baxter.

Friend turned his attention to his salad, chewing away with his head down, trying not to look at the door. He washed the last of it down with some coffee.

Three thirty-two.

He called for the bill. While he waited, he pulled the stone-coloured jacket out of his bag and swapped it for the black one.

Three thirty-seven.

It was the sense of exposure that got to you. Knowing that there was a paper-thin barrier of fate between you and disaster. Feeling that everyone was looking at you, knew who you really were. Even the waiter as he counted out your change.

Three forty-one.

Baxter wasn't coming. Baxter had gone round in circles trying to shake them until he was dizzy with it. Friend was feeling a little dizzy himself as he got to his feet and lurched reluctantly towards the door. He pushed through it with the timing of a drunkard and felt the warm, moist air of Tehran brush his face. Blinking, half-blind in the gloom of the alley, he turned towards Ferdowsi and walked. He should have waited longer in the café. He had left the menu with its guilty secret lying on the table. But who cared? He hadn't even bothered to think about where he would go.

A crowd of teenagers coming out of one of the stores decided it for him. He almost walked into them in his stupor, and they parted ranks to admit him to their heart. The group of eight or nine walked on together, Friend a stumbling simpleton in the middle, a buzzing crowd of happy flies shielding him from the world. They came to the end of the alley and Friend saw a man standing in the middle of the junction, his legs set apart like a politician striking a power pose on stage, one hand stuffed into his jacket pocket. He and Friend seemed to be the only men in Tehran who felt the need of a jacket on such a warm afternoon.

It was Linus Martinson. As the group drew closer, Friend saw with tired eyes the American step slowly to one side to let them pass; saw too in the other man's eyes a look he had seen in many men before. A look that promised violence and death. The broad boulevard of Ferdowsi Avenue stretched out to right and left. With a gentle touch of hand on shoulder Friend moved one of the teenage boys aside, stepped on to the pavement, dropped his paper bag to the ground and ran.

TWENTY-SIX

"Let me put a case to you," said Lascelles, a blissful smile fixed to his face. "A hypothetical case."

"By all means," said Friend.

"An agent in hostile territory is captured by the authorities. He spends several days at the mercy of their interrogators, their torturers, if you like. Eventually he breaks. Everyone does, you know that. Learned it in basic training, I expect. This agent doesn't have much information to give, however: he's not that kind of agent. So the process he is put through is not about trying to get anything out of him. No, it's about trying to put something into him. A story he will end up believing and taking back to his organisation."

Friend looked back at Lascelles, his expression sour.

"Oh, it's easy enough to do," Lascelles continued. "An interrogation is always a conversation to a degree, never just a one-sided business of question and answer. And the more the interrogator talks, rather than asking direct questions, the more background he fills in by way of encouraging the prisoner to come up with those crucial missing details they want, the more the prisoner starts to relax. And that is when he is vulnerable. Soon enough, prisoner and interrogator reach an accommodation, two stories become one. The prisoner doesn't even remember how it came about. No physical violence is involved. I believe the inquisitors here are quite skilled at the technique."

"But I do remember," said Friend. "I remember every bloody minute!" His anger was showing now, anger at their composure, at their indifference to everything he had been through, at Lascelles' insufferable good humour. "They didn't have a story to give me. They didn't have a bloody clue!" He slumped back in his chair, exhausted by the effort of trying to make them understand. It was all to be expected, of course. Derrick Halsgrove had been through the same thing after his long walk to freedom. But then Halsgrove was Halsgrove; he had never been captured.

Lascelles allowed a pause before he continued, hoping to avoid another outburst.

"All right. Perhaps the story wasn't a plant. Perhaps it is all your own work. That doesn't make your deductions correct. And you have to admit that if the Iranians wanted to come up with a story to divide their enemies and bring down glory upon themselves, they couldn't do much better than what you've told us."

That at least, Friend conceded, was true.

"Still," Lascelles continued, "let's leave the question of motive aside for a moment. We need to deal with the core of your argument, your contention that the Tehran Committee was not an opposition group at all but an Iranian intelligence operation. What evidence do you have to back up this claim?"

"The evidence of my experiences. Added to which you have Brian Cochrane's suspicions and the photograph I found in Reza Farahani's office."

"The one you say shows Colonel Hadi alongside the founders of the Committee and Leila Cochrane?"

"The one that does show Colonel Hadi with them all, yes."

"Well now, the problem is that the experiences you claim and the suspicions voiced by an ex-officer of the Service some years ago do not add up to hard evidence. And as for the photograph, nobody outside Iran knows who runs Department 15. We only have your testimony to say that Colonel Hadi even exists."

"He does. I met him. That's him in the photograph."

"We may need more convincing proof if you want us to believe you."

"What about Leila Cochrane?"

"What about her?"

"Why was Colonel Hadi removed from the copy of the same photograph she kept in her home? Surely it was because her husband already knew the other three and Leila wanted to avoid awkward questions about the fourth man. If Cochrane ever came across Hadi in the course of his duties he would have realised immediately that the Committee must be a fake and his own wife must be a double."

"So you are certain that Leila Cochrane was a double agent?"

"I am now, yes."

"And her marriage to Cochrane was a sham?"

"Her whole relationship with him from the beginning was a sham. She must have been a bloody good double."

"I disagree."

For the second time in the day an unexpected intervention from Ms Wilton shocked the two men into silence.

"I disagree," she repeated. "Because her behaviour doesn't make sense to me."

"You've never been a field agent," said Lascelles, gently.

"No, but I have been married. And I do know a few things about this world you inhabit. Mr Friend, would I be right in thinking that an agent working overseas in enemy territory would normally be recalled once they ceased to be of any intelligence use?"

"Yes, that would be standard practice."

"So why did Leila stay with Brian Cochrane after he resigned? Why didn't she return to Iran?"

"So, in your opinion, this means Leila was not a double agent?" asked Lascelles.

"Not at all. I'm sure Mr Friend is right that she was a double at the beginning. But I think that when she received her recall order she refused to comply. She refused to leave Cochrane. I think that's why she died, because the Iranians couldn't trust her anymore. She loved him and she died for it."

Friend smiled at Ms Wilton. "I think you could be right," he said.

Lascelles gave an embarrassed cough and changed the subject.

"I think we're in danger of straying off topic here. In summary, the evidence in support of your contention regarding the Tehran Committee is sketchy at best. How does it tie in with the booby traps in Ali Rezaei's apartment, for example? Surely you don't suggest that the CIA placed those to kill our people, or that Rezaei himself was a CIA agent?"

"Of course not. I think that Rezaei and his VAJA superiors believed that the killings in Cambridge, Hamburg and New York had been carried out by ourselves and our allies. The booby traps were a simple act of revenge."

"So much for that. Then we come to the accusation that it was the CIA themselves who arranged the murders of Professor Sadaghiani and Doctors Qarib and Nassirian. What evidence do you have in support of this?"

"None," said Friend. "But if you want to know the truth about it, ask a few questions yourselves: did anyone matching Linus Martinson's description make a journey to Britain either side of the murder? Did the tip-off about Omid Sourian really come from Mossad, as Damon Bradley claimed? I dare say there will be someone in Mossad we can talk to about that. Is the website that showed Sourian to be a young member of the Revolutionary Guards a genuine one, or is it a CIA fake? I'm sure we have technology experts who can answer that. Why have the CIA offered us so little product from their debrief of Kamal Sirjani? I think it's because they have something to hide. If the answers to those questions come back the way I think they will, then you'll have some pretty strong evidence of American involvement. And from that point you only have to ask why. It makes no sense unless the Tehran Committee was a fraud."

Friend folded his arms and sat back in his chair.

"I'm certain that those answers are being sought as we speak," said Lascelles. He began another of his pauses, looking for a moment as if he wished he had brought some papers to shuffle on the desk; a file to bring out from underneath the other file he hadn't got with him. "Well, now I think we need to address the other thorny aspect of this business."

Ms Wilton was avoiding eye contact again, studying that interesting point on the wall behind Friend that had fascinated her for most of the past few hours.

"Which is?" asked Friend.

"The death of Linus Martinson."

"A non-event. Martinson isn't dead. He was perfectly well when I last saw him."

"Which was?"

"Not long after I saw him on the corner of Ferdowsi and the alley. I bolted north up the main street, but I could tell he was behind me. He may be twenty years older than me, but he was fit and fresh and I was in pieces. I was never going to beat him for speed that day. Besides, I was heading straight back towards Colonel Hadi's men outside the Embassy. So I ducked across the road and into the National Jewellery Museum. I thought that if Martinson was armed he wouldn't be able to get through security and follow me in there. There were too many possible exits for him to cover outside as well. He must have realised that, because it was while I was queuing that he took a shot at me. Here."

Friend rolled up his shirtsleeve to show the dark red mark of a recently healed flesh wound, just below the point of his shoulder.

"Martinson shot you?" asked Lascelles.

"That's right. Only winged me, and he was lucky not to have hit anyone else. But he was a damned fool to try anything there. Dozens of witnesses. Sheer bloody pandemonium broke out. He ran off down the street with half a security detachment in pursuit and I slipped away round the back of the building. That's the last I saw of him."

"I see. Well that's quite a colourful story Mr Friend. But it doesn't tally with what the Americans are claiming."

"I don't give a damn what they're claiming. They're lying and I've told you why it's in their interests to be lying. They want to discredit me and cover up their own actions." He looked from Lascelles's face to Ms Wilton's and back again, hoping for some kind of reaction, for the slightest flicker of interest or belief. There was nothing. He could barely keep the disgust from his face. "So, what is their story, anyway?' he asked.

Lascelles glanced across at Ms Wilton again and got another shrug for his efforts.

"Oh, come on!" said Friend. "Anyone accused of a crime has a right to know the evidence against him. You've asked for enough from me."

Lascelles looked embarrassed. "Well," he began, "the Americans say that you shot Omid Sourian, which is not our problem. But they also say that you later went to Reza Farahani's bookshop, found him and Martinson together, shot Farahani dead and in the subsequent struggle with Martinson you managed to cut his throat."

"Ridiculous! If I had a gun, why didn't I just shoot Martinson as well? And who did they get this story from if Martinson is dead? The whole thing's crazy. I told you what happened. I've no idea who the man in the bookshop was, but it wasn't Linus Martinson. Martinson was waiting for him outside. And what was my motive for killing him and Reza Farahani supposed to be?"

"According to the Americans' story you were brainwashed during your captivity and persuaded to kill them."

"Nonsense. If Hadi's men had got into my head that deeply, they would have known everything I knew about Farahani and Martinson. They could simply have picked them up themselves. They would have learned more than they did from two corpses."

"A fair point, but it's an allegation we have to take seriously." He paused and looked across to Ms Wilton. "What do you think?"

The lawyer gave a dismissive shrug. "Self-defence might do, if a jury could be persuaded to believe his story. To my mind it seems rather... fanciful."

"It's the truth," insisted Friend.

"I dare say it is," said Lascelles. "And I suppose I should also assure you that there is no question of this matter going before a jury."

"So what is it a question of?"

"The Americans are demanding your extradition."

"Extradition to the States? For doing my duty on active service?"

"Well, not to the States precisely. To Guantanamo."

"Oh that's nice. I think I'd prefer the jury. At least that way I'd get to state the case for the defence."

For once Lascelles and Wilton responded with a unified expression. The idea clearly horrified both of them.

"Now, what haven't we covered?" Lascelles resumed as if the distasteful subject of washing the Service's dirty laundry in a public court had never been raised. "There's the remainder of your escape from Iran, of course..."

Oh Christ, thought Friend. *They sweated Derrick Halsgrove for two weeks on his long walk to freedom. I've been here three days already and they haven't even started on mine.*

"...But I don't think we need to go into too much detail on that," continued Lascelles. "Unless you feel there are any legal issues to contend with there?" He looked inquiringly at Ms Wilton.

Friend counted them off on his fingers. "Vagrancy, car theft, assault, numerous traffic violations, possession of an unlicensed weapon, sale of an unlicensed weapon, forgery, possession of a false travel document, bribery of government officials, breaking and entering, trespass on government property, breach of maritime law by stowing away on a freighter at Bandar Abbas, illegal entry into Oman... I think that's it."

Ms Wilton was almost laughing. "You had a busy few days," she said.

"Well then, I think that will probably do." Lascelles glanced at Ms Wilton who nodded her response. "Thank you for your co-operation, Mr Friend."

"What happens now?"

"Now you go back to your room. It's nearly time for supper."

*

Friend's supper—a microwaved shepherd's pie with over-boiled vegetables—didn't interest him very much. Nor did breakfast, lunch or dinner the following day, or anything else in his compact second floor room overlooking Lambrook House's long-disused cricket field. They had allowed him a television and a radio and any amount of books from the house library. He had no real connection with the outside world, and what he picked up from the news merely convinced him that the world outside was as mad as ever.

It wasn't just the cricket field that seemed disused; Lambrook House was quieter than he had ever known it. The grounds were deserted and he neither saw nor heard anyone inside the house save for the three guards who sat on a strict eight-hour rotation in the outer room beyond his bedroom. They were known to him as Ray, Sid and Rashid, each of them in his late twenties; fit, strong and well-chosen for this type of security work. It was their job to keep him in; the boys on the perimeter had the task of keeping anyone else out. Of the three, Rashid was the friendliest, but his friendliness extended no further than a smile of acknowledgement at the start of his shift and a less obvious manner when it came to keeping on his guard against any tricks Friend might try to pull. The other two seemed to expect him to make a dash for it at any moment, and it was clear from their faces that if any such attempt were made, bones would be broken, and it wouldn't be theirs.

Every morning before lunch Rashid would escort him down to the basement where he could spend an hour swimming in the pool and sweating in the steam room. But he was not permitted outside. He spent long hours staring out of the window at the empty field and the trees beyond, thinking of Sourian's wife and daughter and wondering how they were coping with their loss, with their changed reality. Leila Cochrane, too, was much on his mind. Ms Wilton's assessment of her state of mind puzzled him more and more. He could think of no better explanation for why she had stayed with Cochrane than that it was because she truly loved him; because the pain of losing him had been greater in her mind than the pull of a return to her native land. She had chosen to stay, in defiance of her mission and her instructions from Colonel Hadi, perhaps accepting instead of a hero's welcome the chance of a traitor's death. But how did that fit the profile of a woman prepared to spy for her country by marrying a foreign spy and betraying him every day of their lives together? One spoke of a woman ruled by her heart and driven by personal rather than ideological loyalty; the other spoke of an utter coldness, an absolute ability to detach herself from emotional need. Or was the truth of it that Leila had simply overestimated her capacity to sustain that detachment, and had found herself step by step drawn away from her mission into a betrayal that was the reverse of her original intention?

If Ms Wilton was right, there must have come a point when Leila realised that love for her husband had overwhelmed her loyalty to her mission, her duty and her country. Had the knowledge grown in her gradually, or did it come suddenly, only appreciated when the call to return had come and she felt the pain of enforced departure? And then of course the threats must have started. Leila must have known that, once she refused to comply, Department 15 would make certain she would never talk. Her death had been inevitable.

What could she have done to prevent it? To have told her husband would have been to reveal that their whole life together had been based on a lie. How would any man react to a shock like that? Instead, she had buried it all, concealed it in some hidden pressure chamber within from which not even the slightest wisp of steam could be allowed to escape. The stress must have been unbearable. And yet she had managed to conceal it from the man she shared her life with. That was what it meant to be a double, to hide a part of yourself from those closest to you and never let them suspect. Never let them guess that the smallest secret was hidden in your heart, let alone one that was greater even than your life.

TWENTY-SEVEN

Friend had been at Lambrook House exactly a week. For two days after his debrief with Lascelles and Wilton came to an end he sat and waited and wondered whether anyone was truly asking the questions he had posed, and if they were, what answers were coming back.

It was just after lunch on the eighth day when the first news arrived. Security guard Ray had collected the dishes and he had heard the water running in the kitchen for a few minutes afterwards when he heard the bolt slip back on the door. Ray's stern face appeared in the opening.

"Get your shoes on," he said. "You're wanted."

It was probably the first time Friend had ever seen the Director wearing anything other than his usual double-breasted suit. He was waiting for him in the wood-panelled entrance hall, casually clad in an open-necked red-and-white checked shirt, grey woollen flannels and suede loafers. The rolled-up sleeves of the shirt revealed the still powerful forearms that had held together many a scrum thirty or so years ago.

"Morning Sebastian," the Director's Welsh baritone bore more than the usual tunefulness, and Friend allowed himself to hope that he had come with good news. "Lovely day outside, I thought we might…?" He gestured to the door.

"Suits me, sir. I haven't been outdoors properly since Oman."

"How are you bearing up?" asked the Director, once they had crossed the threshold and were striding along the gravel path that separated the main house from what had once been a pretty rose garden. A few pink and white blooms still managed to raise their necks above the strangling weeds and perfume the summer air.

"I'm all right, sir. Just wondering how much longer I'm to be kept here."

"Oh, not too much longer, I shouldn't think. Coming along nicely health-wise, I trust? No lingering problems from your experiences?"

"I'm fine, sir. Apart from my feet, most of the pressure they used was psychological. I mainly needed some rest and good food."

"And they gave you good food here? Things must have changed since my last visit."

Friend laughed. "Well, plenty of rest, anyway. I have no complaints. All the better for some fresh air." He closed his eyes for a moment and breathed in the rose-scented air, feeling the skin of his face tingle at the touch of the summer sun's rays.

"I should think so," said the Director. "Now, I suggest we head across the cricket field towards those trees."

Silently, Friend walked behind the broad, stooping figure of his chief and wondered whether it was the desire for more privacy that was drawing him away from the house, or the need for more time to consider how to broach a difficult subject.

"The first thing I should mention," said the Director as he picked his way along the narrow path which wound through the trees, "Is that Porton Down have carried out a more detailed analysis of the nerve agent used in the Cambridge attack and their conclusions are... interesting."

Friend raised an eyebrow and waited.

"Their report states that it was a highly potent binary organophosphate whose base compound remains inert as a very fine powder until it comes into contact with a fluid with a pH value of between six and seven point five. Tears, nasal mucus and saliva all have normal pH values within that range. Now of course if our killer used his own saliva to leave traces on the door handle you might expect forensics to be able to identify him from it." Friend gave a nod, as some response seemed to be expected from him. 'Wrong. It seems the compound causes severe damage to DNA. They were able to identify fragments of DNA within the samples but too badly degraded to be of any use for identification. Then there was the sweat."

"Sweat, sir?"

"Human sweat normally has a pH value between four and seven, and samples taken from the professor's armpits showed a pH value of six point eight, within the range of values that could work with this nerve agent. So in theory the killer could either have pre-activated the agent with his own saliva, or some other fluid, before smearing it on the door handle, or he could have left it there in its inert powder state and allowed the sweat on the professor's hands to do the work for him."

"Always assuming the professor had sweaty hands, sir," said Friend, his tone of voice making it clear he thought this part of the theory far-fetched in the extreme. The Director ignored the interruption.

"Now we come to its origin. Porton Down could not positively identify the source, but it is known that the Soviets were working on similar compounds in the '80s. Given the level of historical co-operation between Russia and Iran in this field, it's not at all unlikely that the Iranians might have access to something like this."

"But that also makes this sort of agent ideal for someone wanting to frame the Iranians."

"And how would the Americans have got hold of the stuff? Or anyone else for that matter. Can you answer me that?" The Director shrugged and walked on. "But this is just speculation. The plain fact of the matter is that an Iranian dissident was poisoned in Cambridge with a type of nerve agent our experts think the Iranian government might plausibly possess. That doesn't get you anywhere nearer proving your allegations against the Americans."

"Well, the method's crazy, anyway."

"The method? Yes, I agree that using the door handle was risky. Too many variables at play."

"I don't think they used it at all, sir. Look, I know cold blooded murder isn't exactly our type of work, but put yourself in the position of the killer—or the people behind the killer—for a moment, sir. If this kind of nerve agent was what you had available for the job, would you leave it on the door handle and hope the professor touched it before the rain washed it off, or would you find some way to spray it in his face so that it activated on contact with the mucus membranes."

"Using the door handle makes it less likely there would be any witnesses."

"But it's far more likely to fail. Listen, within twenty-four hours or so the killings in Hamburg and New York would be known about, too. We'd have put a wall of security around the professor. This was their only chance to get to him. Why use such an uncertain method? Would you, sir?"

"I don't disagree with you, Sebastian. But there are sterner judges than me to be convinced. It's not a question of arguing over what's plausible or implausible, good tradecraft or bad, but of overturning a deeply held preconception of guilt that, on the surface at least, makes sense to everyone. What else do you have?"

"Well, sir, bear in mind also that the whole case against Omid Sourian rests on him being in a position to place the poison on the door handle. But if it wasn't the door handle at all, then the case against him falls. Wetherby himself said it was impossible that Sourian could have met the professor that day. The timings just didn't work."

"Sound points, Sebastian. But not proof. And anyway, if

someone other than Sourian sprayed the professor in the face in the restaurant, or in the park, why did nobody see it? Why didn't the professor do something about it? These nerve agents aren't instantaneous, you know."

"Yes, I know. Wetherby said much the same thing." Friend turned and looked back at the house, not wanting the Director to see the doubt in his face.

"Look," the Director sounded conciliatory, "I will ask Wetherby to have another look at the toxicology report. Perhaps there might have been a sedative of some kind, given to him in the restaurant. That would explain why he didn't resist when, or rather if, he was poisoned in the park."

"Thank you, sir."

"And as for your other question, I suppose the killer might have chosen his moment carefully, when no one was around. But this is still all very speculative, and you should remember this: even if it wasn't the door handle and the case against Sourian falls, that doesn't mean the case against the Iranians falls. They're still the most obvious candidates for wanting the Committee leaders dead, as far as the wider world is concerned. And, more importantly, as far as our government is concerned."

"But whoever did it wanted to put Sourian in the frame. Why would they want to point the finger at another Iranian?"

"Well, perhaps they wanted us to know it was them, to prove a point to us, but they also wanted to protect the true killer's identity in case they needed to use him in the west again. Or perhaps the professor was killed by IRGC and they wanted to put a VAJA man in the frame to prove how incompetent they are. Any number of theories could explain it." He turned towards Friend, towering over him with his bulk. "The point is, even if it wasn't Sourian, that doesn't mean it wasn't the Iranians. And even if it wasn't the Iranians, that doesn't mean it was the Americans. You haven't even proven the first link in the chain."

Friend gave up, with a shrug. Despite all he had seen and learned. He had no evidence, and without evidence there was no way of convincing anyone.

"But don't be too despondent," the Director continued, his voice now lighter in tone. "I do have some good news to impart. We made discreet enquiries with Mossad about Omid Sourian; the Foreign Secretary even passed a request through the Israeli Ambassador asking for any information they might have on his connection with VAJA. Both enquiries came back negative. The Israelis had never heard of Omid Sourian before this business blew up, so it's safe to say that the little dossier we received from Brother Bradley was a lie from start to finish. If nothing else, that establishes that the CIA have acted in bad faith towards us. And happily, that was enough for 'C' to authorise further enquiries and to take a somewhat sterner line in response to American demands with regard to yourself."

"I'm not going to be extradited?"

"Not just yet. With the help of one of our legal advisors, whom you may have met, 'C' fell back on our old friend *habeas corpus*, and demanded evidence that Martinson was actually dead. Thus far, no such evidence has been supplied."

"So, I live to be extraordinarily rendered another day."

"For the time being, at least. I'm afraid it does leave you in limbo, somewhat. The Americans can't prove that Martinson is dead, but we can't prove that he's alive. And as long as that stalemate continues, I can't say I see much prospect of you being allowed back into circulation. The Americans continue to demand that we hand you over, or threaten that they will serve justice on you themselves if we refuse. There have also been hints of their refusing further co-operation with us. Shutting down every bit of help they give us with operations, signals intelligence, the whole lot. I need hardly tell you that without their help we would find things extremely difficult."

Friend listened in silence. None of this came as a surprise to him; it was more important to know what his masters planned to do about it.

"As things stand, we're playing for time. We asked for

more details about Martinson: service history, photographs, worknames, passports, recent movement records. And that we did receive, at least in part. They sent us details of three work identities used by Martinson and a travel history since January, which, by the way, showed that he was in Langley at the time of the Cambridge murder and for a whole month before."

"That can't be right, sir. He briefed Sourian for the trip and Sourian said it was just three weeks in advance."

"Oh yes, they're lying about that, all right. As it happens we have a record of him ourselves. Derrick Halsgrove had a meeting with him in Tehran four years ago, when he was using the work name Carl Hendricks. Careless of our friends in Langley to have missed that, but then they probably didn't want us to notice that a US passport holder named Carl Hendricks arrived at Bristol Airport from Barcelona exactly a week before the professor was poisoned and flew out of London City bound for Amsterdam the morning after he died. You won't be surprised to hear that we've had some difficulty tracking his movements during the week he was here—not a single clear CCTV image—but we do know he picked up a hire car when he arrived and spent two nights in a smart country hotel between Cambridge and Ely."

"That would work well for getting to the professor's home in the north of the city, sir. And the package that was delivered to him was posted in that part of the county as well."

"Well it's a start, but not much more than that. Linus Martinson hasn't been charged with the murder and I don't expect he will be. For one thing he's officially dead, for another I don't think we've quite reached the point where a CIA agent could be charged for lethal use of a chemical weapon on British soil."

"So much for the trusted ally."

The Director looked as though he was about to launch into one of his periodic anti-American rants, but then he pursed his lips and seemed to hold the thought back, realising this was not the time. He thrust his hands in his pockets, as if trying to contain the energy of his feeling. His voice when he spoke was strangely diffident.

"Trust is never easy in our line of work," he said at last. "And when you do trust someone it's so tempting to take it too far, to become over-reliant on them. That's the other side of trust. Maybe that's how it's become with us and the Americans." He closed the subject with a shrug, and walked on.

Friend looked back through the trees towards the house. Should he feel some sort of anger against the old ally? There, amid the trees and the birdsong with the sturdy façade of the house lit up by the midday sun across the quiet cricket field, and breathing in fresh English air for the first time in weeks, it was hard to feel anything but gratitude for being alive.

The Director continued on through the trees, his eyes raised upwards as if to the heavens.

"To sum all this up, young Mr Friend, you are still in a difficult situation. You have alleged that the whole basis of our intelligence operation against Iran for the last thirty years has been fraudulent. But you have no proof. You have alleged that our most important ally has used a nerve agent against one of our own citizens on our own soil. But you have no proof of that either. All you have in your favour is two small pieces of evidence showing that the CIA have not been completely honest with us. And who on earth expects complete honesty in this game?"

"So what happens now, sir?"

"What happens now is that either we find more evidence to support your tale, or you end up in Guantanamo wearing an orange jump suit."

"I see, sir. It won't be easy for me to come up with more evidence while I'm locked up in Lambrook House."

"Quite," said the Director. "But perhaps I might be able to help with that."

The Director was wearing his enigmatic face; a private smile that could not be read in any line or wrinkle of his features, but seemed to emanate from his person in the most general way.

"The essence of our problem is this: at the moment no one will believe the Americans are guilty because they don't believe they had any motive. Demonstrate that motive, and the whole thing becomes more plausible."

"Demonstrate it how, sir?"

"By finding proof that the Tehran Committee was a sham operation organised by VAJA from the start. If the CIA had found that out from the Sirjani debrief, wouldn't they want to keep it quiet?" He turned to look at Friend. "Now would be a good time to tell me about that witness you have up your sleeve. Will he talk?"

"You mean Brian Cochrane? Perhaps. But how do we get to him?"

"How do *you* get to him, you mean. He's already opened up to you once, so you're halfway there already. He wouldn't know me from Adam."

"All right, how do *I* get to him? Do you think they'd let me out if I ask nicely?"

The Director grinned and patted his portly stomach.

"Sadly, the passage of time has rendered my Wing-Commander's uniform beyond even the gifts of Savile Row's finest. But like any proud old serviceman, I still keep it pressed and ready in the wardrobe, for old time's sake. Do you still have your old dress uniform, Captain Friend of the Rifles?"

"Well, yes," said Friend, uncertain why the subject was being raised.

"And does it still fit?"

"I believe so. I lost a little weight in Iran."

"Then, brother Friend, I believe I may have found a suitable occasion for you to wear it again."

The Director turned back towards the house, and as Friend watched his retreating back he thought for one astonishing moment that he had heard a sort of giddy chuckle coming from his superior's mouth. But it was probably just the creaking of his size thirteen boots as he stomped merrily through the

241

undergrowth.

TWENTY-EIGHT

The funeral of Brigadier Charles Murray-White, MC, at East Devon Crematorium was a suitably dignified affair, in keeping with the deceased's long and distinguished military service. In a career spanning five decades, the old warrior had served in theatres from the Falklands to Bosnia, everywhere earning respect for his cool judgement and quiet heroism amid many varieties of crisis. His death had not perhaps been one the Brigadier himself would have expected, coming as it did from a massive stroke in the middle of a hand of bridge in the lounge of a three-star hotel in Budleigh Salterton. His final words—"Bid three no trumps"—were not the stuff of military legend, but then Brigadier Charles Murray-White had never been a seeker after glory.

Above anything else the Brigadier had prided himself on building a bond with his men. To that end, he had used the short period of leave allotted to him before each of his frequent transfers to study and memorise the names and faces of every officer and man in his new unit. He would spend many a long hour on a sun lounger absorbing himself in his task while his wife slipped quietly away to the shops or the beach, alone. But his effort and sacrifice had been repaid many times over by the loyalty and affection that built up quickly between himself and his men, and more importantly by the way they worked and fought for him.

So it came as no surprise that so many of his old comrades came from far and wide to pay their respects. They were a mixture of ages and units, all neatly turned out in their smartest dress uniforms. Each of them knew intimately what a stickler the Brigadier had been for appearance. Many of them wore the famous red beret of the Parachute Regiment and were of an age to have served under Murray-White during his heroic assault on Hill 33, two days before the Argentine surrender. But there were a sprinkling of other regimental insignia too, most curiously a group of three youngish officers in the uniform of The Rifles, which caused some speculation among those closest to the Brigadier, none of whom could remember him ever having had anything to do with that regiment. Someone said they thought there had been a Rifles battalion involved with Operation Grapple back in Bosnia, but these boys were surely too young to have been involved with that. It was all very curious.

There were also two young, male civilians that no one seemed able to account for. A popular theory held that they were journalists who had gate-crashed in the hope that the Secretary of State for Defence—currently battling a sex scandal—might put in an appearance. But there were others who noted their tough and watchful appearance, the way they had positioned themselves around the room to afford themselves a perfect view of the key dignitaries present, as well as both exits. These others held that the two civilians were in fact part of a discreet security detail there to protect the Chief of the General Staff, General Sir Marcus Firbright, who was seated at the front alongside the Brigadier's closest relatives.

All of this speculation was forgotten as soon as the service got underway. The Brigadier's widow maintained her composure— as her late husband would surely have wished—throughout the vicar's introductory remarks. One small sob was distinctly heard to escape from her lips during the eulogy delivered by the couple's son, James, but she regained herself during the hymns and further readings. Only at the final reading did her emotions really burst forth, and perhaps only then because the reading was delivered with such delicacy of feeling by one of the young officers from The Rifles. This Captain S. Friend—quite young to be on the retired list, as he apparently was—showed himself to be such an accomplished performer that several battle-hardened veterans found their eyes moistening in a way that they were quite unaccustomed to at the words of *Isaiah 40: 1-11*.

At last, the service was over. The coffin was lowered down through the floor towards the fire below to the joyful tune of the Kyrie from Mozart's *Mass in C Minor*. A few moments later, the widow rose solemnly from her seat and began to lead the crowd out through the side door, along the corridor past the crematorium offices and out to the garden of remembrance where a small collection of wreaths and flowers were waiting to be examined. This movement took several minutes to complete, since the doorway was narrow and the company large. No one wished to cause an undignified crush. It was afterwards noted that one of the mysterious civilians had slipped out through the main entrance, past the next funeral party, while the other mixed in with the crowd walking slowly down the corridor. One or two thought they had seen one of the office doors open and close quickly, but whether anyone had come out, or gone in, they couldn't say.

When the first of the two civilians finally emerged out of the dark corridor into the light and made his way around to the garden, he seemed to be looking around for someone he couldn't find. He saw his colleague soon enough, and quickly noted the expression of panic spreading across his face. The other man had come out of the main doors—a breach of crematorium protocols—to make sure he was in the garden before anyone else. The pair came together, then after a word they separated again and began moving about the assembled mourners with swift and careful strides. A moment later, quite unprecedented and unwarranted scenes took place at East Devon Crematorium as these two young hoodlums began forcing their way back through the crowded corridor and bursting into each of the offices in turn.

A short while after this both men were seen running hard up the driveway to a waiting car. There was a third man waiting in the driving seat: a man of about the same age but of South Asian heritage. A hurried consultation appeared to take place. The third man was clearly explaining something to them, perhaps that nothing and no one had passed him in the last ten minutes apart from a solitary hearse bearing a coffin and two top-hatted mourners, emblazoned with the name of *A.J. Bargett & Sons, Funeral Directors*. Both young men climbed in and the car roared off with a screech of tyres.

In the aftermath, it was generally agreed that the two mysterious civilians had not, after all, been journalists. Perhaps it would have been a good deal better if they had been.

TWENTY-NINE

The rain fell cold on Brian Cochrane's face, and the hood of his waterproof did little to interrupt its flow. Why, even in mid-summer, was the rain in England always so chilling? In the Middle East, when it came, it was a cooling balm on burning skin; never would it turn a summer's day to autumn. Here it was like shards of ice cutting into your bones. What he was doing here was still a greater mystery. Something kept drawing him back, every few weeks. It was like the ache of a long-healed wound.

A film of moisture had settled over every surface on the familiar, quiet street, from the paving slabs to the red brick of the terraced cottages which ran down one side, opposite the drainage ditch and the open fields of the Eden valley beyond. When the sun came out the reflections would be dazzling. It had been a sunny morning the day Leila had died; a perfect, cloudless summer morning with the sun barely over the trees and the church clock only just creeping past five. It was still early for a run, even for her.

In his mind's eye Cochrane saw her run; that long, easy stride, her knees picked up high, gathering pace along the straight, just ten minutes from their home. He saw her long hair gathered in a ponytail slapping gently at her back and the faint patches of sweat breaking out over her grey t-shirt. Then he saw her turn her head at the noise of the car engine behind her, raise one hand to her face as the low morning sun reflected off the windscreen. Had there been time to see the driver, or to recognise the car? She was already well over to the side of the road; nowhere to go but into the ditch. And into the ditch she had gone, but only after the impact. There had been no scream, no screech of brakes or roar of acceleration, nobody twitched at their curtains; the street slept on.

Leila hadn't died immediately. She was still alive when the dog walker found her, perhaps twenty minutes later if her shattered wristwatch was anything to go by. The ambulance took another fifteen minutes to arrive, and it was almost two hours before the phone call from the hospital had roused Brian Cochrane from his drunken sleep. In his hurry to get there he had smashed his car into a wall, but it made no difference. Leila never regained consciousness.

The 'if onlys' still troubled him. If only Leila had run along the pavement instead of the road next to the open ditch; it still baffled him why she hadn't. If only she had slept longer and gone out for her morning run after six, as was her usual habit; if only there had been just one red light to stop the car getting to the street when it did; if only he hadn't hit the whisky so hard the night before; if only they hadn't argued as they had. It was a terrible thing to have parted in anger. It was a terrible burden to have carried all these years, telling no one. Wherever she was, he hoped she knew he was sorry.

Cochrane heard no footsteps, but the sound of the rain beating down on the taut canopy of an umbrella made him turn his head.

"What are you doing here?" he asked Sebastian Friend.

"This is where she died, isn't it," said Friend, ignoring the question.

"My wife died in hospital, but this is where the car hit her. She fell into the ditch over there."

"Do you think it was deliberate?"

Cochrane shrugged. "The driver didn't stop. The inquest recorded an open verdict. What are you doing here?" he asked again.

"Loose ends," said Friend.

"What's it to do with me? I told you everything I knew."

"Did you? I thought maybe Leila herself might have told you more."

"Leila? What are you talking about?"

"The Tehran Committee was a sham, a VAJA operation from beginning to end. It was the Americans who shut it down when they found out about it."

Cochrane stared at him blankly for a moment, and Friend wondered whether his response would come in anger or resignation. Instead it was cagey. Cochrane was an old spy, after all.

"Should you even be telling me this?" he asked.

"Strictly speaking, no. But I don't think it matters much, as I'm quite sure you knew already."

Cochrane said nothing.

"And given the obvious implications of what I just said, the fact that you're not shouting and screaming that it's a lot of rubbish means I'm getting surer by the minute."

"What implications are you talking about?"

"That if the whole Committee was a sham, then so was Leila."

Slowly, Cochrane turned away from him and looked out across the street once more. He seemed to see her body flying, tumbling into the ditch. The rain was as cold and hard as ever. The ice was set deep in his bones. Why in God's name had the man come? His grief was a private matter; every bit of it was between Leila and himself. No one else had a right to intrude. Not even if they came from the Service. He hunched his shoulders as if by doing so he could make the rain fall elsewhere and direct Sebastian Friend's inquisitiveness towards some less harmful object.

"The case is closed, Brian," lied Friend softly. "I'm not carrying out an investigation, I have no authority from 'C' or anyone else. This is just to satisfy my own curiosity. This is just the two of us, standing talking in the rain."

"Why should I believe you?"

"Then don't. I'll go away and leave you in peace. Only I'm not sure you are in peace. Why else would you come here?"

Cochrane gave no answer. He was still turned away from Friend, gazing across the street towards the ditch where Leila had lain dying. But it seemed to Friend that he was not about to walk away.

"I'll give you a start," said Friend. He reached into his pocket and brought out something which he raised up to Cochrane's eyes. It was the photograph from his own living room, removed from its frame and held here, on the street, in a stranger's hand. It was Leila and Nassirian and Qarib and Sadaghiani and… Yes, all of them. Slowly, Sebastian Friend unfolded the edge of the photograph to reveal the face of Colonel Hadi, just where it always had been, next to Dr Qarib, hiding in plain sight.

"Why did you keep it, Brian?"

Cochrane blinked. He felt himself to be shrinking in size. Were there tears in his eyes? A moment ago every barrier he had ever erected against the world had been up, as proud and unbreachable as ever, so why now did he feel that all of it was crumbling where he stood? There was sympathy in the man's voice, as if already everything was known to him, everything understood, forgiveness waiting to be dispensed, whatever that might be worth. Already he was seated in the confessional, hands gripped between his knees to stop them shaking, looking up at the grille that separated him from the priest and seeing only the heavy drops of rain dripping from the edge of the umbrella. What would she say if she were there, if when he talked to her she ever answered back with anything other than his own guilty thoughts? Did her secrets matter anymore? Surely his own did not.

"You broke into my home," he said at last. It didn't sound like an accusation, more like a plain statement of a fact that amazed him. How could this have happened? After all these years. How?

"I did," said Friend. "And you weren't home. But I found you here. Tell me about Colonel Hadi, Brian. He was supposed to be your agent, wasn't he?"

It was one of those moments in life when a man feels his actions directed by something external to his own will. Call it conscience or a sense of duty, to Brian Cochrane it felt as though Leila were about to speak through his own voice; that her confession and his own were somehow indivisible. Which was just how it should have been, he thought. Their lives too had been that way.

"All right," he said, turning back to face Friend but looking beyond him, at some distant unseen object in his own mind. "Hadi was still a young lieutenant when I met him. My first big breakthrough: source Qasim. Some breakthrough! Start as you mean to go on, eh? You must have heard of him, you used his recognition signal last time. Leila introduced us. He was part of the whole gang, but he stayed behind when the others went into exile. Said he could be more use to us that way, more use to the Committee. The bastard."

"When did you find out, Brian?"

"Oh, not until later, much later." There was urgency in his voice now, just for a moment, as he sought to make Friend understand. "It was only when Leila…" he paused, still trying to drag it out of himself. "It wasn't until after I left the service. That's when it happened."

"What happened?"

"You must understand, I kept quiet before because I felt I owed it to her memory. But I suppose that doesn't matter now. It started after I left the Service and we moved down here. Not straight away; everything was fine for a few years. We set up the bookshop, things were going well and we were happy. She was a natural at the business, especially the second-hand side of things. I think she got a kick out of visiting people's houses and rummaging through the collections they'd inherited, the boxes they'd found in the attic. Grandfather's treasure trove: ninety-nine percent rubbish, but when you found that one percent of gold, ah but then you had something! Then one day she went off to Wiltshire to look at a collection left by some old Persian guy who'd passed away. She got the tip from one of her London contacts and arranged to go down there and meet his son, just outside Salisbury. We thought she'd be back home the same evening, but then about four in the afternoon she calls me up and says there's more she needs to look at, so the son is going to put her up and she'll travel back the next morning. I asked her if everything was okay, and she said she was fine and that was that.

"I wasn't too worried, but when she got back the next day she was in a really odd mood. Agitated, nervous. I asked her what was wrong and she said it was nothing, she was fine. I wondered whether anything had happened down in Wiltshire to upset her, but all she said was that the books were all too niche for our market, Persian and Arabic stuff, some of it quite old, so she'd given the guy a rough valuation and the name of someone at Christie's they could speak to and he'd given her two hundred quid cash for her trouble.

"After a day or two she perked up again, but then a couple of weeks later the phone calls started. She always took a lot of calls for the business, but these ones upset her. She'd get up and leave the room. After a while she started checking numbers before answering; I think she blocked quite a few, but the calls kept coming. Then she started to think she was being followed; we'd be in the car together and she would be looking over her shoulder at the traffic behind us. She got nervous about being in the shop on her own.

"All this time I was asking her what was wrong: why are you looking over your shoulder all the time? Who are these phone calls coming from that upset you so much? But she just told me I was imagining things and tried to make a joke of it. Silly old

Brian, worrying about nothing. Once a spy always a spy.

"Then we had the burglary. This would be about four months after that trip to Wiltshire. The bastards turned the whole place over, made a hell of a mess, but didn't steal anything. TV, stereo, laptop, jewellery, none of it touched. Then when we got upstairs to our bedroom I saw what they wanted her to see: the dagger left on the pillow."

"Department 15?" asked Friend.

"Just what I thought, and just what I asked her. She broke down and told me that the Iranians had been threatening her, that it had started with that trip down to Wiltshire and then all the phone calls. There was a man who would come into the shop when I wasn't around, as well."

"What were they trying to get her to do?"

"Nothing, so she said. It was just intimidation. First they terrorised her, then they would kill her. She was certain they were going to kill her, she said."

"Did she say why?"

"No. It made no sense to me. Why then, after all those years? She wasn't a threat to them anymore. She just said it was revenge, that they would never forgive her for being involved in the Committee. But here's the thing, I didn't believe her. She was my own wife and I didn't believe she was telling me the truth, or not all of it at any rate. She was genuinely scared, that part I believed, but the rest of it didn't ring true."

"So what did you do?"

"I told her I'd tell the Service. Ask them to give us protection and check security for the rest of the Committee's people as well. She almost threw a fit. Begged me not to do it. Said we should just go away, somewhere they would never find us, change our identities."

"Then you'd have been on the run from both sides."

"It was a crazy idea. But I told her I'd go along with it. I arranged to run up to town one day to speak to someone about passports for us, told her to stay at home with the doors locked.

She wasn't to answer the phone unless it was me. Of course I didn't see anyone about passports; I went to see a little bloke in an electronics workshop just off Tottenham Court Road. Used to be one of our top eavesdroppers. Came back with a nice discreet bit of kit I could use to listen in on her phone. Record the conversations too."

"And what did you hear?"

"More than I bargained for. They were threatening her, all right. But it was because she was one of theirs and they wanted her back. They'd given her a deadline; if she hadn't agreed arrangements for her return to Tehran by a given date they'd come and get us both. Kill me while she was watching, then finish her off. That was one thing. But from the things that were said it was obvious she'd been one of them from the start. 'I don't take orders from you anymore,' she said."

"So you confronted her with the recording?"

"I did. It was the night before she died. I had a good long drink while I was waiting for her to come home. I was already angry and drunk when she told me the truth. She'd been a VAJA double all along. Got me involved with the Committee on their orders and the Committee itself was a VAJA double cross. That was the bit that really took the breath away. I'd been sure there was a traitor in the Committee, but it never occurred to me that the whole bloody thing had been a fraud. And Hadi too, my first and best source, the foundation stone of my whole career. Not an agent at all but the bloody head of Department 15 and he'd been doing me like a kipper for years! Can you imagine what it's like to find out your whole life is a lie? Career, marriage, everything. Maybe if I'd been sober I would have taken it better. She went down on her knees saying she loved me, that she'd always tried to protect me, that if she hadn't loved me why on earth had she stayed with me and opened a bookshop in Edenbridge instead of going back to Tehran. It makes sense now, but back then, in the heat of the moment with my head full of whisky and betrayal, I was in no mood to listen."

"So what did you do?"

"I pushed her away. Left her sobbing on the sofa. Grabbed a fresh bottle of whisky and drove up to a place I know on the greensand ridge, trying to drink myself into a stupor until sunrise. I don't suppose either of us got any sleep that night. That's probably why she went out for her run earlier than usual."

Cochrane looked at Friend, his eyes wide from the horror of his memories. Friend didn't think he would be able to stop them coming now even had he wanted to.

"She must have loved me, you know. Maybe not at first, but later for sure. Why else would she have stayed after I quit the Service? It must have crept up on her over the years, like those marriages you read about in Victorian novels. Funny thing, love. If only she hadn't been out so early! If she'd just gone to sleep and been in bed when I got home, I would have calmed down and maybe we could have worked everything out between us."

He paused, controlling himself, and looked back across the empty street.

"Every light was green that morning. No traffic on the road coming through town and every bloody light was green. Just one red light and it would never have happened."

He drew in a deep breath to sustain him through the last of it.

"I didn't see her at first, the sun was in my eyes, but then she turned. I don't know if she saw that it was me. She never did weigh much, did Leila. She was a tall girl but light as a feather; I could pick her up by the waist with just my forearm and hold her there like that for an age. When I hit her she bounced off the bonnet like a beach-ball, sailed into the ditch like she'd been fly-tipped out of a window. I didn't stop. I was cold, stone cold. Went home and slept off the whisky. When the call from the hospital came in I didn't remember what had happened at first. Don't think it's been off my mind for a second since."

Cochrane felt empty, drained. There was no relief at having unburdened himself of his long-concealed guilt, just a dreadful weariness; the shame that had clung to him ever since that terrible morning was as much of a presence as ever. Perhaps Friend would take him in after all; a quiet chat in the rain was one thing but a confession of murder was another. You couldn't just ignore that. As for his own feelings, they didn't seem to make much difference to him now. A prison was a mental state as much as anything. He'd already been inside for years. There was no hope of parole.

The rain had eased; he could no longer hear it hammering on the canopy of Friend's umbrella, and there were narrow shards of light breaking through the dark clouds overhead. It seemed a lifetime he had been standing here, waiting for Friend to respond, to hear judgement passed upon him. Cochrane turned slowly to meet Friend's eyes.

"Why did you keep the photograph, Brian?"

Cochrane smiled weakly. How could he explain such a thing to this man? What had he ever lost in his life? How much of his truth had turned out to be lies?

"I'm not sure I can answer that," he said at last. "Perhaps it was all I had left that was really true."

Friend placed his hand softly on Brian Cochrane's elbow. "Come along Brian, there's someone we need to talk to."

THIRTY

"I still can't believe it. It's absolutely fantastic!" 'C' slammed the sheaf of papers down so hard on the top of his desk that the whole room seemed to shake. It seemed to Sebastian Friend that the weight of Brian Cochrane's confession, as repeated to the inquisitors at Lambrook House, would be rattling the foundations of more than the home of Sir Richard Graves in the weeks to come.

He watched the Director sit back in his chair and carefully unbutton his double-breasted dinner jacket. The heat in the room was stifling. It was one of those summers of blazingly hot days interspersed with bursts of heavy rain that never seemed to break the heat. All the windows in the house had been thrown open to counter it. The three men were in the private study of Sir Richard's home, a small but handsome Queen Anne mansion deep in the Hampshire countryside that had been in his wife's family for generations.

Friend stood by the open sash window, whisky in hand, making the most of what little breeze floated in and listening with half his mind as his superiors dissected the details of what Cochrane had said. There was a smell of damp, cut grass in the air and he could hear the bees buzzing around a clump of lavender in the garden outside. From somewhere in the house came the sound of a teenager warding off the threat of impending adulthood with the latest variety of popular noise.

Sir Richard was right: it was too fantastic. Not just Cochrane's story but this life of his. One moment he was crawling halfway across Tehran in his prison pyjamas, the next being hurried into a mahogany coffin wearing full dress uniform. And now here he was drinking whisky and soda and wearing a dinner suit he had had tailored in a ridiculous fit of extravagance two years before and never yet worn, inside the private home of a knight of the realm. 'Fantastic' was the word, all right.

Sir Richard had topped up his glass from a soda syphon on a silver tray and was jabbing an angry finger at Friend, the drink frothing over the side of his glass.

"And you, you young upstart. I ought to wash my hands of you for pulling a stunt like that. Causing mayhem at the private funeral of a war hero. I mean to say, was he really your godfather? A strange choice for a bolshy couple like your parents. I've had to haul the warden of Lambrook House over the coals on your account, not to mention three of my best security people being put on suspension pending an enquiry into their conduct and professionalism."

"He did what he had to do," the Director put in quietly. "You had him under lock and key in the most secure facility at your disposal. And he'd still be there now if it hadn't been for that 'stunt' as you call it. Instead of which, at the cost of little more than temporary embarrassment for the security team you sent with him, he brought you a witness to convince you of the truth. Or would you rather have remained in ignorance?"

"I don't suppose he had any assistance from you, did he?" The Director stared back at Sir Richard, his expression blank. "No," the single syllable trailed away on Sir Richard's tongue, making his doubts all too clear. "But be that as it may, you're quite right, Director. It's better that we know the truth, bitter as it is and bloody mess that it leaves us in. The question is what we do from here. But we should discuss that later. Now I think it's time we joined the others."

It was a conference dressed up as a dinner party. Only Sir Richard's wife was the odd one out. Lascelles was there with Ms Wilton, as was a bewildered looking Henry Blake. The Head of SIS's Middle East Desk was now clean-shaven, with all trace of nicotine scrubbed away and wearing a dinner jacket he had probably hired at short notice.

"Ricky, darling, it's too bad of you to neglect your guests like this," said Mrs Graves, rising from her chair in greeting as the three men entered the formal dining room. "Now come along Sebastian, you sit there next to Henry, and Wing Commander, I've saved you a seat next to me."

The Graves' was commonly thought to be among the most successful of Whitehall marriages. She had come from money; a family which for almost two centuries had made, and continually replenished, an ample fortune in tinned meat products. Sir Richard's people were far from poor, but not quite in the same class of plutocrat. His was a solid, middle-class background: minor public school, a first in Greats at Brasenose College, Oxford, then a swift rise through the corridors of power thanks to a winning combination of brains, guts, determination and ruthlessness. Fiona Graves, too, was a strong-willed woman; she commanded great respect for her management of the family business, and for the simple courtesy with which she dealt with everyone she met. Sir Richard, too, could charm when he needed to, but he worked best in private situations. He could never win over a room in the same way as his wife.

Mrs Graves, or perhaps her cook, had provided a suitable light supper for a hot summer evening: fresh local asparagus with hollandaise sauce, cold poached salmon with a green salad, fresh peaches with home-made ice-cream. For almost an hour the seven of them sat making polite conversation, pretending not to think about what was really on their minds. The Director told a string of anecdotes about his time in the RAF and talked lightly about the exploits of two grown up children Friend had no idea he had. Lascelles, fondly referred to by Mrs Graves as "dear Hugo", was his chirpy, effervescent self, while Ms Wilton ("Emilia, darling") sat quiet and demur, saying barely a word apart from a few private exchanges with Sir Richard that seemed intended for nobody else's ears.

Only Henry Blake seemed nervous and ill-at-ease in this company. For half an hour he said barely a word, apart from asking Friend quietly if his bow tie was straight. When at last he relaxed a little, it was only to show his uncertainty.

"I'm not really sure why I'm here," he said to Friend. The words were almost whispered, as if he was worried he might be overheard. "I've never had anything to do socially with 'C', let alone his wife. I barely know who the others are."

"Wing-Commander Owen is my head of section, but we're not Vauxhall Cross so you wouldn't have met him. Lascelles is Cabinet Office liaison, Wilton legal. If you've not had to get involved with them before that's probably a good thing for you."

"I'm not sure I want to be involved with them now."

"Relax, Henry. If you want my honest opinion I think you're here because you're being welcomed back into the fold. Gardening leave is finished. Your slate is clean."

"I don't know about that. My section has been completely bust open by what happened."

"Then you'll just have to build it up again, won't you. Anyway, Middle East Desk is about more than just Iran, isn't it?"

"I suppose so. All the same I'd rather be behind my desk right now, or back in the garden with a smoke, than sitting here in this stupid outfit. A week ago I could barely get out my pyjamas, now here I am hobnobbing with 'C' and his wife in a hired penguin costume. I feel like a bloody waiter."

Blake got his chance to act the part a few minutes later when he volunteered to help Mrs Graves tidy away the dishes. A few minutes later he returned alone, just as his host was circulating the port.

"I think it's time we got down to business," announced Sir

Richard. "We all know why we're here. Our Mr Friend has brought to us a document of quite astonishing content. The confession of our former Head of Middle East Desk, Brian Cochrane, no less. A confession that he murdered, or at the very least was responsible for the death of, his wife, whom he had discovered to be a double agent. Furthermore, his statement that before she died she had told him that the Tehran Committee was in fact a hostile operation mounted by Department 15 of VAJA against the West. In corroboration, I might add, a search of his home revealed recordings Cochrane had made of his wife talking with her Iranian handlers. I suppose there is no question of their authenticity? Our technical people expressed no particular doubts, but all the same." Sir Richard sounded as though there might be a fragment of hope in this suggestion. "Mr Blake, I believe you listened to them?"

"Yes, sir. It was Leila Cochrane's voice all right. I knew her well enough. If you want a second opinion, then ask Derrick Halsgrove. He's back from Baghdad I think."

"Thank you, Blake. No, I don't think we'll trouble Derrick with that for now. He has enough on his plate trying to get well again."

Or perhaps, thought Friend, *you're behaving just like the CIA did, and want to keep knowledge of the Committee's real nature restricted to as few people as possible.*

"Can anyone explain," Sir Richard went on, "why he would have kept such recordings? I find the idea baffling, myself. And the inquisitors didn't seem to press him on the point."

"It may have been his way of punishing himself, sir," Friend offered helpfully. "Or perhaps for the same reason he gave me for keeping his copy of the Farahani photograph: it was all he had left to tell him who she really was."

"I see." From the look on his face, Sir Richard found the idea dubious and distasteful. Far better that awkwardness like this should be kept in the past, where it belonged. "In strict terms, of course, the recordings corroborate Cochrane's statement that his wife was a double agent, but they do not in any specific way confirm his contention that the whole Tehran Committee was a fraud from the beginning. For that we must rely on his statement and the views of Mr Friend, I suppose."

Friend watched as a smile worked its subtle way across the Director's face. He turned his eyes to the ceiling as if in imitation of Ms Wilton.

"We could choose not to believe them if we wished," suggested Lascelles. "That might make things easier. Politically."

"And operationally?" asked the Director.

"But I believe them," said Henry Blake, breaking into the awkward silence with restored confidence. "Now I've been presented with the evidence, it does make sense to me."

"And yet you never suspected a thing?" asked Sir Richard, perhaps less gently than he might have.

"Honestly, no. Perhaps I didn't want to. It was all going so smoothly, so predictably. I probably didn't dare question anything for fear the bubble would burst. Lesson learned, I guess."

"Hmm. Well then, I think we have to conclude that Mr Friend has demonstrated the first part of his remarkable thesis." The general silence served as adequate confirmation. "But that still leaves open the question of the second part: that it was our friends in the CIA who took down the Tehran Committee, used a weapon of mass destruction on British soil, blew all our assets inside Iran—not that they were tremendous assets judging from what we've just learned—and blew up poor Derrick Halsgrove in Baghdad."

"It makes sense to me, sir," piped up Blake again. "From what I know of the Iranians even the rivalry between VAJA and the Revolutionary Guards couldn't account for this sort of action. IRGC might try to take over a major operation like the Committee, but they'd never blow it apart like that. To my mind what happened only makes sense if it was carried out by a third party. The Americans had more reason to do it than anyone else I can think of."

"Yes, yes, Blake, thank you. I think we all accept the logic of Friend's proposition, or am I wrong?"

Again, Sir Richard was met with an approving silence.

"The question is what we do about it. The CIA are sticking to their guns and still maintain that Friend here deliberately killed one of their men in Tehran. We can't prove that he didn't. And even if we accept Friend's thesis about the CIA being responsible for all those killings and betrayals, we haven't got a scrap of evidence to back it up. If the Americans really want to push their case and this gets up to Cabinet level then they can have us twisting on the end of their knife when by all rights it should be the other way round. Am I not right, Hugo?"

"Most assuredly, Sir Richard."

"And did I state the legal position accurately as well, Emilia?"

A curt nod came from Emilia Wilton.

"Then we are in, not to put too fine a point on it, a right bloody mess. If I understand matters correctly there is even some doubt about how that weapon was used. Is that right?"

"If I may, Sir Richard," put in Friend.

"By all means, Sebastian. If you have a theory, we'd all like to hear it."

"Well, sir, we know that the Americans wanted us to think that Omid Sourian had contaminated the professor's door handle. But there are three weaknesses with that theory. Firstly, if the professor picked up the stuff when he entered his house late that morning, then he must have carried it with him after he left. So why did he leave no traces of it in his car or in the restaurant where he had lunch? Secondly, we know there was heavy rain in Cambridge that night, when he was dying in hospital, so why was the sample of nerve agent left on his door handle still so potent after all that rain? All right, the door is partially shielded by the porch, but not completely. Thirdly, and this is perhaps a more minor point, if the professor did pick up the contamination from his door handle, it wouldn't have immediately activated unless he had sweaty hands. You need contact with mucus membranes for this agent to activate. Perhaps he touched his face, or ate something with his fingers in the restaurant, but still, it seems to me that if you want to use a nerve agent with these properties, then smearing it on a door handle is not the most certain of delivery methods."

"And so?" said Sir Richard encouragingly as Friend paused for a sip of Sancerre.

"And so I think the door handle was a complete blind. A lot depends on what comes back from the toxicology report, but my suspicion is that someone spiked the professor's drink in that restaurant, without anyone seeing him do it. Let's assume for the moment it was Martinson; we know he was in the area at the time and we know how good he is. Twice in Tehran he got close enough to me to smell the kebab on my breath before I noticed him. He posts the cylinder to the professor from Ely, with an instruction to leave it in the dead drop down the alley. He watches the professor do this, then follows him to the restaurant and slips a sedative into his beer. Nobody sees him do this, least of all the professor. But that's the kind of operative Martinson is, to give him due credit. A bloody good one.

"A few minutes later, the professor leaves the restaurant. Martinson is waiting outside and tracks him again. He goes for a walk in Christ's Pieces, as he often did. He feels groggy and sits down on a bench. Soon after this, Martinson approaches him, sees that he is for all practical purposes paralysed and sprays the base compound in his face. It immediately activates from contact with the professor's saliva, nasal mucus and tears. A few minutes later it begins to take effect. He starts to sweat, a secondary reaction begins on his skin. He is dying. Martinson is long gone. Nobody has noticed him; the park was quiet and who would notice two men together on a park bench?

"But that's not the end of Martinson's work. First he walks to the alley and clears the dead drop, leaving a few traces of the nerve agent there for us to find. In the evening, while the medics are trying to save the professor's life, he breaks in to his house and strips it of everything to connect him with the Tehran Committee. There might have been something in there that would have revealed to us its true nature. That was the last thing the CIA would have wanted. Their whole operation was dependant on us continuing to think that the Committee had been a genuine dissident group destroyed by Iranian intelligence. Then, when it's dark and the street is quiet, he mixes up some more of the nerve agent, using his own saliva I would suggest and probably in the downstairs toilet, which would explain the traces of the stuff found in there. Then comes the tricky part, the only real risk he is taking. He knows he can't apply the stuff to the door handle while it's still raining, he has to wait for it to stop. At the same time he has no real idea how long it will take for the authorities to work out who the professor was and how he died. At some point, the police are going to arrive to seal the place off. He has to be out of there before they do. So he has to sit and wait, probably in full protective gear, listening for the sound of the rain to stop or the sound of approaching sirens to begin. No way of knowing which will come first. It probably took hours. Whatever else you might think of Martinson, you have to admire his nerve.

"Well, he gets lucky. The rain stops before the police arrive. He impregnates a cloth with the nerve agent, smears it all over the door handle, then bags up the cloth, carefully removes his protective gear, bags that up too and off he goes. That's it."

It was a long time before anyone spoke. Even Emilia Wilton seemed gripped by the image of Martinson waiting in the dark hallway for hours on end.

"Well, it fits with the timings." The Director broke the silence. "We already know Martinson was near Ely around the time that package was posted to the professor. He was travelling on a passport in the name of Carl Hendricks, and Mr Hendricks flew out of London City bound for Amsterdam at 07.40 the next morning. Assuming he was out of the house by 04.00 he would have had time to make the flight."

"If memory serves, the rain stopped well before that. I'm sure he would have had time," added Friend.

"Well!" said Sir Richard. "Any thoughts? Questions? I must say it sounds like a very thorough and logical bit of deduction."

Again, there was silence.

"Then I think we can take this as our working hypothesis, going forward. Though I must say I can't for the life of me see how we go about proving any of this, at least to the point where we can lay the blame firmly at the CIA's door. But perhaps something will turn up."

Friend thought he detected a glance in the Director's direction.

"In the meantime we also need to consider how we manage this situation, going forward, as things stand. Hugo, perhaps you can offer us a little insight about the wider political context. Anglo-American relations in the present day, and so forth?"

"If you wish it, Sir Richard. Well…"

Friend's mind began to wander as Lascelles began to speak. Across the table, he saw the Director reach over to a rectangular silver box from which he retrieved two large cigars. A nod seemed to be exchanged between him and 'C'. The Director raised his ample form from his chair and walked slowly around the table. Reaching Friend's seat, he bent stiffly from the waist and said quietly, "I think we have time for a stroll in the garden before coffee."

The air outside was as muggy as ever, but there was no sign of clouds in the sky, no sense of an impending deluge to break the heat. The Director cut the tip off one cigar with a small pocketknife and offered the other to Friend, who declined with a shake of his head. With a shrug, the Director slid the uncut cigar into his breast pocket and lit the other with a match. He blew his first lungful of smoke out into the evening air and began to walk slowly across the immaculate lawn before he spoke.

"I think we can leave the questions of high policy to the desk jockeys, don't you? Our business is action."

266

Friend felt the familiar tension of battle take hold of his insides. He walked half a step behind his superior across the lawn in the soft evening light. One of the easiest ways to tell the Director's mood was to watch the way he walked. When confident or jubilant he would march out at pace as if on parade; annoyance would have him stomping around angrily, his big feet crashing down on the floor. Sometimes the sound could be heard clearly through the section offices in Mayfair and his team would know to keep out of the old man's way. But at other times, when uncertain or deep in thought, he would move lightly, like a ballet dancer, the long, slender legs that supported his corpulent torso stretching out slowly, the placement of his feet delicate and precise, as if by its exactness he could find the same clarity in his mind.

The sun was almost down, its last rays diffused through the branches of a cherry tree in the corner of the garden. The bees were no longer buzzing around the lavender. Ahead of them stood a clump of rhododendrons, their bright spring blooms now fallen and the remnants dead-headed. Life was closing down as darkness approached. What had the Director and 'C' hatched between them? Still, the Director said nothing.

"What will happen to Brian Cochrane, sir?" Friend could bear the silence and uncertainty no longer.

"Cochrane?" The Director slowed his pace and half turned his head towards Friend. "Oh, let sleeping dogs lie, I expect. You heard his confession. I don't suppose it's in anyone's interests to have it repeated in the Old Bailey."

"No, sir."

And then it seemed that Friend's interjection, although not directly on the subject that needed to be discussed, had broken the dam of silence.

"Do you think there was anything in that cylinder Martinson sent to Professor Sadaghiani?" the Director asked in his most casual manner. "Or was that just another blind, like the door handle?"

"A blind sir. And like the door handle it was an essential part of the plan: a perfectly natural way of getting both the professor and Omid Sourian into the right places at the right times for the CIA's purposes."

"Hmm." The Director puffed at his cigar and strolled on across the lawn trailing smoke behind him. He might have been a banker deciding whether to extend a customer's line of credit, or to reward a junior with a pay rise. Friend had half a mind to ask for one.

"You have to understand," the Director announced, "that we are calling into question more than a century of co-operation between our two countries. CIA and SIS have collaborated directly with each other for over seventy years. We helped set the buggers up in the first place. You can't simply call a halt to all that on the basis of a hunch, or even of a well-reasoned supposition like you just presented in there. You need proof. We need proof. The question is, how do we get it?"

"I'm not sure I follow you, sir."

"Don't be obtuse, Sebastian. Of course you follow me. You remember our conversation at Lambrook House as well as I do. You've done well so far; you proved that the Committee was a sham. But you haven't proved American involvement, or that Linus Martinson is still alive. With those two elements still unproven, the threat of Guantanamo still hangs over you. Don't try and tell me that hasn't been exercising your mind."

"Of course it has."

"Then look here, young Mr Friend. Back in that room," he jerked his cigar in the direction of the house, "they're discussing the political ramifications; how to manage our future relationship with our closest ally in the complete absence of mutual trust. None of that excludes their handing your arse over to the Americans on a plate. After all, look at the question from Sir Richard's point of view: continued co-operation with the most powerful intelligence agency on the planet or the wellbeing of Sebastian Friend? It's not a difficult choice."

The Director expelled another cloud of smoke into the air. There was something about the scent of tobacco smoke in the evening air—good tobacco, not Henry Blake's corner-shop roll-ups—that reminded Friend of something from his childhood that he couldn't quite place. His instinct was to be comforted by the sensation, but he couldn't allow himself to be comforted without knowing the reason why. The long summer evening was drawing in, and bringing with it a chill that was settling in his bones. All of a sudden he felt desperately tired, tired and possessed of an urgent need to have done with this business once and for all. He looked up into the Director's face and met there an expression of cold ruthlessness; somewhere behind those two piercing eyes Friend's superior was engaged in the task of extinguishing any spark of feeling, any small measure of human sympathy in the interest of getting the job done.

"I've been granted authority to mount a small operation," the Director said at last, as the cigar smoke drifted up between their faces.

"What kind of operation?"

"You might think of it as fishing, of a kind. In London. It has 'C's blessing of course, although it's not strictly his area of responsibility. Cabinet approval came through this morning and even our blessed in-laws at Thames House seem disinclined to interfere."

The 'in-laws' were the Security Service, in the Director's unique lexicon; related by marriage to the parent service that was SIS.

"It will, of course, carry with it a substantial measure of risk," the Director went on.

"You want to lure the Americans in." Friend made it a statement, not a question, and uttered the words with a kind of weary inevitability.

"I do."

"And use me as bait?"

"Can you think of better?"

269

And, of course, in all honesty he could not.

"The Americans can only guess how far we have got in our investigations, Sebastian, but what little they can be certain about relates to you. First, that you know Linus Martinson is alive because you saw him in Tehran. Second, that you know Omid Sourian didn't kill Professor Sadaghiani because you spoke to him. Third, that we're starting to believe your story because we're stalling on your extradition. They've probably guessed that you worked out Martinson was Ali and had sent Sourian to Cambridge as a patsy, and from there that you worked out the truth about the Committee. That makes you a threat to them. Their efforts to get rid of you in Tehran and to have you extradited since you got back show a keen appreciation of that threat."

"I see your point, sir. So your proposal is to persuade them that extradition won't do and that they'll need to extract me forcibly instead?"

And that was the best case scenario, thought Friend. More likely they would just try to kill him. More likely, more straightforward and far more deniable.

"Precisely," said the Director, puffing his cigar with added delight.

"Might I ask how?"

"Well, there our options are limited. A blank refusal to co-operate with your extradition might have done it, but that has been deemed out of bounds by our political masters. Our only realistic option, therefore, is to make it seem that your evidence is about to be made public."

"Public?" Friend was astonished. The Director was normally averse to anyone below the highest levels of the intelligence establishment knowing anything about his department or its staff. The idea of operational details being aired publicly was quite beyond the realms of the imaginable.

"A parliamentary enquiry is to be convened to look into the incident in Cambridge. A senior official of SIS will be put forward to give evidence in camera before the enquiry. It will be made clear that this evidence will relate not just to the facts of the poisoning, but also to the true identity and guilt, or otherwise, of Omid Sourian. With that it should be clear enough to the Americans that the officer in question will be you."

For some moments Friend said nothing. He let his eyelids fall and breathed in the soft country air, listened to the twittering of the bird life getting ready for the end of the day. It was an ordinary, beautiful English summer evening of floral scents and birdsong. There ought to be a scene from a Wodehouse novel playing out in the deepening dusk at the end of the garden; the lead character a thwarted young lover using an assumed identity to gain access to the household. This was no place for such a dirty business.

"As I mentioned, it will be dangerous," added the Director softly.

Friend gave a weary sigh. "It usually is," he said.

They walked further out across the lawn, almost as far as the rough hedge and hidden ditch that marked the border with the neighbouring farmer's land, the Director striding ahead thoughtfully, Friend marking his usual place half a step behind. They walked in silence for several minutes before Friend asked the other question that was nagging away in his mind:

"Do you think they would send Martinson, sir?"

"I think it highly probable. An operation the likes of which they've been running relies upon the highest levels of secrecy. You want as few people as possible to know the truth. Martinson ran both the Cambridge and Tehran ends of the business, which itself suggests the use of a small, dedicated operational team. But there's one other fact that makes it more likely they would send Martinson than any other field operative they have: he's the only one who has seen you. He can identify you where others can't."

At a glance, thought Friend. *Added to which, it's probably personal to him now.*

"Then you have to consider that, from the CIA's point of view, the risks would be fairly well balanced," the Director went on. "If the operation went well, they would have restricted knowledge of it to those who already know; if it went badly, they'd calculate that Martinson probably wouldn't be taken alive. They might disavow him altogether, paint him as a rogue operative."

"Yes, that's true. So what would be our objective, sir?"

"At the very least, proving that the CIA lied to us about Martinson having died in Iran. I don't see any realistic hope of hard evidence coming along that will prove American involvement in the poisoning. Our only hope of making a watertight case is to take Martinson alive and sweat the truth out of him. Even if we fail, the fact of them sending a team to extract you helps build the circumstantial case against them, gives us more leverage."

And if they didn't send Martinson, or rigged everything up once more to look like an Iranian operation or… or a hundred other fractional probabilities that were neither more nor less likely than success. Or do nothing. And what then? A return to Lambrook House? A change of identity? Or find himself being dragged on to a plane bound for Guantanamo.

"So, Sebastian, will you do it?"

The Director inhaled a final lungful of smoke and looked up at the sky, as if wishing to spare his subordinate the embarrassment of being watched while he made up his mind. Friend turned around and faced back across the lawn. A faint blush of pink now fringed the blue and back at the house he could see the lights of the dining room coming on through the French windows. Mrs Graves was passing round the coffee.

Weeks before, when Friend had said the same thing to 'C', the words had come swiftly and instinctively, as if from the heart. Now he had to force them out. Their saying was slow, deliberate, final. Like an epitaph.

"I'll do it."

"Thank you," said the Director.

With that, he stuck the dead cigar between his teeth and, with hands clasped behind his arched back, began a slow, funeral-paced march back to the house.

THIRTY-ONE

*PARLIAMENTARY COMMITTEE TO HEAR EVIDENCE
FROM MI6 AGENT DURING ENQUIRY INTO
CAMBRIDGE POISONING*
Tom Westerman reports

*Following the news that the coroner's inquest into the death of
Professor Mansour Sadaghiani in Cambridge in June would
cover only the actions of individuals on the ground, it came
as no surprise when Parliament's Intelligence and Security
Committee announced that it would convene its own enquiry
into the wider geo-political aspects of the Cambridge poisoning.
Far more surprising was the announcement last night by the
Committee's new Chair, Anne Christian, M.P. that the enquiry
would begin as early as next week, with initial hearings scheduled
to take place from next Monday afternoon. For a parliamentary
enquiry to commence so quickly after an incident relating to
Britain's intelligence services is almost without precedent and
speculation is already rife as to why this particular enquiry is
being rushed into being at such short notice.*

*The statement issued by Ms Christian's office last night also
included the tantalising detail that the evidence heard by the
Committee will include the personal testimony of an MI6 officer*

recently returned from Iran. Various independent news agencies have reported the apparent death by shooting of Jamshud Pirouzfar, a.k.a. Omid Sourian, the Iranian intelligence officer who was named as prime suspect in the Sadaghiani case and against whom formal charges were raised recently. Pirouzfar's death has not been confirmed by the Iranian authorities, who have remained largely silent on this matter since the outright denial of any involvement they issued in response to the first accusations levelled at them by the British government. The expected tit-for-tat of diplomatic expulsions has yet to materialise and it is possible that Whitehall is waiting for the conclusions of the Intelligence and Security Committee before proceeding. It is thought unlikely that Tehran will announce expulsions of any British diplomats without the first strike coming from London.

While the un-named Mi6 officer's evidence may relate directly to Jamshud Pirouzfar's part in the Cambridge murder, the wider remit of the Committee's enquiry offers the possibility that it may also deal with the demise of the Tehran Committee; the Iranian opposition group of which Professor Sadaghiani was a leading member. The Tehran Committee is widely believed to be a busted flush following the murders of its leaders in Cambridge, Hamburg and New York and the ongoing secret trials of dozens of so-called 'western spies' in Tehran. But the recent disappearance of some of its middle-ranking members across Europe has caused consternation in intelligence circles, with the suggestion that some have returned to Iran raising the possibility that the Tehran Committee may have been subject to extensive and longstanding penetration by Iranian intelligence services. If the evidence given to the Intelligence & Security Committee next week backs this up, the revelation could have far-reaching consequences for western intelligence operations in the Middle East for years to come.

"Shit", said Damon Bradley. He closed down the browser on his laptop, reached across the desk for his telephone and began a long and urgent call to Virginia.

*

Friend's testimony was scheduled for the start of business on Tuesday, 'start of business' meaning 11am, but the Chair of the Intelligence & Security Committee had been primed to announce as soon as the members convened that the expected deposition from the Secret Intelligence Service would not now take place. At this point the enquiry was to be adjourned for an indefinite period. It was a move that the MP for Worksop and Bassetlaw knew would be unpopular, and had accepted with reluctance only on the unspoken understanding that she would receive her reward for compliance in what members of the House of Commons refer to as 'the other place'.

The following days passed quickly for some and slowly for others. For Sebastian Friend they were a blur of activity: security briefings, operational paperwork, tours of every Service safe house in Greater London.

For Brian Cochrane time passed more slowly. The rolling countryside of north Kent had been replaced by the unlovely grounds of a decaying mansion in Berkshire and he took his daily exercise with little enthusiasm. His guardians offered some sort of company, but it wasn't the kind he sought. The heavy burden of his confession had been lifted from his shoulders, but it brought him no relief from himself, only from Leila. He no longer felt her presence bearing down on him, no longer any tension of unexposed sin, just a terrible sense of emptiness. There was no focus or purpose to his existence; he ate, slept, walked, breathed, answered when he was spoken to. But there was no relish to any of it; nothing he might look forward to. Not even the prospect of freedom. To his growing horror he began to realise that the long strain of his unacknowledged guilt had kept him bound to Leila. Now it was gone, and so was she.

Damon Bradley's existence was rather more in tune with

Friend's. He worked long hours at the CIA station's riverside offices, making endless calls to Langley, to Washington, to his SIS liaison, even to his widowed mother in Rhode Island. He prowled the station corridors with an anxious look on his face, acknowledging no one among his colleagues. There were some days when he disappeared entirely, without anyone knowing where he had gone, or for what purpose. When eventually he returned, there was no explanation and no apparent reduction in his state of anxiety. This was not the open-hearted, sociable Damon Bradley his many colleagues in the local station had known for the last two years. They began to wonder whether World War Three was about to break out and why, if that were the case, their superiors in Langley thought only Damon Bradley needed to know about it.

In the case of Linus Martinson, the days were filled with a sense of growing confidence and optimism. He could leave the panic to others. No one could have been tougher on themselves than Martinson in the aftermath of Tehran. He had got close enough to take a shot at Friend and had missed him. A colleague—a friend—had lost his life. The Englishman had got away, presumably clean out of Iran and was now back in London. The failure had hurt deeply for a couple of days, as he made his report to headquarters and waited for the response. But then he put it behind him. Regret, like so many other feelings, was of no practical use in his profession. Learning from your mistakes, and learning more about your opponent, on the other hand was. And so, for two weeks he had lain in the sun of Dubai at the agency's expense. He had eaten well and put on a little weight, losing some of that lean look that those few who knew him knew so well; he had grown his hair a little until it was shaggy and unkempt and cultivated the beginnings of a goatee beard. What might stand out as unusual in Tehran was perfectly unexceptional in Europe. And he had thought a lot, about himself, and about the Englishman. He was sure he would be meeting him again.

*

In the end, out of the six perfectly reasonable alternatives, they selected the house at Crystal Palace. It was a four-storey semi-detached villa hemmed in between the park and the railway line, and one of the few among its neighbours not to have been significantly refurbished in recent years. Its previous owner had been the local council, who had used it as a temporary hostel for distressed residents, so that by the time the Service took it over there was already an established pattern of people coming and going, residents arriving for a few days or weeks before being replaced by others. And if in recent years there had been a noticeable improvement in the standard of dress in visitors to number forty-six, and a decrease in the frequency of noise disturbance; no one in the neighbourhood was about to raise a fuss about that. If any explanation were ever sought, it was to be found in the property's occasional listing on a website advertising holiday accommodation. And the only surprise to be found there was in the price—surely on the high side for the quality, if the accompanying photographs were anything to go by. For all that, the place always seemed to be fully booked.

Of course, the website photographs of number forty-six bore no actual resemblance to the interior itself. While other, identical properties along the road had been converted into flats from their original purpose as parkside villas, their upper floors overlooking the park's boating lake across the road, the council had divided each floor between three self-contained bedsits. Their cheap partition walls and primitive bathroom facilities had been ripped out in the first weeks after the Service took possession and the house returned to its original layout. On the ground floor, what in adjacent properties would be the garden flat, a well-equipped gymnasium and bathroom had been laid out, to cater for the exercise needs of visitors and personnel who might be cooped up in the property for weeks on end. Above it was a comfortable L-shaped living room and kitchen. The second and third floors accommodated four large bedrooms with en-suite shower facilities, which left only the loft. A fifth bedroom was available, but it was sparsely furnished and rarely used.

As might be expected, the whole property had been furnished and decorated on the cheap. But it was kept clean and tidy by Ted Grant, an ex-boxer and semi-retired Service security man who lived in as permanent housekeeper. It was Grant, too, who maintained the listening devices that were built into each room, activating them when required from their control point in a cupboard underneath the stairs.

Grant was less inclined, or perhaps not so clearly instructed, to keep the property's exterior spick and span. The ground floor windows and front door were hidden behind an expanse of overgrown hedge, and so far had the weeds taken over the path that its concrete slabs had been lifted up by their roots and now constituted a serious trip hazard to the unwary. At the back, a ragged stretch of lawn, much frequented by the local foxes, led down to the railway embankment which rose steeply beyond a tall wire fence. Grant took the trouble of mowing it perhaps twice each year. All in all, number forty-six offered a decidedly shabby look compared with its immediate neighbours.

The house had not been chosen by Friend and the Director for the quality of its accommodation. It was a compact space in a busy area. The park attracted so many visitors in the summer that a strange car parked in the street would attract no attention. Watchers could mingle with hundreds of visitors strolling around the lake. Even at night it was far from silent. The Americans would know they could keep an eye on the place without raising suspicion, while the Director knew that in this dense, suburban setting the opposition would be less likely to arrive in force and start a major firefight. Added to which, the CIA knew all they needed to know about number forty-six already.

"I think they've bitten," said the Director to Friend on the Thursday afternoon, four days after Tom Westerman's article had been published and only twenty-four hours after Friend had moved into the house. Friend moved away from the window and its permanently lowered blinds and came and sat opposite the Director on the sofa.

"'C's had a team on Damon Bradley all week. He made a personal call to liaison last night. Asking for a loan of safe house facilities—did we have anything available they could use for an incoming agent over this weekend? They've used most of them before, of course. Liaison passed the request on to Housekeepers, who offered everything but this one. They will be expecting us to be keeping you somewhere in London, handy for your appearance in Parliament on Tuesday, so the absence of Crystal Palace from the list we gave them won't go unnoticed."

Friend nodded and breathed deeply. There was more. The Director reached into the thin document case beside him and laid a tablet device on the coffee table.

"As I said, there's a team on Bradley. They tracked him to Heathrow early this morning. Terminal Three. That's where you came in from Oman, wasn't it? Well, he was making a pick-up. The team managed to get a couple of pictures."

The tablet flickered to life, a grainy colour image already on screen. A car parked at an angle in the pick-up zone outside the terminal doors, a hunched figure moving towards it. Dark clothing, a hooded top, a single carry-on case rolling behind. Friend used his fingers to enlarge the image.

"Martinson?" asked the Director.

The body was a little broader than Friend remembered, and there was a hint of beard sticking out from under the hood. But the posture was right.

"Maybe. Hard to be sure."

"Swipe along to the next one, then. See if that helps."

Friend did so and was rewarded with the tip of a nose in profile as the man opened the car door. He shook his head.

"Where did they go?"

"To the safe house we offered them. Barons Court."

"Is it wired?"

"Of course. But under the usual agreement all listening devices are turned off while the CIA are in residence. If they need to record anything they bring their own equipment." The Director offered a thin smile. "Of course, Housekeepers do a sweep after they've left to make absolutely certain our friends took everything away with them."

"I imagine the CIA do the same when they arrive."

"Quite. So I don't think we can expect any helpful evidence to drop conveniently into our laps by that route, do you? We'll just have to wait for them, as we expected to. Now, swipe along to the next photograph. There's something else you need to see."

It was a passport photograph of a man in his late forties. Thick set, with dark hair and eyes and a square, Nordic jaw. It took a moment or two for Friend to recognise him.

"Records took the description you gave of the man who tried to kill you in the bookshop and compared it with CIA operatives or private contractors known to be active in the Middle East sector. Is it him?"

"It's him."

"Ismail Djahani. A dual Iranian-American citizen. Not formally on the CIA's books; has his own private security firm with offices in Baltimore which has been known to supply back-up for CIA operations in the Middle East. And just to add a little extra colour to the tale, he also happens to be Linus Martinson's second cousin. One more point to you, I think."

"It'll be personal for him, then. Losing family. All the more likely it will be him who comes after me."

"Just don't expect him to be any less professional."

The Director had more news, good and bad. The good news was that Detective Chief Inspector Wetherby had forwarded on a revised toxicology report showing that traces of a sedative had indeed been found in the professor's body. The forensics team were having a difficult job explaining how it had been missed the first time around. The bad news was that a review of CCTV evidence had failed to find any trace of Linus Martinson tracking the professor on his final journey. But this was no surprise to Sebastian Friend, who knew very well just how good Martinson was at being invisible.

Nothing much else happened on Thursday. Friend spent an hour in the gym before dinner working up a sweat, and then watched Ray and Sid celebrate their return to active duty by half killing each other in an unarmed combat drill. Rashid shared the cooking with Grant. There were five security men in total, but Friend never learned the names of the other two. They were young, lean and fit. There was nothing else to say about them and they had nothing to say for themselves. By day, they spent most of their time scanning the street and the park from the second-floor windows, when they weren't sleeping. By night, one of them watched the street from a parked Hyundai with blacked-out windows while the other covered the rear garden and the railway line. Friend would occasionally hear their whispered signals over the radio as they checked in with each other, or with Ray, who seemed to be in charge. Apart from that he barely noticed them.

External security on the property was limited to motion-sensitive lights on the front porch, the back door into the garden and the iron fire-escape to the side. It wasn't much. The windows were not even barred—it was an offence under local planning laws and anyway it would have attracted unnecessary attention. The single-glazed Victorian sashes would offer little resistance to any intruder. Bathrooms aside, the internal doors had no locks so there was little help inside either. Friend had checked the staircase on the first night: a single step creaked just down from the second-floor landing. That was about as useful as it got.

It was the geese who woke him, as usual, around six-thirty on the Friday morning, honking loudly as they flew over the house to the lake from wherever they spent the night. At dusk, back they came in the opposite direction, just as loudly as before. Not a great deal happened in between. Friend spent long hours reading or sleeping. When he paused to think, he wondered why he felt so calm. There he was, trapped in a cage, waiting for a man to come and try to kill him; a man he knew was all too capable of succeeding. So why did he feel no fear? It could only be, he reasoned, because he was surrounded by friends. The fear, the verge of panic that had overtaken him on the streets of Tehran had been the result of isolation, of having no one around him he could trust.

Not a great deal actually happened during the day, but there were signs of trouble all the same. What was thought to be the same dark blue Ford was observed driving past on three separate occasions in a four-hour period. A succession of young couples made slow circuits of the boating lake with identical baby carriages. A man was spotted on the railway embankment near the back of the house, or at least it might have been a man. A train rattled past before Sid could be certain and when it was gone the man was gone too. As evening approached, the street slumbered. Commuters returned home from the city, ready for the weekend. The parkside villas braced themselves for the influx that came with every sunny weekend. Many, like the residents of the upper flats next door, had left town for the school holidays.

It began when everyone thought it would begin. Just after three in the morning with less than two hours of darkness left. It began just as everyone thought it would: a burst of static over the radio, an urgent voice, quiet but not whispered.

"Movement. Next door garden."

The radio went silent. Friend and Ray sat opposite each other in the living room in utter darkness, Ray facing the window, Friend the door to the hallway. Neither said a word, each of them barely dared to breathe. Rashid was in the bedroom upstairs, Grant covering the front door from the hallway. Sid was floating in between. The other two boys were outside. Friend pictured the one at the front getting out of the car and closing the door behind him, taking care to make no noise.

The silence seemed to last for an hour.

The static burst once more, as if out of nowhere, as if Friend had never heard the noise before.

"Fire escape. Next door."

A pause.

"Halfway up."

It was a burglar; a local break-and-enter merchant who knew the flat next door was unoccupied and was taking his chance. It happened all the time. Friend felt his nerves relaxing. He hoped no one would call the police.

Even in the darkness, Ray seemed to know what he was thinking.

"It's him," he said quietly. "Up the fire escape and in through one of the rear windows next door. Out of the dormer in the loft, across the roof and into the loft this side. Down the stairs."

As if fate wished to confirm his way of thinking at once there was a crackle of static followed by the soft words, "He's inside."

There now followed ten anguished minutes of waiting. Friend listened to the two men outside checking in with each other, watching for movement and seeing none. Sid stuck his head around the door to check that everything was okay. Even Ray couldn't stand it for long and got up to walk around the room. Was he working on the lock of one of the flats next door? The upper or the lower? Was he a simple burglar after all?

Then at last they heard it, from the back.

"Roof. Our side. Dormer window."

Another pause. Sid had been waiting in the doorway. Now he slipped through it and closed the door behind him, taking up position to Friend's left.

"He's inside."

"Copy that. Out."

Ray reached across and slowly turned the volume control on the radio until it clicked to off.

Friend no longer had any sense of the passage of time. He was back in Colonel Hadi's cell, disorientated by the sensory barrage and lack of sleep, he was walking out of the café on Barbod

Alley, his mind in turmoil. There were no footsteps overhead. Would Martinson try to clear the bedrooms first? Would Rashid keep his head and stay out of the way, or would he try to take the American on alone? Ray was standing behind him to his right; together, he and Sid had the doorway bracketed. Their guns were drawn.

Was that a creak on the stair? The three men in the living room would surely have looked to each other for confirmation were it not so bloody dark. Friend could sense a general holding of breath, a tensing of muscles. How long had it been since the creak on the stair? Would the door open slowly or with force? If he could see there was no light on in the room, surely he would go for stealth.

Even before he could finish the thought in his head Friend saw the door whip open. His thumb was already on the switch. The four powerful spotlights behind Friend came on in unison, and instantly he saw the form of Linus Martinson in the doorway, a Martinson wearing night-vision goggles, momentarily blinded and holding one hand up against the light, the light which glinted off the long, clean blade in his other hand.

The rest happened quickly. Before Martinson could rip the useless goggles from his face, the two-ton bulk of Ted Grant hit him from behind and he went down face first as so many others had before. Ray and Sid were on top of him, wresting the blade from his grip, holding his arms. They hauled him upright and as Friend caught his eye the American seemed to laugh, as if the whole damn business had just been a joke and he didn't care one bit about being caught.

There was some fumbling around as Grant retrieved a set of handcuffs from his back pocket and tried to clip them around Martinson's wrists, but Ray and Sid looked to have a good professional hold on his arms. It may have been the momentary distraction of Rashid entering the room, his weapon drawn and ready for action, that caused it, but just for a moment Linus Martinson's left arm swung free. Friend watched as his hand grabbed for the single collar button on the long-sleeved polo shirt he was wearing, tugged it off and crushed it between his teeth.

The end came in a chaos of shouting as Martinson collapsed to the floor. It was a scene played out in spotlight: Friend reaching for the radio and making desperate calls for back-up, Grant turning the American's face upwards and with his massive hands trying to claw the poisoned button back out from his mouth, Sid dashing to the kitchen sink for water. In the middle of it all, Linus Martinson, the spy so lately resurrected, pitched himself willingly and urgently back towards the grave.

THIRTY-TWO

"That's a very interesting story," said Damon Bradley, leaning back in his chair and crossing his comfortably flannelled legs. "But with all due respect, 'C', speaking as your local CIA liaison, I don't think I can agree with the facts you've given, or the conclusions you've drawn from them."

Bradley had listened quietly, politely as the Head of Britain's Secret Intelligence Service took him through each point of the case against the CIA. It was entirely circumstantial. Martinson, if he was still alive, had given them nothing. He swept a speck of lint off the nap of his trousers, as if bored by the whole scenario.

"A very interesting story?" 'C' shook his head sadly. "I summon you to my office, provide you with ample evidence that the agency you work for has used a prohibited chemical weapon on British soil, risking hundreds perhaps thousands of lives, murdered a British citizen, attempted to murder one of my own staff not once but twice, and betrayed all our networks in Iran, dozens of agents facing a death sentence, and your response is to call it 'a very interesting story'?"

"I do call it an interesting story. But that's all it is to me: a story. It doesn't tally with the facts as I see them."

"Which are?"

"Dozens of Iranian agents working for both our organisations being rounded up by local security forces, the murders of three leading dissidents and one of your people going completely off the rails and murdering one of our people in Tehran. And by the way, if your story were true, then that British citizen you're weeping over was an Iranian agent who pulled the wool over your eyes and ours for more than thirty years."

"You're forgetting one thing: we have Martinson."

"Do you? I'm sorry 'C', but you're wrong. Martinson is dead. He was killed in Tehran. I don't know who you've got in custody now but he's nothing to do with us and he sure isn't Linus Martinson."

"Whoever he is, we have CCTV footage of you picking him up from the airport."

A snort of irritation escaped from Bradley. "I doubt that. You can't pin anything on me."

"There's also the fact that it was you who supplied the fraudulent Mossad tip-off about Omid Sourian: a perfectly innocent Iranian spice merchant who thanks to you is now dead, leaving a widow and an eight-year-old daughter."

"Sure, I passed that on, but what makes you think I had anything to do with putting the information together? I didn't even look at that paper. I never heard of Sourian until his name was spread across every front page in the western hemisphere."

"Oh really? How does it make you feel being used like that? And did you really know nothing about the Sadaghiani murder? The CIA carries out a major operation on British soil and their SIS liaison man isn't even told about it?"

"Sure. That's standard procedure. It used to be called 'need to know' but now they call it 'compartmentalisation'." Then Bradley saw the look on Sir Richard's face and realised he had gone too far. He held up a hand in apology. "Sorry, bad joke. But you're right in a way; I would expect to be advised of any major operation involving British personnel or jurisdiction. The reason I wasn't told about this one is that it never happened. That's the truth."

Sir Richard Graves was far too experienced a political operator to have expected that the CIA man would hold up his hands and confess to everything. He would have been told quite explicitly by his masters in Langley to stall, obfuscate, bluster and confuse wherever he could. Above all, admit nothing. All the same, the reality of such a blank denial couldn't fail to have its impact. Sir Richard was not accustomed to feeling so powerless.

"Look, Sir Richard, can we cut to the chase here?" Bradley went on. "You're upset and all that, I can see. I get that. But what exactly are you proposing? If you're really so convinced by your own case then why are you talking to me, Damon Bradley, a mid-ranking guy of no great ambition, instead of asking questions in Parliament and raising all kinds of hell with the State Department?"

"The reason I am speaking with you, Mr Bradley, is to make our point discreetly, as should always be the case with a close ally, rather than raising merry hell, as you put it, in full public view. You are our local CIA liaison. If our positions were reversed, I would fully expect our liaison man in Washington to be consulted first before anything reached me."

"Okay, I appreciate the courtesy and on behalf of the Agency I'm grateful. Thanks. So now you've had a cosy chat with your friendly local liaison man, what happens next?"

"Well, for one thing, we could reveal to your government the truth about the Tehran Committee and the hundreds of millions of dollars the US Treasury wasted funding Iranian intelligence through it."

"With all due respect, 'C', I would strongly advise you not to do that. There's maybe a twenty percent chance they'll believe you on the evidence you have. And even if they do, what action do you think they'll take? Okay, so maybe our funding gets cut, we have to lay off a few people. A few guys with decent tenure get shown the door, but what the hell? The pension's in the bank. We'll be okay, and so will the Agency. But what about you? You get a new Director in Langley, a new hierarchy. You think you'll get squat out of them after doing the Agency that kind of damage? No sir! And how far would you get in the intelligence business without CIA help? I'm sure I don't have to point out to you how reliant you guys are on our co-operation. I'm sorry to have to speak so frankly, but there's not a battle in the world you can fight without our help. If you ask me, you've got a great deal more to lose from this than we have."

"At the very least, Mr Bradley, we will be objecting to your continued presence as liaison officer. Trust once breached in this fashion can never be repaired."

Damon Bradley's heart gave a momentary leap of joy at the thought of being removed from a posting he had begun to find wearisome and a city he had come to loathe. But he recognised the thoughts as unprofessional, unbecoming to the moment. He battened the feeling down and hoped it wouldn't show.

"Well, I'm sorry to hear that, and I'll be sorry to go, but that's your prerogative, of course. Now was there anything else?"

There was a note of suppressed triumph in Damon Bradley's voice that 'C' couldn't fail to notice. He waved him away without another word. He didn't bother watching the American leave the room. He poured himself a glass of water from the carafe on his desk and pondered. Brazen as Bradley's manner had been there was much truth and realism in what he said. An affair like this could cause a permanent rift with the CIA. Even the much vaunted Five Eyes agreement could be holed beneath the water. What would that be without American input? Worse still, it might become Four Eyes without the British, and what then? He would have to go crawling to the Australians for crumbs from the table. It didn't bear thinking about.

He pressed the buzzer on his intercom but didn't speak. A moment later Hugo Lascelles and Emilia Wilton entered the room without knocking and trod their way softly across the thickly carpeted floor towards his desk, as if not wishing to awake the slumbering monster before them.

"Sit down, both of you," he said. He did not offer them water.

"I presume you heard what Mr Bradley had to say?"

Lascelles and Wilton both nodded.

"And what are your thoughts?"

"It's outrageous, of course," said Lascelles at once. "But I'm bound to say that he had a point, however crudely he made it. Much as we would all like to see the Americans held to account for this, I just don't see how it can be done without causing ourselves more damage in the process. And, speaking with my Cabinet Office hat on for a moment, I am quite certain there would be no appetite at Number Ten for the kind of diplomatic fall-out that would result from our taking any of the steps so far outlined. The long-term consequences for our defence, foreign and trade policies might be extremely damaging."

"Thank you, Hugo. An extremely pertinent summing up. Emilia?"

"I agree with Hugo. On the political side, that is. And legally there seem to be very few avenues open to us either."

"So you see no prospect of a prosecution against Martinson?"

Emilia Wilton shook her head.

"Not even under his Iranian identity? He does possess an Iranian passport as well, which appears to be genuine."

"Even if we went down that route, sir, I doubt we would be able to keep the Americans out of it. And what real evidence do we have against Martinson that would stand up in a court of law? There is no forensic evidence to link Martinson with the nerve agent used, nor any kind of evidence at all showing him within fifteen miles of the crime scene. We know he was in the country at the time, but that's as much as we can say. So were sixty-seven million other people."

"Yes, I see your point," said 'C'.

"That isn't to say we can't get him in court on something," continued Emilia Wilton. "Breaking and entering into the safe house, perhaps. But that's about it. The passport he used to enter the country was genuinely issued by the US passport service. Even if we know the name on it isn't his real one, we'd have a hard time proving it in court. And even if we could, I don't see how a court procedure on any of those charges would avoid this blowing up into the biggest intelligence scandal we've had since Philby."

"So what do you suggest we do with Martinson? Just quietly hand him over to the Americans?" asked 'C', adding under his breath, "Dead or alive".

"I'm not sure I quite heard that correctly," said Hugo Lascelles.

"No, I don't think you did. So let me ask again, what do you think we should do with Linus Martinson?"

Hugo Lascelles glanced sideways at Emilia Wilton, hoping for support. But, as ever, Ms Wilton was able to say all she needed to say with a look: *Policy is your line, Hugo. I just do legal.*

"Well, as I understand it," he began, "Martinson is still in a critical condition. He may not survive. If he were not to recover, that would solve this part of the problem."

"I'm not sure his doctors will see things in quite the same light," said 'C'.

"No, of course not. But I agree with you that the prospect of simply handing him over to the Americans is unpalatable and, as Emilia said, the idea of sending him to trial is impractical. I also agree with you that we should not actively seek his death—although might I suggest he be put down as 'do not resuscitate' if it should come to that?"

Sir Richard greeted the suggestion with a resigned shrug. "Well, if he does survive, I suppose all that is left to us is to hold on to Mr Martinson as a kind of leverage."

"Leverage?" asked Lascelles.

"Yes. We keep hold of him, and make sure the Americans know that we are holding him. In doing so we avoid the undesirable consequences of a formal trial or a complaint to the State Department, but we retain the ability to take those steps in future should the state of our relationship with the Americans justify doing so. Langley will know that if they fail to offer us continued co-operation at a reasonable level, we will have little to lose by breaking the Martinson story and the truth about the Tehran Committee all over Washington. The damage for them would be far greater in comparison."

"So, in effect, Linus Martinson becomes the nuclear option in our dealings with the CIA. Mutually assured destruction?"

'C' smiled. Hugo Lascelles might be a Whitehall man to the tips of his exquisitely manicured fingers, but he had a gift for understanding the higher politics of their game that was rarely seen within the Service. There was much of his own younger self to be appreciated in Lascelles.

"More or less," Sir Richard continued. "And since we have him, we might as well sweat him for every last scrap of operational intelligence in his head. Who knows what we might find, or how long it might take." He paused. "Of course, what we are suggesting involves long term detention without trial."

As he said this, 'C' glanced towards Emilia Wilton and watched her squirm in her seat.

"I assume there is some suitable facility for this?" said Lascelles.

There was no expression to be read on 'C's face, but his eyes flickered downwards and his hands toyed idly with the elegant ebony fountain pen he used to sign documents in the traditional green ink. Of course, a suitable facility for the purpose could be found. But it would be expensive. And very dull and dangerous work it would be for those guarding Martinson. Inevitably the Americans would resent this sword of Damocles hanging over them and would do what they could to rid themselves of it. It would put 'C' in the absurd position of demanding large amounts of taxpayers' money for an indefinite period to protect the security of a man who had used a deadly nerve agent on the streets of a British city.

But equally, looking at the alternative view, if, as Emilia Wilton judged, the prospects of putting Martinson on trial were remote, would the Americans even perceive the threat to be a genuine one? Might they not think they could just sit back and enjoy watching their erstwhile ally making a fool of itself in court while issuing blanket denials, denials which the legal processes would do little to undermine?

And then the other thought occurred to him, the one that said that what Hugo Lascelles had suggested was merely the other side of the same tarnished coin displayed to him so unpleasantly by Damon Bradley. But still, of all the options available this one offered at least the appearance, perhaps the reality, of power, of having a card left to play. He looked up again at Lascelles, decided.

"Facilities are one thing, Hugo," he said. "Budget is another. Perhaps you could set up a meeting with our friend in the Treasury."

"Of course, right away," said Lascelles, rising from his chair in the understanding that the meeting was over.

'C' watched them leave, then his eyes dropped to his desktop and his hands toyed with the fountain pen once more. It was as well, at moments such as this, for him to reflect upon the power he held. He had the power to order, or at least request, that a man should die; or that he should disappear, to be seen no more except as some vague cost attribution on a Treasury spreadsheet, or an unwelcome duty on the weekly security roster. He had the power to make the world's largest intelligence agency come to his table or risk the consequences. He had the power to make history; he had the power to make history disappear.

The case file was still open on his screen. He was old enough to remember the real nuclear option; the threat so terrible that it could only be borne if you never thought about it. Perhaps that would come to be the case with Martinson and the Tehran Committee as well. Henceforth the two allies would eye each other suspiciously, never giving voice to the thought of what really lay between them. That would be the future of the 'special relationship'. And Linus Martinson would have disappeared, along with every trace of what had been the Tehran Committee.

As far as the world beyond this building was concerned,

the Tehran Committee had been an organisation of brave and committed dissidents, cruelly broken up and its leaders murdered by Iran's despotic regime. Omid Sourian had been a Department 15 assassin, responsible for the use of a chemical weapon on British soil. The CIA and SIS were the closest of allies, the best of friends; the trust between them as strong as ever. All was just as it should be.

'C' laid his hand on the mouse and moved the cursor to the top of the screen. A single click produced a drop-down menu. The cursor hovered over *'Archive'*. Click. Now a dialogue box appeared, the cursor flashing in an empty field beneath the message *'Select closed access period in years'*. 'C' quickly typed in three figures and, with a final click of confirmation, made history disappear.

END

Did You Enjoy This Book?

If so, you can make a HUGE difference.

For any author, the single most important way we have of getting our books noticed is a really simple one—and one which you can help with.

Yes, you.

Us indie authors and publishers don't have the financial muscle of the big guys to take out full-page ads in the newspaper or put posters on the subway.

But we do have something much more powerful and effective than that, and it's something that those big publishers would kill to get their hands on.

A committed and loyal bunch of readers.

Honest reviews of our books help bring them to the attention of other readers.

If you've enjoyed this book I would be really grateful if you could spend just a couple of minutes leaving a review (it can be as short as you like) on this book's page on your favourite store and website.

Author's Note

The Tehran Committee is of course entirely fictional. But Department 15 is not. Its existence as an operational division of Iran's Ministry of Intelligence and Security is confirmed in several sources, many of them in the public domain. The description in this book of its history and actions - including the detail of the chilling "Chain Murders" - is accurate to the best of my knowledge. It is undoubtedly one of the most secretive and deadly organisations in the world of espionage.

Acknowledgements

Very rarely can any author claim all of the credit for their work. In this case, sincere thanks are due to my agent, Tom Cull, for his enduring faith and hard work on my behalf, to Simon Finnie and Pete Oxley at Burning Chair for their help and advice, but most of all to my wife Katya, whose unstinting support, encouragement and gently-worded criticism have sustained and inspired me every day.

About The Author

Neil Robinson was born in Gateshead and grew up in Newcastle upon Tyne obsessed with books and sport. After studying in Hull and Sweden, he spent six years with the Home Office in London before quitting and setting off to walk across Europe in the footsteps of Patrick Leigh Fermor and in the spirit of vagabond poets.

He returned to the UK with very sore feet and the understanding that he needed a new career. After retraining as a librarian, he took a job at Lord's Cricket Ground where he has remained for the last 15 years. As MCC's Head of Heritage & Collections, his job involves, among other things, looking after the Ashes Urn.

He has written widely about cricket and sporting heritage for a variety of publications and in 2015 published Long Shot Summer, a book about one of the most humiliating years in English cricket history. His fiction writing covers very different ground. A lifelong lover of spy novels, he takes inspiration from thriller writers like Len Deighton and John Buchan and seeks to create novels with a sense of place and character.

Neil lives in south east London, where he spends his free time writing, cooking, hiking, enjoying the odd pint of real ale and following his beloved Gateshead Football Club.

About Burning Chair

Burning Chair is an independent publishing company based in the UK, but covering readers and authors around the globe. We are passionate about both writing and reading books and, at our core, we just want to get great books out to the world.

Our aim is to offer something exciting; something innovative; something that puts the author and their book first. From first class editing to cutting edge marketing and promotion, we provide the care and attention that makes sure every book fulfils its potential.

We are:
- Different
- Passionate
- Nimble and cutting edge
- Invested in our authors' success

If you're an author and would like to know more about our submissions requirements and receive our free guide to book publishing, visit:

www.burningchairpublishing.com

If you're a reader and are interested in hearing more about our books, being the first to hear about our new releases or great offers, or becoming a beta reader for us, again please visit:

www.burningchairpublishing.com

Other Books by Burning Chair Publishing

Burning Bridges, by Matthew Ross

Killer in the Crowd, by P N Johnson

Push Back, by James Marx

The Fall of the House of Thomas Weir, by Andrew Neil Macleod

By Richard Ayre:
Shadow of the Knife
Point of Contact
A Life Eternal

The Brodick Cold War Series, by John Fullerton
Spy Game
Spy Dragon

The Curse of Becton Manor, by Patricia Ayling

Near Death, by Richard Wall

Blue Bird, by Trish Finnegan

The Tom Novak series, by Neil Lancaster
Going Dark
Going Rogue
Going Back

10:59, by N R Baker

Love Is Dead(ly), by Gene Kendall

Haven Wakes, by Fi Phillips

Beyond, by Georgia Springate

Burning, An Anthology of Short Thrillers, edited by Simon Finnie and Peter Oxley

The Infernal Aether series, by Peter Oxley
The Infernal Aether
A Christmas Aether
The Demon Inside
Beyond the Aether
The Old Lady of the Skies: 1: Plague

The Wedding Speech Manual: The Complete Guide to Preparing, Writing and Performing Your Wedding Speech, by Peter Oxley

www.burningchairpublishing.com

Printed in Great Britain
by Amazon